Tithes and Offerings

Book 3 in Detective Trudy Wagner Series

Buttermilk Book Publishing

Myrtle Beach, South Carolina

Typecast in Times New Roman

ISBN 978-0-9978909-9-0

An Actor is totally vulnerable. His personality is exposed to critical judgement – his intellect, his bearing, his direction, his whole appearance. In short, his ego.

Actors and Acting Personality/Alec Guinness

Foreword

Tithes and Offerings is the third novel in the Detective Trudy Wagner series. The readers were first introduced to Trudy in *Road Rage* and then in the follow up novel, *North of the Border*. Various characters from each of the first two are also featured in the third. While the plots in each of the three novels stand alone, to understand the character development and their interaction, it is highly recommended that you read the first two. The setting for this series is Horry County, South Carolina, along the scenic Grand Strand. While the reader might recognize many of the nostalgic venues and locations in Myrtle Beach and the surrounding area, the characters are purely fictitious, and their antics and most situations are not based on real events. Crimes that are, the names have been changed to protect their identity.

Detective Trudy Wagner's approach to crime scene investigations can be unorthodox and outside the parameters set by law enforcement, driving her superiors squirrelly. She is often pegged as a renegade, a lone ranger, skirting normal procedures and policies. Her way, it's not always how you get there, providing you solve the crime and catch the bad guys. Never doubt it. She takes crime fighting seriously and always tends to be drawn into high profile cases. Trudy has her personal struggles though, too quick to put her career ahead of family. She has paid a high price for her poor choice in life's pecking order. Still, she perseveres, job wise. Lessons are best learned through harsh mistakes and the reality of those consequences. Nobody knows this better than she. Perhaps her toughest challenges are ahead. One doesn't always have the luxury of picking and choosing one's poison though. Have no doubt, there are no dull moments ahead in the life of the southern crime fighter.

Dedication in Memory of Faith Wilson

I dedicate the third book in the series to dear friend, the late Faith Wilson, of the Abbeville-Greenwood, S.C. area, who lost her battle with cancer several years ago. Faith was the self-proclaimed president of the T. Allen Winn fan club. We met for the first time when she and her husband, Amon, attended my first book signing and many thereafter. They resided in Myrtle Beach for a while and attended Coastal Carolina football games with us. She loved my Trudy Wagner character and owned all my books leading up to her untimely death. Reader beware. It is only fitting that Faith and her quirkiness is featured in a cameo appearance in Tithes and Offerings.

Love you Faith. You earned your wings and with that, suffer no more. You were the best president I could have ever hoped to have. God Bless. This one is for you my dear friend.

Acknowledgment: The photo used for book cover was taken inside Abbeville's historical Trinity Church.

TITHEs
AND
OFFERINGS

Valdemar listened patiently to the caller, annoyed by the nasally whistling when the person took long deep breaths. Act I did intrigue him thus far. If what the caller described held merit, this could be a most intriguing challenge and Valdemar only accepted those endeavors with seemingly impossible odds. This is what separated him from the vagabond, those run of the mill mercenaries; however, the caller's demands were preposterous. Those contracting him did not have the luxury of delegating the percentages. He took the risk and would be paid dearly for his services. Dickering wasn't optional. He set the tone. He set the price. The caller had no alternative but to agree or seek services elsewhere. Seldom did they ever pass on his stipulations. Valdemar made one thing perfectly clear; refuse and there would be no second opportunity.

This would be his first journey to the South Carolina coastal community. It would be his first contract in the Palmetto State. How quaint, the Palmetto State. Each state had such unique references. The caller had that southern drawl, a Deep South, back woodsy tone. Valdemar echoed the drawl, possessing exceptional mimicking skills. The caller sighed, not amused by his gift. Getting to the point, the contract was sealed, with less than a month to orchestrate it and with the most precise perfection. Valdemar held up his hand as if testifying and then laughed loudly professing he had been moved by the Holy Ghost. With no audience, only he could appreciate his humor.

Pierce Beach House
Sunrise

Welcome to spring break on the South Carolina Grand Strand, thought Detective Trudy Wagner Pierce. The testosterone and hormones were alive and well. Uniforms and detectives alike had full platters and she suspected the menu would continue to be troublesome but entertaining. She stood on the back deck sipping her second cup of Hazelnut brew, enjoying another spectacular sunrise peeking from the depths of the Atlantic. This was Trudy time, that tranquil pause before she hit the trenches in Horry County.

Brady, her beloved, still snored loudly in the bedroom. He needed his rest. His daily wrestling match with Parkinson had been pinning him to the mat two out of three falls most days. The host of experimental medicine had shown promise in the beginning but other than the rainbow of urine colors, none had offered any lasting effect. Brady, forever optimistic and upbeat, had refused to allow it to consume his life. She had tried to follow his example but, she had to admit, dealing with these wacky sicknesses wasn't too easy for her.

Alzheimer's had taken her mom. Would this cruel disease take her husband? Those four dreadful words rang in her head, *there is no cure.* Sometimes a doctor's honesty isn't the best policy. Love will conquer all, right? Love, they had no shortage of that miracle drug. Marrying Brady Pierce, as Lance Rocker would put it, had rocked her world. Trudy glanced at her watch. The old tick tock wasn't on her side and the new sheriff was a hard ass. Unlike Hank Singleton, may he rest in peace, or ex-Sheriff Woody Anderson, he did things by the book, no coloring outside the lines. The new sheriff's military background demanded promptness and discipline. He didn't tolerate slackers or renegades in his department. She had to be on her best behavior if ever she located it.

Woody. She sure missed her old partner. He had held true to his promise, bowing out of the sheriff's position and taking the kids on a long Florida vacation before eventually returning and starting his own business. Woody, in less than six months, had done quite well operating a security business, his version of gunslingers for hire. He also provided training to those wishing to be gun owners, specializing in certification for concealed weapons. Recently he had been contracted by the county to assist in solving cold cases. The boy had done well, life after law enforcement.

Thankfully the crimes along the grand strand had returned to some semblance of normalcy. Trudy had experienced enough high-profile cases to last her awhile. The Road Rage serial killer murders and the Hispanic body parts case had taken its toll on South Carolina's tourist destination and local law enforcement. While they had been both intriguing and invigorating, testing her crime solving skills, she was over it now and ho hum sounded damn good for a change.

She wasn't sure what had become of Lance Rocker. He took a beating during the body parts crime spree, taking too may risks for television ratings, alienating himself from those who had once supported his extreme approach for sensationalism. A part of her said he got what he deserved, but ironically, she missed the bastard and the challenges he brought to the table. One thing for sure, she had seen more than she ever wished to see of her adversary, up close and personal. Those images would forever be etched in her head, not particularly fond images. He had seen her assets and in true Rocker form would view those probably much differently.

"Why I am even going there," she spoke loudly.

"Going where?"

"I didn't hear you, Circus Boy."

Brady cracked a smile. "Guess not, you were enthralled in a conversation with yourself. What's up?"

"I'm just doing my normal babbling. Some people have their morning devotion during alone time. I babble with my second cup of java. It prepares me for the day ahead."

"Sorry, I didn't mean to interrupt. Please carry on while I grab me a cup."

"And put some clothes on while you're at it. I can't be late for work and you're looking a little too up and at'um standing there in that doorway."

"Not to disappoint you but a trip to the john will most likely remedy that little problem."

"Trust me, Circus Boy, there's nothing little about that problem, but my ego has been deflated, so go take care of business. I'm out of here in five anyway."

"Forgot that new sheriff rules with an iron fist. You have to walk the chalk line, no more vigilante tactics."

"I'll wear him down soon enough. My will is stronger than his way. Come give me a big old kiss and hug before I leave and then you can go take care of that distracting problem."

Brady stumbled as he maneuvered the step down to the deck. Trudy moved quickly to steady him in her arms. His balance continued to plague him.

"You'll do just about anything to crash that naked body into me, won't you?"

"And I thought I was being discreet. Play safely out there today and don't pull any of those go off on your own risky moves. Try to keep your clothes on if you get abducted, how about it."

"Now how can a girl be expected to have fun being surrounded by an entourage and clothed?"

"Lessons learned my dear; you tend to always end up in extremely compromising positions when you venture off solo."

"You do make a compelling argument. Have a wonderful day in Knickers-world."

"I'm working a new contract with Coastal Carolina's golf team, teal is real."

Trudy headed out, images of Brady lingering in her mind, good ones and scary ones, his sickness worsening by the day, no matter how they both tried to conceal it from one another."

Conway Police Station
5 AM

A sure sign that the prime time tourist season had begun ramping up; the bad guys had already started practicing their preferred profession, preying on those with the wealth and resources to enjoy a beach vacation. Robberies on the streets and beaches, hotel room invasions, and shootings were on the rise, as were home break-ins. Too often Horry County's finest were seemingly outnumbered and outgunned. Home owner and tourist patience was wearing thin, no one thinking the local police did nearly enough to solve the crimes or capture those responsible. As surely as the humid summer temperatures would rise, so would the crime rate. Law enforcement did the best they could given the hand dealt. Poker faces didn't buy you much when the victims felt the stakes were too high and they were on the losing end.

The new sheriff had his work cut out for him. He had no legitimate reason to bitch and moan though. He had chosen to run for the position and had won it fair and square. For him it came down to the promises he had made while campaigning; put up, shut up or get the hell out of the way and let someone else do the job. It was too early to cry uncle. One cannot lead from the back of the line nor hide from statistics. The numbers don't lie, and crime was in no short supply in Horry County. At least he wasn't dealing with any high-profile cases, those his predecessors had been beaten and battered over. He had taken time to review the files on both, hoping to learn from the mistakes of those who had been subjected to the intense scrutiny. Former constable and interim sheriff, Woodrow Anderson had resigned from law enforcement. Maybe those back to back serial murder cases had just taken a toll on him. He couldn't say he could blame him, given what he had read about both.

With Georgia still on his mind, the sheriff would find a way to transition from the Peach to Palmetto state. He was a definite throw back, an old school cop, a genuine certified Georgia cracker. He had lived his whole life there; red clay running through his veins. He had been born and raised in Dawsonville, most notably known for the bootlegging of moonshine, stock car racing and the one and only Awesome Bill from Dawsonville, NASCAR driver, Bill Elliott. There were other notable drivers from his home town; Chase, Bill's brother.

There were those race car drivers and cousins, Lloyd Seav and Roy Hall, both former moonshine runners. Raymond Park, a former moonshine runner was the first team owner in stock car racing and a cousin of Seav and Hall. There was also one other race car driver, Gober Sosebee. The sheriff had even dabbled in dirt track racing but for whatever reason had gravitated to the lawful side and had only run moonshine a handful of times. Other Dawsonville folks worth mentioning were Jerry Glanville, a head coach in professional football and a driver and professional wrestler Bill Goldberg.

In the early years in law enforcement he had moved around, never far from home and always in Georgia. Eventually he landed in Helen, first as a deputy and then as the sheriff. While Helen Georgia had been a prime tourist attraction, it didn't compare to Myrtle Beach. Those visiting the quaint little Bavarian Alpine Village were not malicious by nature. The worst of the rowdiness occurred during the annual Oktoberfest during September, October and November. Too much consumption of adult beverages, no matter where, can skew the perceptions of those consuming it.

Helen is located on the infamous Chattahoochee River, with Georgia's Route 75 getting you to and from there. Last count, 430 people lived there year-round. The town's survival depends on the tourists. Helen had been a former logging community. As the logging declined, those living there tried a new tactic, resurrecting it by transforming it into the alpine theme. All buildings had to conform to the Alps theme. It's had its ups and downs but has somehow remained on the tourist radar screen. Like Charleston, South Carolina, it offers carriage rides. Another close by draw is over in Cleveland, the Babyland General Hospital, birthing place of the Cabbage Patch Kids.

One more notable name had caught his eye before moving to the area and vying for the sheriff position, and he would have to keep a wary eye on this one. Detective Trudy Pierce, formerly Wagner, had managed to be slap dab in the middle of both serial killer controversies. Colleagues had warned him of her tendencies of reckless lawlessness, often being too much of a renegade, taking on cases her way or the highway. Insubordination would not be tolerated on his watch. While he sincerely appreciated good detective work and the swift apprehension of the bad guys, breaking the laws to do so would not be allowed and would be dealt with severely. Criminals break the rules; police officers enforce the law to the letter, end of story. He had already had his little talk with her, warning her and laying down the ground rules. He had told her in simple terms that he had no qualms about locking her ass up if she broke or bent the rules to serve her own agenda. She knew where he stood. He just hoped she abided by it, for both his and her sake.

He had never been married, except to the military and then law enforcement. Sure, he had his needs like any man, but he handled it his way. He never took advantage of any woman to satisfy his own vices. At an early age, boys learn quickly how to do the needful to fend off natures' persistent urges. Like riding a bicycle, one never forgets. Sure, he dated from time to time and thoroughly enjoyed female companionship, but he had never been in a real relationship. That required commitment. Time didn't allow for such distractions. It made a man weak. Weak men were prone to make mistakes. He never made mistakes. Mistakes get you hurt or worse, killed. He was alive and well for a reason. The military had taught him well, too well in some folks' opinions. There was a right way to do everything. Taking short cuts or choosing the wrong way dealt harsh consequences, often deadly ones.

He considered himself fair and balanced, reasonable to a point, passionate about his job, intent on doing what he had been elected to do, protect the innocent, even for those too stupid to know they needed protection. Those who reported to him were duly sworn and expected to do the same. Subordinates attempting to compare him to his predecessors Sheriffs Hank Singleton and Woodrow Anderson were wasting their time barking up that tree. While both men had probably been likable and had done the best they could, weakness had surely run through their veins. Each man had failed royally at being a leader by allowing those under them to do as they pleased, bending and breaking the laws they had been sworn to uphold. He would bring law and order to this out of control tourist trap, restore the integrity of the position and do it effectively and efficiently. The fat would be trimmed, lean and mean would surface to the top.

There was no place for politics in his department. The county council, if like others, was in for a rude awakening. No one would be advancing their personal agenda while he held this position. Gratuities and favors were nothing more than bribes. Bribes were unlawful. Those offering them were common criminals and would be dealt with as such. He was hired to do a job. If he wasn't doing it, then fire him. If he wasn't doing it the way they had envisioned him doing it, then get over it or fire him. Think long and hard though before dismissing him without just cause. His integrity was his livelihood. Pretty simple, tread on it and be prepared to face the most uncomfortable circumstances. He was small in stature. He had even earned the nickname of Napoleon because of his size. Those dubbing him thusly had not been too far off the mark. Like Napoleon, he was a visionary and strategist. Some might say he suffered from little man syndrome, but they would never be so careless as to say that to his face.

Computers were grand tools for those too lazy to do their job. He used them only when he had to and not because he didn't know how. Hard work paid off in huge dividends. There was nothing shameful about simply rolling up your sleeves and digging into a case the good old fashion way. Spread across his desk was a series of folders, each numbered and ranked according to their urgency to be solved, number one being the highest-ranking current case. Due diligence on his part, each of the folders had been researched and had been assigned a ranking number and would be divvied out at the morning's debriefing meeting. He had already selected who would receive each one. There would be no dithering or taking up important meeting time to make the assignments during the meeting. His meetings were structured to last no more than ten minutes. Get to the point and send his officers out on the streets to do what they were trained and paid to do.

His mantra: never become involved in his officers' personal problems. Doing so posed too many risks and even more liabilities. He didn't share his personal life with any of them and he didn't expect to be pulled into their little dramas. He had seen it too often, officers blaming their behavior or poor judgment calls on a rocky home life. Excuses were just another form of weakness. Keep it strictly business while on the clock and never socialize with those directly under your command. Departmental human resources took care of the rest. No one forced a man or woman to become a police officer. Expect long hours away from family and friends, being underpaid and under appreciated by the public, and the strictest code of conduct with unimaginable expected high standards.

He didn't expect to be loved or even liked by his officers, the mayor or the public he served, but by damn they would respect his office and position as sheriff. Anything less would be unacceptable. He didn't rule by controversy, but if controversy existed, it only existed because he chose to allow it, and it would most certainly exist on only his terms. Chaotic behavior had no place in his world. Same code of honor as the military was applicable. Never leave a fellow officer behind. Your life for his or her life. Anything less would clearly lead to disciplinary action delivered personally by him. Being on his wrong side was uglier than imaginable. Was he a hard ass? Sure he was, but he was a consistent and fair hard ass. Absolutely no one received special preference.

He had managed to secure a modest house minutes from his Conway office. Rent had been reasonable. It had been completely furnished and it had all that he required; one bedroom, a kitchen, a bathroom and small den with the yard maintenance included. When not working he could be found at the local indoor shooting range. His marksmanship was superior to most. Weapons were his one and only passion and he possessed a mini arsenal of legal firearms. He maintained them in a climate-controlled storage facility, having seen too many home gun thefts. He ate most meals alone at home. He kept it simple, having grown up with not too many perks. With a can of Spam, pork and beans, two pieces of bread with mayonnaise, slice of onion or tomato, he would be living in high cotton, a meal fit for a king. Canned tuna, Vienna sausage and potted meat were staples in his pantry along with a variety of canned soups and vegetables. He preferred things simple and down to earth, no frills and fancy restaurants for him. He always brought a brown bag lunch to work and shied away from fast food joints unless he was in a crunch for something to eat.

He glanced at his wrist watch, a seventeen-year-old Timex. It was a few minutes after six. His dayshift officers should be reporting to duty within the hour. He had arrived just before five. Long hours and hard work always paid off in this line of work. The bad guys didn't punch a clock. You had to think like them to beat them at their own game. He believed once you latched onto a hot trail you stuck with it to you reached the end of it. You didn't just pause and pass it off to the next shift. Breaks were made. They didn't happen by chance.

McDonalds
6:30 AM

Trudy was still thinking about Brady's condition cruising north on highway 17 bypass when the call came over her radio. An altercation was in progress at the drive-thru window at McDonalds. She was less than a quarter of mile away and reported she was on her way to the scene. Trudy began humming the jingle, *you deserve a break today.*

As she approached the golden arches, she observed a white Mercedes sedan wheeling out of the parking lot quite erratically. A man was standing next to an SUV, waving his hands wildly and pointing towards the Mercedes. Reacting to a hunch Trudy followed it. Apparently upon seeing her, the driver floored it and fishtailed out onto Highway 707, heading towards Socostee. She radioed in that she was now in pursuit of the suspect vehicle and requested back-up. The driver changed lanes numerous times, cutting off one driver and then almost T-boning a second one as he sped through a red light. After the near miss, the driver of the Mercedes pulled into the parking lot of a strip mall and stopped. Trudy eased in behind the vehicle keeping a safe distance. A city policeman, blue lights flashing, entered the opposite end of the parking lot.

The officer had opened his door and had drawn his weapon, yelling for the driver of the Mercedes to exit his car, hands up. Trudy, also with her weapon drawn approached from behind. The door opened, and the driver did as he had been instructed. Trudy, with the better angle, pushed the man forward against the car and cuffed him without incident. Peeking inside, she noticed what appeared to be .38 caliber revolver and a box of ammunition on the passenger side front seat.

"What's with the gun?"

"It's perfectly legal. I have a concealed weapons permit. It's in the console if you don't believe me." She flipped the man around, so she could see his face and then motioned for the officer to check the console.

Trudy removed his wallet from his back pocket. "Gordon Wise, I presume."

"Look, this inconsiderate asshole cut me off at the drive-thru. I honked my horn and he gave me the finger. I sort of lost it."

"Hold that thought, Cowboy. You have the right to remain silent when questioned. Anything you say or do may be used against you in a court of law. You have the right to consult an attorney before speaking to the police and to have an attorney present during questioning now or in the future. If you cannot afford an attorney, one will be appointed for you before any questioning, if you wish. If you decide to answer any questions now, without an attorney present, you will still have the right to stop answering at any time until you talk to an attorney. Knowing and understanding your rights as I have explained them to you, are you willing to answer my questions without an attorney present?"

"Got it."

"Not that simple. Are you willing to answer my questions without an attorney present? This is where you say, yes or no officer, I understand and am willing or not willing to speak to you."

"Yes officer, I understand, and I don't need a damn attorney, but that bastard who cut me off does."

"Drive-thru rage, not exactly how I envisioned starting off my morning. Please tell me you didn't threaten the other guy with your .38?"

"I want a lawyer."

"Perfect…Office Evans please take Mister Wise into custody. I'll circle back and take statements at the scene."

"I get cut off and you lock me up," yelled Wise. "That's what's wrong with this country; the laws protect the damn criminals. Where are my rights? I was in line, he wasn't. There is no justice when you can't wait your turn at McDonalds. There's only chaos and a complete breakdown of the society. I should have shot that SOB while I had the chance."

Déjà vu, Trudy experienced flashbacks of an irate Tim Ford, Edward Bradshaw's murderer, during the infamous Road Rage serial killings. Ford was serving a sentence for that murder, after having attempted to allow Joseph Preston, the real serial killer, to take the rap. She and Woody Anderson had busted his chops, but only after he had thought he was free and clear. She still enjoyed viewing the video of her nailing Tim Ford with a right hook as he was caught red handed resisting arrest during his recorded confession. She sure missed Woody though and smiled, remembering how rocky their start had been when Sheriff Hank Singleton had introduced her as his new partner. Those were some good times. Trudy returned to her cruiser and double backed to take the statements of the witnesses.

Horry County Police Station
Sheriff Buster Ferguson's Office

Trudy knocked then entered the sheriff's office. He was on the phone but motioned to her to have a seat. She envisioned Hank sitting behind that very desk. The leather chair swallowed up the new sheriff. Hank had been a big old grizzly bear by comparison to the cub now sitting there. Ferguson was maybe five foot, seven or eight, weighing no more than a hundred forty pounds. He was clean shaven, sporting a crew cut, possessed a chiseled square chin, a flared disjointed, flat nose, looking as if it had been broken more than once.

He had the blackest eyes she had ever seen on a human, almost shark like. His image was GQ perfect, uniform starched and creased, not one single wrinkle; spick and span from head to toe. He appeared a bit too perfect, too diva like for her taste. He had looked this way since day one of his swearing in ceremony. In contrast, Hank had been more of a man's man, slouchy, burley, sweaty and just rough enough around the edges to make you appreciate him.

Hanging up the phone, Ferguson immediately began thumping his fingers on his desk in a most irritating manner. He leaned forward, eyeing her unlike Hank, who would rear back in the chair. Trudy locked eyes with him as if in a childhood stare off. Who would blink first?

"You missed my morning meeting detective. You do understand this is mandatory. No one simply chooses to skip it."

"Sir, I didn't simply choose to skip it. I was side tracked at McDonalds and…"

"McDonalds trumped my meeting. Highly unacceptable."

"Might I be allowed to continue, sir? I had not planned on stopping there."

"What, you had a sudden fast food urge."

Trudy had all but reached her frustration overload. "I intervened after hearing a call by the dispatcher, sir. We had a maniac waving a loaded .38 at the drive-thru window. Fifty-six-year-old Gordon Wise had gotten upset about how a man had pulled into the drive-thru lane, cutting him off. He then went on a tirade pointing a gun at the man, a McDonald's employee and a group of kids nearby. During his ragging fit, Mister Wise also threatened to kill the driver of the car during the heated exchange before driving off in a white Mercedes sedan. I arrived just as Wise sped away and I pursued him. The incident ended with Wise pulling over and surrendering. The .38 and a box of ammunition were resting on his front seat. The state had issued Wise a concealed weapon permit back in February. The road rage incident went too far and Wise overreacted."

"Road rage. You have certainly been in the middle of those, haven't you detective? Might I assume you played this one by the letter of the law?"

Trudy didn't immediately dignify that comment with a response, fearful of what she might say. She stood, regrouped and then said, "Protocol was followed. He was given the Miranda. Officer Evans, also present, took custody of Mister Wise and brought him to the station while I returned to the scene to interview the witnesses, sir."

"Very well, here's your next assignment, detective," he said, pushing the manila folder across the desk. "You are dismissed."

Trudy calmly retrieved the folder, nodded and exited the sheriff's office. She proceeded down the hallway, grabbing a cup of coffee, black, and then headed outside to her cruiser. Placing the coffee in the cup holder, she switched on the ignition and then banged the steering wheel, unleashing her very own tirade of very unprofessional off-color rants, purposely excluding any mention of Sheriff Buster Ferguson's name. Man, how she missed Hank, even wished Woody hadn't walked away from the position. Those words now haunted her. She had told Brady that she would eventually wear him down. Once a drill sergeant, always a drill sergeant, so it appeared.

Trudy took a couple of long, deep breaths, inhale, exhale, breath in, breath out. She then opened the folder. "Is this his version of a sick joke?" Someone was stealing donuts from Krispy Kreme. Two stores had reported missing pastries. She'd be the laughing stock of the force when they caught wind a cop was investigating the theft of donuts. She was tempted to march back into Ferguson's office and slam it down on his desk. He was either testing or punishing her. Based on the road rage comments, she leaned towards the punishment theory.

She switched off the engine, still furious but nothing she could really do about the sheriff or his treatment of her. She almost wished Sam the sadistic sheriff was back, almost. That blackmailing bitch had gotten her just reward. She pitied the person who had received her body parts, compliments of the brothers Hawthorne, responsible for murdering Hispanics for their vital organs. The Hawthorne brothers were doing time at the Lieber Correctional Institute in Ridgeville. She dreaded going back inside and meeting with her CSI team.

"First McDonalds, now Krispy Kreme. What's next, Chucky Cheesy?"

The rapping on her window caused her to jump, spilling coffee on her trousers. Detective Tim Burroughs, one of her team members, leaned over, peeking inside, and of all things, had a powered donut in his hand. The sugared white powder was coating the corners of his mouth with a light dusting also down the front of his shirt and on his tie. Omens were leaping at her from every direction. The signs said this day was going nowhere but downhill fast. Tim stepped back as she opened the door. She pointed to his mouth, then just reached over and wiped his face with her fingers. While he had improved by leaps and bounds as a detective, his eating habits were completely horrific, more resembling those of a five-year-old.

"You missed this morning's meeting. We were concerned. Is Brady all right?"

"Brady is doing as well as expected. Sorry, I left word with Roberts to let you know I had been delayed because of an incident going down at a McDonalds. He didn't tell you guys that I called?"

"Not a word. I don't much care for our new team member. He's a back-stabbing suck-up."

"Gee Tim, tell me how you really feel about Detective Lee Bowdon."

"Sorry, but that's the way I see him."

"Do the others agree with your assessment?"

"You should probably ask them. I've told you how I see him. What about you, are you satisfied with his performance?"

"He's done nothing but what I've asked."

"Of course not. That's what suck-ups do. You remember the character Eddy Haskell in those old *Leave it to Beaver* reruns, don't you? He's our Eddie Haskell. I'd watch your back. He's a gold-digger, just saying."

"Tim, cut back on the donuts, please. It might curb these sugar highs."

"I'm only telling you this as a friend, not a snitch. It's not any of my business who you pick to be on the team. We'll make do, but he better not drop the ball when we need him covering our backs."

"That's a serious accusation, Tim, and so unlike you."

"You trained me to be observant. One last thing, he can be a bit overbearing and crude. You know, like the big bad bully on the playground, he's always flexing his muscles and flaring his tail feathers."

"A bully, a back stabber and a suck-up, is there anything else I need to know about Officer Bowdon?"

"Besides being a racist and homophobic…"

"Okay Tim, I get it. I'll have a chat with him. After all I do have a bone to pick with him for not delivering my message. Please assemble the others. I'll be there momentarily."

Trudy phoned to check on Brady.

Brady picked up on the first ring. "Hello dear, did you want an update on how many times I've fallen this morning or my drool output?"

"Both, if you're keeping records. How's your appointment going with CCU?"

"Tough sell so far. The new coach is eager to make changes, but I don't think having the team dressed in teal knickers is on his transition list. This damned walker isn't helping my cause."

"The doctor didn't say you had to use it all the time, only when you felt the need."

"The need struck me like a bolt of lightning shortly after you left, babe. Sadly, I would have never made it to car or here without it."

"Why didn't you call me?"

"You can't be on call 24/7. You should know that by now. I can be stubborn as the next one, and using the cane was bad enough, but reality is reality, and the walker saved my butt today. It is what it is, and it isn't getting any better. We both know it. Trust me, when it comes to it, I will not hesitate in asking for your help. Just be patient, your turn will be here soon enough. How's your day going?"

"It's just another day in the neighborhood; Wonder Woman fighting crime and tracking down the bad guys, those innocent until we show them just how guilty they really are." Tears formed in her eyes, but she maintained control over her voice, or she thought she had.

"Hang in there. I wish I could promise you it was going to get better, but we vowed to always be honest with one another. Life sort of sucks right now. The last thing I ever wanted was for you to have to be a caregiver again."

"You're lucky I'm so good at it."

"Lucky indeed I have to go now. Maybe I can play up the poor pitiful cripple angle and guilt the coach into a contractual commitment."

"Peddle that snake oil, Circus Boy. Love you and see you tonight; I'll pick up a dozen donuts if the hot now light is on."

"Love you more and make mine crème filled."

Myrtle Beach International Airport
Delta 875

Valdemar exited the plane with but a single carry on, preferring to travel light. He would make purchases as he required them. He breezed through the gate and walked nonchalantly through the airport terminal, noting how small and quaint, not at all resembling the monstrosities to which he had become accustomed. He paused and purchased a copy of the Myrtle Beach Sun News and a Zero candy bar. He had a weakness for the combination of caramel, peanut and almond nougat covered with a layer of white fudge. He ripped the paper with his teeth and then took a bite, pure white ecstasy. Next stop, Alamo Rental Car. There he presented his identification and the receipt for a Mustang convertible.

"Welcome to Myrtle Beach, Mister Johnson," said the chunky attendant with a name tag sporting Ervin.

"Jeremiah, please; Misters are for the elderly. Point me to the nearest watering hole, Ervin. I badly need to quench my parched throat. Feels like I've been dogging a herd of mangy bison."

"With that accent, you must be from Texas."

"Fighting words where I come from Ervin, but you're just a young pup and don't know any better. Okalahoma, Old Caw City to be exact. It's just a little old ghost town with a population that suits my disposition. I'd love to chew the fat with you but that horseless wagon is screaming old Jeremiah's name. I got myself some young and wild sand fillies to break. Rride'um hard and put'um up wet. Where can I find myself one of them titty bars?"

Vladimir smiled, looking at Ervin in the rearview window. The boy was watching him drive off; perfect, he bought it. *Life's like a play; it's not the length but the excellence of the acting that matters.*

"As in a theater, the eyes of men, after a well-graced actor leaves the stage, are idly bent on him that enters next…William Shakespeare," quoted Valdemar.

The entrepreneur inhaled his surroundings, top down and indeed the warm breeze blowing his black flowing mane that is after he had removed his Stetson and freed his hair from its confinement. He skirted past the carnival atmosphere of the Pavilion, taking a right, down South Ocean Blvd and soon arrived at his destination, Hurl Rock Motel. He pulled into a parking place and retrieved the voucher and a brochure from his bag, reading it one more time just for the hell of it.

The Hurl Rock motel caters to families and golfers. We feature great rates and personalized service. We feature the MOST AFFORDABLE RATES and the CLEANEST ROOMS in Myrtle Beach. Along with our personal service and friendly family staff, you will enjoy a quiet, relaxing stay. Our family is looking forward to meeting your family again or for the first time.

All rooms have a refrigerator. Some guest rooms adjoin if needed. All efficiencies come fully equipped with a full-size refrigerator, stove, microwave, coffee pot, toaster, and include dishes, 2 pots, 1 frying pan and utensils.

All Cash specials are based on payment in cash

'*Tomorrow I will purchase a set of golf clubs and vittles for my little chuck wagon round up, but first I must prep for my next performance. Go strip off your clothes that are a nuisance in this mellow climate. Get in and wrestle with the sea. Wing your heels with the skill and power that reside in you, hit the sea's breakers, master them, and ride upon their backs as a king should...Jack London.*'

TV Channel 4, News on the Twelve
Marion County Police Station

"Summer Knight, reporting for Channel 4 News at the Marion County Courthouse, where the Atlantic Beach Mayor has again been arrested. Highway Patrol troopers arrested Mayor Paisley Heaton in Marion County for driving erratically. She was charged with Driving Under the Influence. For an unknown reason, Heaton was taken to the hospital before being taken to the Marion County Detention Center. This arrest, like her previous one, came one day before a scheduled court appearance. Because she was in jail during the time of her court appearance, the judge granted her a continuance. A new court date was set but did not happen because Heaton requested a jury trial. No date has been set for the jury trial."

"The Mayor has a history of arrests spanning over the past three years. Previous altercations with law enforcement include Heaton not stopping for a stop sign and side-swiping several parked vehicles. Police charged her with Hit and Run. The day before she was due in court for that incident, local police arrested her at the Town Hall. They charged her with Trespassing and Disorderly Conduct. Six months prior to this incident, Horry County police arrested Heaton in Little River. She was charged with Reckless Driving, Failure to Use a Turn Signal, and Resisting Arrest. Police dash-cam video shows officers asking the Mayor to get in their patrol car numerous times."

"Channel 4 will be following this story and updating as it evolves; Summer Knight reporting. Back to you Virginia..."

"How is this woman still a mayor," asked Summer.

"That has everyone along the Grand Strand scratching their heads," replied Mike, her camera guy. "You want to go grab a bite over at T-Roys while we're here? My favorite dish has got to be their Shrimp and Grits, but you must try their fried mushrooms and fried broccoli on the appetizer menu. They are the bomb."

"Sounds great, I'm famished."

"Summer, you have a treat coming over the next few weeks. We have spring break, the Harley Rally and the Atlantic Beach Bike Fest and I'm sure we'll have opportunities to cover all the excitement."

"I'm staying at a friend's condo until I can find a place. It's located in Windy Hill. Atlantic Beach is just next door and it seems very peaceful."

"Bike Fest will change your mind, I assure you. Expect over a half million attending these events."

"This is certainly a change from Salt Lake City."
"Yeah, this is not Mormon country for sure. I particularly look forward to your take on the two bike rallies."

Summer Knight, twenty-seven years old, black hair, fair skinned, petite build, pretty with or without makeup, very conservative background, had just relocated to Myrtle Beach three weeks ago to take the position with the local television station. She was a complete opposite of one of the former area news legends, Lance Rocker. She was a real sweetheart by comparison. Mike wasn't so sure she had what it took to survive the beach world. Time would tell.

Over lunch at T-Roys the conversation worked its way towards the Road Rage serial killings. Summer, like everyone, was intrigued by the case. Mike had been here for the entire time, so he held her undivided attention. He even skimmed over the Hawthorne brothers' murder, another Grand Strand serial murder case. She was spellbound, putty in his tale spinning hands. He was just as enthralled by her stories of Utah. Mike had never lived outside of Horry County, born and raised in Aynor. He still lived there. He laughed, telling Summer that Aynor was the gateway to Myrtle beach.

Summer utilized her reporter skills to 'excavate' the grand strand dig, learning what she could over lunch about former Sheriff Hank Singleton, officers Anderson and Wagner and new Sheriff Ferguson. Mike read her like a book and had a new appreciation for Summer Knight. Maybe she would do just fine here.

Highway 17 Business
Surfside Beach City Limits

On the way home, after a grueling day, Trudy in route down Business 17 spotted a yellow and blue golf cart exiting Main Street. It crossed the roadway in the dark, without lights, carrying a small child as a passenger. She engaged her blue lights, but the cart only sped up in response, veering onto the frontage road and then through the Piggly Wiggly parking lot. She made a right turn onto Holmes Town Road then a right into the parking lot to essentially head him off at the pass. Trudy sounded her siren and the driver pulled into a parking spot and stopped. Relieved, Trudy anticipated no more than maybe the issuance of a quick ticket and then she would be on her way.

She identified herself and then inquired as to why he was driving without his lights. The gent had slightly slurred speech and had no coherent response to her question. She was not surprised. What did surprise her was a Ziploc protruding from his front shirt pocket, a green leafy substance clearly visible inside the bag. Trudy, playing it close to the vest, first asked for the man's driver's license. He couldn't produce one, mumbling something about leaving it back as his place. The child, a girl, sported only a bikini. Trudy gauged her age at around five or six. She asked him his name, but he refused to answer, now appearing quite nervous for the first time. Trudy then asked him to empty all his pockets, starting with his shirt pocket. He clasped his pocket with his right hand and then ran like hell.

"Nothing is ever easy," Trudy sighed, calling for back up as she began her foot pursuit.

The man wearing flip flops sounded like a horse. He weaved between parked vehicles, side swiping and careening off most of them. Quickly he lost one flip flop then discarded the second, now running barefooted on the rough asphalt. Still, she had to hand it to him, he was quite the sprinter. She was gaining no ground. The distance was widening. This wasn't his first police rodeo apparently. She could see him clinging to his shirt pocket, not willing to risk dropping his pride and joy. Most felons in his precarious situation would have tossed the bag but not her boy.

An SUV backing from a parking spot both halted her progress and blocked her view. She lost sight of slue foot. Had he ducked behind the rows of cars? She stood motionless scanning the horizon ahead. An elderly couple had stopped two parking aisles away and was staring downward. Trudy instinctively started moving in that direction. A head popped up and looked in her general direction. He was off again, and this time disappeared around the side of the building. She heard sirens, saw the blue lights; the cavalry had arrived. She quickly explained the situation and pointed to where flip flopless had last been seen. Officer Hal Skipper took up the foot pursuit while Trudy returned to check on the child.

"Hello, sweetie, I'm Detective Wagner but you can call me Trudy. Please don't be frightened. Everything will be all right. Can you tell me your name?'

"Pearl…are you going to arrest my daddy?"

"We just need to talk to him for now, Pearl. Can you tell me your last name?"

"Easton…are you going to arrest me?"

"Certainly not…how old are you, Pearl?"

Pearl held up five fingers. "I'll be six soon."

"Pearl, can you tell me where you and your daddy live?"

"I can show you."

"How would you like to ride in a police car then? We'll ride there together."

"Mama told me never to get into a car with strangers."

"You mother is a wise woman. We're no longer strangers, now are we? I'm Trudy and you're Pearl. I don't think your mother meant it wasn't okay to help the police, do you? Here's my police badge. Tell you what. You hold onto it for me until we get you home."

Pearl took the badge and Trudy helped her into the backseat of her cruiser. The little girl pointed towards Holmes Town Road and then right. Her house was located only a block and half away. Trudy radioed Officer Skipper, telling him to break off the chase and join her there. She waited until he arrived, exercising restraint; having promised she would curb her one-woman posse tactics, not something that came easily. Skipper positioned himself at the back of the residence, a single wide mobile home. Trudy explained to Pearl that she was just going to check on her father and for her to remain inside the vehicle. She approached the front door with caution, refraining from drawing her weapon, not wishing to terrify the little girl. This could be a risky move given that drugs appeared to be involved.

Trudy knocked on the front door, identifying herself and requesting entry. No one responded. She realized Pearl still had her badge. No time to get it now, she repeated it a second time; still, no response. She checked the door knob. It turned and clicked. The door wasn't locked. She spoke loudly a third time, this time stating that she had his daughter, Pearl Easton, wishing to return her safely to her home. Still no response. Possibly he had not made it here yet or had not come here at all. Trudy whispered into her microphone to Skipper that she was going inside. After opening the door and scanning the room, she pulled her revolver, but only after being out of Pearl's view. This had been a risky maneuver and against protocol, but she didn't want to frighten the little girl.

"Hal, I'm in. The den and kitchen area appear clear. I see three doors down a short hallway. I am assuming a couple of bedrooms and maybe a bath. Layout is straight forward for a mobile home."

Trudy rapped on the first door, announced her presence, stepped aside and shoved the door open. She took a deep breath. This type of situation was always high risk. An ambusher had the advantage. Too many officers lost their lives to a trigger-happy suspect. Taking another deep breath, she peeked into the room, both hands on her weapon, with absolutely no hesitation to use it if need be. No officer wanted to discharge their firearm but failure to be willing to do it often led to worse circumstances.

A single sized bed and the feminine décor indicated this had to be Pearl's room. The room offered no hiding places except the closet. The double sliding doors were open. Fortunately, she could see it in its entirety. No one was standing among the hanging clothes; one down and two to go. The stakes just rose higher. She reported the results to Hal and backtracked into the hallway. She told him to hold tight, she was about to see what was behind door number two.

Trudy advanced with her back to the wall until she reached door number two. The third door was located directly at the end of the hall. This had to be the bathroom. She knocked, identified herself and then pushed open the door after finding it unlocked. As in the bedroom, there was no place to hide, except behind the shower curtain, inside the tub. In the movies, too many bad things usually lurked behind shower curtains.

Time for a more creative tactic; she scooped up a fresh bar of soap from the sink and tossed it over the shower curtain, hoping to catch a reaction if anyone was lurking there. The soap ricocheted noisily but if anyone was hiding there, they didn't make so much as a gasp or whimper. She rushed the curtain and yanked it to one side. She almost fell backwards, facing a tub full of mature marijuana plants nearly as tall as she; the Ziploc puzzle solved. Door number three remained. Could Mister Easton be hiding there? If so, how willing was he prepared to protect his investment. She reported to Hal what she had just found.

The obvious predicament, there was no place to hide from a direct assault from this room at the end of the hallway. She would be a sitting duck and an easy target. She attempted to improve her odds. She crouched as low as she could, gambling that if any shots were fired, Easton would be targeting someone standing. This time she made no announcement. She reached up and grabbed the knob and like the others, it was unlocked. She turned it, hunkered down and then shoved it open, finger and trigger ready to fire. The room was darker than the others making her standout in the doorway. She fell into the room on her stomach, double fisting her gun.

"Don't shoot," pleaded a slurred voice.

By dropping to the floor, her aim directly aligned with the underside of the queen-sized bed. Looking down the barrel of the gun, Easton had been caught completely off guard, and in no mood to be shot between the eyes. Her eyes adjusted, and she clearly saw him scrunched underneath the bed. She instructed him to come out and stood as he crawled from his confined little hiding place. Trudy ordered him to place his hands over his head and then cuffed him.

He still had the Ziploc in his shirt pocket. It really didn't matter now, given what she had discovered in the bathtub. Trudy alerted Hal that she had her man in custody. She also instructed him to contact SLED and DSS. Daddy was going to jail. Pearl would be heading to the Department of Social Services, a sad ending for an innocent little girl. The South Carolina Law Enforcement Division would complete the drug search and assess the value of the find.

Trudy stayed with Pearl until DSS arrived. She soon discovered that the mother no longer resided at the home and hadn't been for over a year. She was being detained at Horry County's J. Reuben Long Detention Center. She had recently been picked up on prostitution and drug possession charges. Poor Pearl had never stood a chance with parents like these. Only for the little girl's sake, Trudy had regretted now having to tell her that her daddy was indeed being placed under arrest. Good, bad or ugly, he was still her daddy. After the prolonged detour, she finally headed home.

Trudy entered the house but didn't immediately spot Brady. Doing her second room to room search, weapon holstered this time; she located him on the back deck sitting in the dark. The Parkinson had been getting worse and bad days were winning out over the good days. He never complained. He just pushed on; dealing with life's dealt hand much better than she. They had once discussed having children but given the circumstances that had fallen to the back burner. She couldn't help but smile, thinking about how she had first laid eyes on him at the Hot Fish Club in Murrells Inlet. He had been wearing those gosh awful golf knickers and argyle everything. It was then that she had dubbed him circus boy. He had resembled an escaped clown from the circus for sure.

Brady had entered her life at the worst possible time. She had just relocated to Horry County to take care of her mother in the latter stages of Alzheimer's. With a serial killer taking its toll in the tourist town and caring for an ailing mother, the last thing she needed was a boyfriend. The love interest had been her salvation though, an escape from the craziness. She had sadly juggled her priorities terribly, often rating her mom and Brady second and third in the pecking order behind solving the case.

She had allowed the Road Rage murders to consume her life. She paid for those sins with the tragic loss of her mother, passing off her daughterly responsibly to Brady. He, instead of her, had been by her mother's side when she had breathed her last breath. Tough lessons are often the hardest to swallow. To use Brady's golf lingo, she had no mulligan option. She had promised she would not make the same ill-fated mistakes and so far she hadn't, placing family first. She was about to step out onto the deck when her cell phone rang.

"Hey Allison, how's my little sister doing?"

Allison lived in Atlanta with her husband and two children. Theirs had often been a strained sibling relationship, but they had grown closer after their mother's death. While it still had its ups and downs, mostly it had been on the upswing.

"Whoa, calm down. Take a deep breath, stop the sniffling, blow your nose and please repeat that again, slowly this time."

Walterboro, Colleton County, S.C.
Olde Café House

The little restaurant was an unassuming building on one of the main roads into Walterboro. Sitting alone he pushed the last of his meal about his plate with his fork, contemplating his next move. Sadly, he had no Plan B, C, D or even F. Options were not readily available and offers weren't exactly falling from the trees. To compound matters he had just gotten fired from the Press and Standard, the town newspaper. Locals had been outraged at his article about how the town had gotten its start and name. When pressed, he could not back up his findings. Given the bad PR, none of his contacts would step forward to support his article.

He had dug too deeply into the ugly side of slavery and depicted the town's founders as ruthless tyrants. It was a badly skewed article designed for sensationalism. Neither blacks nor whites had appreciated the tar and feathering of their town. The article had completely re-written history with no basis for truth as far as they were concerned. There is a fine line between reporting factually and embellishing. Push the embellishment too far and you can get crucified quickly.

History books had painted a much different picture than one man's depictions, an outsider now banished from the land. Existing and readily accessible records indicated Walterboro had been founded in 1783 as a summer retreat for local planters trying to escape their low country plantations from the onslaught of malaria. The original settlement was located on a hilly area, covered with pine and hickory trees and had been appropriately named Hickory Valley. Paul and Jacob Walter, two brothers who owned plantations in nearby Jacksonboro, brought Paul's small daughter Mary there after she had been sickened by malaria, a common disease amongst the families who built their plantations in the marshy areas of the low county. Rice was a big crop. Because of Mary's illness, Paul and Jacob had gone looking for a healthier location to live during the summer months when mosquitoes took their toll.

In 1942, Walterboro became home to the Walterboro Army Air Field. The base was established to provide advanced air combat training to fighter and bomber groups. It also hosted the largest camouflage school in the United States, as well as a 250-person Prisoner of War Camp. In 1944 the air field changed commands and became an advanced combat training base for individual fighters, primarily the black trainees graduating from Tuskegee Army Air Field in Tuskegee, Alabama. Over 500 of the famed Tuskegee Airmen trained at Walterboro Army Air Field between April 1944 and October 1945. The base closed in October 1945 and returned to its origins as a local airfield. Today Walterboro is dotted with historic homes dating back to 1820, and a downtown that has changed very little in the past 75 years.

One cannot tarnish rightfully earned southern heritage for the sake of sensationalism and dub it journalism. Southerners are not forgiving souls when it comes to ruining their reputations. Cries came from those declaring his lies were fighting words for true blooded born and raised folks from Walterboro. Others were just a blink away from becoming a lynch mob. He took everything with a grain of salt, accustomed to riling the locals with his unorthodox approach to reporting it as he saw it or as he visualized it as getting the best mileage. There was no such thing as bad publicity. The worst and ugliest could be parlayed into something beneficial and profitable; well, usually. This had been his toughest sell to date, but he hadn't tossed in the towel just yet. The wheels were turning in his scheming head. He motioned to Norma-Jean the waitress that he could use a refill on his coffee. He then immersed himself back into deep thoughts of damage control and profiteering.

At the hint of approaching footfalls he held up his coffee cup without looking up. A couple of seconds passed, and Norma-Jean had not refilled it. Thinking here we go, she recognized me, he looked up. He locked stares with two behemoths, one black, one white, neither cracking a hospitable smile. These guys probably weren't members of his fan club or avid autograph seekers. Local critics, okay, he thought, get this over with, give me the two thumbs down and get it out of your system. Each of his new-found friends eased into chairs on either side of him. Both placed their enormous hands on the tables apparently neither astute to etiquette, elbows off the table. The white guy spoke first.

"You're him, aren't you?"

"Him, who do you think I am, big fellow?"

"It's got to be him," said the black guy. "He has a smartass mouth and has those pretty boy looks."

"I just want him to say it, Henry."

Getting quickly bored with the situation, he responded, "And just what is it that you request that I say to your pal, Henry."

"Caleb, listen to the way he talks down to us. He can't be anybody else."

"Look boys, if this chat is going to be lengthy, can I at least have Norma-Jean pour you some coffee or bring you menus?"

Henry crashed a thundering fist down on the table, rattling the dishes and silverware, turning every head in their direction.

"I take that as a no or possibly a maybe later."

"You don't want to piss off Henry any more than he is already pissed, I promise you. Hell, boy, you've already pushed my rile button a might too hard. Just say it."

Henry nodded his head, half smiling, but there was nothing warm or sincere in it.

"As it does appear you two gentlemen fully comprehend the English language, can you be more specific in your line of questioning. Just exactly what is it that you require me to say to satisfy your obvious curiosity?"

"You're Rocker, the bastard who wrote that article about our town, aren't you?"

"We haven't been formally introduced, but I take it that you are Caleb and your friend is Henry. I am indeed Lance Rocker. How can I be of service? Apparently, you're not pleased with my featured article in the Press and Standard. While I do appreciate your criticism, not to worry, I'll not be doing a follow up in your quant little newspaper. We have parted ways, their loss, not mine."

Both stood up, towering over Lance. Not to be outdone, Lance stood too. They still dwarfed him, big boned country boys; big old pissed off country boys at that. Lance had two approaches to situations like this; wit and sarcasm or pouring on the suck-up charm. Something told him neither option was viable. These boys hadn't come calling with the intent of him winning them over. On the contrary, they had already drawn their opinions and there would be no swaying them otherwise. He did have one advantage. They were in a public place in plain sight of plenty of witnesses. Surely these two Neanderthals had better sense than to do something regrettable and incriminating. Henry reached over and grabbed Lance by his shirt. Maybe they preferred an audience instead. Caleb placed an iron claw hand on his shoulder. Their breaths smelled of hard liquor and this early in the morning that spelled a heap of trouble.

"What are you boys up to this morning?"

Lance peeked around the mountains blocking his view and spotted a deputy standing there. Lance sighed. Miracles do happen. He recalled how he had been deputized during those Road Rage killings and even held this position during the Hawthorne brother's Hispanic killings. A fellow comrade in uniform was a welcome sight. Both of his breakfast guests simultaneously released him in response to the officer's inquiry, apparently recognizing him and respecting his authority.

"Henry, Caleb, just what are you boys up to with Mister Rocker?"

Lance read the name on his shirt. "Deputy Beers, would you care to join us for breakfast?"

"I'll have to decline your invitation, Mr. Rocker. Boys, I'm going to have to ask you to take your little discussion outside and settle it there. This is no place to make a public scene. People are trying to relax and enjoy a leisurely breakfast, read their papers and prepare for a rigorous day ahead. None of us see ourselves as slaves to our ho-hum jobs. Ya'll have a good day, you hear."

"You heard the deputy, let's go have ourselves a little parlay," smiled Caleb.

"Outside, newsboy," said Henry, both men grabbing Rocker by an arm and escorting him towards the exit.

Lance looked about, searching for any signs of intervention. The patrons buried themselves in their newspapers and meals, none making eye contact or even watching the unfolding saga. These two vigilantes were doing what most didn't have the courage to do. Lance felt as if he was being marched to the gallows. Possibly that's what these two brutes had in mind, justice served southern style, no racial lines, a town standing united. They were going to rock his world like it had never been rocked before.

2nd Avenue Pier
110 N Ocean Blvd, Myrtle Beach

"What a wonderful sunrise, Brady; the perfect place for breakfast."

"And they have an elevator, the perfect amenity for me. Thanks for taking the morning off away from crime fighting to accompany me to my doctor's appointment."

"That's the least I could do after dropping the bomb on you last night."

"I wouldn't call it a bomb. You sister needs you right now. I guess we're both just taken aback by her keeping the divorce hush-hush."

"We talk weekly, and she never mentioned they were even having problems. She still hasn't divulged what prompted their break-up. I guarantee there's more to this than meets the eye."

"You'll have plenty of time to talk about it when she arrives in a few days."

"Without the kids, that's odd too."

"Maybe she just needs a break away from the situation. Try to cut her some slack."

"It's not like Allison to be away from her children for any reason."

"It wasn't likely she would be splitting with her husband either, was it?"

"Uncle, I give. Let's just breathe in the sunrise and sounds of the waves."

"You don't have to twist my arm."

She reached over and gave Brady a big old long kiss just as the waiter arrived. He blushed slightly, fumbling with his order tablet and fidgeting with his pen. "Are we ready to order?"

Brady looked over at Trudy for her to place her order first, but she was preoccupied gazing out the window towards the beach. "Crap," she said as she leapt up and made a hasty exit to the pier.

Both Brady and the waiter watched in dismay as she trotted out onto the pier and began yelling at someone below. Both turned to see where she was venting her anger and spotted a lone teenager, standing in knee high breaking surf, naked as a Jaybird. The boy responded by giving Trudy the finger. A small crowd of walkers and joggers had gathered to observe the nude boy's behavior. He gave them the finger too and then began shaking his genitals at them. When Brady glanced back at the pier, his wife was gone. This spelled bad news for the dick-jiggler entertaining the beach goers.

Trudy arrived and flashed her badge. "Out of the water, now!"

He waved his pride and joy at her and then backed deeper into the surf, the waves crashing against his back side, his front side still in full few. The water's cooling affect made his genital flaunting less of a visual display; the turtle retracting inside its shell so to speak. He backed deeper, spouting curses, still firing off one finger greetings. Trudy had had enough. She removed her shoes and socks and began walking into the ocean. Her other police equipment was locked in the trunk of their car. The boy continued to taunt her and yell crude remarks.

The crowd of onlookers had doubled in size, many snapping photos or recording the incident. The boy was now in nearly chest deep water, the breaking waves and swells posing obvious balancing problems. Trudy used an old tactic, figuring the kid was just intoxicated enough to fall for it. She cupped one hand to her face and then screamed and pointed, yelling shark. He took the bait and attempted a turn, the waves staggering him sideways and then slightly backwards. She closed the distance to within three feet before he turned back; realizing too late that it had been a trick.

Trudy calculated one quick lunge and made it count, wrapping her arms around his waist, taking them both under. They surfaced coughing and gasping for air. She was face to genital, but quickly released him and flipped the boy around, penning one arm behind his torso, inflicting a world of hurt on Mister Nude Grand Strand. He cried out in pain. Trudy ignored his protest and dragged him toward the beach, the crowd having nearly tripled, more than twenty people gathered about. One emerged from the crowd, offered her a hand and then relieved her of the exhibitionist. Detective Sylvester Stone, a member of her CSI unit, had just so happened to be out for his morning jog when he noticed the commotion.

"He's a little young and wet behind the ears for you, isn't he?"

"He's currently wet behind almost everything right now, as am I but don't let the cold water fool you. I think he's older than he presently looks. Are you a beach gawker, Sly?"

"Yeah I do my best gawking while on my morning beach jogs. Why don't you let me take Tiny off your hands? I'll call it in and have the City Blues pick him up."

The kid's discarded clothes were on the beach along with a twelve pack with over half the bottles missing, three empties nearby. Young Jason Gore, 19 years old, from Danville Kentucky, would be arrested and charged with public nudity, public intoxication, under aged drinking, unlawful possession of alcohol, and disorderly conduct. He would then be incarcerated at J. Rueben Long until eventually being released on bond to his parents. His 19th birthday celebration would not be soon forgotten. He would be grounded possibly until he reached 21 years of age. Embarrassed, the Gore family would not be vacationing in Myrtle Beach again anytime soon.

Dripping wet, Trudy rejoined Brady, now propped on the railing of the pier. "Sorry, I'm on duty 24/7 and the youngster was parading his goods in public. I'll have to skip breakfast though and run back by the house to change before your appointment."

"It's not the first time I've seen you sopping wet, but I must admit, the clothes don't do you justice. I like my recollection better."

"Better drop those thoughts. It wouldn't fare so well, me being arrested for public nudity and performing obscene sexual acts on the pier. Ferguson would have my hide. I'm already reduced to donut crime investigation; oxymoron for cops."

"Was that Sly I saw on the beach?"

"Indeed, it was. He took junior off my hands. Sly is my right-hand man for sure. He really stepped up to the plate during those senseless Hispanic murders. Doctor Demento, the one and only Lincoln T. Hawthorne, had practiced his body parts removal operation and perverted interests way too long. I wonder how it's going for him on death row down at Leiber. It had to be injury to insult, his brother, Eugene turning states evidence on him and becoming a witness for the prosecution to save his worthless hide."

"I like and truly respect Sly too. What did Woody call him at our wedding reception, the Black Avenger?"

"Woody never was one to mince words and he'd never shy away from racial profiling."

"If I remember correctly; Sly embraced the nick name, saying he was The Mandingo of the department."

"You have to remember; neither Woody nor Sly hardly ever take an alcoholic drink. Rocker was mixing the beverages and fueling that fire."

"Maybe Woody would be a good match for your sister, Allison."

"Those two, six kids between them, I don't think so."

"Could be a match made in heaven…"

"Or one directly out of the bowels of hell…just stay out of the cupid business, Circus Boy, how about it? I really don't need Woody Anderson as my brother-in-law and all those kids in tow when they come for an extended stay."

"You do make a compelling argument."

"Let's get me out of these wet clothes and you to your doctor's appointment. They haven't had you peeing teal yet."

"And if they do, I might just have to take that in stride and try for that Coastal Carolina contract again."

Missing Links Golf Super Store
Myrtle Beach Location

Valdemar strolled down the aisles in search of the perfect set of golf clubs. He wasn't a golfer but what did that really have to do with anything. Many individuals who played the game of golf had no business doing so. A gent eventually intervened and assisted him in purchasing a most expensive set of Callaway clubs. With the Missing Link's staff in tow, Valdemar selected an appropriate golf bag, shoes, golf balls, glove and tees. All individuals employed by the store wore unique attire. The gentlemen sported knickers of various colors, argyle socks with matching vests and caps. The ladies accessorized with plaid kilts, knee high socks, white blouses and the signature caps.

"Just curious, why the odd uniforms," asked Valdemar in a Jersey accent.

The young man smiled and then explained. "It is our theme. The originator of Missing Links started out just selling knickers and all the clothing accessories. He eventually branched out into tools of the trade and adopted the super store concept used by others. What makes us stand out is the Scottish wears. Our creed is *Look Good, Feel Good and Play Good*. A matter of fact, there's Mister Pierce now. He visits all his stores regularly."

Valdemar turned to see a gentleman wearing burgundy knickers, matching black, white and burgundy argyle socks, a black vest over a white shirt, and a matching burgundy flat golf cap. Pierce propped himself on a walker, apparently suffering from some sort of handicap. Valdemar noted he had a contagious smile and calming demeanor, a man of confidence.

"What does a guy have to do to meet this Mister Pierce?" He laid out the Jersey accent to the perfection.

"Follow me. I'll introduce you to him."

"Good morning, Mister Pierce. This gentleman would like to meet you, sir. I'm sorry; I didn't catch your name."

"I'm Joseph Cafiero but you can call me Joe."

"Pleasure to meet you Joe. Likewise, just call me Brady. What brings you to Missing Links?"

"Everything actually. I'm just taking up the game of golf. My wife says I need to get out of her hair and do something somewhere that is out of the house. I retired recently. She says she's seen me too much already."

"Sometimes retirement can be a tough adjustment, especially for those who aren't used to having the retiree around 24/7."

"I've got to have one of those outfits like you're wearing if I'm going through with this fricking crazy idea of hers. Might not be such a bad idea if I got myself some lessons too. I don't want to go out there and stink up the joint and piss off the real golfers."

"We can certainly fix you up with a set of knickers and all the accessories. As for lessons, I know several golf pros in the area and will gladly make recommendations or referrals."

"You're a real champ, Brady Pierce."

"Are you vacationing, moving here or already live here?"

"Vacationing but scoping it out. My wife says we're relocating here so the move is in the works. House is already on the market back in Jersey. Beach weather beats Jersey weather hands down."

"I can suggest a real-estate agent if you don't already have one."

"Thanks…that would help out a lot having one down here."

"Here you go, I just so happened to have one of her cards, Karen Massaro, she's a sweetheart and will fix you right up."

"She sounds like she could be from Jersey."

"We say folks from New Jersey are locals. You see more Jersey tags here than from most anywhere else. A running joke is we hope the last arrival switched off the lights because there can't possibly be anyone else left in the garden state."

"You guys down here have some of the funniest sayings. I guess I'm going to have to learn to eat grits and talk slower."

"Trust me, if you did, you'd no longer sound like a Myrtle Beach local. They are more of you than us here."

"I'll have to remember that one."

"Good to have met you, Joe. Kyle, please assist in selecting something snazzy for Joe. Give him the local's discount. Here you go, Joe; contact this guy for lessons, tell him I sent you and to give you my special rate."

"I'll do that. Thanks Brady. You take care."

Within thirty minutes Valdemar had closed out the transactions, had loaded the merchandise in the Mustang and headed southward on bypass 17. He wasn't sure why the highway had been named a bypass; it seemed quite congested. Top down on the Mustang, the alleged New Jersey visitor motored through Murrells Inlet, Pawley's Island and now passed over a bridge with a sign welcoming him to historical Georgetown. He made a slight detour off 17 and drove down Main Street near the Harbor Walk. Old store fronts dotted both sides of the street of the historical district.

As in anywhere he visited, he had researched the history. Georgetown was the third oldest city in South Carolina. The historical little town was located on Winyah Bay. Second only to Charleston, it is one of the largest seaports in the state. By 1840, Georgetown produced nearly half of the total rice crop in the United States and became the largest rice-exporting port in the world. Wealth from the rice created an elite European-American planter class. They built stately plantation manor houses, bought elegant furniture, and extended generous hospitality to others of their class. Their relatively leisured lifestyle for a select few, built of the labor of thousands of slaves, lasted until 1860. Rice also supported Charleston artisans: fine furniture makers, jewelers and silversmiths, to satisfy the tastes of the planters for refined goods. Plantation owner, Joshua John Ward owned the most slaves in the United States, some say reaching as many as 1000. Many of the old plantations are still standing today.

Valdemar, somewhat of a history buff, relished towns like Georgetown. He was driven to learn everything about the places he had been a contracted assignment. History had painted a tough road traveled for the southern city. Georgetown had suffered great economic deprivation during the Great Depression. The Atlantic Coast Lumber Company went bankrupt early in the depression, putting almost everyone out of work. In 1936 help arrived. In that year the Southern Kraft Division of International Paper opened a mill; by 1944 it was the largest in the world. Then there was Hurricane Hugo in 1989. It struck south of Georgetown with extremely hard winds, an intense storm surge that damaged Georgetown along with nearby areas.

Valdemar continued, exiting the town's city limits to a more rural setting along the long-deserted rice fields and bordering swamps. He came to a sign identifying a public golf course, Old Plantation Golf Resort and the Live Oaks Church of Contemporary Teaching and Healing. He made the hard left and leisurely drove down the picturesque roadway until he reached the golf course. It bordered the live oak lined entrance to the church. Minutes later, the inexperienced golfer wearing a lime green golf shirt and white shorts stood on the driving range with his newly purchased equipment and began striking golf balls. The oppressive humidity and searing sun made this a short-lived adventure. Nevertheless, he had completed what he had set forth to accomplish.

On his return trip he again motored down Main Street and this time parked in front of the Thomas Café, an obvious local's favorite. A sign on the door stated it had been a casual and cozy landmark since 1929. This cafe offered Low Country dishes for breakfast and lunch. He settled on a sweet tea and side of She-Crab soup, rich and like bisque, consisting of heavy cream, fish stock, Atlantic blue crab meat, traditional crab roe and small amount of sherry. He had greeted his waitress, using a Bostonian accent. He sported a Boston Marathon tee shirt and faded jeans shorts, sandals with nylon black socks extending a foot above his ankles. He purchased a slice of key lime pie to go.

Valdemar arrived back at the Hurl Rock Motel sometime before 3 PM, engaging his Oklahoma persona to perfection, having changed his clothing for the fourth time. The cowboy discreetly checked on others of his party that had begun to arrive. All were met with courtesy greetings, strangers passing but being cordial. As was the routine, authorities would be ill pressed to connect any dotted lines among patrons. Following his explicit guidelines, they too would take on the rolls of multiple personalities during their stay, almost schizophrenic like behavior if detected from a more astute and detailed orientated observer. Authorities would find it difficult to assemble suspects in the wake of the completed contractual assignment.

Detail, deception and diversionary tactics assured Vladimir's services remain in high demand for those willing to fund the project to meet his price tag. Perfection was costly; satisfaction guaranteed. He had never had a disappointed client to date. Mistakes among his crew were not tolerated. Those floundering in any manner were dealt with swiftly and severely. There were no second chances. His team understood and accepted these consequences. Insubordination wasn't an option; like wedding vows, until death do us part. No one under his watch ever received a divorce, nor asked for one.

He had hand selected every one of them and would trust any of them with his life. He had on numerous occasions. Never would anyone remember seeing them together, not even in speaking pairs. Details of their assignments and the plan had already been discussed in detail long before any of them had arrived. Here, they just bided their time waiting for the opening curtain and Act I.

Just Another Day at the Beach

The headlines were filled with an assortment of wild beach activities.

A man and a woman were arrested after police said they were seen having sex in front of their hotel window in plain view of the public. According to a Myrtle Beach police report, Skeeter Levitt, 20, of Wyoming and Rose Manzoni, 23, of Florence were having sex at a motel on North Ocean Blvd. in front of a window visible to the public. It happened around 11 p.m. with the drapes open. Pedestrians told police they could see the couple performing various sexual acts. Both were arrested and taken to the Myrtle Beach City Jail. They were charged with engaging in a lewd act in public.

A Conway man was in police custody pending charges being filed against him that he tried to elude police on his moped after being identified as a suspect in a storage shed burglary, according to a Horry County police report. The 37-year-old man was being held at J. Reuben Long Detention Center pending formal charges being filed against him, according to jail records. Officers were called to the scene at about 1:30 p.m. Sunday to Dirty Branch Road in the Conway area for trespassing after a 79-year-old man reported he saw the man currently in police custody and another man leaving his backyard on separate mopeds, according to the report. The victim followed the suspect while staying on the telephone with 911 dispatch operators.

The other man went in the opposite direction and no additional information about that suspect was listed in the report. An officer saw the victim in his vehicle following the suspect on the moped and began chasing the suspect, according to the report. The suspect refused to stop for the officer, who had his blue lights and siren blaring. The suspect drove about 40 mph on U.S. 701 South and then turned back toward the Conway city limits, according to the report. Two Conway police officers set up a roadblock at the city limits, but the suspect drove around it. Several Horry County police officers were involved in the low speed chase of the suspect on the moped to monitor traffic and safety conditions during the incident. The suspect tried to turn his moped around in the road.

A Conway police officer stopped and grabbed the suspect by his shirt and pulled him from the moped, which caused the moped to crash into the patrol vehicle, according to the report. Officers noted there was light traffic in the area at the time of the incident and troopers with the S.C. Highway Patrol completed a crash report. The suspect was taken by EMS to Conway Medical Center to be checked for injuries and officers planned to charge him with burglary, failure to stop for police and damage to the patrol vehicle, according to the report. The victim identified several tools and items found in the bag and on the moped as being stolen from his shed, which had a broken door.

In an unrelated incident, a man died, and another was injured in a hit-and-run crash at about 3 AM. The victim was pronounced dead at 11:45 A.M. at Grand Strand Regional Medical Center, according to Horry County Deputy Coroner. The victim died from multiple blunt trauma due to being struck by a motor vehicle. Police are looking for a newer model Nissan Pathfinder SUV who they say was involved in a hit and run collision. The S.C. Highway Patrol said the collision was between a moped and the SUV, according to a press release. The moped was struck, and the riders received life-threatening injuries and then the SUV fled the scene. The crash occurred on U.S. 501 near the old Waccamaw Pottery Bridge in Myrtle Beach. Police say the vehicle is silver or white in color, with noticeable damage to the left front of the vehicle. Anyone with information about the collision or about the vehicle of interest and encouraged to contact the highway patrol.

Sheriff Buster Ferguson stood before his assembled officers reeling off the cases that had occurred over the weekend. The list was long and more detailed than usual. His meeting had gone well past his self-imposed ten-minute guidelines. The disgruntle sheriff apparently steered them down a path that would equate to nothing but Monday unpleasantness for those beginning their work week. He remained calm and composed but an obvious facial tick told another story, contradicting his cool and collective demeanor.

No one uttered a word. His officers just waited patiently for the other shoe to drop. Crime was obviously on an upswing and the quirky side of beach life ever so prominent. The veterans on the force missed the late Sheriff Hank Singleton, a grizzly bear in size by comparison to Ferguson. He would have never used this tactic to make his point. The old guard wasn't impressed, more pissed and insulted by Ferguson's approach. Those rookies who knew no better were shaking in their boots, hanging on his every word.

"Officers, you have heard the facts, a cankerous oozing sore on the underbelly of Horry County. Is anyone in this room beaming with pride over the department's job performance thus far? Those who pay our salaries most certainly will be questioning our effectiveness. Some of you may be naïve enough to defend that argument, saying we caught the bad guys. While apprehension beats the alternative, it does not satisfy the intent. The taxpayers will not buy such a lame defense, nor will I."

Buster paused and scanned the room before continuing. "Too much emphasis is placed on capturing the lawbreakers and not preventing the crime. I can see on your faces that you think otherwise. How does one prevent a crime that you have no way of knowing will be happening, correct? Simple, you can't. Sure, there are opportunities to predict crime where the statistics support the likelihood and we do beef up patrols accordingly and seasonally in those areas. What about that couple who makes whoopee in the window or golf carts and mopeds disrupting traffic patterns or even being utilized for getaway vehicles? How can we possibly prevent those?"

Buster again scanned the room, searching the souls of those assembled before him. "It starts with every one of you. We can't stand on the mantra of that's the way we've always done things. They break the law. We try to catch them and bring them to justice; sometimes we win, sometimes they do. No, that is no longer acceptable, not on my watch. Continual improvement, never settling for less, not doing things the same old way, that is the key. We must become innovators. We WILL become innovators. How much time do any of you really spend talking with the public; not after a crime has been committed but before?"

Buster eyed his officers and then continued.

"Neighborhood watches have been formed for a reason. More eyes, more presence, more awareness, more communication with thy neighbors is a formula that works. Too many law enforcement officers think their job consists of cruising around until the call comes in that a crime has been committed and then they act and react. Idle time is an opportunity to meet and greet and develop a bond with those paying your salaries. Show them you really care, and they will care and be more responsible. Networking is more effective. There is strength in numbers. Stop thinking you're the Lone Ranger and more like you're the Texas Rangers, with more resources available to utilize."

He paused again, searching for any indication that they were with him.

"We must dispel the police stereotype. We're not just a bunch of fat cats riding around, trigger happy just waiting for the next crime to be committed. All those eyes that we're not tapping into see much more than we do. All we must do is spend the time to make them aware, train them what to be suspicious of, and to call us at the first sign of activity, before the crime has been committed. Sure, there will be false alarms, but continual improvement is just that. We learn. They learn as we go. We adjust, retain and improve. Are there any questions?"

Trudy spoke up. All those around her, including her team, scrutinized her boldness. This was almost like one of those situations where a volunteer was needed and everyone in the room but one took a step backwards, leaving that person out on the limb alone.

"Thank you, Sheriff. I for one do concur with your approach. Might I make one suggestion though? "

"You have the floor, Pierce. Make it quick though."

"Before you herd us into the streets to make nice with those who pay our salaries, might there be some training and guidelines established first? Let's face it. Not everyone in this room is equipped with the technique and protocol to do as you have asked. While old dogs can certainly learn new tricks, it does require teaching to ensure we're all operating from the same play book so to speak."

No one came to her defence or clapped, whooped or hollered to acknowledge she was spot on, not even her CSI team. Buster's facial tick became more noticeable, not something that indicated he embraced or appreciated her frankness or boldness or suggestion. Upstaging Sheriff Buster Ferguson might not be the wisest career move for anyone, not even if it wasn't meant to sound condescending. Detective Trudy Wagner Pierce, now working her forth Horry County sheriff since moving back from Ohio, had not learned her lesson when it came to keeping her mouth shut or coloring outside the lines.

"Time does not presently allow for discussions in this matter. Everyone is dismissed, everyone but Detective Pierce. Please consider what I have said as you begin your day on the streets and highways. Focus on prevention and detection, not reaction. That will be all."

Whispers and rumblings could be heard as the officers exited the war room. While many agreed with her assessment, most didn't envy Pierce's current situation and decided to give her wide berth. She had called out the Sheriff so to speak and he was not a man accustomed to being questioned or critiqued. Little man syndrome was never more prevalent. Making matters worse, a woman had upstaged him in front of his department. No one wanted to be in her shoes right now.

Trudy, not one to be shy to take on controversy, didn't flinch at the Sheriff singling her out for a private discussion. She instead interpreted it as at least he had been listening to what she had to say. She might end up investigating a Dunkin Donut caper next. Why worry, the worst he could do was fire her. Nothing she had said came close to insubordination. She had a room full of witnesses, not worth much given how they had remained silent. If he canned her, she'd just have more time to spend with Brady.

Sly and Tim waited for her in her office. "Well," inquired Sly, "Should we help you pack up and exit the premises or are you still our fearless leader?"

"Wishful thinking I'm sure. Surprisingly the sheriff asked me to research and see if I could find what he calls sensitivity training, getting along with thy neighbor so to speak, the right approach to winning them over to our side."

"Doc Dallas might have some suggestions," spoke up Tim.

"Great idea, round her up and then you and she can investigate an incident in Loris. Seems we have a repeat offender abusing a horse out that way. The horse owner caught the suspect and held him at gun point until local police arrived. The official offense is buggery."

Sly smiled, "You and the doc should have a fine time on this one."

Tim shrugged, not getting it.

"Research it before you arrive," advised Trudy.

Longs, S.C
Horry County

Detective Tim Burroughs and CSI Team Doctor Dallas Solomon, psychologist, had arrived on the scene first, following the arrest. Trudy had asked Dallas to accompany Tim, based on the circumstances surrounding the reported occurrence. Tim was uncomfortable with the subject matter and had avoided discussing the specifics of the case with Dallas during the ride to the little community, 14 miles northwest of North Myrtle Beach. It was a small unincorporated community within Horry County located at the intersection of S.C. 9 and S.C. 905. The town consisted of a post office, a gas station and few small businesses.

Pulling into the yard, Tim spotted a woman standing outside the stable. The suspect in the crime had already been transported to J. Rueben Long. This must be the lady who had caught the perpetrator red handed or at least red something. Tim's face flushed dreading what must be done. Sometimes he liked it better when Trudy utilized him as just the computer geek. While he thrived on the thrill of the pursuit, the formalities of the interrogation weren't his cup of tea, but it did come with the territory.

"Hello, you must be Anna Kessler," said Tim.

"That would be me in the flesh."

"I'm Detective Burroughs and this is Doctor Solomon. We're with the crime scene investigation unit. I understand you had a little situation here."

"Guess you could say that. You're a tad too late, detective. The policemen that answered my 911 call have already hauled him off."

"Yes ma'am, we're aware of that fact. We're here to further the investigation."

"What's there to investigate? He's guilty. I caught him at it and called the police. Maybe this time the law will actually lock him up and toss the key."

"This time?" inquired Dallas.

"Second time he's been here; well as far as I know any way."

Tim dreaded the next question but somehow mustered up the nerve to ask, "Can you tell us exactly what happened?"

"I can, but those other officers have already written this up. It seems to me you could get the lowdown from them."

"Yes ma'am, we probably could be like I said, our job is to conduct a more thorough investigation. If it doesn't put you out, we would appreciate you indulging us."

"Got nothing better to do, I suppose. Where do you want me to start, this time or the last?"

"Let's stick to the most recent first."

"Just happened, not much longer than an hour and half ago. I was inside, cleaning up the kitchen when I heard Cookie making a commotion in the stable. I recognized the panic in her whinnying. I knew right off the bat that something wasn't right. We have coyotes around here, so I figured I best check on her. I fetched my shotgun and slipped out the backdoor to nail me one if I had half a chance."

"And what did you observe," asked Tim.

"It was no coyote though. It was him again, Vernon Rudder. God must have intervened and stopped me from emptying both barrels. I told him britches and hands up before I cut loose and ask questions later."

"You caught him in the act of buggery," asked Dallas.

"I did and it's damn disgusting. Let me be the first to tell you so. It looks like we got more company coming. This sort of thing sure draws the attention, doesn't it?"

Tim and Dallas turned to notice a television van pulling into the yard. The logo on the side indicated it was the Channel 4 News team. Parking next to their car, two people exited. Just what we need, thought Tim, something like this on the local news putting Horry County on the map for all the wrong reasons. Any publicity is supposed to be good publicity, right…wrong.

"Hello detectives, I hope we're not intruding. I'm Summer Knight and this is Mike, my camera man. We're here to interview Anna Kessler on the Vernon Rudder buggery incident."

"Come on over honey, I was just about to tell Detective Burroughs and Doctor Solomon what happened. It'll save me from having to repeat it a third time."

"Mrs. Kessler, this is an investigation. I don't think it would be appropriate if it was filmed."

Anna smiled. "Pish-posh, young man. It's all going to be a matter of public record anyway, so why not?"

"You may stay Miss Knight, but no camera," said Tim.

"Deal, no camera it is, Detective Burroughs. Please call me Summer."

Without thinking and quite taken by the newswoman's beauty, he replied, "And you can call me Tim." This drew an odd look from Dallas and a slight smile.

"Thanks Tim. Please, continue with your questioning of the witness to the buggery."

Just the mere mention of the word sent Tim into a whirlwind of dread. Now he'd have to survive this recount with a larger audience, in front of a news woman at that.

"Well, it's not much to it; at least the catching him part. Like I said, I was inside, cleaning up the kitchen when I heard Cookie making a commotion in the stable, whinnying something terrible. Can you imagine what poor Cookie must have been thinking? I knew right then that something wasn't right. She doesn't carry on like that unless something has her spooked. I fetched my shotgun, thinking it might be coyotes. There is no short supply around here."

Tim swallowed. His mouth felt dry. He almost stuttered his next question. "So, you're at the barn and then what?"

"There's that black man, Vernon Rudder, pants down to his ankles, standing on a cinder block poking my sweet innocent horse. She's never even been with any other horses before and here's this no good for nothing bastard doing this to her. I had my fingers on the trigger but if I had pulled the trigger, I would have hit Cookie too."

"Then what," asked Tim.

"I yelled at him to pull up his britches and then hold up his hands, so I could see them. I told him to step off that damn cinder block and away from my horse. I backed his black ass into one of the empty stalls and then called 911. That's about it."

"Did you converse with the gentleman while you waited on the officers to arrive," asked Dallas.

"Gentleman! Anyone who would rape an innocent horse can't be confused with being anything close to a gentleman. Well, it takes a while to get out here so yes; I had time to talk to him."

Before thinking, Summer spoke up, "What did you say to him?"

Tim gave her a courtesy smile. Actually, it was more than that. His portly face was flushed again. Tim had become a cracker-jack detective, especially after having had Trudy as a mentor, but still at a glance he could be easily pegged as Piggy from *Lord of the Flies*. Still there was no denying it, he was quite smitten by the news gal.

"I scolded him royally. I told him it was sick for a fifty-year-old man to be doing this to poor helpless animals. I don't get it. This is the second time he's been caught doing this and both times here at my barn with Cookie. He was already on probation for that first time. That charge resulted in a three-year jail sentence for him, but the sentence was suspended to probation. They let him wiggle off the hook and look what he does."

"Did he respond," asked Summer, sort of taking over the investigation. Tim said nothing. Dallas eyed Tim then Summer, assessing the situation.

"Yeah, he did but can you really believe what anybody might tell you while staring down the barrel of a shotgun. He told me he had been struggling with schizophrenia and had not been taking his medication. He said he was very sorry for letting his family down and for doing things like this. He told me he wasn't brought up doing stuff like this and that he was in the wrong for it. He swore that he would try his very best to admit to his wrongdoings and that he hoped I could accept him for who he was and the things he had done in the past."

"Did you accept his apology?" asked Summer.

"Hell no. I told him to save that crap for the judge and that he was damn lucky I hadn't scattered pieces of him around the barn. I took the safety off just to put the fear of the Lord in him."

"Is that all," Tim finally asked.

"Back in the day they used to hang horse thieves. I wonder what they would have done to a horse fu…"

"Thank you, ma'am, for your statement," interrupted Tim. This time it was Summer who cracked a smile.

"You can do your televised interview now if you'd like," added Tim.

"That's okay. I think I have enough for my report. Besides, you heard her; I don't think she's up to repeating it again, even for the camera."

"Buggery is a fascinating subject," interrupted Dallas. "It's a British term, very close in meaning to the term sodomy, and is often used interchangeably in law and popular speech. It may also be a specific common law offence, encompassing both sodomy and bestiality."

Tim's face again flushed red as a beet. Summer engrossed in the subject hardly took notice. Tim looked at her, thankful she wasn't looking at him. He would have probably blushed if he already wasn't doing so.

Dallas continued. "In English law buggery was first used in the Buggery Act 1533, while Section 61 of the Offences against the Person Act 1861, entitled *Sodomy and Bestiality*, and defined punishments for the abominable Crime of Buggery, committed either with mankind or with any animal. The definition of buggery was not specified in these or any statute, but rather established by judicial precedent. Over the years the courts have defined buggery as including either anal intercourse by a man with a man or woman, or vaginal intercourse by either a man or a woman with an animal, but not any other form of unnatural intercourse; the implication being that anal sex with an animal would not constitute buggery."

Tim wiped his forehead, the back of his neck and then his mouth. Sweat was pouring down his back like a river, following the crack of his ass. He leaned against the cruiser to conceal it. He didn't know how to stop Dallas without appearing to be a wussy.

"Buggery is illegal in South Carolina though," added Summer.

"Quite so, our Mister Vernon Rudder can surely bear testament having now been incarcerated a second time. In English Law such a case had not come before the courts of a common law jurisdiction to test the criminal implications. If it had, I find it highly improbable that a person would be exculpated of a crime associated with sex with animals only by reason of the fact that penetration involved the anus rather than the vagina."

"Times have indeed progressed," said Summer, now glancing over at Tim, sensing his discomfort for the first time. She thought it refreshing for a man to be embarrassed by sexual conversation, even if it involved something as vulgar as horse buggery. "Do either of you have time for a break, maybe even lunch? I'd relish the fact to discuss this further for my report." Mike nodded it was okay by him.

Dallas answered for both, sensing Tim's hesitation. "We'd be delighted; any thoughts, what might be nearby."

"There's Casa Villa Mexican Restaurant," said Mike.

Summer rolled her eyes. "Do you know where every single eating place is, Mike?"

"Lived in these parts all my life; what can I say? I have to feed this face regularly."

"Hispanic it is," added Dallas.

Tim nodded his agreement, just happy to spend more time with Summer Knight.

River City
Murrells Inlet

"Brady, how did you read my mind? I was in the mood for a big old burger and fries. I'm on the verge of drooling just thinking about double clutching a *Three Alarm Fireburger*." She followed the menu with her finger, mouthing the ingredients; *Cajun spiced, smothered in hot sauce with jalapenos, pepper jack, lettuce, tomato and spicy chipotle mayo, all for just $6.99.*

"It wasn't difficult. You had already had a long day and the cook was sort of out of commission."

"Not a good day, huh?"

"From cane to walker again in the snap of your fingers; I'm betting that wheelchair is closer than either of us would like to believe."

"It's not like you to be so pessimistic."

"Kicked, punched and beaten down, just having one of those pity party days I suppose. Reality is knocking on the door. The doctor has warned us that the Parkinson was progressing at an alarming pace, much more than he would prefer. The guinea pig days are over. That magical medical breakthrough simply doesn't exist yet. It's time for you and me to get serious and plan for the inevitable."

"Who are you and what did you do with my husband. This is so un-Brady like. You're not a quitter."

"I didn't say I was tossing in the towel, my love. I just think that it's time we begin planning for the next stage of our lives. Remember, we agreed that you would not take this on alone. We will employ at least a part time caregiver when that time arrives."

"I don't want to have this conversation right now."

"I know. Neither do I but putting it off is not an option. Let's face it. I'm going downhill fast. I know it and I know you know it. Denial is pointless. We have the long-term healthcare so paying for it isn't an issue. It's the mental preparation I'm more concerned about; maybe mine more than yours. You've been there. You at least have a leg up on it after taking care of your mother with the Alzheimer's."

"Yeah, right, you saw what a complete disaster I made of that."

"You're no longer that person. You learned from those mistakes so stop beating yourself up over it."

"That's just it and you know it. I never did beat myself up over it. I justified my actions all the way to the very end. You were with my mom when she died, not me. I didn't mean to say it like that."

"What, the die word; there is no cure for Parkinson. We've known that from day one. We must make the most of what time we do have left and we will. We are born, and we inevitably die. It's the cycle of life. Mine is just at an accelerated pace I'm afraid. We can't stop it. We must learn to cope and do what is necessary."

"Maybe I should take a leave away from the force and spend more time with you."

"See your priorities have indeed evolved but let's face it, you could never be happy being the 24/7 caregiver. You'd drive both of us crazy. No, you'll need a break away from this and your work is an escape path. Besides, I've been thinking."

"You thinking this can't be good, Circus Boy."

"When Allison arrives for her visit, I want you to invite her to move in with us."

"The drugs have completely warped your brain, me and my sister under the same roof, permanently, I don't think so."

"Not permanently…"

"Oh great, you want her to hang around with me until you kick the bucket." Trudy couldn't believe what she had just blurted out. "Brady, I didn't mean…"

"Fact is fact and that's exactly what I want you to do. I couldn't have phrased it better myself. The day is coming, sooner than either of us would like but, yes, please promise me you'll ask her."

"I can't. I won't."

"Then I will if you give me no choice."

"Come on Brady, this is like mixing oil with water; we'd kill one another."

"You said you've grown closer since your mother's death."

"She's divorced and has, for some ungodly reason, lost custody of her children. We haven't grown that close because I didn't know anything about either. With what we've got going on, we certainly don't need her emotional package."

"Have you not considered she might need you about now?"

"I hate it when you rationalize every single little thing. I'm the last shoulder she should depend on and I have the track record to back it up."

"Who knows; she might be able to help if you give her half a chance."

"Let's get one thing straight, Circus Boy. I sucked at being a caregiver, but I was the caregiver poster child compared to Allison. She hightailed it back to Atlanta and stayed there until our mom died. She'll just screw this up for me and you both, I promise you."

"For me, give this a chance, please."

"Ah man, not the poor pitiful puppy dog look; you know how I hate that. I see through your little plan. You're bribing me with this damn burger and fries, aren't you?"

"I'm just taking my lovely wife out to dinner at one of her favorite eateries."

"Can we compromise and do this on a probationary basis?"

"What...set some sort of time limit and if it doesn't work you kick her ass out of the house; I don't think so."

The meal arrived. Trudy smiled at the waitress and welcomed the brief reprieve.

"Damn it, Brady, this is fighting dirty, below the belt."

"Trust me, below the belt will come later, Phase II of my plan."

"Damn it to hell, Brady. All right, I'll ask her, but if she says no, there will be no groveling. We drop this, okay?"

"If she says yes, there will be no stipulations or time limits, okay?"

"I'm warning you, we'll have no privacy with her here. She's so needy and intrusive."

"That's why I say we introduce her to Woody."

"I can't do that to Woody."

"Why not allow Woody to decide. We can invite him over after she arrives."

"You're really into this, aren't you? Okay smartass; let's just see who breaks first with Allison under foot."

"Care to make a side wager?"

"Name it."

"We'll discuss it over dessert."

"We never order desert here."

"And we won't start now."

"Doubly evil, aren't you?"

"Bad to the core; taking advantage of every open opportunity while I'm still up to it. Besides, hooking her up with Woody would get her out of the house. Eat your burger, detective, then my walker is open for business."

"Walker…kinky…"

Myrtle Beach Gentlemen's Club

Detective Sylvester Stone and Detective Parnell Roberts were on the scene investigating a series of vehicle break-ins. Suspects were non-existent, almost as non-existent as witnesses and those willing to admit their vehicles had indeed been broken into at Myrtle Beach's only *all nude revue*. So far, a couple of bouncers and the cashier at the entrance door were the only willing participants in the investigation and only because their rides had been compromised during the robbery. They worked there so they had nothing to hide. In total, seven vehicles had been damaged in the little crime spree. Three belonged to these gentlemen. License plates were being run on the other four, all with broken passenger side windows, the owners supposedly still inside and avoiding the interrogation. The detectives had been granted permission to enter the premises by the owner/manager.

Detective Parnell Roberts had just arrived in Horry County two weeks ago and because of previous experience had been assigned to work with Trudy's CSI team. He had twelve years of police experience under his belt. He had worked crime scene investigations for the past three, but in a much smaller venue, Clover, S.C., in York County, a stone toss from Charlotte. Clover was most recognized by history buffs for the pivotal American Revolutionary War battle of Kings Mountain just eight miles away. A railroad had operated from Yorkville to Gaston County, N.C. A water tank for the railway's steam locomotives was constructed midway between Gastonia and Yorkville. According to lore, the overflow of water from the railway's water tank fertilized a patch of clover and the stop was called "the clover patch." The town was officially incorporated in 1887. It later became the home of several cotton mills, many of which operated until after World War II.

Clover, with a population around 5000, just didn't hold enough excitement for the likes of Parnell Roberts. He leapt at the venue change to the east coast when he realized they were fishing for a detective. Parnell had been born and raised in Chester, a nearby town, also lacking the luster to captivate a sleuth such as himself. Parnell, a southerner through and through, talked the talk and walked the walk. He dipped snuff and cursed like nobody's business.

At six eight, topping out at nearly three hundred pounds, he could hold his own in any sort of tussle. Parnell wasn't muscular but was big boned, stout as an ox, and had quite the temper when riled. He proudly sported a shaved head and bushy red mustache. He had served two years in the marines before being discharged for being just a tad too feisty, even for a marine; often challenging the authority of his superiors. That had carried over into his policing, not one to take crap off anyone, ranking or not.

Parnell had been Sheriff Buster Ferguson's first hire. It takes a good ole boy to appreciate a good ole boy apparently, so said some officers in the department. To Trudy it just didn't wash. Ferguson was a ball buster, rules and regulations to the tee, spit and polished all the way. Parnell Roberts was almost an exact opposite. Does the myth that opposites are attracted to one another apply in law enforcement? To make matters worse she had been tasked with having the reject from Deliverance join her team. Possibly that had been the sheriff's motive all along, just another way to bust her chops. Too pig headed, it would take more than the likes of this one Bubba to break her down. Trudy partnered him up with Sly to investigate a series of car break-ins, figuring low hanging fruit such as that case should keep him out of immediate trouble. Sly was an excellent mentor, leaving Parnell in good hands.

"We're going inside, huh, Sly?"

"Yes, Detective Roberts, we're going inside. How else do you perform a thorough investigation?"

"It says there on that marquis that this place is a nudie bar."

"Yes, it is an adult entertainment establishment. We have quite a few in Horry County."

"That's not what it says. It says that they are all nude. That means they are naked, not topless and no pasties."

"Your schooling must have been exceptional in York County."

"Naked, like, wearing no clothes, nothing; is that even legal in these parts?"

"Loop hole, they can't actually sell any type of alcohol inside."

"That doesn't make a lick of sense. Grown men visiting a joint where they have naked women head to toe, and they can't even get liquored up. That alone ought to be against the law."

"BYOB, they can bring their own inside."

"Get out of here. You mean I could go in there and take whatever I want to drink, and nobody can tell me to leave."

"Those are the house rules and the law."

"You ever been in there before; I mean, when you're off duty?"

"No, I can't say I have. Matter of a fact, this will be my first time on duty."

"Clover sure didn't have naked women prancing around the stage. You had to go into Charlotte, but still they just stuck their titties in your face for a buck, that was about it. I think they did bust a few for prostitution and trafficking drugs from time to time. All naked revue, now don't that beat all, here in the great Palmetto State, Bible belt central."

"Myrtle Beach is anything but Bible belt country. Tourist towns are a bit more liberal with what is allowed. We have casino boats leaving out of Little River and some have been lobbying for years to allow actual casino hotels here along the grand strand. Blue laws are not enforced. You can purchase beer in the grocery stores and order a drink in a bar or restaurant on Sundays."

"If that don't beat all. Hell, if I would have known all this crap, I would have been vacationing here years ago instead of going to the Great Smokey Mountains."

"History lesson is over. We have an investigation to conduct, Detective Roberts."

"Come on now, it's Parnell. We're riding buddies. There's no need for this Detective Roberts bullshit."

Sly was none too pleased with his redneck gunslinger sidekick. He couldn't fathom how this man could have held down a police job with this sort of unprofessional behavior. Southerners are sadly stereotyped as such in movies and books. People like Parnell Roberts just provide credence to the myth, dumb hick, trash talking, uneducated sounding, and tobacco chewing bubba-jay. He, like, Trudy, didn't get it; what had Sheriff Ferguson been thinking?

This could only dumb down the perceived image of officers under his watch. Visiting northerners crossing paths with Parnell would have a feeding frenzy. Keeping tight reins on this potential renegade was going to be a chore. The man had a garbage pit mouth and Sly could only imagine what his approach to an actual investigation might be. Fact, he was about to find out and in of all places, a gentleman's bar. Parnell was possibly the furthest thing from a gentleman, southern or otherwise.

Frankie Costello, the owner, escorted them inside, not too willingly. He just wished to get this over with quickly and hopefully not send his patrons running for the hills. Many were visiting golfers and businessmen, strangers for the most part and not in fear of being identified. There was a a few locals, some single, others married, those who didn't wish to be recognized. It shouldn't be difficult to determine which was which. Those heading to high ground or avoiding eye contact would float to the surface belly up like dead fish. Several of the compromised vehicles were sporting South Carolina License plates. The easy way would be to just make an announcement over the PE system, but Frankie Costello would never agree to anything like that, fearful of destroying his night's business. By evidence in the parking lot, the place should be wall to wall with would be dollar stuffers.

They made their way inside. It took a few seconds for their eyes adjust to the darkness and the spectacle of strobe lights and excessively loud music. Then the circus like spectacle unfolded in all its glory. The bare as the day they entered the world young ladies were on stage vying for the dollar bills being offered up for a closer look at their goods. Sly glanced over at his cohort, obviously awe struck by the nakedness being flaunted at every turn.

Talking above the noise, Sly laid out a game plan, but before they could act on it, two gals grabbed them by their arms, acting as the welcome wagon. Sly promptly flashed his badge and to Parnell's dismay they quickly made a hasty retreat. He instructed Parnell to retrieve the list of license plates, names of the title owners and vehicle descriptions of those damaged outside and to begin working the crowd, locating the owners. He was to ask if any late arrivals had noticed anything suspicious outside. In the meantime, Sly accompanied Frankie to a back room to review any video footage of the parking area.

Bingo! A camera had indeed clearly captured two culprits breaking and entering the various parked vehicles. Frankie, red faced, recognized them. They were two of his newest recruits, having only started to work tonight. Sly asked Frankie why he hadn't already viewed the footage. His excuse, he had arrived just minutes before the detectives, having been contacted by a bouncer reporting to work, who had discovered the windows broken and alarms sounding. This case was going to be an easy one to solve so it appeared. The girls were still here. Frankie suggested that his latest bouncer be questioned too. Patrick Yenicek, one of the bouncers, had recommended the hiring of the two young ladies. He had his suspicions that the three of them were in this together.

Exiting the office area, Sly spotted Parnell book-ended by two young ladies, one completely nude and the other scantly attired and may as well have been. Frankie shouted in Sly's ear and motioned to the female suspects and the bouncer not too far away. Sly approached Parnell, tapping him on his shoulder from behind.

"Hey man, this isn't what the hell it looks like, really," Parnell trying to defend his most compromising position with the two young ladies obviously groping him vigorously.

"Fine work Detective Roberts. Please cuff and Miranda them." Sly then zeroed in on the bouncer.

Yenicek had been around the block a time or two. He caught the look too. Making no bones about it, he hauled ass, running down a hallway. Before pursuing him Sly asked where the hallway led. Frankie said to pretty much everywhere, to the restrooms, dressing room, private dance rooms and office, but more importantly, a rear exit. Sly phoned for back-up as he sprinted down the hallway. A big busted blonde stepped aside nervously. A valet, a sleazy looking fellow standing in the bathroom doorway, pointed towards a door, nodding he had seen the escapee.

Sly burst through the door and into a sea of naked and half naked women. None attempted to cover themselves. Parnell would have been in redneck heaven here. One helpful brunette pointed towards another door, apparently feeling no loyalty to the bouncer. She mumbled something about him being a big prick as Sly passed. Sly charged through the next door exiting into the parking lot. The suspect, Patrick Yenicek was sprawled on his back, holding his throat and gasping for air. Standing over him was Detective Roberts, patting his forearm, motioning that he had just clothes lined him.

"The lariat, I learned it from Stan Hanson, does the trick every time."

"Lariat…Stand Hanson," questioned Sly.

"Three hundred pounds, all Texan, spitting tobacco, swinging a bull rope with a giant cow bell attached to the end of it, and screaming his head off, a man's wrestler, where have you been, under a rock?"

Sly just shrugged, still having no clue who he was babbling about.

"My turn to deliver a history lesson then; Stan 'the lariat' Hanson stormed onto the wrestling circuit in the mid-seventies. He was a big ole, all brawn, Texan, wearing the cowboy hat, leather vest, boots, the real McCoy. He got his start and reputation over in Japan. During a title match, he broke ole Heavyweight Champion Bruno Sammartino's neck while they were going at it in a match; used the lariat, his version of the clothes line. The power of the lariat became legendary on the circuit after that. It's a real man's version of a close line." Parnell patted his forearm again and smiled.

"Lariat, right…"

"Not to worry, the gals are cuffed to the dancing pole on stage. The good old boys are drooling inside, thinking it's part of their damn act. I played a hunch when I saw this feller make the mad dash with you in hot pursuit and headed him off at the pass. He'll be feeling that tomorrow for sure. I'm figuring he must be tied into this too."

"You figured right, probably the mastermind and I have a hunch too that there are a string of similar unsolved break ends matching this MO."

"We did good then, didn't we partner?"

"We did well indeed; nice work, Parnell."

"That's some place in there. I might just mosey back in there when I got myself some downtime; strictly investigative of course," winked Parnell as he spat tobacco juice on Yenicek's shoes.

Sly smiled. "Knowledge is a powerful tool."

"Bull crap and you know it," laughed Parnell.

Live Oaks Church of Contemporary Teaching and Healing
Georgetown County

Reverend Jonah Blackwood sat in the church's study preparing for the most prestigious upcoming event. He labored over the speech, avoiding the urge to speak from the pulpit to stir the congregation, attempting to walk the straight and narrow, and stick to the ceremony as scripted. Besides, most of the congregation would not be those of his immediate flock. Not to his particularly liking, there would be assigned seating, an event more resembling a rock concert he feared. He had prayed about it before committing the church, but in the end had allowed sizable contributions to influence his decision. Churches had operating budgets too and there was no denying this would wipe the slate clean, making them debt free for the very first time. Money excluded, how could he turn away a former member of the flock, one who still paid his tithes tenfold, even if he hadn't attended services in many years?

The Reverend, long of tooth, would be eighty this fall and for the first-time contemplated retirement a second time. He had come out of retirement when a friend approached him seven years ago about starting up this new church, a new-fangled concept that intrigued the old pastor. It was high energy and targeted at the young. It hadn't made much sense why he had been chosen to lead the mostly newbies. Why not hire a high energy youngster? It had been explained that they wished to have an old-style man of the cloth, mingled with a new image; old time religion with a twist.

Jonah, sporting a thick wave of grey, compelling green eyes and an almost Billy Graham like demeanor, the church for whatever reason had flourished nicely, more so than most new start-ups. The church itself had undergone a complete makeover, while not losing site of its one-hundred-year-old foundation. Décor offered illusion, making those who visited think they had ventured into a world long forgotten. It complemented the long drive lined with ancient live oaks to a tee.

A welcomed knock at his door disrupted his deliberation and second guessing. Associate Pastor Garrett Moore eased the door open after Reverend Jonah granted him permission to enter. Garrett was the pastor in training, Jonah's protégé. He had been with the church for nearly four months now. While young and exuberant, the congregation had been slow to warm up to him. Jonah constantly coached him on being less political and opinionated, and to focus more on the scripture as it was intended.

It had surprised Jonah how this young generation of church attendees had latched on to him instead of the youngster. Garrett reminded Jonah of a young Robert Redford. The females certainly swooned in his presence, none of them driven by old time religion but, still, his sermon delivery lacked the punch to reel them in. Some things just take time Jonah reminded himself. One thing for sure, he better accelerate the learning curve if he planned to exercise his exit strategy.

"What has you so perturbed, Garrett?"

"He's back, that filthy derelict is hanging out on the front steps again."

"Have I not corrected you before, son? Every man belongs to the Lord's flock. Please refrain from calling him a filthy derelict. Less fortunate yes, but men in need must never be shunned or turned away. Remember, he who cast the first stone. Please invite Noah in. Offer him a meal and an opportunity to address any hygiene issues he may have. We should have fresh clothes in our clothing closet."

Exasperated, Garrett returned to the front of the church but thankfully Noah had moved on. Noah, he scoffed, probably fabricated to con the many churches he has visited. Garrett had no time or patience for such foolishness, especially not now. The event was rapidly approaching. Failure wasn't an option. He and the elder pastor certainly shared this sentiment. All seemed to be going as planned. This would be one like no other; placing the small southern community on the map. Glancing down the long driveway he thought he spotted movement on the right near one of the live oaks maybe fifty yards away. Scanning the outlying perimeter, he saw nothing further. Possibly he had only caught a glimpse of one of the many huge fox squirrels, a flicking grey tail along the side of a tree. That's all, nothing more.

Garrett relieved that Noah had moved along, returned to his chores inside, grateful to have stumbled into this opportunity as a free-lance associate pastor. It had been the perfect fit; well at least for his bidding. He hadn't exactly wooed the congregation yet, but everything takes time and must run its course. Everything would work out in due time. Destiny had an assistant in the wings. How did it go? Things always worked out in mysterious ways or something like that.

Noah watched from the underbrush, curious and alert. There was something about this place; his senses were seldom wrong, even now. Odd, he thought, how a gift had become a curse. Still, it could not be ignored or dismissed no matter how hard he wished it away. Destiny had offered the invitation. He had accepted, unwillingly at first, but now he was certain he had made the correct decision. It was but a waiting game and patience he had plenty as well as all the time in the world. It would play out in due time. It always did and not always as one would wish. Happy endings could go bad in a blink. No one knew better that him.

Suck, Bang and Blow
Murrells Inlet

Sheriff Buster Ferguson met with a group of organizers for the upcoming Harley Rally, his mission to ensure everyone was on the same page. Those planning for the rally were polite and quite genuine, not the abrasive biker types. He intended to do what needed to be done to make this work for the community, the bikers and the officers working the event. Through the discussion it became apparent that this was no event for the Hell's Angels or Outlaws. Most of the Harley Riders were doctors, lawyers, factory workers, and people from all walks of life. These were just common folks looking for a few days of fellowship and rowdiness, sowing a few seeds along the way. Sure, there would be those that would misbehave. Consumption of too much alcohol played a large part, but the goal, minimize the risks of fatalities. So many bikers and tourists in the area at one time surely introduced dangerous scenarios on the highways, a recipe that rarely ever served up an equal helping.

He had asked Detective Pierce and her team to join him if for no other reason than a show of support. After all, most of the detectives had worked rallies in the past. They could offer suggestions for improvement. He especially respected Detective Stone's approach and understanding of human behavior. He had warmed up to Pierce a tad but still didn't completely trust her and her vigilante ways. She had that reputation of going out on her own, but still, he could detect good qualities. Possibly she could be salvaged and remain part of his team of elite. Time would tell. Things always worked out one way or the other.

After the meeting, Ferguson and the detectives gathered outside of the Suck, Bang and Blow, Four Corners. This would be one hell of a congested area based on what he had been told; an adult carnival and a traffic sore spot. Soon he would have the largest police force in the state at his beck and call. It didn't come cheap either. Following on the heels of the Spring Harley Davidson Rally would be the Memorial Day Bike Fest, bringing in an entirely new bunch of bike riders and a supporting cast of non-biker participants. He and the detectives would soon have the same powwow with Atlantic Beach organizers. One could never be too prepared when it came to these sorts of things.

"How do you think this went?" asked Buster, looking for honest feedback.

"I think they'll try to do their part but with several hundred thousand arriving, try is about all one can expect," spoke up Trudy.

"Suck, Bang and Blow, what a hell of name for a place," chuckled Detective Parnell Roberts.

"Not really that odd once you understand the mechanics of the four-stroke engine," explained Sly. "An internal combustion engine cycle is completed in four piston strokes; includes a suction stroke, compression stroke, expansion stroke, and exhaust stroke, thus suck, bang and blow."

"I'll be damned. I was thinking something a lot more different."

"Hopefully this got your mind out of the gutter then," added Trudy.

"Speaking of mind in the gutter, Burroughs, how did that horse fu…"

"Detective Roberts, curb that foul mouth of yours and show a little respect for the position," snapped Buster. "I'll have none of my officers disrespecting this department. Do I make myself perfectly clear?"

"Yes sir," answered Parnell, just before he spat tobacco juice onto the pavement.

"Get rid of that bad habit while on duty. Trust me, you'll not wish me to tell you again."

Parnell spat the content of his mouth onto the pavement and wiped his mouth with the back of his hand. "Done, sir."

"What's with him," whispered Trudy to Sly.

"Hard to figure him," replied Sly. "He's perfectly capable of playing good cop, bad cop, a regular one man show, all with ill manners."

"Sheriff, if we're done here, might we be dismissed? We have Krispy Kreme rustlers to round up."

"Dismissed Pierce, and capturing a thief is no laughing matter."

"Sorry for the levity, Sheriff; just trying to mesh with the neighbors. A sense of humor can often break the ice and make friendly."

"Research, Detective Pierce?"

"Bad habits…guilty as charged…"

"I see through your little scheme…deflection for a teammate, interesting given the circumstances…take this motley crew out of my sight and be careful out there."

"Duly noted, sir."

After they were out of earshot of the sheriff, Trudy let it fly. "Parnell. What the hell were you pulling back there? You are treading on thin ice, an eyelash away from insubordination. Pull that crap again and I'll have your balls."

Parnell stuffed another large pinch of snuff in his cheek and eyed Trudy. Tim Burroughs made a step in the crude detective's direction but Sly grabbed his arm.

"Let it go, Tim."

Parnell saw him. "Anytime you feel froggy, bring it on Timmy boy."

"Enough, both of you, especially you Detective Roberts, if you wish to remain in this unit, you can that frigging smartass attitude."

Parnell spat but not in her direction, realizing he might be pushing it. "Yes sir, ma'am."

"Loose that snuff too. You heard the sheriff."

Parnell mumbled something. Trudy stood her ground and held out her open hand. "Now!"

He plucked the wad from his mouth and plotted it into her hand with the slightest of smiles. He then stepped back, saluted and spin around of his heels and then stepped away. Trudy shook her head in disgust.

"I'll ride back with him," spoke up Sly.

"Fine by me...Tim you're driving. I have some calls to make."

"Brady...?"

"He's my first. Woody left me a message too."

"Tell that ex-deputy-constable-sheriff, Woodrow Anderson hi for me. I heard his business is doing really well."

"He seems to be happy for once, long time coming after Janice's murder."

"Good for him. Woody has always treated me descent," replied Tim.

"He and I had a rocky start, but I think we eventually grew on each other."

On the ride back to Conway, after checking in on Brady and attempting to reach Woody and failing, she and Tim chatted, small talk mostly. Tim was such a likable guy on or off duty. He didn't put on for anyone. He was the same through and through, usually an easy read. That's why the conversation took her off guard.

"Have you had contact with the new news woman, Summer Knight?"

"No, not directly but I have caught her a couple of times on Channel 4. Wasn't she on the scene for the buggery incident over at Loris?"

Tim's face reddened. Trudy thought it might by the mere mention of buggery but relying on woman's intuition she sensed something else. "Spill it Tim. You have a thing for her, don't you?"

"We have a date this weekend. We have a lot in common. Plus, she's super nice and almost as geeky as me."

"Tim Burroughs, you've been smitten, haven't you?"

"I guess. I do like her."

"Where are you two kids having your first date?

"I'm not sure. I want it to be somewhere nice though."

"Aspen Grill, call and make a reservation. It's the perfect place for a romantic evening."

"Whew…that's a load off…thanks…I was thinking Bubba's in Surfside."

"There is certainly nothing wrong with Bubbas. They have killer fried pickles and dollar PBR. A walk on the beach is a stone's throw away."

"I thought about it because she really likes fried pickles."

"Make that you second date destination, Tim. Do the Aspen Grill this time. Tell you what. I'll have Brady make the reservation for you. He and the owner are tight. He'll do something special if Brady asks him. Settled, okay?"

"Thanks, I'm not the best at this sort of thing."

"You'll do just fine. You've already asked her out. That's a step in the right direction."

"Maybe not. She asked me out but told me to pick the place."

Trudy smiled. "We women are quite liberated. Who would have thought a bra burning party would have gotten this started?'

"A what?"

"Never mind, Tim. It was before our time. Change of direction, you don't care much for Detective Roberts, do you?"

"Does anyone? You called him a prick." Tim's face flushed again when he said it.

"None of us are perfect. I rewrote the book on imperfections and risky calls. I had a knack for dragging along the rest of you. We're lucky we didn't all receive our walking papers."

"Might have come to pass if your risky calls hadn't paid off. None of us wanted to turn over the Road Rage case to the Feds. As for the doc and those Hispanic murders, you just did what any of us would have done, given the circumstances. You thought you were rescuing Doctor Hawthorne at his clinic."

"And what did I get for my heroics…a tranquilizer needle and almost ended up with my body parts being served on a silver platter. We lost one of our own because of my carelessness."

"I could say the same thing. I lost my partner on that Tank fellow's front porch, blown away in one clean shot."

"Okay, enough, we're cops, and crap happens, right? We get ourselves in bad situations and if we're lucky, we get our asses out of them in one piece."

"Thanks for suggesting the Aspen Grill."

"I'm happy for you, Tim. I hope this works out for you."

"It's just a first date. We're not engaged or anything like that."

"Beginnings often have happy endings."

Tim smiled. "I would like that."

'What you say we stop by Dairy Queen in Conway and get an ice cream. I suddenly have an incredible craving for something big and chocolate, three scoops minimum on a waffle cone. Treats on me."

"I like your choice in cravings."

Pierce Beach House
Sisterly Love

Trudy remained on pins and needles, unable to sit still, nervously flitting about; mannerisms Brady had not witnessed during their relationship. He thought about intervening but that would require much effort on his part. The Parkinson had worsened, even more than he had let on. Hiding it was not really an option though and he would never intentionally keep his condition concealed from Trudy. Her stubborn pride unfortunately weighed in heavily. The cane had become all but useless except for mere balancing if he was only standing and making no attempt to walk. He had the bruises to prove recent bad decisions of only using it.

The walker barely served his purposes now. He made do but there was no denying it, a wheelchair loomed in his very near future whether Trudy wanted to come to terms with it or not. The rigidity was winning the battle just as the doctor had diagnosed. Thankfully his libido was still in tack. Well, with help from his beloved. They had always had an interactive relationship, aggressiveness welcomed from either party. It frustrated him watching her fret so over the arrival of her sister, Allison. It wasn't that she didn't want her to come; she just wasn't sure how this was going to play out. Second thought, she really didn't want her to come.

Allison had kept the secret of her marital problems from her. Trudy had thought they had grown closer and they had, but maybe not close enough to confide in her. What she couldn't figure out was why her ex-husband had the children and not her. Trudy could not visualize Allison being an unfit mother. She worshiped those kids, always had. Had she had an affair? That seemed so unlike her too, but sometimes things just happen. She could picture neither of them committing adultery. Then what happened? What went terribly wrong with their relationship?

"Please pour us a drink and make them doubles. We both need it. You're wearing me out."

"Sorry, this waiting is driving me nuts, Brady."

"Take it slow when she arrives. All will work out in due time."

Trudy made them a triple instead, Apricot Brandy instead of the hard stuff. She didn't wish to be zonked when Allison finally arrived. What was taking her so long? She should be here by now. Had something happened? Had she been in an accident? Now she was thinking like their mother, bless her soul.

"I'm too young to become my mother."

"Why did you say that?"

"From the brain to the lips, what can I say? I'm becoming a worrywart just like mom used to be before..."

"Hey, those were good times before the bad, right?"

"Back then when I was on the receiving end I didn't think so; all those curfews I had to break. I led Allison down the path as she got older. Boy did I set a hell of an example for little sister."

"What about a quickie? That usually mellows you out."

Trudy sat down in Brady's lap, hugging and kissing him. "What would I ever do without you, Circus Boy?"

Their eyes met, reality hitting home once again. The chiming of the doorbell rescued them from inevitable gloom and doom. The wait was over. Trudy downed the rest of her drink in one swift gulp, retrieving breath spray from her pocket as she headed towards the door. Brady slid the walker over and after three attempts made it to his feet. Brooding over his condition served no purpose. It was what it was, and he would deal with it one day at a time or maybe one step at a time, so it seemed. He made it to the foyer. Trudy and Allison were on the porch, talking, sort of. Neither of them was smiling nor embracing in a warm sisterly hug. Brady finally made it to the door and slowly eased it open.

"Hey Allison, long time no see, great to have you here."

Her jaw unhinged as she stared at him standing there propped up with the walker.

"This old thing. It's just a new golf apparatus for developing upper body strength. It hasn't caught on too well yet and isn't exactly leaping off the shelves at my stores. Some say it's just not sporty enough, too dated. We're redesigning it though."

Allison approached Brady cautiously and then gave him a hug, handling him as if he were a fragile old man. "That's no way to greet your brother-in-law." He squeezed her tightly, almost too tight, just to make his point.

"How long have you been like this," she asked, never being one to hold back any punches, Trudy's blood kin through and through.

"It comes, it goes. It's in come mode right now."

"You didn't say anything about Brady being…"

Trudy cut her off in mid-sentence. "You didn't tell me you were divorced and without your children so don't start on me, Allison."

"I knew I should have dressed for the occasion. Don't make me go referee on the two of you. Allison, can I get your luggage from the car?"

That drew the look from the detective and a smile from Allison.

"I'll help her with her things. Why don't you mix us a pitcher of Margaritas?"

"Pablo the barkeep at your service, my dear…"

Outside Trudy continued her questioning.

Allison quickly responded. "What, am I some sort of crime suspect? What's next, a line-up?"

Trudy threw up her hands. "Fine, we can talk later."

"What, an ultimatum now, sis? Just let up a little, how about it? This is tough enough without your senseless crap. You'll get your answers. Just not now…okay?"

"Sorry…to take a page out of Brady's golf manual, I need a mulligan for the hospitality wagon, don't I?"

"You better have a cartload of do-overs up your sleeves. This is going to be a long round."

"Where'd you learn golf lingo?"

"I took lessons once, but we realized golfing was not exactly an aphrodisiac in our marriage."

"Did golf ruin it for you?"

"No, silly, golf had nothing to do with it. Patience please, and a little breathing room would be greatly appreciated." With that they hugged like they meant it.

Aspen Grille
Myrtle Beach

Tim Burroughs perused the menu, torn between the Braised Black Angus Short Ribs and Seared New Bedford Sea Scallops. He had already ordered North Carolina Oysters, after finding out that Summer Knight liked them too. A bottle of Domaine Chandon Cab 2009 had been served. It had been arranged by Brady. Tim had all but decided against the ribs, fearing he would wear them. The waiter took Summer's order, Braised Black Angus Short Ribs, Bacon braised Brussel sprouts and fried spinach. Tim ordered the same.

"This is some place, Tim, an excellent choice."

Tim, with research as his life, responded, "Chef and owner Curry Martin reopened the Aspen Grille in 2009. Dishes are based on traditional Southern cuisine with Chef Martin's own personal twist. The dining room features warm woods and original art, making it a relaxing respite from the hustle bustle of the world outside. Food alone doesn't make a great dining experience. It must go hand in hand with excellent service. Never overbearing, but always helpful, their knowledgeable and attentive staff is trained to ensure the time spent here is enjoyable and truly memorable. I'm glad it pleases you."

Summer smiled, deciding not to confess she had read almost those exact sentences in the 'About Us' section on their website. She liked Tim and didn't wish to embarrass him.

"I've never had a better glass of wine. You've certainly outdone yourself on our official first date."

First, does that mean there would be a second and third, Tim wondered, mustering up a wide grin. Thank your Detective Trudy Pierce. "First impressions are important. Everyone judges you by that very first interaction."

"I agree. I was impressed by you when we met in Loris. That had to be a difficult case to investigate. Animal buggery is a touchy subject."

Heat escaped Tim's collar. He felt the flush wave approaching up his face like a tsunami. There was no quenching it. He opted for a verbal distraction. "Nothing is ever really just routine. Each case is analyzed and investigated to the best of our ability. A detective must rely on instinct as well as fact. The crime scene holds plenty of secrets if you take time to collect the puzzle pieces. This one was easy. The offender had been caught in the act, not much intervention required by us."

"That's why I enjoy being a news investigator. Every day is a challenge. It is so invigorating. You meet so many interesting characters and follow such compelling stories."

"Yeah, it can be a rush."
"I followed some of the high-profile cases here. You were in the middle of them, weren't you?"

"Goes with the territory, one must be prepared to react in an instant, but research breaks the cases. The internet and social media are ripe for the picking."

"I agree. I'd fall flat on my face if not for the research."

"Tell me, Summer; am I merely a research vehicle?"

She reached over and touched Tim on the hand. "If you're asking if I'm using you; the answer is not yet." She then smiled. "Tim, we have a lot in common. I sensed it the minute I met you."

Love at first sight, thought Tim. Impossible.

"We value the same morals and work ethics. I can tell you came from a loving home, one that believed in family values, working for what you wanted, no hand-outs. I, too, come from that background. I don't compromise my values, even for a headline story."

"No one can be that intuitive."

"You said yourself that you rely on instinct, right?" She squeezed his hand. "I'm a computer geek too, I must confess. I was captivated by you sometime back, even before I relocated here. Those same high-profile cases reeled me in, Tim. I saw you spread your wings and become who you have become. I must admit, I liked what I saw. You played such an important part in those cases."

"You make it sound almost as if you moved her because of me."

"In a way, I guess I did. Please don't get the wrong impression. I'm no stalker or perverted serial killer. I saw a man that I wanted to get to know for all the right reasons. Tim, you're a diamond in the rough, and there aren't many out there like you."

"I'm flattered but a little creeped out."

"Don't be. I mean, don't be creeped out. Take a chance on me and let's see how our relationship pans out."

"We're in a relationship?"

"Figure of speech, Tim, but let's take it slow if you think you might like me as much as I like you."

"Summer, you're more than I could ever hope for as relationships go. You're beautiful. You're intelligent. You possess excellent taste in men."

They both laughed and agreed to give this a try and see where it would take them. Tim had never been in a relationship, so he had no benchmark. He did like Summer Knight, had liked her from the instant he had seen her. Why someone would be interested in a chunky geek like him remained to be seen. What did he have to lose, other than his virginity? He flushed red from thinking the thought.

"Okay Tim, confess. What were you just thinking?"

"It's too early in our relationship for true confessions. To be honest, I've never been in a relationship. This is new territory for me."

"Let me guess, Tim. You're a virgin. You don't have to answer. I am too and that's no bull. Firsts must never be squandered, don't you concur. My mother instilled in me to protect mine and save it until marriage. I'm old fashion, I admit it."

Tim nodded. "I just can't believe we're having this sort of conversation on our first date. It seems a little too much too soon."

"Please don't think I'm promiscuous because I'm the furthest thing from it. I don't bar hop. I don't smoke. I avoid the so called in crowd. I commented earlier about the excellent wine. Heck, I could count on one hand how many times I've even tasted wine. In social situations, I tend to carry an alcoholic beverage around forever, pretending I'm sipping on it. My family was God fearing and never drank."

Tim remained silent, unsure what to make of the circumstances. He was taken by her, no doubt, and wanted to believe what she was saying. It just didn't add up though. He was the furthest thing from a catch. He knew it and she should know it. She was rambling on. He continued to listen, captivated but the analytical wheels turning inside his head. He feared she was using him but using him for what reason. He had nothing to offer, no path to a blockbuster case or information on any cold cases. What then? Should he just ride it out? She was so beautiful, and they did seem to have a lot in common, even their virginity, if she had been truthful about hers. Again, was it an act and would he have his heart broken. Well, he had never had his heart broken so how bad could it really be to have that happen?

The waiter delivered their meal. Tim didn't remember what he had ordered and if it had indeed been tasty once he had finished. Summer Knight had stolen his heart for better or worse. No argument, he had never felt happier or more suspicious. He would go with the flow, keeping in mind that if it didn't work out, he hadn't set himself up for the ultimate fall. On the bright side, he temporarily had the makings of a social life, one that didn't equate to bowling with his pal Richard. Maybe Summer liked to bowl. He'd hold out for a second date and reassess the data.

High profile loomed in the not so distant future, a game changer for those not expecting lightening to strike a third time. Statistically lightning strikes along the grand strand laying claim to the second most lightning strikes in the United States. This brewing storm had nothing to do with weather patterns but would certainly be a dozy. Enjoy Tim, while you can. The grand strand was in the crosshairs one more time. The beginning of both bike weeks was quickly approaching and with it evil would find its comfort zone.

Pelican Baseball Field
Myrtle Beach

Disguised as a loyal fan of the minor league squad, Valdemar sported a Pelican jersey and hat, booed the umpire and tossed out a few derogatory opinions concerning balls and strikes. A legion of associates was scattered about the first two rows along the first base line. Each was boisterous, chugalugging the dollar drafts and making themselves noticeable, some sporting Pelican logo merchandise while others wore tee shirts and hats supporting various venues about Myrtle Beach. While each was unique, they ironically blended into the crowd gathered to witness their team whipping up on the visiting Hellcats.

Valdemar firmly believed that the best way to not be noticed was to be noticed. Suspects in any crime were typically those attempting to keep a low profile, someone remembering something odd in a person's behavior. The person or persons slinking about, staying in the shadows, acting nervous, tended to be the ones witnesses remembered. A true chameleon blended into its surroundings by becoming its surrounding. There was no place in his occupation for hide and seek. Be loud, likable and one of the gang. Engage in conversation. Don't avoid social contact or interaction. Those who would remember you would never remember you as acting odd or suspicious. Thusly, you were quickly dismissed as being a suspect in their memory. Criminals flew under the radar and not in plain view.

Beer, popcorn, hotdogs and supporting attire were just props and costumes. Acting a bit intoxicated and overly zealous simply made people laugh or join in on the antics. Potential witnesses would be more prone to remember those antics instead of a face or description. Valdemar and his supporting cast had been in Myrtle Beach for eight days and had crashed the tourist community taking on almost every venue, vacationers to the core. They never moved as one but eventually ended up in the same locations. Talking in a unique theatrical code, meetings were covertly accomplished, and plans were forwarded. The curtain would go up in less than a week. The grand opening would be nothing short of spectacular. Perfection would be a given. His handpicked ensemble never faltered, every scene performed in one take, the bench mark set for the actors' guild.

Quoting from Poe, just above a whisper, Valdemar leaned to an associate sitting beside him, "If you wish to forget anything on the spot, make a note that this thing is to be remembered."

The man decked out in a Beaver Bar tee shirt and cutoff jeans replied, "Stupidity is a talent for misconception."

"Indeed, there is eloquence in true enthusiasm that is not to be doubted," volleyed Valdemar. "Did you leave your glasses at home; that was a strike, my ass," he yelled at the home plate umpire.

"I have, indeed, no abhorrence of danger, except in its absolute effect - in terror," replied his associate, "The Hellcats wiring your payment to an offshore account, ump?"

"Deep into that darkness peering, long I stood there, wondering, fearing, doubting, dreaming dreams no mortal ever dared to dream before…over here, I'll take a cotton candy," he waved down the vendor.

The next row down another associate spilled his beer on a grey-haired lady sitting in front of him, slurring his speech, tossing in an occasional expletive. Instead of blessing him out, she joined in, dropping an F-bomb, scolding the umpire for alleged bad calls too. The ruse played out as designed, all for one and one for all, locals supporting the home team. All the time, Valdemar confirmed the details of the operation with talking details of the operation in code, Act II in the publics' eyes, enjoying the national pastime under cloudless beach skies.

The game went extra innings, the Pelicans winning on a wild pitch in the thirteenth, the runner scoring from third. Those depicted as diehard fans filed out of the stadium, and over the next couple of hours all eventually ended back up at Hurl Rock Motel. Some were a hair shy of seeming to be drunk and disorderly, while others remained in their rooms, and a spattering even made their way across Ocean Blvd and to the beach. It was just another typical day from the desk clerk's perspective.

Gary, the desk clerk, had witnessed worse and had seen better. He stayed shy of all the monkey business unless neighbors complained, fights broke out or patrons went skinny dipping. He was slow to react on most disruptions, enjoying the cheap entertainment. Besides, by the time police would arrive most disturbances would have run their course. The owner made it perfectly clear he didn't want any business lost over minor altercations. Never jump the gun. Keeping that in mind, Gary tolerated most of the actions and just minded his own business.

The Trestle Bakery and Café
Main Street Conway

Trudy entered the doorway just ten minutes past the hour, having Saturday off and really hating to be up before 6 AM. She couldn't pass on an invite by Woodrow Anderson, her former partner and resigned sheriff of Horry County. It had been months since their last meeting, their work conflicting with any opportunities. She had been tempted to bring Brady and Allison along but didn't, figuring Woody would have told her to bring Brady if something hadn't been up. He was sitting alone at a table near the back, face buried in the menu.

"Good morning Woody and this better be good to ruin my opportunity to sleep in."

"Missed you too, Detective. Have a seat and order whatever you want, I'm buying."

"My, my, what happened, you hit the lottery?"

"I got your butt out of bed on a Saturday morning. The least I can do is buy you breakfast, right?"

"What's up?"

"Let's order first then we can catch up on old times."

"You are okay, aren't you Woody?"

"I'm fine. You're fine. Let a friend buy you breakfast, how about it?"

"Something's not right. I can read you like a book, Woody. Cut the being cordial crap and tell me why I'm here."

"No need to argue with you, I get it. But we're still having breakfast and I'm buying."

"Spill it."

"I had an old buddy contact me from Walterboro the other day."

"Walterboro, okay. So what did this buddy have to say about that quant little town?"

"Rocker, he just recently got his butt fired by the local newspaper."

"Rocker, working at a newspaper; how the mighty has fallen."

The waitress arrived to refill his cup. "Coffee, Hon?"

"Please, Hon," mocked Trudy.

"Ready to order?"

"Give us a minute," she answered.

"Sure thing, Sugar."

"Okay so Lance Rocker has fallen on hard times. That must take away from his face time. What did he do to get fired?"

"Apparently he concocted some sort of story that tarnished the town's founder's reputations. The town folks were not too happy. He got canned due to the negative feedback."

"I hate it for him but why the face to face to tell me?"

"He's missing."

"What do you mean he's missing?'

"Like poof, gone, he's missing."

"Trust me, he'll pop back up. He's probably just shacked up with a hot little honey licking his wounds and her. He'll be back at it, a thorn in someone else's side in the blink of an eye."

"I'm serious. He's missing. The landlord to his apartment found his door standing wide open. All his belongings were still there. His car was parked out front. The apartment door had been kicked open. And no, I had nothing to do with it. I still don't have much use for him, but I've gotten way past wanting to kill the a-hole."

"Okay, so he's missing, I get it. Why the hush, hush meeting?"

"My friend with the police force said they're leaning toward foul play, not that any of the folks really care one way or the other."

"Rocker always makes an impression wherever he goes. What evidence do they have?"

"Two local good ole boys were seen escorting him from a restaurant after a verbal altercation."

"So, what did these two goons have to say about that?"

"An anonymous tip was called in, but the snitch wouldn't cough up the guys' names, fearful of retaliation."

"Again, I hate it for Lance but what does any of this have do with us?"

"My turn to say you do remember Detective Shannon Chestnut's Aunt, District Attorney Claudia Livingston, the one you were so concerned about after it was reported she committed suicide in Wilmington last year. They reopened the case under the insistence of the family and now they're leaning away from the suicide assumption."

"Is this your way of eating crow, Woody?"

"Connect the dots, Detective."

"You scold me for being paranoid over her suicide and now you're telling me you think her death and Lance Rocker's disappearance are somehow linked?"

"Just something to contemplate is all I'm saying. Hey, you opened this can of worms when the district attorney died. Now I'm just willing to consider your hunch."

"Woody, who could possibly want to harm Livingston and Rocker?"

In unison they both said, "Tim Ford."

"But he is still in prison, right?"

"Yeah, however, his attorneys have been working vigorously for a new trial. Sources tell me that she had been subpoenaed to testify about the search warrant she issued us."

"My turn to be the naysayer then; why would Ford have her murdered after having her subpoenaed?"

"Suicide makes a good argument for guilt, something to hide."

"You're thinking too much like me now Woody. Why Rocker then and not you or me?"

"Who says we're not next? Rocker is just missing, no body, no connection on the books. I'm just running the scenario by you for now. Our hands are sort of tied. I'm no longer in law enforcement and besides, both cases are outside Horry County, one's out of state, North Carolina."

"Then what do we do?"

"Pierce, I didn't call you here to solve it. I just wanted to give you a heads up, something to consider. Remember you first planted the seed. I just say for now let's stay on alert. We really have nothing to hang our hats on. You had a gut feel and I'm just sort of willing to consider it after Rocker came up MIA. Like you said, he'll probably resurface and be a pain as always."

"I agree. We've certainly learned our lesson going off halfcocked and vigilante. You've got my attention though. Keep me posted if you hear anything else. Now you owe me breakfast and I want a slice of Rocky Road German cake to go."

"Spoken like a true officer. Tell you what, I'll have them box up a whole cake and you can share it with those scoundrels at work."

"I take bribes, no shame. By the way, my sister is visiting with us for a while. You remember Allison. She and her husband have split, divorce is final."

"I've seen that look in your eyes. Don't go there."

"You know her, so it can't be a blind date. Your kids are in Wilmington, come on over for a home cooked meal."

"You don't cook, remember?"

"Steak on the grill, Brady's treat."

"How is Brady doing?"

"Let's just say he could use some male bonding with two females in the house."

"For Brady, then, but don't you pull any of your matchmaker crap. I'm happily unmarried right now; too busy being self-employed and raising my chaps. I don't need any distractions, got it?"

"Got it. See you tomorrow around six."

"I'll bring dessert."

"It better not be my Rocky Road German cake."

Woody flagged down the waitress. "We're ready to order now."

"You got it, Sugar."

Myrtle Beach Indoor Shooting Range
Highway 17 Bypass

Sheriff Buster Ferguson recreated like he did most Saturdays, firing his assortment of weapons at targets at the indoor facility located on Highway 17 Bypass. He had become a regular, everyone greeting him like the character Norm in the *Cheers* sitcom. Buster enjoyed nothing better than firing off round after round, consumed by the sheer power of a weapon at his finger tips, the smell of gun powder and the adrenalin rush it promised. Wearing his ear protection, even though there were others about, he became lost in the solitude, just him and his weapons of choice, shredding the bull's eyes on the targets he faced. When not at work, he lived an almost reclusive life style. He didn't require the company of people but that didn't mean he lived a happy existence.

Buster allowed his work to consume him. There was little left at the end of a day to share with anyone. That alone sent the sheriff plummeting into the darkest and deepest of pits, not that he recognized or acknowledged the bipolar disorder. At work he was a machine, seldom dogged by mood swings. When those spurts of sadness and hopelessness did plague him, usually when he was alone, he vented at the shooting range, his perfect cure, making him feel euphoric and full of energy.

Thus far he had kept it in check and concealed. Most people in his situation would have already sought psychological counseling. You must first admit you have a problem to treat the problem. Even if Buster had realized his illness, he would have never considered a shrink. Doing so would equate to weakness and prompt others to question his ability to lead. No, the gun range offered the perfect therapy to keep it in check, a potentially dangerous prescription at best.

Sheriff Buster Ferguson, like most officers, had never fired his weapon in the line of duty. He as all trained officers knew if you pulled your weapon you better be prepared to use it. There was no such thing as shooting to wing a potential assailant. A wounded person could still kill you. He had only personally known one officer to have ever fired his gun and it had happened during a convenience store robbery. The officer had stopped for coffee when the young man came barreling out, a fistful of dollars in one hand and a pistol in the other. The officer had just exited his vehicle, was no more than ten feet from the robber when he yelled the command to freeze and drop your weapon. Instead the startled youth pointed it at him. He fired, dropping the young man dead with one shot.

The boy was large for a twelve-year-old. He had been brandishing a replica of a forty- five, difficult to distinguish at a glance. Faced with a split-second decision the officer had indeed stopped a robbery in progress, being there at the right time, but at a terrible cost. The boy had been carrying a pellet pistol. For seventeen dollars it had cost him his life and the livelihood of the twenty-four-year officer who had slain him. The officer was never able to return to active duty after that. He remained on administrative assignment, even after he had been cleared. While under the care of a physiatrist and showing some progress, he left his session one afternoon, visited the crime scene, as he had done numerous times since, and then drove to a secluded wooded area.

The next morning two men scoping out a new hunting area spotted his cruiser, the door open and the officer slumped inside. Crime scene investigators had found a neatly folded suicide letter on the dash explaining his anguish in slaying the boy. The officer's police issue fire arm was still in its holster. He had taken his life with a forty-five he had purchased earlier that day. He had been engaged with plans to marry three months later. Buster, only a rookie himself, a year younger, had suffered his first severe bout of depression afterwards. He just thought he was reacting as his fellow officers must have been reacting. He drove to a secluded logger's dirt road three days later and fired an assortment of personal guns, not stopping until he had completely run out of ammunition. An old deserted, rusted out truck had been the victim of his venting.

His undiagnosed bipolar disorder continued to get the better of him. Most of the time it only happened two or three times a year, but it happened. Guns blazing were his constant rescue and never had it stricken him while on duty, or at least not to a point where it completely debilitated him. His job and challenges of the day served as his rescue vessel when firing a weapon was not a viable option. Relocating to the life style offered by the beach should have offered stress relief, but instead the burden of policing a tourist destination had only worsened his condition.

A recent physical had identified high blood pressure and now he popped a pill every day to control it. Saturdays he always visited the shooting range, making time for it even when he shouldn't have had time. Twice in recent weeks he had even dropped by during the workweek. Telltale signs indicated it was becoming less affective, that is if one is astute at detecting the obvious. Buster hadn't noticed and just made his way one day at a time.

No one in the department had sensed his edginess. No one was close enough personally to him to have questioned it, had they noticed. Most gave him wide berth. Some officers had dubbed him Napoleon, others the Little Georgia Fire Cracker, but none of the nicknames had made their way back to him. Little man syndrome had never been more prevalent. All kidding aside, no officer under his watch questioned his fairness. Sure, he expected the moon, but dishing it out only made his officers stronger and more confident. There were those who didn't particularly like him but even those few respected Sheriff Ferguson.

Deputy Parnell Roberts was most certainly on that list but then again, he despised most ranking officers. Even Trudy straddled the fence, unsure if the sheriff really did have a bone to pick with her because of her reputation as being a bit rebellious or was she just paranoid. No, paranoia had nothing to do with it. He wanted to bust her chops, to break her for sure and prevent her from pulling any crap under his jurisdiction. She shouldn't really blame him, given her record. She had been fortunate both with Hank Singleton and then with Woody as sheriff when she had pulled her most bone headed stunts.

Buster loaded his arsenal in the trunk of his car, having relieved the mounting tensions one more time. With the Harley Davidson Bike Rally and the Atlantic Beach Memorial Day Bike Fest rapidly approaching, his first real tests as sheriff of Horry County loomed up close and personal. His predecessors had had their hands full. He intended to raise the bar and set the new benchmark for police excellence in both events. Never had he ever failed to do what he set out to accomplish, but even he realized this would be his largest and most visible challenge to date.

He would rise to the occasion, but he understood this could be a make or break career phenomenon. Buster would only be as strong as the weakest link under his watch. He had his attention focused on Detective Pierce, damn determined to prevent her from going off on one of her little unauthorized tangents. Others had turned their heads when she had pulled her stunts. His objective was to never allow her the freedom of reins to even get there. She had been the focal point of several of the county's, if not the country's highest profile cases. Her crime scene investigative methods were off the unorthodox scale, but had been admittedly effective, that is if you turned your head to unlawful methods. Given some circumstances she had and might bend the law to ensure the criminals were apprehended.

The so-called Road Rage case had however reared its ugly head once again in recent headlines. Tim Ford, while he hadn't been the road rage serial killer, he had played an intricate part in steering the investigation away from him. Ford had attempted to hide the murder of Ed Bradshaw, a man he had allegedly killed, among the many committed by the actual serial killer. Detectives Pierce and Anderson had captured his confession on tape. Their technique for obtaining the confession was being questioned once again, this time by a team of new lawyers in the case. If proven unlawful, Ford could be set free due to a mistrial being declared.

Even though this had not occurred on Buster's watch, he now wore the sheriff's badge and Pierce was still a detective in his department. This could only result in the worst of bad PR if Ford was granted a new trial or set free. Buster had more than enough on his plate with the upcoming biker events to be worried about what hadn't happened yet. He had never met Woodrow Anderson and could thank his lucky stars that the ex-sheriff had moved on to greener pastures, resigning and starting a security guard business shortly after the Hawthorne brothers' body organ murders. From what he had heard, he and Pierce were the perfect toxic recipe when it came to not following police protocol.

At least he had one less headache to deal with. It was still hard to figure just how the doctor and his brother had concealed the murders of illegal Hispanics for all those years, all for the sake of selling organs for primo bucks on the black market. Both men were behind bars, again thanks to Pierce and Anderson, and that TV guy, Lance Rocker. Small blessing. Rocker had moved on also.

Now sitting behind the wheel Buster stared from the parking lot, bypass 17 bustling with traffic. He contemplated heading back to his apartment via 544 or 501. He opted for 544, lesser of the two evils so he had learned to appreciate. He could almost visualize Pierce utilizing her siren to clear a path home, but he wasn't Pierce. Most recognizing the sheriff's vehicle would give him wide berth of their own accord. He had but one stop to make, the Food Lion and a short grocery list.

Buster had a taste for skillet fried beef cube steak, smothered in peppers and onions, with tater tots as the only side. He needed flour, cooking oil, eggs and a half gallon of buttermilk and maybe some spring onions. He might splurge and pick up some Rocky Road Ice cream and root beer for a homemade float. His belly let out a little growl of approval. The grocery store would be on his way. Before pulling out he called the station just in case he needed to stop by there too. Nothing pressing caught his attention. For the moment Sheriff Buster Ferguson's world was nearly perfect. Enjoy while you can, so they say.

Pierce Beach House
Sunday, Doubling Down

Brady Pierce had been experiencing a tougher morning than most, possibly his worst to date. Stiffness had made the simplest of movements excruciating and agonizingly slow. He was the grill master. Somehow, he had to reach deeply and make this happen. For once he wasn't sure he had it in him to pull it off. There was no concealing it and he had promised Trudy he wouldn't, so he didn't. She told him she would cancel the cookout. He talked her out of it, saying if he couldn't, she'd have to do the honors. The thought of her grilling made both laugh. They needed it too.

Woody arrived on time and as promised had brought dessert, a cheese cake-turtle style and a dozen trestle cookies. Trudy couldn't help herself and sampled a cookie. She bushed crumbs from the corners of her mouth. She still wasn't too keen on this match making, Woody and her sister. Brady seemed convinced it could work.

"I started to bring donuts. I take it this is okay instead."

She held up one finger as to say wait one second. "Hand over what's in that box."

"I think we should open it after the meal."

"Really, you bring goodies and then tell me when I can eat them. You're a bad guest, Woody."

"Lighten up, Trudy. You're acting like a bad host," said her sister.

"Hi Allison, it has been a while. How are you doing? Bad question, sorry."

"I'm fine, Woody, and good to see you too. Excuse my sister and her crude behavior. Let me take that." She retrieved the cake box and took it to the kitchen.

"She's looking good, don't you think."

"Stop the bull crap, Wagner."

"It's Pierce."

"No. I'm talking to Wagner. Pierce knows better."

"Touché."

"Where's Brady?"

"He's out on the deck, minding the grill, sort of."

"What does sort of mean?"

"He's watching it and waiting for you to come out, so he can direct you how to grill."

"You're psycho babbling, Wagner and I meant Wagner this time too."

"He's having a tough time today, rigidness and balance, so he could really use your help, Woody."

"Then he's got it. Direct me to the master chef and the little grasshopper will do his best."

Trudy joined Allison in the kitchen. Little sister was propped against the counter, arms crossed and eying her, foot patting up a storm. This was always a bad sign. Amy, their mother, would coddle and baby her until the mood passed. She wasn't Amy and she didn't possess a motherly bone in her body. Trudy didn't waste any time in calling her out.

"You have a bug up your butt, spit it out, or maybe that was a bad choice of words."

"I heard that."

"Heard what, me asking Woody to help Brady with the grill?"

"Yeah, that too. Please don't try to be matchmaker. I had my suspicions and you just confirmed them. Woody is a nice guy and was widowed for all the wrong reasons. He deserves a good woman, one that will stand by his side next time for the whole better or worse thing."

"Talk to me, Allison. I'm struggling to read between the lines. What really happened between you and…?"

"Stop it, not now; I told you I wasn't ready and I'm still not."

"Uncork that bottle of wine then and let's get this party started."

"You do it. I'm going to check on Woody and Brady. I need some air."

"Plenty outside, knock yourself out sis."

Trudy opted for something stronger, a gin and tonic without the tonic, and a double at that. This hush-hush game of Allison's was wearing on her. What had caused them to split, and worse, divorce? Something stunk to high heavens and this detective wasn't going to be happy until she got to the root of it. The kids, why had he gotten full custody of the kids? Why hadn't she fought for her rights? What was she thinking; maybe she had. Allison wasn't talking. This was so screwed up. Everything was so screwed up. The sheriff had it in for her, and then there were Allison and Brady's situations.

Listen to me she thought, lumping this together as usual, work and family, poor me and how everything is impacting my life. Woody said it, stop the bull crap Wagner. I'm better than this. I was beyond thinking like this. The old Wagner rearing her ugly head again, me, me, me…like hell it's going to be like this. Evil be gone, go haunt easier prey. This is Trudy Pierce you're messing with now. She mixed her second drink, this time with tonic and a slice of lime before joining the others and taking their drink requests. Brady settled for brandy, Woody had a beer and Allison opted for club soda.

Brady struggled through it. Allison and Woody were cordial, but both were on to Trudy. Neither blinked or gave her anything to hang her badge on. Woody had been stung before and wasn't ready for a relationship. Allison definitely wasn't ready. Trudy regretted she had even suggested this little outing. It was a train wreck. They ate, they made small talk and then it ended early. The approaching Monday had never looked better from Trudy Pierce's perspective.

Myrtle Beach Pavilion
Three Days before the Harley Davidson Rally

Dressed in khaki shorts and a Harley Davidson Rally tee-shirt, flip flops and hair now perfectly braided, Valdemar walked among the sea of tourist, munching on a tub of buttery popcorn and breathing in the ambiance of the carnival like atmosphere. Rumors were that the local owners of the amusement park were contemplating dismantling the icon. He had read in the Sun News about the outpour from the voice of the people and venders. Shop owners were protesting such a senseless suggestion. The Myrtle Beach Pavilion had apparently been the focal point for generations of visitors, rich in history for the young and the old.

Valdemar felt compassion for those clinging to its continued operation and existence with the Atlantic Ocean as a backdrop. It seemed to flourish by the look of the abundance of ants scurrying from one ride to the next. Ah, but according to the owners of the property, this was misleading. Once the summer season ended, the amusement park went dormant, hibernating through the fall and winter, awakening again only when spring arrived. Pity, history should always take precedence over monetary gain, so Valdemar believed.

Others of his little ensemble mingled among those from faraway places, New Jersey, Ohio, New York, Pennsylvania, West Virginia, Maryland and Canada, according to the array of license plates in the parking areas and highways. Valdemar wondered if anyone still actually resided in the state of New Jersey with the influx of Jersey plates. His supporting cast adorned an assortment of souvenir attire, Bowery and Mother Fletcher logo shirts, I Luv Myrtle Beach tee-shirts, one with the Confederate Flag emblazed on front *The South Will Rise Again*, a Gay Dolphin baseball cap, Ripley's Believe or Not Visors, Panama Jack straw hats, and Harley Davidson do rags and shirts. They were the perfect mingle in the menagerie.

The motor cycle gatherings were finally approaching. Soon the next act in his orchestrated play would be set into motion, the curtain rising in all its glory and splendor. Rehearsals had been ongoing; each role being perfected with no adlibs anticipated. Of course, this was one sided. One could not predict the consequences, actions and reactions of those stand-ins not scripted in the plot. Disruptions to the flow would not be tolerated and those doing so would be dealt with swiftly. While he had allowed for a threshold of error, maintaining the strictest of schedules was crucial to the operations success, the curse of being anal, what physicians now called Obsessive-Compulsive Disorder, *OCD*.

Valdemar had been this way all his life. There was no need for a second opinion. Obsessed with perfection to the finest detail had always ruled his life. Failure to follow through would certainly produce uneasiness, elevated anxiety and cause severe emotional distress. Quickly this transformed into paranoid and psychotic delusional behavior, compounded by irrational decision making if gone unchecked. Because of his failure to seek medical assistance, there was no magic pill at his disposal to balance the ensuing chaos.

These incidents most often alienated him from the situation, making it virtually impossible for anyone to interact or rationalize with him. It simply had to run its course, often with ugly and tragic results. Ironically Valdemar had always been able to maintain his composure while under contract. Afterwards all bets were off. It could be a different story. As with many emotional highs, comes the inevitable drop off the cliff. The downward spirals experienced by Valdemar were excruciating to witness. He trusted only one with his secret, his confidant, Ligeia, not her real name of course.

Ligeia, thusly named by Valdemar from the Edgar Allen Poe short story entitled *Ligeia* was so beautiful, passionate and intellectual, raven-haired and dark-eyed, emaciated, with some strangeness, as was the character in the story. Her forehead was faultless. Her eyes were divine orbs. She possessed immense knowledge of physical and mathematical science, and a proficiency in classical languages, again molded from the mind of the great Poe, the perfect mentor. Valdemar remained captivated by her knowledge of metaphysical and forbidden wisdom, character development honed under him to conform to the image he desired. In the short story Ligeia becomes ill, struggles internally with human mortality, and ultimately dies, but in Valdemar's depiction her life is sustainable through willpower. He preferred his outcome to Poe's tragic ending.

Valdemar discarded the half empty popcorn tub in a trash receptacle and then ambled his way through the crowd of thrill seekers, young and old. The chameleon disappeared among the oblivious, as did his supporting cast members. Ligeia passed by slightly brushing against his shoulder. Strangers they remained among the ebbing tide of tourists, all according to plan. She paused to watch the children on the Merry-Go-Round, smiling and waving at the little munchkins.

Just ahead, now boarding the roller coaster were Doctor Tarr and Professor Fether, more characters from the pages of Poe. Hop-Frog appeared focused as he tossed baseballs at bottles, one of the gangway's Carney style money grabbers located on the Pavilion grounds. Prospero posed statue like as an artist using charcoal rendered a comical caricature. High above, Tamerlane sat in the stationary vessel at the crest of the Ferris Wheel, having a bird's eye view of the little amusement park.

Dupin exited the restroom and stopped to ask a police officer where he might find a good place to purchase food. Valdemar smiled and clapped his hands at this bold move by one of his rising stars, a fearless protégé indeed. He has learned well the deceptive maneuver; no sane criminal would ever intentionally converse with a lawman if he intended to rub the crime in his face. For that very reason, the lawman will never make the connection or remember the face of a potential suspect. Maintaining a high visibility delivered less memorable profile in the end. Lastly but not least, Ethelred snapped photographs of scantly glad beach twits, flirting with the recipes for jail bait, prompting a fatherly figure to intervene. After a brief exchange of photographic preferences, Ethelred promptly gave dad the finger accented by a series of vulgarities before departing and exiting the park.

Valdemar rated the little outing as an overall success. The highly visible achieved anonymity. His touring company of actors has passed as everyday tourists, loud, boisterous, obnoxious, most assuming the personalities of migrating northerners, accents perfected to regionalize their suspected origins. The rumbles of invading Harleys had signaled the beginning of the early arrivals for the rally. It officially kicks off in three days and in five days comes the reaping of the rewards, the diligence of practice becoming reality. Valdemar quoted Poe to a threesome of youngsters sitting on a park bench. "The true genius shudders at incompleteness and usually prefers silence to saying something which is not everything it should be." They looked at one another and shrugged, then walked away. Valdemar filled in the blanks for them, "crazy old man."

Ocean Blvd
Myrtle Beach

Detectives Tim Burroughs and Parnell Roberts pulled up in front of the beach front hotel and were immediately met by the day manager of the motel. The two officers had been in close proximity at Mammy's Kitchen having lunch when the call had come in. Francine Broadwater, probably in her mid-fifties, was livid to say the least, proclaiming this had never happened at their family and pet friendly motel. There was a fine line to be drawn in being too friendly, so said Francine. An incident like this could tarnish their reputation. She demanded that the offenders be arrested and then she would process their check-out, eviction to be precise.

"I knocked on their door before I called you, after I witnessed in plain daylight firsthand what they were doing. It took them forever to respond and when he did, I could see and smell the obvious sex on Mister Lee's sweaty, half naked body. You know how men get all worked up in the middle of intercourse. I'm not naïve. I know these sorts of shenanigans are common place at the beach but fornicating in plain sight is blasphemy and just downright perverted. They could have at least pulled the curtains closed. Their window faces the sidewalk for heaven's sake. After that nice couple with the two tiny tots brought it to my attention and all but dragged me to their room window, I stood there for a least at a full minute. They never looked up. I was tempted to rap on the window."

Parnell smiled, giving Tim a little wink and nod. "Describe just precisely what you witnessed, Mrs. Broadwater."

"You can't be serious. I have to tell you exactly what I saw?"

"You called, and you are a witness. If we are going to make a potential arrest, we must have the supporting evidence. In this case it is your statement describing what you saw, your word against theirs."

Tim could see that Parnell was obviously enjoying this line of questioning, making the poor woman squirm, but he was right, without her account they could do nothing. At least no horses were involved this time; none that had been mentioned so far. She did say it was a pet friendly motel though. Tim allowed Parnell to take the lead and assumed the role of stenographer.

"I saw them, isn't that enough information?"

"I'm afraid not. We do require the details for our report." Parnell spat tobacco juice in a nearby trash can, shocking Francine and disgusting Tim. He wiped his chin with the back of his hand, mostly just habit. He still had not heeded the sheriff's warning about his bad habit.

Francine agonized through the graphic and quite acrobatic details of what she has seen. It became evident to Tim and Parnell that she must have been standing there much longer than a minute to have been able to describe in far more detail the aspects of the encounter. This included visible tattoos and a birthmark, both in the lower extremities. Parnell was shocked that she hadn't waited until they had finished before knocking on the door. He loved his job; never a dull minute in the beach community.

Next came the second knocking on the door. After the introductory formalities and an explanation for why the couple was being arrested, the pissed off occupant of room number 103 unleashed a verbal assault. With hands flailing and F-bombs flying, Bobby Lee Rydal made it perfectly clear he had paid good money for the room, and what he and his girlfriend, Bonnie Sue Mason and he did there behind closed doors was their business. He claimed he didn't know that the curtains were pulled wide open, and that Bonnie Sue always got a case of the horniness after sunbathing on the beach. They were on vacation and enjoying themselves. Was that a crime?

Yes, rebutted Tim, attempting to reply, only to be interrupted and met with more verbal vulgarity. Bonnie Sue had chimed in, getting in her two cents worth, giving the detectives quite the peep show. Wearing an oversized tee shirt and obviously nothing else underneath, she exposed the alleged culprit in the crime, neatly shaven with the incriminating birthmark adjacent to it. Tim looked away. Parnell didn't. He instead instructed Tim to cuff Mister Rydal while he moved in Bonnie Sue's direction to do the same. She reacted by placing her hands on her head. That delivered exactly what she had intended, the tee shirt riding high and above her thighs. Her squirming and partial resistance only enhanced the view and confirmed the evidence did incriminate them.

That's when Tim got it, catching her grin and flirtatious looks, and then seeing the nod of approval by Bobby Lee Rydal, the quick little wink the giveaway. These two had known exactly what they had been doing. They were full-fledged exhibitionist, risk takers, doing stuff like this for the sexual thrill and the rush. Obviously, they hadn't anticipated on it being reported and them being arrested though, but now that they had, they had incorporated it into their sick little game. Tim saw a pair of shorts on the sofa and before Parnell cuffed her, he motioned for Bonnie Sue to put them on. She did but did so in a way to further promote the peep show and flaunt her goods. Tim's face reddened. Parnell never flinched, sponging in the choreographed spectacle. Why pass up a freebee was Parnell's mantra.

After reading them the Miranda, the couple was hauled off to face criminal charges for public nudity, being involved in a lewd act and resisting arrest. Rydal had jerked his hands away from Tim, shouldering him to delay being cuffed so he could watch his girlfriend exposing her nether regions, all for the hell of it. Until bail was set, they would be spending time at J. Reuben Long Detention Center sporting their new bright orange jump suits. During the booking phase, records indicated this wasn't their first brush with the law concerning their exhibitionist tendencies. Priors showed up in four other states over a period of three years, all in high traffic tourist destinations.

"Well that was certainly a hell of a way to top off lunch; some desert, wouldn't you say Timmy ole boy?"

"Tim," Burroughs replied to Detective Parnell Roberts.

"Don't ruffle your tail feathers, no harm, no foul. We're all on the same side, right, good versus the evil doers, fornicators and exhibitionist included."

"I'll file the report and meet you at Detective Pierce's office."

"Got to see a man about a dog, then I'll meet you there in about ten, Timmy."

"TMI," whispered Tim, just happy to be rid of him for ten minutes.

Tim optimizing a few minutes of free time called Summer Knight. Their second date had been set for this coming weekend, dinner and a movie at Broadway at the Beach. His hopes were squashed. Summer had been assigned weekend duty as replacement anchor after the usual anchor had taken an unforeseen leave of absence due to a family crisis. While disappointed he understood she couldn't pass on such an opportunity, as in his profession, schedules could change in the blink of an eye. She offered him a rain check for the following weekend. Tim had to decline. He had already committed to extra duty during the Memorial Weekend Atlantic Bike Fest. Still, Tim remained optimistic, just having a reason to juggle a schedule for a girl topped his usual decision making, bowling or pizza night.

He arrived at Trudy's office about the same time Parnell did. The man was a slob, half of his shirt tail tucked in, the other half flapping in the breeze. Trudy picked up on it too and had him rectify it. She also prompted him to remove the snuff from his cheek again. Hand held out, she confiscated his Skoal. She didn't need any crap from the sheriff. After hearing a brief summary of their recent arrest, she had another assignment for them. Just great, thought Tim, still stuck with this moron. He liked it much better when Parnell partnered with Sly. Unfortunately, this was Sly's day off.

The assignment was one right out of the pages of dumb crook news. A man had called in the theft of his moped and a bag of weed. Officers had apprehended him but uncovered a grizzly scene, a badly decomposed body in a drainage ditch. It was near a shanty town occupied by a small group of homeless. Chances were that no witnesses would step forth. The homeless rarely cooperated with police unless they were looking for a warm jail cell for the night and then they might confess to most any petty crime.

Earlier during the shift, just before the sheriff's morning debriefing, Trudy had shared the cake from the Trestle with her team. She saved a slice for the sheriff and had delivered it to his office. He hadn't been there, so she left it along with a plastic fork and napkins on the corner of his desk. He had just summoned her to his office. She wondered if the sweet tooth bandit had hit Duncan Donuts this time. What was left, The Donut Man on Kings Highway? She figured she may as well get this over with and headed to his office.

Ferguson was on the phone when she arrived. He glanced up at her but didn't so much as mouth hello or motion for her to have a sit or anything. Just as well, whatever he wanted, she just as soon get this over with and then go back to her office and do something productive, well out of the line of fire. He chatted for a couple more minutes, almost prompting her to leave and come back later. Unfortunately, the call ended in mid-thought.

"Pierce, are you the one who deposited that cake on my desk?"

Sighing she replied, "Busted, guilty as charged."

"Rocky Road, that's my favorite. I don't think I have ever tasted better. Did you make it?"

Oh, how she was so tempted to take credit, but she didn't. "It came from the Trestle Grill and Bakery in Conway, actually a Rocky Road German cake."

"Ah yes, I pass it every day on my way to and from the station. I'll have to schedule a stop, so it seems. Thank you very much for saving me a piece. That certainly got my morning off to a great start."

"You're more than welcome, sir."

"Carry on then."

Trudy restrained herself from cutting cartwheels down the hallway; what a surprising breakthrough and pure luck of the draw at that. She had almost saved that last piece for Brady but decided better because she didn't have one for Allison. So, Napoleon had a sweet tooth for Rocky Road, who would have ever figured. She might have to make this a weekly ritual. Nah, he might develop diabetes and blame her. She decided to just enjoy a little morale victory and not push the cake. She certainly didn't want others pegging her as his favorite. In the seclusion of her office she did cut one cartwheel. Busted, the sheriff walked by just as her hands contacted the floor. She thought she saw him laughing but from an upside-down position she couldn't be quite sure. She had to admit, it had been one of her best cartwheels, at least as an adult.

The Police Station
Detective Trudy Wagner's Office

The Harley Davidson Rally was now in full swing. The distinctive sound of their engines could be heard from Georgetown to Little River. Day two and there had been no fatalities. Most warnings and tickets had resulted from burnouts, speeding and DUI incidents. There had been three vehicular-cycle collisions but no serious injuries. Law enforcement was in abundant supply at the Harley Davidson Dealership in Myrtle Beach, at Suck, Bang and Blow on Business 17 four corners, and in Murrells Inlet Suck, Bang and Blow and the Beaver Bar, mostly to assist traffic flow. Vendors were in no short supply.

Trudy sat at her desk filing some paperwork, exhausted from an almost fourteen hour shift she had pulled. The vibrating in her pocket signaled an incoming call. She retrieved the phone, "Brady, I'm just about done here."

"Long day, but these biker events are bears, aren't they?"

"Long but not really that tough; I just pretend I'm a tourist until the next crisis arrives."

"I just wanted to remind you we have that event Sunday. You will still be able to go, won't you?"

"Yeah, I've worked it out in my schedule."

"By the way, I'm allowed to invite two, VIP treatment all the way. I took the liberty to ask Allison. I hope that's okay."

"Perfect."

"I figured as much. Go ahead. Invite Woody and give them a second shot at lustful bliss."

"I'll call him now and then I'll be on my way. Love you, Circus Boy."

"Love you more. Be careful and I'll keep the bed warm for you."

She waited impatiently through the third ring before Woody finally answered. "You've got to be kidding me, Wagner. Do you know what time it is? I don't keep cop hours anymore."

"This is important. Brady has an extra VIP invite to this celebrity thing Sunday. I just thought you might like to attend it with us. Allison is going."

"I get it. You're at it again but no can do."

"Come on Woody. Just give it a chance, one more time, how about it? She could use some company."

"No, I can't. I really mean it. I can't. I'm working. I've already contracted to man the security for a gig that day. It's one with a hefty paycheck, my largest to date. I'm going to head it up, no mistakes, reputation on the line."

"Bummer, you're not just making up this crap, are you?"

"It's legit, sorry. Tell her hey for me. Now I'm going back to sleep, if I can."

"Damn it," she said after she ended the call. She heard footsteps in the hallway and a second later Sheriff Buster Ferguson was standing in her doorway.

"Late night, Pierce?"

"Late night for you too, sir."

"I was on my way home and just thought I'd stop by and clear a few things off my desk, head it off at the pass before Monday. I stopped by the Trestle the other day for lunch. Thanks for recommending it."

'Lunch or more Rocky Road German..."

"Yeah..."

"Sir, since we're both sort of off duty right now, can I ask you something personal?"

"I guess, but if so, you better call me Buster."

"Buster…sorry, I'm not sure I can get the hang of this."

"Only when we're not on duty and only when no one else is around, got it?"

"Got it, sir…I mean Buster. Do you have any plans Sunday afternoon?"

"Nothing specific other than staying a step ahead of this motor cycle circus. Why do you ask?"

"Trust me sir…Buster, this is just a preview. The real circus doesn't arrive until Memorial Weekend. Buckle up then."

Sunday, 6 AM
Conway Police Station

Tim Burroughs had the day off but was bored so he decided to take care of a backlog of records. He was responsible for making sure all reports were maintained electronically. He enjoyed this assignment, anything to do with computers being his strong suit. Plus, it was always quite entertaining reviewing some of the unique cases in the beach resort. He smiled as he perused one involving a coach at the local university.

The cheerleading coach at a local college had been arrested on charges stemming from resisting arrest and public intoxication. The police report indicated that officers were called to a residence at 12:30 p.m. the day before after a woman refused to get out of the bed of a man's pickup truck, and when officers arrived, they found the 31-year-old coach sitting in the bed of the truck and a 29-year-old man inside the truck who said the two had been in a relationship. When officers asked her to get out of the truck, she did but became "loud and boisterous and used profanity while standing in the roadway," according to the report. When officers arrested her, the coach resisted and reportedly kicked officers until she was handcuffed. Charges included resisting arrest, assault while resisting arrest/assault on police officer, public disorderly/public intoxication and criminal domestic violence.

"Two bits, four bits," rallied Tim. In another college related incident...

Two Horry County school buses had been sideswiped as they were stopped in traffic on S.C. 707 Tuesday morning, according to Lance Cpl. Sonny Collins report. A vehicle came off Big Block Road, over accelerated and lost control on the wet pavement before striking the buses. The driver had been charged with driving too fast for conditions and for not having a S.C. driver's license. A total of 51 students had been on the buses, which were headed to Early College High School and the Scholars Academy. There had been no serious injuries.

All were solved so quickly.

A paunchy man who says he is looking to buy a home is targeting female real estate agents in Horry and Brunswick County, N.C., with odd and inappropriate behavior. Interviews revealed the suspect was stated as being just creepy, making them feel very uncomfortable. The man will call female agents about property, identify himself as a vice president of the Hanes Corporation, and insist that they are the ones to show him the property. The man, who used the aliases of Eric Mullins, Steven Mullins, Alex Mullins and possibly Steven Kincaid, carries a green portfolio with him to the showings. At some point, he pulls out Ziploc bags with panty hose in them and begins a conversation that eventually leads to lingerie. The man has not attacked or touched any of the agents but added that his behavior makes them feel very uncomfortable. The man was said to be driving a white SUV with Georgia license plate. He is described as 6 feet 4 inches tall, paunchy with thinning black hair. He also has worn gold-rimmed glasses, according to information.

"I hope he doesn't fantasize about horses."

A motorist says a man helped push his broken-down car off a highway, then robbed him. Case is still under investigation, no suspects.

A 30-year-old man told Myrtle Beach police he was hit in the face with a stick and had his moped stolen when he stopped while driving along 15th Avenue South near Yaupon Drive. The victim told officers he was driving to the store about 1:45 a.m. Thursday when he saw two men and they asked him for a cigarette. The victim said he stopped to tell the men he didn't have a cigarette. One of the men hit him in the face with a stick and then stole his hat and tried to steal his jacket, according to the report. The victim said the other man took the moped and drove away. The victim chased the suspect, who hit him, but was not able to catch him as he ran through several yards, according to the report. Officers checked the area but were unable to find the stick or the suspects. The victim complained of an injury to his face, but officers noted in the report there were no visible injuries on the victim's face.

A New Jersey man was arrested on petty larceny charges after stealing a golf cart and took a joy ride at Broadway at the Beach. He was arrested at 2:30 a.m. after a security guard saw him and another man riding the golf cart "at a high rate of speed" on the sidewalk. A Broadway at the Beach maintenance worker parked his golf cart in front of Key West Grill at about 1:30 a.m. and left the key in the cart while he continued working. The maintenance worker said he saw two men get onto the golf cart and drive away. The worker chased after the men and a security guard was able to stop the cart and detain the driver. The other man ran away from the scene, according to the report. There was an unspecified amount of damage to the golf cart.

Mopeds are the root of evil, as are golf carts, thought Tim, but this one takes the cake.

Police were still looking for a woman accused of assaulting 37-year-old woman at a dance club at Broadway at the Beach. The suspect stepped on the victim's foot during the "Electric Slide" and the two started fighting, according to the report. The suspect left and then came back with an unknown man and the three started to purposefully bump into the woman on the dance floor starting another argument. The couple and the unknown man are accused of punching the woman in the face, then beating her more when she fell to the ground. The woman was treated for deep red bruising on her face, chest and arms.

Then there are strip clubs…

A dancer had been arrested at a local gentleman's club. The report states the victim, a 31-year-old male, was at the club having a good time with his friends. He put money down on the table they were sitting at, when the offender and another dancer came to the table, tried to take the money and dance on him. The victim declined the offender and asked her not to take the money.

The offender, a 25-year-old exotic dancer tried two more times to take the money, the third time even sitting on the victim's lap and starting to dance on him. When he declined her dance the third time, she told the victim that he had a "sweet receding hairline," to which the victim replied "Yeah, and you're a snaggle-toothed [expletive]".

At this point, the victim and multiple witnesses said the dancer started striking the victim in the face, hitting him five-to-six times. The victim and his friends then left the club and called police.

Responding officers said when they arrived, the victim was holding a towel of ice to the left side of his face, and had welt forming under his left eyebrow. When police approached the dancer, she claimed the victim pushed her which prompted her to strike him. Police spoke to witnesses who corroborated the victim's story, placed her under arrest and transported her to the Myrtle Beach jail.

"Snaggle-toothed, now that's funny…"

Tim took a break and perused local news on the computer, pausing when he spotted one related to Conway.

It's unclear where the Conway resident was going last month when he was charged with driving under the influence on Interstate 95 near Latta, but for S.C. Highway Patrol troopers he was hard to miss driving a large John Deere tractor that was reported stolen from the City of Conway. The driver of the tractor was charged with driving it @ 1:30 a.m. while intoxicated down the busy interstate.

The tractor was reported stolen from a job site in Conway later that same day and Conway police had made several pleas for information regarding the whereabouts of the piece of equipment. But unbeknownst to Conway officials, the tractor had been at a Florence impound lot since the day troopers arrested the man. Conway police are investigating how he came to be in possession of the tractor at the time of his arrest,

He has not been charged in connection with the theft of the tractor. Conway officials had offered a $1,000 reward for information leading to the recovery of the tractor.

Police were called to 1700 New Road after workers from the city's street department went to work and found the tractor was gone. Workers told police that the day before they were at the site and picked up another piece of equipment and the tractor was there. But when they reported to work about 7:45 a.m. the next day to retrieve the tractor, it was gone. The tractor is 2008 JD-6415 John Deere tractor with an enclosed cab with City of Conway decals and Street Department number stenciled on the hood. A Tiger 360 Heavy Duty Flail Mower also was attached to the tractor. Additional details about the DUI arrest were not immediately available. The investigation into the theft of the tractor continues.

Tim had remembered something about the incident but what stuck out even more in his mind was the murder of Sonny Boggs, an old farmer driving a John Deere who had crossed paths with the Road Rage serial killer, Joseph Preston, leading to his senseless murder. Tim suddenly didn't want to be here. He longed to be with Summer, but she was working. There was nothing left to do but pick up an extra-large cheese burger pizza on the way home.

Pierce Beach House
Sunday 9 AM

"Are you going to be okay with this, Brady," asked Trudy.

"You forgot, I suggested it. Besides, given the circumstances I don't think we have an alternative plan."

"We could just not go."

"What about our two invited guests? Would that be fair to them? Does it bother you seeing me in a wheelchair and worrying about what others might think?"

"Me, screw what others think. I was thinking of you. This will be your first time out in public in it."

"This is my first time in it period, so I may as well bite the bullet and share it with the world. Reality is this might be our way of life now, Circus Boy in his most challenging role, *Iron Sides*."

"This might just be a temporary hiccup."

"Not according to my doctor; he's been preparing us for this day for awhile. You've heard him just like I have. Whether you wanted to believe it or not, now that's another story. Let's face it, my time has arrived. It beats the alternative."

"Hush, don't say that."

"I was referring to falling down. The getting up part is challenging but not nearly as painful."

Trudy's face reddened.

"Don't beat yourself up over that assumption. We all die sometime. Destiny chooses our time. Chances are I will outlive you, given your poor choice of careers and crime fighting methods."

"Thanks a lot. Now you've probably jinxed my livelihood."

"Life's too short to fret over this. Let's just enjoy it while we can, okay?"

"Okay, long as I get to be the driver. I'm going to cherish my stint at finally being in control of this marriage."

"Push me where you might. I was a push-over from day one, the first time I laid eyes on you at The Hot Fish Club."

"And you were dressed like a circus clown in that outrageous knickers outfit. You said it was your marketing strategy."

"It worked didn't it? I landed my largest account that day, you."

"I was drunk and stressed out, too vulnerable to resist. Did I mention how horny I was? I would have jumped the bones of any old snake oil peddler that night. As you recall, I bought you the first drink."

"As described in the marketing module…it worked flawlessly…hook, line and sinker…reel them in."

"You were fishing the hole with the right bait, that's all."

"Red wigglers, satisfaction guaranteed every time."

Trudy plopped down in Brady's lap. "I love you so."

"I love you more. What you say we take this for a little spin?" Trudy attempted to get out of his lap to take the reins. "That's not exactly what I had in mind."

"Maybe this wheelchair isn't such a bad idea after all, Circus Boy."

"Hey, what are you two up to," asked Allison, appearing at their bedroom doorway.

"Just taking the chariot for a little spin," replied Brady, with a little wink.

"Oh, sorry, finish your test drive then. I just wanted to confirm the time we're supposed to leave."

"In about thirty minutes, give or take," replied Brady, glancing at his watch.

"Plenty of time to work out the kinks, *Iron Sides*," added Trudy.

"I'll pull the door closed then. It will give you two a bit more room for your test drive."

"Excellent," replied Brady.

"See to our guest, Allison, if he arrives before we finish the obstacle course."

"Just make sure it doesn't become a crash course," she said, closing the door behind her.

Ten minutes later the doorbell signaled the arrival of the guest. Allison did her last second primping before responding. "Hello, I'm Allison, Trudy's sister. You're obviously Sheriff Ferguson."

"Please, call me Buster."

Hearing the doorbell Brady and Trudy sped up their little liaison and wheeled into the den five minutes later. Allison smiled. The sheriff was clueless. This was only the second time Brady and the sheriff had ever met; the first being shortly after he had been sworn in. At that time Brady had only been using a cane sparingly. Brady brought the sheriff up to speed on his condition, the abbreviated version of course. First impression, Brady liked Sheriff Buster Ferguson. Still, he was a far cry from the good ole boy himself, the long-deceased Sheriff Hank Singleton.

"I'd like to offer the services of my vehicle," said Buster. "There's plenty of room for everyone and your wheelchair. It's the least I can do since you were so kind to invite me to join you. I'm not in my police issue, if that's what concerns you. It's a 1993 Suburban, purrs like a kitten. She's in mint condition for most old girl's half her age. She's got over 250, 000 miles on her but don't tell her."

Trudy saw the twinkle in his eyes and a side she had never seen at the station. He really did love this vehicle with a sincere passion and took pride in keeping it…her in tip top shape apparently. She spoke up and confirmed that they'd take him up on his offer. Brady signaled that they should get going. After assisting Brady into the front seat, Buster loaded the wheelchair in the back. Trudy noticed what resembled a long foot locker, probably tools and extra parts of the old gal. The suburban was indeed in excellent shape, as clean inside as out. It had certainly benefited from the TLC.

Brady co-piloted, directing Buster's attention to points of interest along the way, Huntington Beach State Park, Brookgreen Gardens, locations of the numerous golf courses throughout Pawley's Island, and all the favorite eating places. Trudy observed from her catbird's view in the backseat that the two were hitting it off quite well. Or maybe Brady just needed some testosterone interaction for a change. He had always been accustomed to being out and about, visiting his stores and various golf courses, making business calls and participating in charity events. His deteriorating physical condition had brought much of that to a grinding halt, to his regret and hers alike.

"Ahead is Winyah Bay," said Brady pointing to the bridge. Here is the confluence of the Waccamaw River, the Pee Dee River, the Black River and the Sampit River. The bay generally serves as the terminating point for the Grand Strand. Off to the left is the river front of Georgetown and the historical district, live oaks lining every street. If time permits, we should swing through there on our way back."

"You have been a gracious tour guide, Brady Pierce. You missed your calling."

"Southern history can't be beat. I've lived in the low country and the Grand Strand all my life."

"I'm a southern boy myself, the Peach State, a Georgia Cracker, red clay running through my veins. Savannah, now there's southern charm at its finest."

"You betcha and Charleston is another hour down 17. If you haven't been there, mark it on your to do list."

"Only if you're my tour guide…"

"That can be arranged for a nominal fee of course." Both burst into laughter.

Trudy nudged Allison and nodded in their direction, granting them her approval of manly bonding. Her sister was deep in thought, barely aware of her surroundings. She nudged Trudy in response, missing the point. Not the time or place thought Trudy, but when, Allison? She had seen those facial expressions before, in the mirror when she too had struggled with the demons. She wished she had could help Allison, but stubbornness flowed through the family's veins. She should be better at helping Allison, but she hadn't been much of an older sister, much less a role model.

At a time like this their mother, Amy, could smooth everything out; the Amy of their childhood, the Amy before Alzheimer's had stolen her mind and sentenced her to a terrible death. The Amy she had deserted in a hospital with Brady standing by her side when she had taken her very last breath. Demons are relentless. Now they had invaded her space too. They were determined to worm their way back into her life. Not going to happen she professed. I'm Pierce now, not Wagner; take your bad medicine elsewhere, and leave my sister the hell alone while you're at it.

"Make a right up here. Another twenty minutes, give or take, and we should be there. More southern charm than you can possibly withstand is heading your way."

Buster smiled and engaged his right turn signal. He felt more relaxed than he had in long time, even better than going to the shooting range. He had never thought anything could beat firing off a few hundred rounds. This transition from the mountains to sea just might work out after all, that is, if he could keep his demons at bay. This fended off any sign of weakness. Right now, he felt like Hercules, in charge and in control, invincible, but still a mere mortal, no matter how he wished he weren't.

An invisible demon road shot gun in the white 1993 suburban. It had its pick of troubled souls, each with their personal crosses to bear. Persecution never had it so good, a foursome doomed, not a mulligan among them. Past, present or future, take your pick. The endgame would separate the winners from the losers. Under cloudless sunny southern skies, a darker day there had never been.

Live Oaks Church of Contemporary Teaching and Healing
Georgetown County

Brady pointed out the Old Plantation Golf Resort as they passed. "Do you play golf, Buster?"

"Not my cup of tea, no insult intended."

"Too bad, the coast and low country have some of the most beautiful landscapes and scenes/ Live oaks, marshes, the remnants of long-ago abandoned rice fields and plantations are plentiful. The wildlife is beyond the imagination, all assessable via the cost of a round of golf. Tell you what; I have inroads with most of them, tour guide at your service. When you have a little free time, I can schedule a few no golfing visits."

"Sounds like a plan. You're a very gracious host, Brady Pierce."

Sounds like a date thought Trudy; this macho madness love fest was getting just a little too difficult to witness. "Are we there yet," she mocked in her best kid's voice, receiving a stern shoulder punch by her quite embarrassed little sister.

"Almost Buster, take the next left turn just around the upcoming curve."

"It appears to be some sort of road block or detour ahead," commented Buster.

Four men wearing khaki shorts and bright red sports shirts, baseball caps and side arms had set up temporary barricades at the entrance to the dirt road, the very next left turn. They flagged down the suburban after seeing the turn signal blinking. Buster pulled to a stop as directed. One of the four men approached the vehicle. Buster eased down his window.

"This is a private function today. Do you have an invitation and if so, please present it now? If not, I'll have to ask you to exit the way you came."

"Woody, what are you doing here?" asked Trudy from the backseat passenger side just behind Buster.

"What are you doing here Detective Pierce? Oh…hey Brady…Allison."

"Is this why you turned me down, you're working security?"

"Oh, this is what you were inviting me to attend?"

"Here Woody," said Brady, handing the VIP passes to Buster to show him.

"I guess you're clear and free to enter then. Do you have any idea what's going on at the church, if you don't mind me asking?"

" You took a job and don't even know why. That's lame even for you Woody."

"Cut him some slack, Trudy. This has been hush-hush. Even I haven't seen the invite list," added Brady.

"Look, they hired my company because Horry and surrounding counties have all the cops tied up for the bike weeks. They wanted security at the entrance to the church. They got security. Deal was that no news media or uninvited guests will be allowed to pass this check point. You are neither, so your chauffer can drive you on down."

"Woody allow me to introduce you to our chauffer, Sheriff Buster Ferguson. Buster this is ex-sheriff Woody Anderson."

Not missing a beat, Woody responded, "Moonlighting sheriff? I'll have to keep that in mind when I'm short on staff."

"Pleasure to finally meet the infamous Woodrow Anderson, I have heard and read a lot about you and your approach to law enforcement. Do you incorporate and practice the same work ethics in your personal business?"

"Sorry I missed your swearing in, sheriff. I was brushing up on my ethics and couldn't work it in my schedule."

"Buster, I do apologize. He isn't always a smartass. To clarify, he had taken his kids to Florida on vacation at the time of your arrival."

"Permission to go join the secret festivities granted, and for the record sheriff, she taught me everything I ever learned about being a smartass. You kids have fun. Let them through Drew."

"Keep out the evil doers, Woody."

"I rest my case, sheriff. My mentor has spoken. See you later, Wagner."

"It's Pierce."

"Not today it isn't."

"No hiding the fact that you two were partners in crime…I mean law enforcement," said Buster, as he drove down the live oak lined drive.

And you have a smartass streak too thought Trudy. Damn, you're growing on me, sheriff. What a coincidence, ending up here at the same place after all with Woody. The ride to the church was quite picturesque, ancient live oaks lining both sides of the single lane dirt roadway, moss clinging to their limbs, the limbs stretching outward forming a canopy created by the heavens for sure. A quarter of a mile later they spotted a church, one that appeared to have defied time by the looks of it, rich in southern heritage.

One mystery remained. They were VIP's to what? Brady had told her very little, only that there would be celebrities attending, but who and attending what? She thought he was playing this too close to the vest, but he had confessed he didn't know the entire story. He stuck to his story, saying he had been sworn to secrecy, had had to sign a nondisclosure agreement. There were but four cars parked out front. It was early yet, accordingly to Brady. As Buster parked the suburban, two gentlemen stepped outside to greet them.

"Ah Brady Pierce, my son, I am happy you were able to attend," stated the elder of the two.

"Reverend Jonah Blackwood, how's that golf game?"

"Not as long and not nearly as straight, but I can't deny, it has a hold on me. Sometimes I think the devil had a hand in making this my vice. Allow me to introduce you to my associate pastor, Garret Moore."

Brady still seated in the front seat, introduced Trudy, Allison and Buster, all of whom had exited the suburban. He waited patiently as Buster assisted Trudy in retrieving his chariot from the back. The Reverend Jonah Blackwood joined them after Brady had been settled into the wheelchair. He promptly took the reins and pushed Brady towards a side entrance with a handicap ramp, then paused and turned to the others.

"I do apologize for all the secrecy surrounding the Lords Day of worship. I, too, had to sign one of those nondisclosure documents. We are expecting a few of our normal congregation and some special guests. Lunch on the lawn will follow. The women's auxiliary serves up some fine fixings."

"Speaking of, reverend, this is a fine church you have here," spoke up Buster. "It reminds me of one I grew up in as a mere chap. I was...am Baptist."

"Live Oaks is the new wave for worship. An old dog such as me did have to learn a few new tricks. This is not your grandmother's church, but it is supported by generous, God-loving folks. You'll find our style of worship a tad unorthodox by Baptist standards but being in church, no matter what the denomination, is a God wink, I always say."

"I try not to judge a book by its cover, Reverend Blackwood. It's what's on the pages inside that hold the spine together."

"I like that. May I use it in sometime in one of my lessons?"

"Be my guest."

Trudy continued to be impressed with the sheriff and how he related to strangers. The man seemed at ease in their company. She was glad she had invited him.

"He's something else, isn't he?"

"Who," Trudy asked Allison.

"Buster, who did you think I was talking about? He's quite the charmer. I can't understand why you stay at such odds with him. Did you invite him just to gain suck-up points?"

"Same reason I invited you, little sister."

Low Country Hunt Club Grounds
Colleton County

Groggy, he looked about, met with nothing but darkness, the hood over his head concealing his surroundings. Gagged and shackled to a chair, an uncomfortable cane back chair at that, he couldn't see the minimal rays of light penetrating the darkness, windows boarded, the room empty except for him and his chair. His head and face ached something fierce. His memory was a blur, as was any time reference. He wanted badly to run his tongue over his lips, but the gag restricted that maneuver. Still he could almost feel the dryness, parched and cracked for sure. A growling stomach indicated he was past due for a meal. Moisture between his legs indicated he had pissed in his pants.

He shook his head about to clear the cobwebs, wishing instantly that he hadn't. It throbbed with vengeance. He considered the fact that he may have suffered a concussion. There were no sounds except from the whistling made by intakes of fresh air through his nostrils. One nasal passage was completely closed, meaning his survival hinged on the second one remaining clear. The urge to pee again suddenly hit him. He made no attempt to hold it. Wet was wet. The fresh urine penetrated his senses, quite pungent and sour the second time around. A shiver overcame his body, his body ravished by a series of chills. He couldn't tell if anything was broken or just how much blood he may have lost in this ordeal. Were his kidnappers going to return to finish what they had started or was this it, a slow death, stashed away, out of sight and out of mind?

Reality suddenly rocked his world. His clear nostril was becoming clogged. Breathing was now a major concern. He shifted the chore to his mouth, but the positioning of the gag prevented even less intake than his nose. He quickly abandoned that idea and breathed in deeply with the one good passage, not nearly enough to sustain him for long. He tried blowing out through it to clear it, but it only made matters worse. Panic and suffocation were overwhelming him. He had become lightheaded and began squirming in his chair. It could have only been worse if he had been under water. Both nostrils were totally useless. Death seemed seconds away. He tried his mouth again, but it was no use. Not only was he gagged but duct tape had been used also. Duct tape, a man's solution to everything. It was certainly working. Lance Rocker blinked his eyes frantically, his chest heaving and then just like that, it was over.

Live Oaks Church of Contemporary Teaching and Healing
Georgetown County

"Looks like it's petering out, Woody," commented Drew, one of his security team. "No cars in the last ten minutes."

"I have it at twenty-nine vehicles, guessing forty to fifty folks minimum, given that we didn't get a look at who was riding inside those four limos. We're to ride this out until everyone leaves. We have a four-hour window from what I have been told."

"What could be so important that they need to hire us," asked Leo, another one of his team.

"Their business, not ours; there's no need us losing any sleep over it."

"I hope we're not protecting some sort of Mafia gathering," added Drew Proctor.

"Long as they're not disposing of bodies or making any hits at the church, their money spends like any other," replied Woody.

"That sounds odd coming from an ex-sheriff," said Leo.

"Trust me, I'm not going to knowingly accept dirty money or contribute to a crime. I used my contacts on the force and did a thorough background check. Those fronting this are legit and are not gangsters best I can tell."

"I can't shake the creepy feeling about this. Maybe it's just being out here in the middle of nowhere, looking down that road with all these damned odd trees."

Woody smiled. "It's just the Yankee coming out of you, Rydzewski. Never trust anyone from the south, right? We're all slow-witted bumpkins."

"Come on Boss, you know better. Besides, I'm from West Virginia, not Jersey."

"Rydzewski isn't a good old coal miner's name. You must have been a relocated union boss."

"You damn well know that wasn't on my resume."

"I damn well know you weren't born and raised in West Virginia."

"Hey, guys, here comes another vehicle," interrupted Drew. "By the way, I was born in Raleigh, North Carolina, and Woody's right, you're not a southerner."

"Where's Al," asked Woody.

"He said something about finding a dog," replied Leo. "Why is he so interested in dogs all of a sudden?"

Simultaneously Woody and Drew sounded, "Yankee."

The Town Car had three occupants, two men and a woman. After flashing their invitation, Woody waved them through. He then scanned the perimeter for Al but there was no sign of him. He prompted Drew to go looking for him. He and Leo manned the cattle gate just in case any more late arrivals showed up. He could barely hear music coming from the direction of the church somewhere at the end of the road. The event, whatever it was, was in motion apparently.

Speaking from the pulpit, just after the music director had finished an opening hymn, Reverend Jonah Blackwood welcomed those attending the morning's service. There were only six individuals in the choir, three men and three women. Trudy sat on the first pew, the one reserved for the handicapped. Brady unfortunately fit that category, now confined to the wheelchair. They shared the pew with an elderly woman with a walker and a middle-aged gentleman on crutches.

Buster and Allison sat directly behind them. Allison had already recognized at least one person on the opposite side of the church, Julia Whitaker, twenty-three years old, twice nominated for Oscars in supporting roles, already collecting one last year. She was accompanied by a much older man. He looked familiar, but she couldn't place a name to the face. This event was taking an interesting twist whatever it was supposed to be. Allison looked over at Buster and they exchanged smiles.

Trudy glanced about, estimating less than fifty people in attendance in the tiny church. She noticed something odd. There were no children in the congregation. Possibly they were corralled in another area, but the old-style church didn't look as if it could have many other rooms within its confines. She still couldn't figure why this was a VIP experience and why access was so limited. Brady offered no explanations.

"This is a special day for Live Oaks. One of our very own and a founding father, has come home for a joyous occasion. Please welcome Franco Morrissey, our brother, but better known these days for producing and directing award winning films."

Reverend Blackwood stepped aside as Morrissey approached the pulpit, giving him a warm hug. Morrissey pulled a piece of paper from his jacket, his notes. He smiled and eyed the congregation, appearing to be taking in a panoramic view. He patted his heart with his hand to the warm applause.

"I first wish to thank Reverend Blackwood for his hospitality and for agreeing to allow me and a few of my friends to join in today's worship. I promise you that we will not disrupt your Sunday in the Lord's house. On the contrary, I am here to join you. At the end of the service you are all welcome as my personal guests to join me and my bride to be, the lovely Julia Whitaker as I take her hand in marriage. Please humble me with your attendance. You are somewhat of a captive audience I must confess. After the ceremony and brief reception, you are free to go as you please. My guests have agreed to allow photographs and autographs to any of you wishing to have mementoes. Think about it. You, the congregation are getting an exclusive and jump on the paparazzi. Do as you wish with the photo opt. My friends and I will be making a worthy contribution towards the fund for construction of all structures required to support this church."

To that, the chapel erupted in applause and a standing ovation. They were about to witness famed producer and director Franco Morrissey wed an Academy Award winner, actress Julia Whitaker.

"This church and the Live Oaks grounds have been in my family for generations. The church was built by my father, an immigrant to this amazing country back in the heyday when Georgetown dominated the world in supplying rice. He was the original Episcopal pastor, long before the conception of the Church of Contemporary Teaching and Healing. Enough of the post worship day activities. I do apologize for derailing the flow. Please Reverend Blackwood, tend your flock and lead us back down the righteous path."

Trudy leaned over to Brady. "Just how much of this were you privy to?'

"None actually, like I said, I had to sign a nondisclosure. I understood celebrities would be attending. I just had no names. I didn't have a clue a wedding would be performed after the regular church service. I do recognize some seated on the front pew with the groom."

Allison elbowed Buster and smiled. Buster had no clue who these people were supposed to be. He spent very little time watching movies, not unless a classic John Wayne western was slated to be shown on one of the nostalgic channels. He never read the tabloids or kept tabs on who's who in Hollywood. He was more concerned with being potentially trapped here, not having to attend a damn wedding. Of course, he had the keys to the suburban if he pulled rank and decided to leave.

Now it made sense, thought Trudy. Somehow the good reverend had convinced the church members to exclude bringing children; most likely the master of ceremonies didn't wish any disruptions during his wedding. She wondered how Reverend Blackwood covertly pulled off this one. And this better explained why Woody's services had been contracted, no news media. How had this been kept a secret? Of course enough money can buy most anything.

Reverend Blackwood stepped back up to the pulpit. "I do hope none of you have any ill feelings towards an old con man and his mild attempt at deception. My sermon should most certainly serve as the set-up for the festivities to follow." Someone in attendance shouted 'Amen'.

Three masked individuals with automatic weapons entered the doors to either side of the pulpit. The congregation gasped. More armed and masked thugs entered the front doors of the church, guns aimed, blocking the aisles of any possibility of escape. Reverend Blackwood approached one of the men but was met with the barrel of the gun in his face. His associate pastor stepped forward and was immediately met with the butt of a firearm, sending him to the floor unconscious.

Trudy looked back at the sheriff, neither carrying their police issues. Both felt naked and as helpless as the congregation. Brady placed his hand on her knee, making sure she tried nothing foolish. She counted eight of them, armed and apparently dangerous. Allison instinctively hooked her arm under Buster's, terrified by the unfolding saga, as were the nearly fifty others. Buster thought VIP my ass.

Old Plantation Golf Course
Georgetown County

Noah had given the church wide berth after being harassed by the rude associate pastor. Apparently, he and the main pastor were not on the same page when it came to the church's outreach to the less fortunate. Hindsight, he should have stayed in Myrtle Beach where more assistance seemed available for the homeless. That lifestyle rubbed him the wrong way though, competing for shelter and food, often having to defend his turf and belongings against those seeking to take what he had, even if what he had didn't amount to much. On the street the meek had no chance of inheriting the earth; not that he was meek by any stretch of the imagination. He could fend for himself in a heartbeat if he so chose to do it. Noah just wasn't willing to give into violence over such trivial stuff. Unfortunately, nothing was trivial on the streets he had learned. If anything was worth possessing, someone else always wanted it.

Noah had first hand experienced of the ugliness associated with being one of the less fortunate. He had seen just how kind some people could be also. His perfect balance fit his living on the edge of civilization, being better adapted to wilderness survival than most. If push came to shove, he could live off the land. He found it less stressful and demeaning than begging on the streets for handouts. Most shunned those standing at busy intersections holding the poor pitiful signs asking for money or a job. Too many undercover television specials had exposed this type of thing as a simple con, following the perpetrators back to their homes and cushy lifestyles where they lived the life of tax-free imposters.

The world as he once knew it was being transformed into one not promoting hope and prosperity but one of laziness and entitlement. Big government seemed more determined than ever to push the middle class into poverty and dependency on the powers that be; a happy constituent being one that had everything provided them by the wealthy few that worked hard for a living. Noah had had his fill of government's attempt to control every aspect of his life. He didn't need their handouts. He despised the abundance of programs intent on destroying the American dream and even worse, the American family household. If he had been a product of the sixties and seventies, he would have most certainly been part of the anti-establishment movement, a hippy with long hair and a bead, wearing bellbottoms and beads, and chanting love and freedom to all. His present looks were only missing the bellbottoms and beads.

Noah mostly dressed in army camouflage attire. It served two purposes. One, it offered him better concealment when living in the woodsy terrain. Secondly, contributions flowed more freely with people feeling sorry for a war vet. It pulled on their heartstrings. Begging and panhandling, playing the poor pitiful card didn't come easy for Noah. That's why if given the choice, he was happier and better suited for the outdoorsy away from townsfolk living.

Sadly he, too, had learned to play the game. Beggars could not be choosey. Standing six foot, one and even in his present leaner condition, most others in his situation didn't challenge him. But like in any food chain, there were those who positioned them on the top of the pecking order. These could be the most ruthless and dangerous, ones that wouldn't hesitate to take a human life to advance their agenda. Ironically, it mirrored the politics and world of today.

Having distanced himself from the church, Noah had constructed a makeshift encampment in a wooded and grassy area between the twelfth hole of the golf course and the church. He was adjacent to the tee box so there was no chance an errant golf shot would find its way to his position. Noah was far enough away so that golfers seeking a place to piss would not venture deep enough into his domain. The golf course and surrounding area provided plenty of game for his snares. There was no shortage of huge fox squirrels and rabbits. The ponds offered an ample supply of cooters. The turtle (cooter) meat offered up meals any given time.

The golf course also provided him with fresh drinking water from strategically placed water coolers. A bathroom was a short distance away to provide him with other creature comforts. With no beverage cart girl or roaming rangers, he had only to watch for golfers during the day. There were no houses located on the golf course, so people traffic was held to a minimum. Noah always scouted his camping areas before choosing one.

He had just used the facilities and was heading back to camp, skirting along the number twelve fairway, when he heard the familiar sounds of gas engine golf carts motoring in his direction. Crouching, he soon spotted four carts carrying two people each speeding down the cart path. Oddly they sped past the number six tee box, cut directly across the seventh fairway and were fast approaching his position near the twelfth. Possibly one or more golfers had a sudden urge to visit the facility, but why all four carts then? He stayed put, watching them continue their path directly towards him. They zipped by the restroom and past him before veering though a narrow trail and then vanishing.

Curious, Noah bird dogged them. By the time he caught up with them they had parked and were busy accessing their various golf bags affixed to he back of the carts. He noted their position, probably less than one hundred yards from the little country church. Their behavior was quite odd for golfers. Soon it became evident that he had stumbled into something he should have ignored. He quietly backed away, deciding this was absolutely none of his business. It was time to fold up camp and get the hell out of Dodge.

Live Oaks Church of Contemporary Teaching and Healing

"Brothers and sisters, all rise, and before any of you act on the urge to utilize your cell phones to alert family, friends or the dreaded police, please allow me to point you to my left where my associate, Hop-Frog, has a loaded weapon held to the head of your beloved reverend. Please heed my warning or you will have his blood on your hands. Do I make myself perfectly clear? Before the man of the cloths' lifeless body contacts the floor, Ethelred and Dupin positioned at the rear of the church, will unleash hellfire from their automatic weapons that will make quite a bloody mess of the center pews of this gracious church. In layman terms, don't try anything stupid or most certainly you will meet your maker sooner than you anticipated. I promise you there will be no survivors if you so choose to test our intentions."

Trudy reacted by feeling for her revolver that wasn't strapped to her side. Feeling somewhat naked under the circumstances she looked over her shoulder at the sheriff. His face was blood red and the man was obviously quite pissed to be caught in this situation, whatever this situation might be. Brady reached over and touched her hand. A murmur spread over the congregation. Some weeping could be heard. The man standing before them banged a hand gun like a gavel and then returned it to Pastor Blackwood's temple who had been delivered front and center by Hop-Frog.

"Now that I have your undivided attention it is time to show your love by giving. Ushers, Doctor Tarr and Mister Fether, please come forward as we prepare to give thanks for the Tithes and Offerings. There will be a slight twist in what you might be accustomed. Please remove your clothing and pass it to the ushers. For the men this includes coats, shirts and trousers, socks, shoes, hats if you have them and underwear, with everything intact inside your various pockets. Women, same applies and please include your purses. After all, are we not the Lord's children, each equal in his eyes? Okay, I admit, some will most certainly be less or more equal than others in this state, but one should not be envious of thy neighbor or poke fun at thy neighbor for being less fortunate. Don't forget the '*thy shall not covet*' part either. This is not intended to be a mere peep show."

"Hold on there. You can't expect us to strip down to nothing," protested Buster. "Certainly there is another route to take, one less embarrassing for these fine folks."

"Thank you, sir, in the second pew for volunteering to demonstrate for the others what I have just explained. Please step front and center and shed those dreadful clothes so that the others of the congregation shall be compelled to follow by example."

Buster crossed his arms and said, "Absolutely not."

"Tamerlane, please execute the young lady standing to the defiant one's right."

"Hold on a second," replied Buster, glancing first to Trudy and then to Allison by his side.

"Must I remind you? I have a schedule to maintain. Disruptions upset my little apple cart. I do not appreciate my apple cart being disrupted. Is that perfectly clear for you, Brother? Do what I ask or watch the first of the flock unite with the heavenly body above. Can I hear an Amen?"

"Amen," replied Hop-Frog, poking the barrel of his weapon firmly against Reverend Jonah Blackwood's head.

"Enough of this crap" shouted Ace. O. Diamonds the professional wrestler, followed by an outcry from many in the congregation.

"Please, calm down…all of you. We better do what he asks." Buster walked and then stood before the pulpit, turned and faced those thankful it was him instead of them.

"Might I ask your name, Brother, before you graciously demonstrate the disrobing technique for the others?"

Buster wanted so badly to announce exactly who he was, but training had taught him otherwise. "I'm Adam West." He assessed the various masks being worn by gun totters. He thought he recognized some of the characters. He had indeed recognized the names Valdemar and Hop-Frog.

Valdemar chuckled. "By some chance were your parents devout fans of the 1960's Batman series?"

Not cracking a smile, Buster answered. "They preferred Bruce Wayne, but our last name is West. Bruce Wayne West just wasn't to their liking. What villain persona have you and your thugs assumed, the Edgar Allen Poe Dead Poet Society?"

While Trudy appreciated the sheriff's motives, shifting the focus to him and away from the others, even she could see he was toying with fire. His smartass mouth was riling up their host.

"Discard your clothing. This senseless debating is disrupting my schedule. Pass me your wallet first. Let's reveal your identity as you reveal everything else."

Bad news, Trudy reacted, making every attempt to derail exposing his identity. "Hey Raven Boy, why all the silly ass games? Why not just get on with this? What do you really want?"

"Contestant number two come on down. Perfect. A man and woman will lead the congregation to nakedness, a scene fit for the Garden of Eden. Don't bite that apple though."

"And you make an excellent serpent if I might be so bold to add."

"I'll take the crazy bitch's place. I have nothing to hide. Let's just get this over with, please."

Trudy gave her the eye. What was Allison doing?

Julia Whitaker stood, quickly disrobed and tossed her clothing to the floor. She had done her fair share of nude scenes and had nothing to hide. Methodically others followed suit, passing their clothes to the ends of the pews. Allison stood nude beside an equally naked Sheriff Buster Ferguson. This was a memory Trudy would rather not have etched in her head. She assisted Brady in removing his after she had disrobed. Within five minutes every one was naked as a flock of jaybirds. Most avoided any sort of eye contact. A few gawked, more interested in seeing what others had to offer than taking time to comprehend the serious situation that lay ahead.

Trudy whispered to Brady, "This is getting old, me being nude every time the next big case comes along. Maybe it's a sign we should become nudist."

"I know him."

"You can't possibly know everyone wearing knickers."

"No, I mean it. I know him."

Valdemar shifted his gaze in their direction. "Must I remind you? I granted no permission to talk to thy neighbors. My ushers are a bit trigger-happy so please comply with my wishes."

Trudy reached over and grabbed Brady by the hand and squeezed. He returned the squeeze and remained silent as instructed.

"Now that wasn't so difficult was it? Next, please assemble in the center aisle and follow Ligeia to the left side of the chapel. There we'll be taking portraits of the modest free congregation. In the meantime, please step forward if I call your name."

Calling names, this was getting just too creepy thought Trudy.

"Franco Morrissey, acclaimed director and producer and your bride to be, the award-winning Julia Whitaker, please stand before me. World renowned cardiologist and lecturer, Paula Cameron, please join them. Governor Marcus McDonald, how I do enjoy your weekly program; there is life after a governorship. Phil Locklear, real estate mogul extraordinaire, and I must say, quite endowed, step forth. Derrick Shumway, aka Ace O. Diamonds, nine-time World Wrestling champion and action film movie star. Sorry the steroids didn't treat you as well as Mister Locklear. Ouch, no porn scenes for you. I do beg your forgiveness. I am not exactly practicing what I just preached. You can't help your short comings. Ah yes…Graham Firth, CEO, multibillionaire, owner of three sports teams. Impressive. And last, but not least, Fabio Fuentes, entrepreneur and closet drug lord. Money can indeed buy your way into inner circles. I have before me all my favorite flavors from society row. I recognize you and the congregation is now familiar with your crevices and fannies, long and short of it all."

Reluctantly each of the individuals named did as instructed. The remainder of the congregation proceeded single file to their appointment with the designated photographer, Professor Fether. All poses were the same, hands down by your sides, up close and personal, full frontal from the knees to the head. Before returning to their seats, each person could rummage through the piles of clothing until they at least located their original outer garments or something suitable to wear. Shoes, socks, underwear were excluded to speed up the process.

Trudy, standing in line nude behind Brady's wheelchair, equally wearing his birthday suit, watched and waited. Just what was this masked maniac up too now? Allison and Buster had filed in line behind them. TMN, 'too much nakedness' prevailed, and in a church of all places. Weaponless, Trudy and Buster had no choice but to obey the leader's requests. Biding her time wasn't an easy task for Trudy. Reality, too many lives were at stake to pull anything foolish; even she got it. She just hoped there were no boneheads in the congregation. Sometimes in an incident such as this it only took one to set off a chain reaction of epic proportions. With all the fire power being flaunted about, these folks meant serious business.

"Contrary to belief, the emperor without his or her clothing does make a difference, doesn't it? Professor Fether, please be so kind as to snap some mementoes of my celebrity guests, individually and then in group poses. I shall set the stage for the interactive group poses, something most provocative and risqué, the paparazzi Holy Grail of all exposés."

In pairs and in groups, Valdemar positioned his quests in poses that would make Larry Flint blush. This was defined as an insurance policy against retribution, but retribution against what. Photo opts completed, everyone was instructed to return to their pews, all except the celebrities being flaunted up front. Fabio had taken a backhand from Valdemar after threatening to kill the host. Valdemar instructed Hop-Frog to promptly go 'Bobbitt' on him if he made another sound. Fabio covered his privates with both hands and remained silent.

"Allow me to explain why we are gathered here, and, no, it is not to hear another wonderful all inspiring sermon from your pastor or to witness the wedding of these two. My request is quite simple of those capable of making my wish come true. The eight standing before you are to have one billion dollars transferred to an off shore and secured account. I'm not interested in even shares being contributed. Pool your resources. The final tally is what's important."

"If any of you divulge the intent of our little arrangement to those on the phone, everyone is this room dies. I've taken all the necessary precautions to keep this our little secret from law enforcement, news media and so forth. Don't undo these arrangements by doing something completely idiotic. Let me make this perfectly clear. Disobey and you all die. Do not insult me by saying this figure is unachievable. I have researched your portfolios. You have exactly two hours to complete this task. All phone calls shall be monitored as will the account. You do your part and I will ensure that every one of you is rewarded with the gift of life. Fail me and you will be sealing your death and the deaths of those gathered here. It is no more difficult than that. Choose wisely and save your excuses."

Security Check Point

Woody and his security team were basically in hurry up and wait mode now. Whatever was going on down at the end of the road had to run its course. Once the guests departed his job would be fulfilled. Waiting was not a Woody Anderson strong point. His guards were on the clock and couldn't care less if they were staying busy or not. One troubling issue remained. They had not been able to locate Al. Woody now thinking he must have gone AWOL. It was a stretch to conclude he had, given he had no transportation. Why would he though? This was a paid gig, easy money.

Woody decided to widen the search, telling Drew and Leo to stay put. It suited them just fine, better to stay in the shade and out of the heat and humidity. Leo had gotten a scare earlier along the banks of a nearby pond. A gargantuan alligator had slipped into the murky marshy water as he approached. Leo claimed it must have been at least a twelve-footer if not larger. Alligators were no strangers to these parts. Copperheads, rattlesnakes and cottonmouths were probably a more dangerous threat when roaming about. No one had snake chaps either or a harpoon for the giant lizard so said Leo.

Paralleling the opposite side of the church's drive, an area they hadn't searched, Woody moved cautiously through the overgrown brush. Thirty yards in he jumped two whitetail deer, nearly causing him to piss his pants. Luckily, he was out of sight of his two guards, saving some embarrassment. He no longer heard any music or singing coming from the church. It was still out of sight somewhere down the end of the live oak lined lane. Perspiration dripped off the end of his nose, his clothes already drenched. He snagged his shirt on a vine with razor sharp thorns, ripping the material and drawing blood from his arm.

Woody paused and called out again for Al. He received no reply. He hoped he hadn't succumbed to a heat stroke or heart attack. After another fifteen minutes of searching he came within eye contact of the church. The assortment of vehicles was parked to the right, an area packed down with crush run material. He decided not to go any closer. His contract stated that he was just supposed to man the main entrance. He surely didn't need to jeopardize it by doing something stupid.

To quicken his trip back he returned via the driveway. Woody detected movement from the corner of his eye, the area near where he had last seen the leaping deer. He stopped, focused and listened but saw or heard anything out of the ordinary. He shook his head, displeased with his sudden jumpiness. Proceeding, there it was again, a flicker reflecting off something, movement for sure that time. He eased down on one knee in the middle of the narrow roadway as if to wish himself into blending in with his surroundings. Hardly breathing now and not blinking he zoomed in on where he thought he had detected something, determined to wait it out this time. Still nothing caught his eye. He wiped perspiration dripping into his eyes with the back of his sleeve.

There it was again, a fuzzy, shadowy silhouette but no doubt real, not the result of an overactive imagination. Woody suddenly had the feeling he was being stalked. Stalked by who or what? His first impulse was to call out to the phantom apparition and announce he was armed. Doing so might prompt the person or thing to flee. No, he wanted to get a close look, ID the trespasser first, and then flash his credentials and gun if deemed a threat.

Could it be Al playing some sick prank? If so, he should know better. Never pull crap like that on people packing loaded weapons. Woody developed a plan in his head. He turned and continued his trek towards his men. Once he reached the next huge live oak, a dead spot between him and the other. He used the massive trunk to conceal his movement. He parked against the tree, his back against the trunk. Now with his gun drawn, gripping it with both hands, he stood on ready. Somewhere on the other side of the oak a swig snapped. Woody circled the trunk and approached from what he hoped to be behind the unknown stalker. There he was leaning against the tree. Woody recognized the uniform. He had found Al Struthers.

Before he could call out to him, the man slumped and then began sliding to the ground and tumbling downward, crashing with a loud thump. Woody took a step and he was grabbed from behind, around his throat, his oxygen supply cut off immediately. Wooziness overcame him, and he dropped his gun. When he woke Woody was propped against the live oak. Al was propped up next to him. One glance told Woody the man was dead. His skin was an ashy grey and upon closer observation he could tell he wasn't breathing. Someone kicked Woody's foot. He looked up to see a stranger now holding his gun. Woody prepared for the inevitable. He too was about to meet his maker at the hands of the mystery guest.

"I didn't kill him if that's what you're thinking."

The stranger offered him a hand up. Woody reluctantly accepted. After he was on his feet the stranger handed him back his weapon, gripping the barrel to gesture he meant it. Woody didn't immediately respond. He instead assessed the figure standing before him. The man said nothing else, continued to meet Woody with his stare. Dressed in army camo-fatigues, sporting black nappy hair and an equally scruffy beard, the light skinned black man stood at around six feet tall, lean but not skinny. His eyes were brown and quite alert for a homeless gent if indeed he was. A scar graced his right cheek to just above his eye, but the eye appeared undamaged by the old wound.

"Where were you taking Al Struthers?"

"To you."

"Why?"

"By the uniform, he's one of yours, right?"

"How did you know we were here and why are you here?"

"Not important but what is important is what's happening at the end of this road."

"Are you saying it has a connection with Al's murder?"

"Murder, your words not mine. I wasn't a witness to his death. A coroner should make than assessment."

"What exactly is going on here and how are you involved?"

"You ask a lot of questions."

"Former occupational habit, sorry…"

"You were a cop."

Woody nodded. "In another life… I'm guessing I better call the Georgetown sheriff's department though."

"I'd suggest holding off on that thought."

"Get to your point. What's really going on here? And I think it's high time you told me your name."

"Name's not important either but if it makes you happy just call me Noah. Everyone else does."

"I take it that's not your real name then. I know. It's not important right now. I get it."

"Call me Woody, short for Woodrow Anderson, my real name. Formalities over, tell me what the hell you do know about Al's death and just what the hell is going on here? This better be good because I'm not exactly liking this conversation so far."

Eggs Up Restaurant
Pawley's Island, Georgetown County

"Thank you for meeting me here Tim."

"Thanks for inviting me, Summer. I figured I wouldn't see you today."

"Time off for good behavior, I suppose."

"How's the bike coverage going?"

"Interesting event but there's really nothing to write home about."

"Sorry, you've already missed the prime murder and mayhem events here. Quiet is better, at least from my perspective."

"Tim, unfortunately the warm and fuzzy stories don't hold the viewers' attention or interest very long. We're a society programmed to feed off tragedy and drama I'm afraid. Bad news trumps good news hand over fist. Murder and mayhem boost ratings. I knew that going into this profession, so I shouldn't whine about it."

"There's always a bad side to every job. It's taken me a while to warm up to the cruelty mankind inflicts on itself. Somewhere along the way we've lost the concept of love thy neighbor and do unto others as we'd have them do unto us."

"I agree. Too many people practice the opposite. Do unto them before they have a chance to do unto me. We're a lot alike, Tim. That's why I like you and your ethics. You're a believer in mankind wanting to do the right thing."

"Sure, I believe, but I've come to the realization that I can't transform the world, not even one puzzle piece at a time. I've been sucked into the sandpit, rolling with the punches and just hoping it all works out to something close to a happy ending. Sadly, most of the time it doesn't."

"So, what do we do about it, Tim?"

"Right now, I'm going to cherish the time I have with you."

Summer smiled and reached across the table and touched Tim's hand. Tim placed his other hand on top of hers. Could this be love he wondered? He surely hoped so. Tim's phone rang, and he reluctantly answered it. Summer watched as Tim's facial and physical expressions underwent a terrible transformation, concerned and breathing hard.

"Not presently. Yeah, I understand. Don't worry. I won't. Yeah. I said I won't. I'm all over it. Consider it a done deal. Crap…just un-fricking believable…No…I get it. Will do. You too." He ended the call. "I'm going to have to bow out, take a rain check. Sorry Summer."

Intersection of Highways 501 and-544
Conway

Detective Parnell Roberts, on his way home, witnessed the incident in its entirety. The driver of the pickup rear ended the SUV just as the driver pulled forward after the light had changed to green. The pickup driver apparently angered by the incident, rammed the SUV a second time intentionally and then the driver exited the truck. The man banged on the window of the SUV. Parnell could see a frightened woman at the wheel as he was still sitting at the traffic light heading westbound towards Conway, the others heading eastbound towards Myrtle Beach. Before he could wheel around to intervene, the female driver pulled away. She was obviously fearful of her safety.

The rear bumper of her SUV had been entangled in the front bumper of the late model truck. As she pulled away, the truck towed behind her before breaking free. The irate truck driver consumed by a fit of road rage never saw the approaching vehicle. The force of the truck struck him from behind. He ended up face first on the asphalt pinning him underneath the truck. Parnell completed his U-turn and parked his car behind the truck. Exiting he could hear the pinned driver cursing up a storm, still pissed at the SUV who had now fled the scene of the accident, one that had not been her fault. Approaching the front of the truck, Parnell's senses were bombarded by the unmistakable smell of alcohol.

With some effort he freed the intoxicated man from underneath the truck carriage only to be greeted by a wild swing. The force of the missed punch and ensuing spin sent the man crashing back face first on the asphalt. Parnell identified himself and ordered the man to remain in his facedown position while he retrieved his handcuffs. Of course the man didn't heed his warning. He tried to stand, wobbling on all fours. Parnell placed a size thirteen in between his shoulder blades pushing him flat on his belly again. He warned him to stay put this time but quickly realized that resisting arrest was going to be this perp's MO. Parnell handcuffed him and then yanked him to his feet. He gave him his Miranda and asked if he understood. Archie Allen, the name on his suspended driver's license, DUI forth offense now, pending confirmation with the breathalyzer, was led tiptoeing to the back of Parnell's vehicle.

Parnell handed the impaired driver over to the highway patrolman once he arrived. Archie submitted to the test once he calmed down and blew an impressive number, indicating he could be categorized legally as a dead man walking, or driving in this case. Both Parnell and the patrolman shook their heads in disgust. The woman involved in the incident had pulled over at a Burger King on Singleton Ridge Road and had then called 911 to report the incident. She explained she had fled the accident, fearful for her own life, describing the incident to the 911 dispatcher. As Parnell returned to his vehicle, he received a phone call.

"Yes and no…I was heading home but this stupid ass drunk ran slap dab into the back of a SUV on 501. I saw the whole damn thing and held him until the highway patrol arrived. The sot blew twice the legal limit on the breathalyzer. Get this. It was his fourth damn DUI offense, the A-hole driving with a suspended license of course. He probably won't even remember doing it. They better put his ass away this time. Yeah…yeah…I'm done, what's up? Son of a b…damn straight, count me in. I'm on my way. I got one stop to make and I'll meet you there. Son of a bitch…"

Little River
River Gate Community
Doctor Dallas Solomon's Waterway Condo

Doctor 'D' answered the doorbell on the first ring, expecting the guest at her door.

"Hey Doc, I'm a few minutes early. I hope that won't be a problem."

"Not at all, Sly, it takes very little prep time for me. Let's go."

Sly was tempted to utilize the siren but thought better of it. He needed time to think. Darting through, in and around traffic at breakneck speeds would only serve as a distraction. He required some thinking time but that might be easier said than done. Dallas had immediately engaged in conversation.

"Sly, do we have any additional information?"

"Details are sketchy. You know as much as I know about it as this point."

"Is this associated in any way with the ongoing bike rally?"

"Who can say? Events such as these often attract the riff-raff, someone looking to make a quick buck by hook or by crook, pun intended. I personally don't quite understand enough of what's going on to make a stab at a motive. The whole cockamamie story is just too bizarre and difficult to believe. Hearing and seeing it firsthand might convince me otherwise."

"If the evidence reinforces our worst fears, then what do we do?"

"Let's take it one step at a time and not jump to conclusions just yet."

"I'd suggest we go solve the mystery then. My detective juices are on high alert, Dallas, doctor and detective at your service," she replied with a tone of sarcasm in her voice.

"I just hope we're not dealing with a bunch of lunatics."

"Sly, have you considered this might be a mere diversion for something much larger? With the biker distractions, and then this, specific banks could be prime targets."

"See, you are wearing your detective hat after all."

"No crime has been confirmed yet to support my theory."

"Maybe not, Dallas, but at least you're thinking it through, entertaining other possibilities, more so than me thus far. I'm still hedging towards this being a mere hoax, nothing more."

"We can only hope. There have been a precious few dull moments since I joined the merry band of crime scene investigates. It has been my honor to know every one of you. I still miss our fallen comrade, Detective Kirk Cardoon. Captain Kirk, our forensics expert was taken too soon doing what loved to do."

"Now we have Parnell Roberts. Most feel we have traded down. The jury is still out for me but so far so good."

"I shall refrain from judging the detective until I become better acquainted with our latest edition."

"He's raw and rough around the edges but I think he'll do just fine. One thing for sure, life here comes at you fast and furious. It's put up or shut up time for our Grand Strand rookie."

Live Oaks Church of Contemporary Teaching and Healing

Trudy assessed her options, drawing nothing but blanks. At least everyone was fully clothed once again; well, almost. The rich were still standing front and center, clothing not optional. Most of the distraction was now history, although she would have a tough time blocking out those images of her superior once this ordeal was over. This Valdemar and his assembled cast from a cheesy Batman sitcom couldn't possibly think he could cash in on one billion dollars on such short notice and then get away with it. He was one ambitious bastard that was for sure.

In her mind she began assembling the facts. There were eight of them, armed and extremely dangerous and more than fifty guests, unarmed and scared to death. Only she and the sheriff were trained police officers, unarmed and drastically outnumbered. The bad guys fortunately didn't realize trained good guys were among them. That was something to hang their hats on. Valdemar hadn't divulged an escape strategy yet, pending securing his ransom of course.

Woody and his security force were a stone's throw away but what good did that do. They weren't privy to the chaos inside the church and it wasn't likely he would wander in to check on the activities. If he did, his men were certainly no match for this fire power. Valdemar professed a four-hour window to pull this off. Engaging in delay tactics seemed a plausible plan, weak, but at least something. One cannot be too choosey when insurmountable odds are stacked against you. Trudy wondered what the sheriff might be thinking. Surely the wheels were turning in his head too but chatting about it didn't seem a possibility.

Old Edgar Allen Poe's patience for chit chat among hostages was nonexistent. Those automatic weapons being waved about were convincing deterrents. If only she could get her hands on one of them…then what, instigate a shootout and have the senseless slaying of innocent people potentially on her head. She had reformed…right…no more vigilante tactics...everything by the book. Well, maybe saving your butt was just cause to bend the rules a tad if needed. Lucky her if she did. Her superior would witness her rebel ways first hand and potentially support her dismissal.

Trudy perused the perimeter for the zillionth time, noting the position of each of what… the kidnappers, extortionist, blackmailers or terrorist for lack of better descriptions? She looked for any sign of weakness and, as before, saw none. This had been well planned, leaving little wiggle room for counter actions. Worst case scenario, the plan worked, the money was collected, and everyone lived to see another day. Why not just allow it to run its course and play out? Why couldn't she just sit on the sidelines and do just that? It wasn't her nature to just give in, plain and simple. She was a cop. These were criminals. Her job was to enforce the law, not allow it to happen unchallenged. Pig headed, inherited from Amy Wagner, her mother, rest her soul. Besides, she had the welfare of her sister and husband resting in her hands…family first...right, no place for gunslinger antics. What was she to do then? Becoming another cow in the corralled herd just wasn't her way. A bull in the china shop…no doubt.

Covertly as possible, keeping her eyes on this Valdemar character she whispered to Sheriff Buster Ferguson sitting behind her, just over he left shoulder, "any ideas?"

Allison elbowed Buster and nodded towards her sister, and in the slightest of whispers, barely moving her lips, repeated what Trudy had asked.

"None," Buster replied, "what about you?"

She simply shook her head no. Brady squeezed her knee and again said what he had attempted saying much earlier. "I'm telling you I know this guy," he, too whispered.

Too much whispering…busted…

"Do you have something you'd like to share with the congregation? I would ask you to stand but that might sound a bit cruel given your current situation," stated Valdemar.

"Don't," cautioned Trudy.

"Ah, and you, who might you be…Mister Ironsides' spokesperson?"

Obviously he hadn't recognized Brady yet and she wanted to keep it that way. She stood, and stepped forward, slightly blocking Brady from direct view from Valdemar.

"We're all just a little anxious. When can we get out of here? Why do you need us? We have absolutely nothing to do with you raising this money."

"Possibly not directly, but one can never tell if I might require your services in brokering the deal. Most respectable people appreciate the value of human lives. As a contingency and a failure to meet the terms of the contract you could be most valuable. I don't foresee this becoming a hostage scenario, but one can never predict the unpredictable. And if the rich and famous fail to meet their obligations, penalties could come at a deathly cost. See, you play an intricate part in that little scenario if my terms are not met swiftly. Do we understand one another?"

"You actually intend on murdering innocent people?"

"My intentions are to enforce my proposal. As in any investment the stakes are high, and coddling is for the weak. Guilt is a powerful instrument. No one really wishes to have the blood of another on their hands. We are not on the brink yet. Ultimatums are currently not in play. Please dispel those thoughts. One hour from now, if progress is not being made, I'll open the conversation up to the penalty phase. I assure you it will be strictly a democratic process."

This conversation had stirred a rumbling of comments from the others, becoming a bit too vocal for their own good, soon pointed out by a disgruntle host. A mere nod and Ethelred walked over to a random pew and slammed the butt of his assault weapon against the head of an unsuspecting elderly man, prompting screams from his wife as he toppled over into her lap, blood gushing from an open wound.

"Silence," demanded Valdemar. "It's golden, might I remind you with a second gesture of ill will."

Silence quickly prevailed.

"This is no mere game of who wants to be a billionaire. I lose, you lose. There are no life lines or opportunities to phone a friend."

A lady a few rows back raised her hand.

"Please stand and speak clearly and coherently."

"I have to go to the bathroom."

Valdemar chuckled. "This is no movie my dear. No one will be allowed to visit the facilities. If I allow you then I open the option to everyone else in the room. We'll not be distracted as escorts to the restrooms. Do what you must do to relieve yourself but do it where you stand. Before the floodgates open, we'll not be serving beverages or food on this flight. Surely everyone can make do. Once the money is confirmed in my account you shall be rid of us. If I were you, I would vent those frustrations to those controlling your destiny, those standing to my right naked as the day they arrived from their mother's womb."

Reverend Jonah Blackwood had heard and seen enough. The elder pastor stood and walked towards Valdemar, throwing caution and his safety to the wind. Associate Pastor Garrett Moore, having recovered from his unconscious state, called out to him. He turned and offered him a brief smile but never slowed until he was a mere three paces from the lead intruder.

"Sir, these people need not be treated as animals. Surely you have some decency and compassion."

"Pastor, tending the flock is admirable but totally unacceptable in my house and, yes, this is my house now, not yours or your Lord's. Humor me and I shall opt out of the lease option once my demands have been met. Please return to your seat."

Blackwood took a step closer. Buster now gripped the back of the pew in front of him and was on the verge of standing, having seen and heard enough also. Allison sensing this placed her hand on his knee, digging in with her fingernails. Buster winced and looked over at her. She mouthed no. He moved as if to attempt to stand and she dug them in defiantly. Buster mouthed ouch.

Out of the blue, Brady wheeled into action, bringing the wheelchair to rest between the two men and announcing, "Enough."

Valdemar grabbed the foot rest of the wheelchair and in one quick movement flipped it backwards sending Brady toppling out of it and onto the floor. Trudy stood and rushed to his aid, as did the Associate Pastor, Garrett Moore. Hop-Frog was upon them, shouldering Moore before grabbing and tossing him to the floor. Valdemar had magician like retrieved a jaded dagger from his clothing and now had it to Trudy's throat.

"Enough is the appropriate term. Enough of the heroics and theatrics. Return to your seats and consider yourselves extremely lucky. You, on the floor, stay there face down as a reminder to those who may be thinking foolish thoughts."

A trickle of blood appeared on Trudy's throat as she slowly did as instructed by Valdemar. Keeping Brady face down might just keep him out of harm's way. If he truly recognized the masked Valdemar's identity it might not set well if Valdemar also recognized him. Brady had not been able to recall where he had seen or met him. Perhaps it had been at a golfing event, given that he had keyed in on the knickers. Maybe Valdemar had been a participant that hopefully hadn't noticed Brady.

Pastor Blackwood had assisted his associate pastor back to his seat. The younger man had a welt appearing on his right cheek from the fall he had taken. He waved off Blackwood indicating he was okay. Moore took in the scene, patting his foot nervously from where he sat. Rubbing his burning face, he wondered just how bad this might get before it was over. He prayed no one else would try to interfere and just allow it to run its course. He had certainly escaped a much closer call than he had intended.

Moore had momentarily assumed the role of a hero. Those in the congregation would remember vividly how he had tried to protect the crippled man in the wheelchair. He had served the church as protector and defender of the flock. Even Blackwood would be impressed. Moore fought back a smile, suddenly finding himself staring at the nude posteriors of the rich and famous, serving as a reminder of the urgent task ahead, collecting one billion dollars or die at these people's hands. He for one had no intention of being a victim of their penalty clause. Every lamb didn't have to be sacrificed to appease the gods. It was too early to count out the tithes and offerings from those who could certainly afford it.

Security Checkpoint

Woody had radioed Drew Proctor and Leo Rydzewski, only telling them to stay alert; momentarily heeding Noah's warning to not contact the authorities. This certainly wasn't Woody's first rodeo at not following protocol. He still wasn't buying the entire story of what little bit the homeless guy had shared with him, but he couldn't argue the fact that Al was dead. With the absence of any obvious wounds who could say he hadn't died of natural causes. Noah said his neck had been broken. Maybe, maybe not. Woody wasn't a doctor. It could have happened during a fall.

Other than karate chopping him initially, Noah had not resisted, had even handed back over his gun. That didn't mean he had to trust him though. This could be some sort of setup. Possibly this Noah character had murdered Al and had his sights set on the rest of them. Woody had already witnessed firsthand the work of serial killers. Who's to say Noah wasn't one, roaming about, killing for fun or maybe just for the purpose of survival. That's why he allowed Noah to carry Al's feet, walking ahead, him bringing up the rear. As awkward as this method was, it allowed Woody to keep a watchful eye on him.

Woody played back in his head what Noah had shared so far. He had seen eight individuals in four golf carts veer off one of the cart paths of the golf club next door and drive towards the church. He had watched as they stopped shy of the church. Noah had remained hidden as he observed them removing an assortment of weapons and electronic equipment from golf bags that he said weren't actual golf bags. Once they had organized and masked themselves, they proceeded to the church, a couple spurring off and doing a perimeter sweep. Noah thinks that during the perimeter sweep is when they had crossed paths with Al Struthers, but he had not witnessed an encounter, deciding to follow the main group.

The story became sketchy at best after the strangers ventured inside the church. It was tough for Noah to position himself close enough without being detected, so he said. One window concealed by a fence for the air conditioning unit allowed him his only access. Woody had a tough time understanding why a homeless guy would risk being shot just for curiosity's sake. It made absolutely no sense. The air conditioning unit had just knocked off, allowing him to hear some of what was going on inside.

The apparent leader had warned those inside to make no calls to the police, news media or friends on their cell phones or another intruder would slay Pastor Blackwood and then the congregation. He had heard something about removing clothes before the unit cycled back on, drowning out most of the dialogue. He spotted two masked men returning from their perimeter sweep and deserted his eavesdropping post. The intent of the raid had not been disclosed. Woody would have to see this with his own eyes before determining an action plan. For all he knew, this Noah character could be suffering from some sort of paranoia disorder or drug induced state. Those with emotional or psychological issues were prime candidates for the homeless circuit, not that he was unjustly stereotyping the man.

Woody tried to formulate a game plan. First things first, secure Al's lifeless body and then be prepared to dish out some serious damage control to his other men. Somehow, he would have to justify with them not calling this in yet. Neither of the other two had a police background so maybe it would be easier than anticipated to convince them. Al Struthers on the other hand had retired from law enforcement. Look where that had gotten him. Woody paused, prompting Noah to stop and look back at him.

"Change in plans. Let's leave Al here for now. You and I are going to pull a little recon back at the church. Not that I don't believe you, but I need to see this first."

"Are you sure this is a good idea? These guys mean business and they have you out gunned and outmanned."

"Not if I call this in once I see what I'm dealing with."

"Did you not listen to what I shared with you? They said that they would murder everyone inside at the first sign of any resistance or media coverage. Do you want that on your conscious?"

"Okay…let's just see how close we can get and go from there. That is, unless you have concocted this whole story and don't want me to see that none of it is true."

"Suit yourself but humor me please and allow me to take the point."

Woody noted, taking point, military term, maybe this guy had been a soldier, now homeless because of PTSD. Many folks having served in the military returned from duty suffering from post-traumatic stress disorder. It used to be called combat fatigue or maybe caused from guys being shell shocked, but the medical profession embraces coming up with new labels and acronyms for everything. Call it what you will. Woody had witnessed firsthand what it could do to people, to friends and to foes on the streets.

The military garb this Noah was wearing fits the pattern. What didn't fit was the fact that so far Noah was showing none of the telltale signs, fatigue, slower reaction times, indecision, a disconnection from one's surroundings, and inability to prioritize. On the contrary, he seemed alert and on top of his game, other than the cockamamie yarn he might be spinning. Possibly he was just hallucinating. Woody would take all this in stride until evidence supported fact.

Noah moved away from the church, giving it wide berth. Woody instantly became suspicious, placing his hand on his holster. Still, the same guy had handed him back his gun. It didn't make sense he would harm him now when before he had already had the upper hand. A lot of this wasn't making any sense. Concealed by the overgrown terrain skirting the church yard, Noah led on and Woody followed several paces behind him.

Noah stopped, holding up his hand and motioning with obvious military signals his intent. Stop and come closer. Woody read them loud and clear, advanced to the man's side and then parted the branches to get a better look. There they were, as had been described, four abandoned golf carts sporting the Old Plantation Golf Resort logo. It was becoming a bit more believable seeing the deserted carts so far away from the course.

Noah, using two fingers, pointed to his eyes and then to the church, remaining quiet just in case others were within earshot. He then pointed to the back of the church, a possible entry point. Skirting the wooded area, they circled until they had a better view. No guard was stationed outside. The windows were stained in typical church fashion and the back door was solid, no glass pane. The two chanced it and quickly positioned themselves at the back of the church. Woody cocked his head and listened but could only barely make out muffled talking. Noah tested the doorknob…locked. The three windows were sealed too. Woody edged to one side of the church while Noah did the same on the opposite side. Coast was clear both sides. Something didn't feel right to Woody. Why were there eight alleged individuals and no guards posted outside?

Woody signaled to Noah he was going to move towards the front of the church. Noah acknowledged he would do the same from his side. Slinking beneath all side windows the two men advanced. Within a couple of feet from the front Woody paused, his back against the building and took a deep breath. He removed his gun from its holster and eased forward. A hand grabbed him from behind. Woody spun and pointed his pistol between the eyes of his assailant. With not so much as a flinch, Noah placed his finger to his lips and motioned for Woody to follow him. Woody composed himself, thankful he hadn't just shot his cohort between the eyes. He followed Noah back to the safety of the woods before the man explained his actions.

"Sniper on the roof watching the driveway, that's why there are no posted guards in plain sight.

"How could you have possibly seen on top of the roof from your vantage point? I couldn't see on the roof."

"Cigar stub on the ground, still smoldering…"

"So, what...a patrolling guard could have dropped it."

"It ricocheted off my nose. Cigars don't rain from the sky."

"Funny, smartass..."

"I backed away, got a better view. The dude is packing military vintage sniper equipment, A-one, badass firepower. He could take out anything local police could offer up and do it from over a quarter mile away if he so desired. No one will come down that road and live to tell about it."

"Why not secure the back?"

"No need, there's no real access except by way of the golf course. I walked the area many times. Possibly they have that sealed off too would be my guess."

"The million-dollar question, what the hell are they up to in there? What significance could there be in this out of the way church?"

"I'd be asking who is inside. There lies the key. The church is just a convenient location. Who passed through your security check point?"

"Most were just locals I am assuming. There were six limos, didn't see anyone but the drivers, all presenting passes. I do have friends inside, a Horry County detective and her husband and sister. The Horry County sheriff is a guest too."

"Do they have enemies that would pull a stunt like this? This seems awfully sophisticated for mere revenge, but we can't discount anything."

"You ask a lot of questions for..."

"A homeless guy," Noah finished the sentence. "Homeless doesn't mean I'm some stoned and out of reality loner looking for the next handout to buy my drugs or wine. You're profiling."

"All right, point taken, I get it. Then who the hell are you?"

He smiled, "Noah, without an ark."

"Well we're up the river without a paddle and we can't just creep around out here and do nothing." Woody retrieved his cell phone and began keying in numbers.

"You can't be serious? You're going to get these people killed if you call this in."

Woody placed his finger to his lips and then proceeded, his mind made up. This wasn't going to just come clean with the wash. Intervention was the only solution. He just hoped, like Noah had pointed out, that he didn't have the blood of innocent folks on his hands once this was set into motion. Doing nothing was not an option, not with his friends inside. He was one man down already. Al Struthers' death had to be avenged. The senseless murder and now he was sure of it, had left a wife and two children behind. Security guards were not supposed to fall prey to crap such as this. Most considered guard positions pie jobs, gravy after retiring. He dreaded having to break this news to next of kin.

Signing that nondisclosure agreement had been a costly lesson. Woody now wondered if those footing the bill were somehow involved. It made sense to him. If they were behind it then he could almost be considered an accomplice. He shuttered at that thought. Still why all this and what was going on inside? Worse still, how would it end? And to think, he had opted out of police work for this very reason. Maybe he was just cursed or something. He hoped his ex-partner and the others were okay inside. Criminal type didn't take to kindly to police officers interfering in their plans. There were those who would jump at the chance to harm or torture law enforcement officers if given half a chance. The more he contemplated what could be happening inside the little church under siege, the less Woody liked it.

Inside the Church

"Peep show over, photo opt a complete success," announced Valdemar. "Now please accompany Ligeia, Professor Fether and Doctor Tarr. Your fund raiser telethon begins now. We must achieve our goal of one billion dollars and maintain my schedule."

"Can't we at least put our clothes back on," complained Ace, the wrestler.

"Mister Shumway, I do feel your pain given your obvious tiny little problem, but house rules stand until we have reached our intended goal."

Ace mumbled an F-bomb. It didn't go unnoticed.

"Perhaps I should reconsider my original goal and target two billion instead. You have the acclaimed world wrestling champion to thank for me considering amending by original arrangement."

Ace turned and dropped a second F-bomb, telling Valdemar to kiss his butt. Hop-Frog moved in quickly about to administer a severe blow to the side of his face when Valdemar halted him.

"I'm a fair man. We shall split the difference. The new goal is one and half billion. The clock is ticking. You have your instructions. Make your calls. The transactions will be monitored as will your conversations. Consider the consequences before you disrespect me. If it is even perceived you are chatting in code, the call will be ended, and you will be executed promptly, no plea bargaining, no jury, no trial, just an immediate death sentence. With your untimely departure the burden of fund raising will fall on those you leave behind now having to make up the difference. On second thought, the goal will be raised to two billion. I can be a somewhat greedy gentleman when I sense your hearts are not into this. Think long and hard my friends, long and hard. The clock is set. You have exactly two hours. Word to the wise, do not disappoint me."

It was Buster's time to speak up. He used a different approach than previously. This time he raised his hand.

"Ah yes, my brother, the disrobing model, what might you have on your mind?"

"If these fine folks meet your aggressive goal, do we indeed have a gentleman's agreement that you will not harm anyone, set us free once you have departed."

"Indeed, I am not compelled to earn a reputation of being a mass murderer. Do not be deceived, my brother, I nor any of my assembled cast, will hesitate to slaughter the lambs of this chapel if given no alternative. Practicing your best behavior while I am your host is encouraged. The success of the fund raisers determines the ultimate outcome. Do we understand one another? There is no fuzzy line."

"I do. I just don't like not controlling my own destiny."

"You can become a player easily. The price of admission is one million dollars. That goes for any of you in the congregation."

A gentleman in the back raised his hand. He was granted permission to stand and speak.

"What does one million dollars buy us…our freedom?"

Valdemar smiled. "Every one-million-dollar contribution raises the thermometer. It lends to us meeting our goal as in any fund-raising marathon. The sooner it is met, the sooner we shall part company. Do you have a million you would like to donate, sir?"

He shook his head, no.

"Then sit your ass down and stop wasting my time. Are there any others?"

Brady still lying flat face down raised his hand. Trudy mouthed, *no Brady*.

"My fine fellow, do you have a favorite charity in mind?"

"I'll contribute four million if you will release some hostages."

"Four million is a mere drop in the bucket when compared to our overall goal. I'm afraid it would not prompt the release of anyone. I am intrigued however by your offer. Who might I be addressing?"

No Brady. Don't tell him who you are. Remain face down.

"I'm…I'm just curious. I don't have that kind of money."

Good answer, Circus Boy.

"Bad answer my friend; I have no tolerance for such foolishness. Examples, why do I always have to lead by example? Hop-Frog, please remove the handicapped gent from my sight and teach him some manners."

"One hundred fifty million in the account," announced Ligeia.

"Not a bad start," stated Valdemar. "That calls for a round of applause, wouldn't you agree?"

The congregation mustered a weak response.

"You can do better than that. After all, this should be as important to you as me, more so if you take time to consider the consequences."

A louder applause ensued.

"Much better, thank you."

Associate Pastor Garrett Moore had stood and clapped, prompting a stern stare of disapproval from Pastor Blackwood. Moore paid him little attention and clapped louder. Valdemar turned and nodded his approval. In the meantime, Hop-Frog had begun dragging Brady by his collar towards an exit door.

Trudy stood and yelled, "Stop, please stop. My husband is not well. Surely you receive no joy from inflicting injury to an already broken man. His days are already numbered. Please don't shorten the time I have left to spend with him, I beg you."

Brady overheard her banter, nice work he thought.

"Hold it a second, Hop-Frog. My original selection for disrobe model is begging for mercy. Such loyalty is hard to come by in today's marriages. State your name my dear."

"Trudy…Trudy Wagner…"

"And your husband is afflicted by what cruel disease?"

"Parkinson, an extreme case…if you draw pleasure from inflicting pain then allow me to substitute for him…do with me as you will…"

"No," yelled Brady.

Allison stood, "Take me instead."

Buster stood next and volunteered and then Pastor Blackwood. One by one other members of the congregation stood, all vowing to take the stranger's place, all except the associate pastor. Garrett Moore remained seated until it was too late to correct his terrible mistake. Valdemar signaled for everyone to be seated and then instructed Hop-Frog to allow the associate pastor to take Brady Wagner's place. Moore begged for mercy now and even asked to speak with Valdemar privately. Hop-Frog escorted him out of sight but the screams from the other room left little doubt that punishment was being severely served.

"Trudy Wagner, please take the wheelchair and retrieve your husband. Adam West, you may assist Trudy with her beloved."

Buster quickly assisted Trudy in positioning Brady back in the chair. Distractions were becoming too dangerous. Pit pig headiness didn't give in without a fight. Trudy had to come up with a plan and very soon.

"Life lessons often require tough love. The associate pastor is not ready to serve the house of the Lord, I fear. He has chosen to place himself above all. That is unacceptable for a man of the cloth would you not agree, pastor?"

Pastor Blackwood replied, "Fear, not lack of faith influenced his decisions."

"But look about you. Everyone here, man or woman, was willing to take Brady Wagner's place except him. To me that speaks volumes. You should beam with pride, a church united. I would on the other hand consider finding a replacement for your apprentice. It is my humble opinion that this man is not worthy of that position." The screams continued.

Pastor Blackwood beckoned, "Enough please."

"Vengeance is mine. I will repay...says Valdemar...Romans 12.19, the newly interpreted version."

Security Check Point

Woody and Noah arrived with the body of Al Struthers. Leo Rydzewski spoke first, not at all a surprise.

"What the hell happened to Al? How bad is he hurt?"

"Al is dead," replied Woody.

"Dead, what happened," asked Drew Proctor.

"We're not sure. Noah thinks his neck is broken."

"Noah? Who the hell is this Noah?"

"Calm down Leo. Noah found him and helped me bring him in."

"How do we know this Noah guy here didn't have something to do with it?"

"Take my word for it, Leo; he didn't."

"I better call for an ambulance."

"No, hold off on that call."

"Yeah Leo, can't you see an ambulance can't help," added Drew.

"Guys we have a little situation developing and we have to be very careful how we handle it," spoke up Woody.

"Situation…what kind of damn situation…we're not going to like this, are we?"

"No Leo, you're not. The church has been commandeered by some sort of tactical force, at least eight of them. Everyone inside is being held hostage for reasons undetermined. Those same thugs may be responsible for Al's death…I'd say most likely."

"Hells bell," said Drew. "We better call this in, right?"

"Wrong," replied Woody. "We can't do that."

"We're not trained for engage and rescue, Woody," said Drew.

"I didn't sign up for this. Al is dead. This is frigging crazy. You don't pay me enough to be taking on this kind of shit."

"Leo, calm down for a minute. Let me explain the situation."

"Hell, you just did. Terrorist of some kind have taken over the church. That's way above my pay grade. SLED or the FBI or the damn governor should be contacted."

"That's just it, Leo. They have vowed to kill everyone inside at the first sign of the law or news media."

Drew jumped in. "How do you know that?"

"Noah overheard their threats."

"You're taking his word. He looks like a wino or something."

"Leo, I trust this man. He and I have pulled recon at the church. All of this is real. We can't afford to react hastily. People could die."

"Nope, we're not equipped to handle this shit, end of story."

"Sorry Woody, I have to agree with Leo. We're in over our heads. We need to call for reinforcements."

"Drew, I can't allow that. Sorry boys. I apologize for my actions. I'm going to have to cuff you."

"Like hell you are," protested Leo, now reaching for his side arm.

A spinning kick delivered to the side of his head dropped him to the ground, out cold. Drew held up his hands, wanting no part of this after witnessing Noah's attack. Woody patted him on the shoulder while removing his gun. Noah assisted with handcuffing them back to back against a small pine after positioning them on the ground, Leo still slummed and down for the count.

"Noah, you didn't have to do that."

"Maybe, maybe not, but the situation has been brought under control."

Drew, please bear with me on this. I'll compensate both of you for the risk and you'll not have to be part of it."

"Part of it…part of what...are the two of you going to take on the eight of them?"

Three vehicles approached in the distance. A panicky expression formed on Drew's face. He looked at Woody and then towards the approaching cars.

"You better warn those folks to stay clear of this mess," said Drew.

"No need…that's the Calvary." Woody winked.

Inside the Church

Another lady had reluctantly raised her hand. Valdemar asked her to stand and state her name and reason for disrupting his proceedings. Trudy observed, wheels still turning in her head. There had to be a way to shift the tide before this debacle got tragically out of hand. No doubt these intruders were capable of doing what had been warned if their little fundraiser flopped. Murder was murder, whether it was one or fifty victims. One thing for sure, this had been planned and calculated for quite some time. Two billion was a lot of money to raise in just two hours not just pledge it but deposit it in an actual account. Two hours, that was her time table. Think…

"My name is Faith and I am feeling quite nauseous. I get these real bad headaches if I go too long without eating. My doctor says I don't handle stress very well either. Since moving to the beach a few months ago I really freak out at those four way stop signs. When cars start to line up at the four way stop signs down here, I get really nervous and lose count as to whose time it is to move next. I'm looking around like Me? Him? Oh my? I usually move when someone blows the horn. I have to take medicine to regulate my anxiety and that's what causes the headaches if I don't eat after I've taken it."

"You are quite long-winded Faith. Is that a side effect of your medication?"

"Not that I know of, but it can cause bouts of gas. Sometimes I get light headed and giggly if I take it too soon after the last dosage. It's not supposed to be addictive but I'm not sure about that. I keep taking them and refilling the bottle."

"So just exactly what is it you require?"

"A pack of crackers would be nice. Cheese crackers if you have them. Lance brand would be even better. If you don't, I'm going to need a barf bag or a trash can. Living here along the coast has sort of upset my metabolism. Who what have thought that?"

"You moved to the Carolina Coast from where?"

"Abbeville, South Carolina. I always wanted to live right on the beach. We sold our house and moved here. We had a lake there but no ocean. Nothing beats the sound of crashing waves on the beach. Do you have any cheese crackers or not?"

Trudy was shocked that their host had allowed this to play out, but it gave her an idea.

"I have cheese crackers in my study," spoke up Pastor Blackwood.

"The preacher has cheese crackers," repeated Faith.

"You do make me smile, Faith, but there is one problem with your request. I allow the dear reverend to bring you these cheese crackers and then what next, a cold beverage, sandwich, an endless flow of requests."

"No sir, I promise, I would not ask for anything else. I've already wet my pants, just like you told us to do. I didn't even ask to be excused or anything. That should count for something."

Valdemar rolled his eyes. "Not you dear, but what about the remainder of the congregation? Would they feel I was showing preference. I can't risk a mutiny. It would be a bloody mess."

"Three hundred million," announced Ligeia.

"Prospero find something equivalent to a barf receptacle and deliver it to our bold and candid Faith please. Now please young lady…sit…and do not raise your hand again. Learn to take your turn at the four way stops…remember clockwise."

"Are you going to kill us? It's really contributing to my stress level and headache just thinking about it. I just came with a friend. I don't know any of these people. Well I have seen some of Julia Whitaker's movies and my husband likes wrestling. Ace O. Diamonds isn't one of his favorites though. He says Ace fights too dirty and talks too much crap. I really think wrestling is fake but don't tell that to my husband. I should have stayed at home with him, shouldn't I?"

"Please have a seat."

"You are going to kill us, aren't you? My horoscope said I'd cross paths with a stranger today that would forever change my life. I thought I might hit the lottery or something, but I try not to think negative thoughts."

Trudy shook her head and whispered, "I wonder if she knows Marian, Woody's cousin."

"Reverend, bring her the cheese crackers please. Ethelred, accompany him."

"I get it. This is my last meal…right? I should have asked for something else then."

"Prospero, please assist Faith in taking her seat. Use whatever means you see fit."

"All right, I'll sit but you better hurry up with those crackers or a trash can, Mister Val-de-mar."

Taking advantage of the distraction Brady turned to Trudy. "I know him, Trudy. He came in one of my stores a couple of weeks ago, bought that outfit and golf equipment; dropped a wad of money. He had a Jersey accent then though. I gave him the name of a realtor. He said his name was Joe…Joseph Cafiero. He was loud and friendly. I usually read folks pretty good. I would have never envisioned him pulling this."

"Maybe that was his intention. This fellow is a smooth operator. He wanted to be noticed."

"Do you two have something you'd like to share with the congregation," asked Valdemar. "Please, no cheese crackers."

"I was just telling Brady how intrigued I was by the names you've given your hired henchmen. Adam West said they sounded like Edgar Allen Poe characters. I was just curious why you picked Poe characters. That all."

"First, please refrain from calling them henchmen. We're all actors in the grandest of productions today. Adam West was spot on. I commend him for recognizing Poe's work."

Buster tipped an imaginary hat and winked at Valdemar. He would have preferred pointing a not so imaginary gun at him and pulling the trigger. He wondered what Pierce was up to now. Surely, she wasn't going rogue again. Nothing he could do if she was. He assessed the situation, piecing together a plan of his own. Allison clung to him like a tick, very distracting but he didn't push her away. This was difficult for everyone. She seemed much different than Pierce but he had only met her today so what did he really know.

"Edgar Allen Poe characters, they are interesting alias choices," continued Trudy.

"Four hundred million and counting," announced Ligeia.

"All is well with the participants, I assume."

"Best behavior thus far," replied Professor Fether.

"The wrestler is still bitching but nothing we can't handle," added Doctor Tarr.

"You have my permission to neuter him if necessary."

"Snip, snip," said Doctor Tarr, forming his finger like scissors and touching Ace's genitals.

"Where were we Mrs. Wagner? Ah yes…the origin of today's rolls."

"Please…I am all giddy just thinking about it."

"Your sarcasm is quite offensive. Be thankful I am thick skinned and do appreciate your twisted wit and charm."

"Forget her," spoke up Buster. "I'd like to hear this."

"A captive audience…the very best kind…" chuckled Valdemar, "You are interested in the method to what you presume is my madness, Mrs. Wagner. Edgar Allen Poe's legacy was confounded with lunacy for sure, magnificent reading for those inspired to do so. There will never be another Poe."

"Hop-Frog, an odd name…"

"Indeed, Hop-Frog or as many know it, *The Eight Chained Orangutans*, was a Poe masterpiece first published in 1849. The title character, Hop-Frog, a crippled dwarf taken from his homeland, becomes the jester of a king, a man particularly fond of practical jokes. Hop-Frog takes revenge on the king and his cabinet for striking his friend and fellow dwarf Trippetta. He dresses them as orangutans for a masquerade. In front of the king's guests, Hop-Frog murders them all by setting their costumes on fire before escaping with Trippetta."

"Hop-Frog, the man behind the mask can be ruthless as well. When I first met him he lived in deplorable conditions and had been, as the Poe character, badly mistreated and abused. I offered him a life, a new beginning. Before departing his former world, he promptly rectified the wrong doings and delivered swift justice to his three tormentors, locking them in a basement and burning them alive, orangutans up in smoke. To answer the question perched on your lips he would do the same to everyone gathered here and never bat an eye."

"I apologize then. Henchman being applicable to Hop-Frog was way too kind."

Valdemar applauded and laughed, "Point taken Mrs. Wagner."

"You've certainly set the hook. I look forward to hearing the stories behind the other masks." Trudy had to keep this animal preoccupied as best she could for as long as she could.

"I'll share one more for now to quench your apparent insatiable appetite. Doctor Tarr and a Professor Fether are from a Poe short story, a dark comedy, The *System of Doctor Tarr and Professor Fether*. The plot basically centers around a hospital for those deemed unsuitable to live in society. Those which we don't understand are often locked away and treated unfairly for society's protection. The staff for whatever reason has replaced the system of soothing with a stricter system. The story's narrator refers to this as the work of Doctor Tarr and a Professor Fether. Eventually the patients, granted a large amount of liberty around the facility, overthrow their doctors and nurses and usurp their positions, locking them up as the ones, pegging them as the lunatics. These lunatics were led by a man who claimed to have invented a better method of treating mental illness, and who allowed no visitors except for "a very stupid-looking young gentleman of whom he had no reason to be afraid. The narrator asks how the hospital staff rebelled and returned things to order. Just then loud noises are heard, and the actual hospital staff breaks from their confines. It is revealed that the dinner guests were, in fact, the patients who had just recently taken over. As part of their uprising, the inmates had treated the staff to tarring and feathering. The keepers then put the real patients back in their cells while the narrator, who is the "stupid-looking young gentleman", admits he has yet to find any of the works of Dr. Tarr and Professor Fether."

"I'm not sure I follow the analogy, your reason for naming those two guys over there based on these characters."

"Simple my dear. Both were dealt an unfair hand at an early age, brothers ages nine and ten, committed to a facility after being accused of murdering their parents, but not before torturing them in the most unique methods. I solicited for their release, lawyers excavating loopholes in the judicial system to grant them clemency. I had stumbled upon their case while under contract of another client. Both adults then, living their lives in the most deplorable conditions, their story tugged at my heartstrings. If ever I require information from an uncooperative participant, I can rely on the brothers to convince them otherwise."

"You seem to surround yourself with crazies."

"I would caution you, Mrs. Wagner, to not frame them as such. The eccentric does not take lightly to being stereotyped. Practice common courtesy in their presence and perhaps you might forgo their wrath in return."

Buster spoke up. "Forget her. I'd surely be interested in hearing more when you have the time."

"Mister West, likewise, I would be interested in hearing more about your background if indeed time allows. Perhaps I will have Ethelred seek your credentials from the Tithes and Offerings collected earlier. One can learn insurmountable information from a man's wallet. Mrs. Wagner, if that time arrives, you might assist by pointing us to your purse. The two of you certainly intrigue me. I am a people person. Personalities fascinate me. You fascinate me."

This isn't going according to plan thought Trudy. If time allows, and if he locates our identification, our shields will tip him off and the consequences might be severe. In that event, I certainly hope law enforcement officers fascinate him too. Tar and feathering aren't my idea of accessorizing.

Security Check Point

"That didn't take too long," commented Woody.

"Moonlighting becomes us, given the situation," replied Detective Sylvester Stone.

"I've added all of you to my roster to make this legit."

"Give us the details," said Detective Tim Burroughs. "By the way, this is Summer Knight. She's with one of the local television news affiliates."

"No news media, Tim. Didn't I make that perfectly clear," fumed Woody.

"She's my date, off duty, just like me."

"I carry a concealed weapon permit and can shoot," added Summer.

"For the record, I'm packing too," stated Doctor Dallas Solomon. "I'm an excellent shot. We can never have enough backup, correct?"

"Man, oh man," sighed Woody.

"And I have a butt load of firepower in my truck," grinned Detective Parnell Roberts. "I see you've already apprehended a couple of them, and they were disguised as your security force."

"Those men do work for me."

"Trader bastards. Is there no loyalty," snapped Parnell.

"No, they're not disloyal, not exactly. Let's just say they are remaining neutral until this is finished."

"Who's that gent," asked Sly, pointing to Noah.

"Son of a pioneer, I know you," interrupted Parnell.

"I don't think so," Noah quickly replied.

"Oh yeah, damn straight, I know you. I don't forget a face. You're one badass I'm telling you."

"You are mistaken."

"Mistaken, my big ole fat butt. You served about the same time I did over in Operation Desert Storm. I've seen the results of your handy work first hand. You were with the 75th, kicking butt in Iraq and Afghanistan, the elite of the elite. I salute you, sir. It is my honor indeed to be here with you. Hell, I always wanted to be a Ranger. Don't tell me. I know your name. Just give me a second…it's on the tip of my tongue…Malone, that's it…you're the one and only Mighty Malone, kick ass and the hell with taking names. You were part of the Special Forces from Task Force 121 assigned to capture and kill Saddam Hussein, weren't you? Hell, yeah you were, Operation Red Dawn, damn right."

"What is it now, Code Name Noah," asked Woody.

"Felix…Felix Malone...busted…and I'd appreciate it if you folks would forget you ever saw me once this is over. I'm officially retired. I have no forwarding address and I would prefer to remain among the anonymous for personal reasons."

"Pleasure to meet you Felix," said Woody, offering him his hand. "Given your experience, I request that you take charge of this mission, rescuing those inside and catching the bad guys."

Parnell grinned like a possum. "Catching them, hell Woody, you're barking up the wrong tree. Malone specializes in eliminating the opposition. We'll just be here to clean up the carnage left behind."

Woody recapped the scenario as best they knew, including the sniper atop the church, the time line and threats if any signs of intervention were detected. An assortment of weapons had been brought, the most impressive being that owned by Parnell, including several assault rifles and one Uzi. Woody raised an eyebrow when he brought it out, but had to admit, it was a welcome sight given the circumstances. Felix Malone, aka Noah, began laying out a plan. First, they must neutralize the sniper and do it quietly.

"Seven against eight, but we have an ace in the hole, Mighty Malone" smiled Parnell.

"Just Felix, okay…"

"Nine against eight if you set us free," spoke up Leo, Drew nodding his agreement.

"Guys, this could get rough not to mention we're not really following protocol. Maybe you should just stay put. It keeps you safe and absolved from any wrong doing."

"We have a famous Ranger leading the charge. I'm okay with all the other stuff, not calling it in and everything," said Leo. Drew nodded again.

"More can't hurt," spoke up Sly.

"Maybe not, but I'm responsible for all your lives, remember. Hindsight, I should have done this by the book."

"When have you ever followed the rules," said Tim, patting him on the shoulder.

"He has a point," said Dallas. "You're no longer a Sheriff, a constable or a detective."

"But most of you still have careers ahead of you in law enforcement."

"Moonlighting is not a criminal offense. You said we are technically on your payroll," replied Sly. "Besides, Detective Pierce is in there. I'd have this no other way. Screw my pension."

"Hey Sport, you called us; forget about it," said Parnell.

"Actually, I just called Tim."

"Fine, it's on my shoulders, I accept full responsibility for anything that happens, including all the accolades once we rescue those inside and put the offenders behind bars or in the ground."

Summer squeezed Tim's arm, proud of her man's assertive behavior. Tim had never felt more the confident hero with his pistol packing mama standing by his side. He kept those thoughts to himself though.

Woody removed the cuffs from Leo and Drew and returned their pistols. Parnell gave them their choices from what remained of his mini arsenal. Both chose shotguns.

"As planned then, let's proceed," announced Felix Malone. "No heroics or gunslinger antics please. You do as I say when I say, got it. Those inside are depending on us getting this right the first and only legitimate attempt."

"Lock and load, baby…" added Parnell.

Felix Malone, civilian, would never forget…

Ranger Creed

Recognizing that I volunteered as a Ranger, fully knowing the hazards of my chosen profession, I will always endeavor to uphold the prestige, honor, and high esprit de corps of my Ranger Regiment.

Acknowledging the fact that a Ranger is a more elite soldier who arrives at the cutting edge of battle by land, sea, or air, I accept the fact that as a Ranger my country expects me to move further, faster, and fight harder than any other soldier.

Never shall I fail my comrades. I will always keep myself mentally alert, physically strong, and morally straight and I will shoulder more than my share of the task whatever it may be, one hundred percent and then some.

Gallantly will I show the world that I am a specially selected and well-trained soldier? My courtesy to superior officers, neatness of dress, and care of equipment shall set the example for others to follow.

Energetically will I meet the enemies of my country. I shall defeat them on the field of battle for I am better trained and will fight with all my might. Surrender is not a Ranger word. I will never leave a fallen comrade to fall into the hands of the enemy and under no circumstances will I ever embarrass my country.

Readily will I display the intestinal fortitude required to fight on to the Ranger objective and complete the mission, though I be the lone survivor.

Rangers lead the way

Inside the Church

Hop-Frog returned with Associate Pastor Garrett Moore in tow. The obvious was evident. His face showed signs of bruising and swelling, both nose and mouth were bloody, and he limped and swayed as Hop-Frog dragged him along, unable to stand or walk without assistance. He and Valdemar immediately made eye contact. Locked in momentarily, the gazes were at opposite ends of the spectrum; Valdemar satisfied with the results. Moore was a combination of being pissed and almost pleading for leniency.

"He's one whiny little bitch, demanding he must speak to you privately," stated Hop-Frog as he shoved Moore into his seat.

"I have no more time for these senseless interruptions. Keeping this congregation in check is as difficult as herding felines. They continue to disrespect me by disregarding my rules."

As if on cue an elderly woman near the back stood up, forgoing the raising of the hand protocol. Valdemar rolled his eyes, tempted to make an example of her. Before he could hail one of his demented cohorts to address the ill-mannered old hag, she intervened.

"Hey Sonny, you talk a lot of crap for a man hiding behind a mask. Manners, you have no clue what manners are. Rules...screw your silly rules. You were not raised right apparently. Rule number one...respect your elders. Rule number two...respect the confines of the church. Rule number three...do to others as you would have them do to you. ... Luke 6:31."

"Who might I be addressing?"

"Fanny Mae Davidson..."

"Miss Davidson, for curiosity sake, might I inquire your age?"

"Rule number four...never ask a lady's age. At my age that rule doesn't mean a hill of beans though. I'll be ninety-seven next month. I'm fit. I'm fiddle. I still drive, and I was least offended when you asked us to take off our clothes earlier. On the contrary, I was all giddy with the prospect. It's been nearly thirty years since a man asked me to remove my clothes; not since my Bill suffered his heart attack, dropped dead right there in the kitchen as I was serving him his gravy and biscuits. I miss having a man in my life, but all the good ones are chasing the skirt tails of the flirting airheads. They have no idea what they are missing, passing on years of experience for those empty-headed floozies."

"I'm either in a parallel universe or the southern version of the Twilight Zone. Miss Davidson, please have a seat. I'm not really interested in your spin on today's proceedings."

"What are you going to do, take me in the back and rough me up too?"

"Do what he says, Fanny Mae," said another elderly lady sitting beside her, tugging on her arm.

"Leave me be, Gertie McCarthy. I'm going to have my say and he's going to hear me out. I'm too set in my ways to just sit here like a bump on a log. He has no call treating us like this. And he's not even man enough to do it face to face, hiding like a little Halloween trick or treater behind the goblin mask, making believe he's a creation out of the head of Edgar Allen Poe."

"Please sit down, don't push this man, Miss Davidson," spoke up Buster, now standing and facing her.

"Some sheriff of Horry County you are, young man. Oh yeah, I know who you are. I've seen your picture in the Georgetown Times, Sheriff Buster Ferguson. You're just as bad as these masked men, hiding and pretending to be Adam West and all. Our Georgetown sheriff would have never allowed this to go on this long. I'm just standing up for everyone here. That Faith gal got her crackers. I'm borderline diabetic. Where are my crackers?"

"Oh crap," whispered Trudy.

"Do as…The Sheriff…suggested Miss Davidson. Comply or die. This conversation is over, but I do thank you for the pertinent information."

Gertrude McCarthy tugged on her friend's arm, dragging Fanny Mae to her seat. Fanny Mae didn't appreciate it but stayed put, Gertie whispering to her frantically, pleading her case. "Pish-posh," whispered Fanny Mae in response, too old to be fearful of what might happen to her. Gertie locked her arm through Fanny Mae's to make her point.

"Revelations...from the mouths of babes and octogenarians...a lawman among us...an elected official, poker faced lying one at that. Adam West the disrober demonstrator is in fact Sheriff Buster Ferguson of Horry County, no less. The right arm of the law has concealed his identity for what...CYA perhaps. Or, did you have something else in mind...a one-man gang with a plan to derail my fundraiser?"

Buster said nothing; stood his ground, arms folded, and defiant, poor choices given the circumstances thought Trudy.

"Sheriff, do you have any other dirty little secrets you'd like to share?"

"Collect your blood money, run and hide if you think that's possible, but leave these innocent folks alone. We get it. You're the mastermind, the extortionist, the man behind the mask as already pointed out by Miss Davidson. By the way Miss Davidson, I don't blame you for exposing me. He would have found out soon enough after finding my shield."

Allison stood, hooking her arm through Buster's. "If you're considering doing him harm then you'll have to do the same to me."

"And me," said Pastor Blackwood, also standing.

One by one various members of the congregation again stood, united, rallying to Buster's support. Trudy stood too, as did Brady, springing from his wheelchair, standing at attention and unwavering. A riled Valdemar head motioned to Prospero, nodding some sort of understood signal. Prospero swiftly moved up the aisle and stopped adjacent to Buster. Punishment was delivered swiftly, the blow from the gun stock sending the sheriff to the floor. Disappearing between the pews Trudy heard him make a crashing thud, Allison unable to restrain him from falling.

"Next," asked Valdemar, prompting the others to begin taking their seats. Even Trudy and Brady knew it was futile to buck the bastard. Only Pastor Blackwood held his position.

Valdemar turned to face him. "Reverend, this is quite symbolic, standing up for the flock, but please have a seat. Your point has been taken. I will not ask a second time."

Blackwood took his seat, point also taken. Associate Pastor Garrett Moore then raised his hand.

"What part of this demonstration did you not understand," asked Valdemar.

"I really do need to speak with you…in private."

"We'll not be speaking in private, nor will you say another word. Heed my warning. Your next lesson tutored by Hop-Frog shall be your last. Do you understand?"

"But…"

"Hop-Frog, he does not understand."

"I do…I really do."

"One half billion mark," announced Ligeia. "One hour three minutes remaining."

Valdemar walked over to the gathered phone calling nudists. "Shumway, are you shrinking to minuscule proportions or is it just me. Steroids or God-given, one wonders. Now for a more serious note, people, this is quite disappointing…only a third of our goal achieved thus far. Might I remind you that failure to obtain our goal will result in horrific consequences? A photograph is worth two million words I suppose. Dupin, would you be so kind as to randomly select a wallet or a purse from the Tithe and Offerings pile? Please bring it to me now. A wallet…excellent…Luke Paul from Bucksport, thirty-seven years of age, one hundred sixty-five pounds…come on down, front and center. Don't be shy. I have your driver's license and can easily identify you. Besides, I'm sure you didn't hesitate standing moments ago to rally to the sheriff's support."

Luke Paul stood. Ethelred escorted him to the front of the church, positioning him in front of Valdemar. Hop-Frog stepped directly behind him, forcing him to his knees. Luke stared at the floor, refusing to make eye contact. Trudy looked back at Allison. She was still squatted on the floor tending to an unconscious Buster Ferguson. Trudy then took a step forward, still not sure what she intended to do, but she had to do something.

"Look at me Luke Paul. To quote Poe, *I have great faith in fools; self-confidence my friends call it. All religion my friend, is simply evolved out of fraud, fear, greed imagination and poetry.*" With that Valdemar gave a slight nod.

Hop-Frog placed his hands on each side of Luke's head; snap, the man tumbled to the floor, neck broken, dead before he made contact. Trudy froze. Inside she screamed, wanting nothing more than to rush those standing there, attack them, take their weapons and open fire. Her training compelled her to stand down, the events hopelessly spiralling out of control.

"*Words have no power to impress the mind without the exquisite horror of their reality*, so said Poe. One hour, one billion dollars…"

Moonlighters, Rescue in Process

Sticking to the wooded and secluded areas, well away from the roadway leading to the church, the unlikely gaggle of rescuers forged onward. Their faith had been placed in the hands of ex-ranger and homeless guy, Felix Malone. Mighty Malone, the kick-ass bad-ass as Parnell had so eloquently put it. Their first objective would be to take out the sniper positioned atop the church, easier said than done. If successful that would still leave seven more inside the church, each brandishing an assortment of militia type weapons as observed by Malone.

Woody had confirmed the threat was indeed real. He had no choice after seeing the evidence first hand but to believe the rest of the story. He hoped he hadn't made a grave error by agreeing to do this without contacting forces better equipped to handle hostage situations. Coloring outside the lines this time could lead to dire consequences if judgment proved him wrong. One man already down, he should have known better than to go this route. Still, he had done just that with very little hesitation. His gut had told him that time wasn't on their side. Any delay might be costly to those being held captive inside. Besides, if Malone had overheard it correctly, such force would only worsen the situation. Perhaps the element of surprise offered them the slightest edge.

Woody assessed the forces challenging the well-organized counter force inside the church. Sure, with Sly, Tim, and this new guy, Parnell, being police officers made the odds better. Dallas, while not tested under fire, seemed confident enough. Drew and Leo were at least gun totters but had not been challenged. Baptism under fire wasn't necessarily the best way to prove their net worth. Tim's gal friend, the news woman, had said she held a concealed weapon permit. She should know how to handle and fire a gun, but there is a vast difference between paper targets and people, potentially those firing back at you with live ammo.

Woody gave much credence to their ace in the hole, the ex-ranger. What still worried him though; why had Malone dropped out of society? Was he emotionally stable? If things really heated up, would he crack or go flash back? With so many people's lives at stake he needed no unexpected surprises.

Woody's mind drifted to his kids. Just as quickly he dismissed the thoughts from his head. He must stay focused on the task at hand. A cloudy head got you killed. He was either in this or he wasn't. There were friends inside that church, end of story. He sure hoped Pierce didn't pull one of her bone headed stunts. It would be just like her to take them on single handed, figuring the odds were in her favor outnumbered eight to one. He had certainly learned his fair share of bad habits from her. He had been 'Mister Play it by the Book' until partnering with her. Those road rage killings had been the beginning of the end of his career in law enforcement.

The Hawthorne brothers' case had been the final straw, that and having pulled that stint as the acting sheriff. Woody could no longer be what it took to be an officer. He had simply crossed too far over the line too many times, ignored his ethical oath and saw no path back. And now look at him. He was slap dab in the middle of another fine mess. Learned bad habits don't die easily. He was ignoring proper protocol once again. Three strikes…

Tim Burroughs was both excited and fretfully concerned about having Summer Knight along. He had finally found someone he genuinely liked. The last thing he needed was to get her killed. He tried to dismiss such morbid thoughts, but they clung to him like a tick on a hound. He would never ever forgive himself if anything happened to her. He was tempted to send her back, even though he knew she would never listen to reason. This could potentially be a blockbuster story for her if they didn't totally botch it up. It could boost her career, even though she had not mentioned that as her motivation for being here.

Tim hoped he was the front runner in the motivation race. He couldn't help it. He still had his doubts as to why she would be interested in someone like him. Low self-esteem had been his mantra for way too long, especially when it came to a love life. Funny, what did he even know about the subject. He had never had one until now. Just don't screw it up he kept telling himself. His emotions ran the gambit, also thinking about Trudy and Brady inside. The sheriff and Trudy's sister also made it all too real. He briefly smiled, thinking about how many times they had bailed Trudy out of similar situations. He too thought about the three strikes and you are out rule. How long would luck be on their side in these bizarre and dangerous situations?

Parnell Roberts was pumped. He had a chance to be part of a major operation under the leadership of all people, Mighty Malone, a seasoned and proven ranger. Kicking ass and taking down the bad guys created an adrenalin rush. He had lived for this day, dreamt it and soon he would experience it firsthand. He sought Malone's approval and recognition for exceeding excellence. *Never shall I fail my comrades. I will always keep myself mentally alert, physically strong, and morally straight and I will shoulder more than my share of the task whatever it may be, one hundred percent and then some.* Ranger creed, live it, breath it, thought Parnell. This was his chance to do both, a fantasy come true.

Parnell hoped Malone would allow him to take out the sniper. He was more than ready to volunteer given the opportunity. Parnell Roberts, the next American hero, had a nice ring to it. Going above and beyond, foiling a terrorist attack or whatever this was. He would be recognized worldwide for his heroics. He could envision a book opportunity, his memoir, and then a movie deal. Heck, he might even have his own action figure and video game. His mind raced with the possibilities. Parnell had to come up with a catchy name though, one that suited his badass persona.

Sly was uncomfortable with the situation, but as had the others, been swayed by the 'what if' factor. Jeopardizing the lives of those inside, especially Detective Trudy Pierce, gave him no wiggle room in making his decision. If the ex-ranger's recon was point on, did they really have a choice? Woody seemed to trust him. That was good enough for Sly. He trusted Woody's instincts. Still, these commandos sounded as if they were prepared for almost anything. Even more concerning, they'd not hesitate in killing everyone inside if the scenario didn't go their way. One miscalculation could blow this up in their faces. There were too many unknown variables for his taste, too many uncertainties to impact success. Sly looked over at Dallas. She had been part of the team for a while, but she wasn't a cop. Neither were a few of the others. These outliers screwed up the stats royalty. Sly wasn't overly confident but tried not to be pessimistic. He did try to remain realistic. The odds were not in their favor.

Summer Knight, just two paces behind Tim, struggled with her emotions. Butterflies bombarded her insides, fear and excitement equally battling for control. Seeing Detective Tim Burroughs in action and seemingly in control made her want him more than ever. She couldn't claim perspiration as the only source for the wetness overcoming her. For once in her life the news story had become secondary. She and Tim shared this rare bond and attraction. She wasn't sure if he even realized the extent of it, at least not like she did. Relationships had never come easy for her. She had never had anything close to what she and Tim had shared, and they really hadn't traveled that far in the journey yet. Instinct told her it was right though. She had found her man. Summer had to exercise restraint to keep from smiling, realizing how under these circumstances she was fantasying about Tim and not the events rushing towards them like a runaway train. She took a deep breath, attempting to refocus on the seriousness of what lay ahead. Tim remained up front and center. She closed the distance and placed her hand on his shoulder. He stopped dead in his tracks and turned around. Dallas, just behind Summer, nodded her approval, reading them like a book.

Noah, no, the mighty Felix Malone, pushed onward, visualizing the scenario. He remained focused, clearly many steps ahead, a chess player contemplating moves and counter moves. For the moment his mind and actions operated as that of a machine. In the darkest recesses other forces battled to take control. Noah wanted nothing to do with this. The Mighty Malone disagreed. This mission was of the utmost importance. Walking away into obscurity made more sense. Noah had worked long and hard to distance himself from this sort of thing. Malone embraced the opportunity to complete the mission. It was a tossup, a battle of wills; the slightest could sway the decision one way or the other. Getting from there to here had been a long journey, one not without hiccups along the way. Reopening the door now could undo it all. Noah blinked uncontrollably, paused briefly, almost swaying and falling. Mighty Malone seized control and quickly picked up the pace. The success of the mission rested in their hands. Who would prevail? A catastrophe hinged in the balance.

A Church under Siege

"Okay, you've proven your point, Valdemar," spoke up Trudy. "Please, no more."

"I thought it might draw your attention to the perils that lie ahead if the goals are not met. Mrs. Wagner, has the congregation granted you spokesperson duty on their behalf? I do apologize for missing your appointment."

"Cut the pretend crap, how about it? This Poe put-on farce has run its course, okay? You're in charge. You have your damn demands and you have demonstrated the consequences if not met. We get it. I'm with the sheriff. Collect your money and leave; no need taking more innocent lives."

"You disappoint me Mrs. Wagner. Just moments ago you sounded so sincere in wishing to understand how I so named my actors in this little play."

"Knock yourself out. Talk. Just stop the bloodletting. I'm all ears."

"Who are you, Mrs. Wager? What is it that makes you so qualified to challenge me? What position do you hold in my universe that influences your behavior? Could you be a lawyer perhaps? Maybe you are a woman of the bench? Obviously, you are accustomed to being in charge. Why is it so important that you think you must control the outcome? Confessions cleanse the soul. How does that commercial go, ah yes, *you can pay me now or you can pay me later*? Is law enforcement you fancy also? Speak the truth my dear or should we locate your credentials and view them together?"

"I have a confession."

Trudy whipped around at the sound of her sister's voice. Allison stood. What the hell was she up to? *Tend to the sheriff and stay out of this, Sis. Don't mess with fire...please.* Trudy looked back at Valdemar. Wearing the mask provided him with the ultimate poker face. She started to continue her conversation but Valdemar held his finger to his fake plastic lips.

"Speak my dear. Don't squander your turn and ask for cheese crackers or a pass to visit the facilities. I'm in no mood for such foolishness as you have observed."

"Trudy is my sister. She has been kind enough to allow me to temporarily move in with her and her husband, no questions asked; or at least she has given me some breathing room with explaining why my marriage is over."

"Moved in, I thought you were just visiting. When were you going to tell me it was more to it?"

Brady grabbed Trudy by the hand and whispered to allow Allison to speak. Buster's head craned up over the back of the pew resembling a turtle's antics. It didn't go unnoticed.

"Ah, you have joined us once again, Sheriff Ferguson. Please have a seat and allow the young lady to speak her peace. Your name?"

"Allison, like I said, Trudy is my older sister. She invited me here. I wish I would have declined that offer."

Valdemar let out a slight laugh from underneath the mask. "Please continue with your confession my dear Allison."

"I have… had two children and I had what should have been a wonderful marriage. On the surface most would have described it at wonderful. There were no signs to point otherwise. My sister never had a clue. She didn't even know I had divorced. Amy, our mother never knew either that my marriage was always in peril. Perhaps her disease prevented her from detecting it. She suffered from Alzheimer's. It might have been a blessing she has been spared all this."

You could have heard a pin drop. The congregation was enthralled by her confession, or maybe it was just a needed distraction. Trudy wiped perspiration from her forehead with her open hand. Her face felt flushed. As bad as she had wanted to hear this, now was not the best time to air the dirty laundry. Then it suddenly dawned on her. Allison was doing this to protect her. Drawing attention to her had distracted Valdemar from pursuing the police angle, possibly only a brief reprieve, but a delay just the same.

"There are usually two sides to every conflict, every breakup; not so in this case. It is completely one sided. There is only one at fault. I stand before you as that guilty party. For that reason, I have received the ultimate penalty, not just a badly broken marriage but a divorce, and the loss of my children too. I deservingly both. I contested neither."

Still woozy, Buster offered his hand to Allison, realizing her anguish. She accepted it, squeezed his hand lightly to show her appreciation. Trudy stood in shock, concerned about where this was heading. She hoped her sister was just fabricating some wild tale to pacify Valdemar. The look on her face clearly painted a different picture. A tear rolled down Allison's cheek. Trudy, now oblivious to her surroundings, hung on her sister's every word, heart pounding; now regretting having hounded her earlier.

"In any marriage some things are forgivable. Mine is not the case. My sins are incomprehensible."

"Allison, stop…this is not the place."

Valdemar replied, "I disagree, Mrs. Wagner; if not in a church, where then?"

"He's right. The time and place are perfect, long overdue."

"This is crazy, Allison," blurted out Trudy.

"Sis, trust me, you have no idea just how crazy."

"Eight hundred fifty million in the account," announced Ligeia. "Ace O. Diamonds has tapped out."

"Sorry to interrupt your confession but I must attend to this personally. Hop-Frog, please escort Mister Teeny-Weenie front and center."

Trudy paid little attention to Valdemar's request. She instead locked onto Allison, more than ever fretful about where this confession thing had been headed. Thankful it had been disrupted. Whatever her sister had to share needed to be said alone and just between her and Allison. She didn't want the world to hear these confessions at the same time she learned of them.

"Tell me, Shumway, why is it you have thrown in the towel? You're supposed to be of champion caliber, fight to the finish, and never give up, right? Your battles on paid per view have ranked among the most ever watched. How is that you dare insult me by tapping out? Am I not a worthy opponent? This troubles me greatly."

"I'm busted. I've called everyone I know. You said a deal was a deal so long as we raised the money collectively. The others are still trying."

"There lies the problem. They are still trying but you are not. This makes you much less valuable."

"Look, I did my part. Cut me a break."

"Ligeia, exactly what were our world belt holder's contributions?"

"Seven million…"

"Seven million…do you take me for a complete idiot? That is nowhere near your net worth in assets. You insult me. I completed my research thoroughly on each of you. You are a liar. What am I going to do with you, Shumway?"

"It's tied up. I can't get my hands on it, not for this or anyone."

"On the contrary, you have bonds and stocks that can be cashed in. Would you care to reconsider? I have the precise numbers."

"Those no longer belong to me."

"I'm aware of your reckless gambling, Shumway. Are you telling me you have gambled away your investments too?"

"Yes."

"I see. You have an addiction to gambling. It is sad to leave this earth with nothing to your name."

"Please…don't kill me. There must be another way."

"Perhaps after all you are an entertainer. Obviously, all that wrestling is fake, correct? You mesmerize your fans by acting out the roles. Possibly there is a solution though."

"What can I do, anything, just ask."

Valdemar clapped his hands. I have the perfect event for you. It combines entertainment and wagering. Win and you live. Fail and you die. We'll call it Valdemar's Little Death Match. Are you in? Please just nod. You really have no other options."

"Enough Valdemar, can't you see how you are traumatizing this man?"

"Mrs. Wagner, to experience trauma is good. Only a living person can feel trauma. You do feel alive, don't you, Ace? Now, please no more interruptions. Our contestant must concentrate and prepare for his greatest and most challenging match."

"Who do I have to wrestle?"

Valdemar laughed. "You'll be competing with yourself."

"Absurd," replied Ace.

"Doctor Tarr, you are a wealth of information, especially as it refers to the human anatomy."

"I am. How can I assist in this little competition you have chosen for the world champion?"

"Little, how amusing…Doctor Tarr, answer me this, what is the average length of a male's erect penis?"

"Studies conducted with measurements vary 5.1 to 5.7 inches."

"Shumway…Ace. O. Diamonds allow me to present you with your challenge. Prove to this audience that you can measure up. We shall forgo measurement in its pathetic little flaccid state. Your goal is to obtain an erection of a mere 5.1 inches, the lower end of the average male's. Do this and you live to wrestle another day. Fail to achieve or exceed this goal and you die."

"This is a load of crap. What are you, some sort of perverted sick-o?"

"On the contrary, I have no interest in your manhood, flaccid or erect. This is simply a wager. You enjoy gambling. I am just allowing you the opportunity to bet on yourself. You control your destiny, not me. Steroids can be quite damaging to the anatomy, now can't they. Prove us wrong. It's just that simple."

Leave him alone came the cries from several church members. Valdemar's henchmen cheered him on as if this was indeed a pay-per-view extravaganza. Trudy turned her head in disgust as did many others in the congregation.

"Do any of you have a ruler or measuring tape? I do wish this to be a fair contest."

"I have a six-foot tape measure on my key chain," spoke up Dupin.

"Wonderful, you shall be the judge and jury then. One last piece of information, an important rule for the contender. On my go you will have ninety seconds to produce your evidence."

"You're joking," decried the wrestler.

"I assure you I am not. Surely you can achieve an erection in that time, can't you? All right. Never say I am not reasonable. You have two minutes. Dupin, you may be the time keeper also."

"Let me just go back over there and try to scrounge up more money."

"You've already admitted that you have exhausted all avenues. Scrounge is the perfect analogy, I must confess. The wager begins in five seconds. Don't squander any precious seconds. Five...four...three...two...one..."

Rescue Ranger

The Mighty Malone had successfully maneuvered through the wooded perimeter with his rag tag regiment in tow. He had placed a wide stand of trees between them and the church, pausing near the edge of the golf course's fairway. He was tempted to scope out the clubhouse, just in case more intruders were posted there but time was of the essence. He'd deal with that situation later if necessary. The prime focus for now, take out the sniper and do it undetected by those inside. He would not be able to utilize a firearm. The risks were elevated thusly. From the sniper's present position, crossing the pitch of the roofline could easily alert him before he could close the distance and neutralize him. Still if anyone could pull this off, he could. The others weren't trained, would botch it up royally. Perspiration dripped down his back. Noah's hands were tingly, almost numb. Mighty Malone flexed his fingers, regaining control slowly but surely.

"I'm going to require a distraction. Without one, I'll never be able to close in on our gunman on the roof. He has strategically placed himself in the best possible position, one I would have chosen. Before anyone volunteers, let me warn you, he can take you out in the blink of an eye from any distance you could ever fathom. If he does, we're screwed. You'll be dead and those inside will be alerted of our presence, game over, bad guys win."

"I've got this," spoke up Parnell.

"No, not you. To be blunt, I need those trained to be close by just in case. Sorry folks, I don't mean to belittle your value but…"

"I'll go," said Dallas. "I'm a doctor, not one trained in assault tactics. I understand perfectly what you are insinuating. I'm expendable. Plus, the gunman will not be expecting a female and shouldn't be threatened by one's sudden appearance. I have that going for me, right?"

"Do what you can to distract him, short of waving at him or flashing your breasts. Remember, you don't know he is there. If he detects any sign that you do, you're dead."

"Not to worry, the furthest thing from my mind I assure you," said Dallas.

"Lance Rocker would have certainly appreciated that you take the low road if he was here," spoke up Tim Burroughs.

Summer elbowed Tim in the ribs, fully aware of *Mister Rock Your World's* reputation from his involvement in the road rage murders and his publicized affair with then Detective Woodrow Anderson's wife. Sadly, she had fallen victim to the killer and Rocker had been a temporary suspect in her death. Some had even thought Rocker might be the serial killer; that is until the killer struck again while he had been in jail. Summer Knight had left few stones unturned when doing her research of the high-profile case.

"Doc, circle back but stay concealed until you reach that slight curve in the drive, then do your thing. Good luck."

"Improvisation is not a problem, I performed with a group in college. I toured in France and Italy one glorious summer with a theatrical group of my peers. Besides flashing my breast, I do this second best. I embrace the arts and theater, always have. I'll have your gunman eating out of my hand. He'll never know what hit him. Don't squander the opportunity Mister Malone."

"Five minutes then work your magic Miss Dallas."

"Break a leg," added Sly.

"Stash your weapon before you make your appearance," warned Malone. "With that scope he will be able to see the finest details.

"And details he will view," she added before departing.

"Do you think she can pull this off?" asked Parnell

"Absolutely," replied Woody.

"Roberts you come with me. The rest of you stay put."

"How do you plan on ambushing that dude? You said yourself you can't shoot him. We have no silencers."

"Not your concern…you just keep him in your scope if I fail. Shoot him before he shoots me."

"I thought you said no gunfire."

"It won't matter at that point, those inside hearing his shot or yours. I'd prefer it being yours if things turn ugly."

"You're a ranger, remember. You live for this crap."

"I'm a rusty ranger…remember. I can die doing this shit." With that, Malone vanished behind the church. A ladder stood against the back wall, compliments of the gunman. Without making a sound he eased up the rungs and slipped onto the roof. The high roof pitch concealed him from view. Moving like a cat he inched his way along the opposite side of the roof line, and then ascended the roof just shy of seeing on the other side. From his vantage point he could see the drive as well as the sniper. Malone glanced at the watch borrowed from Woody. She should be making her move now.

Doctor Dallas Solomon suddenly appeared in the middle of the drive, less than two hundred yards from the church. She had removed her jeans, sporting her teal tee shirt that barely covered her thighs. She was barefooted and braless. Her hair was no longer in a bun but instead flowing freely like a lion's mane. She was ranting in her cell phone, tossing her free hand about, looking to be having a most uncomfortable conversation with the person on the line. She kicked up sand from the drive several times. Malone was sure he had heard a few f-bombs being dropped loudly at her imaginary caller. Good idea he thought, the gunman might be reluctant to shoot her while she was on the phone.

From his perch Tamerlane watched through the scope, crosshairs on the target. His finger was a mere squeeze away from taking out the interloper. He exercised patience, evaluating the threat. Valdemar had derived his name from an epic Edgar Allen Poe poem first published in a collection in 1827, *Tamerlane and Other Poems*. The poem itself follows a Turkic conqueror named Tamerlane. The name was a Latinized version of 'Timur Lenk', the 14th century warlord, though the poem was not historically accurate. Tamerlane ignores the young love he has for a peasant in order to achieve power. On his deathbed, he regrets this decision to create a kingdom in exchange for a broken-heart. This Tamerlane was quite heartless and as ever bit ruthless as the Turkic conqueror.

Dallas squatted and then picked up a stone and tossed it at one of the live oaks as she unleashed more unladylike language. Tamerlane currently viewed her as posing no threat, but he continued to monitor her antics. He moved the scope up and down the length of her body, assessing the animated lady's curves and obvious braless breast. Malone had to give her credit for a performance worthy of an academy award nomination. He pulled himself to the pitch of the roof and cautiously peered over the other side. The sniper appeared clued to her performance. The distraction was working perfectly. Now it was his turn.

In one swift move, the Mighty Malone launched himself over the roof and sliding into second base on a collision course with the gunman. Reacting, the sniper pivoted, but from his belly flat down position he could not bring his weapon around fast enough to squeeze off a shot. Malone caught him squarely in the face with both feet. Both men tumbled off the roof, the rifle dislodged from the sniper's hands as he thudded to the ground, breaking the fall of his attacker who landed on top of him. Malone and sniper labored to recover from the wind being knocked out of them. The sniper had snapped an ankle bone. Malone retrieved a Bowie hunting knife from his belt and plunged it deeply into the bad guy's thorax shushing any opportunity for him to scream, severing his spinal cord and killing him instantly. Hopefully no one had heard their crashing freefall, or it had been all for naught. Parnell, having seen Malone disappear over the other side of the roof quickly converged. The mighty Malone was already standing by then, the sniper's gun now in his possession.

"We need to replace him on the roof. Fish the others, find one who can fire this rifle with some semblance of accuracy and stage them as double."

Dallas had remained in character, even after detecting the assault from her peripheral vision. She only glanced towards the church after she detected an arm waving about. Quickly retrieving her clothes and handgun, she soon rejoined the others. Malone had already hauled the limp body of the dead man into the edge of the woods, one down and seven more to go. He commended Dallas for her performance.

The previously reluctant Leo had taken up the sniper position on the church roof. A bored and overly cautious security guard now embraced his role seriously. Malone had given him instructions to just lay low, no shooting unless the others realized he wasn't their comrade. Don't play hero. Pretending just guaranteed casualties. The goal remained, rescue and avoid engaging in a gun battle. These people were obviously seasoned professionals. Professionals rarely ever lost, not without inflicting significant collateral damage. From what he had overheard, bloodshed, theirs or their hostages, posed little concern. He had no way of knowing two people already lay dead inside.

Fundraising Day-mares

Marc Drayton was getting antsy, like most in the congregation. He had witnessed too much and had just about had enough of this senseless crap. It was plain as the nose on his face, they were all going to die at the hands of the money-grubbing maniac. He talked up a plan among those closest to him. Few were taking the bait. Marc, a debt collector by profession, continued to plead his case to those who would listen. Only a handful of others were showing any signs of being on board. He persisted though, professing his way was the only way any of them had a chance in hell.

"We must use our numbers and rush them. We have the element of surprise on our side."

Calvin Thomas half bought into it but made a compelling counter argument. "They'll just start shooting and mow us down if we can't get our hands on a couple of their weapons."

"They're going to do that anyway if they don't collect the two billion. I say they'll kill us either way. We're witnesses."

"How can we be a threat to them as witnesses? They're wearing masks. We don't know who they are or what they look like, Marc," added Trevor Hester, his wife JoEllen nodding in agreement.

Penny Morgan, an elder of the church, spoke her mind on the subject as a naysayer. "Marc Drayton, you hush up now. All of you. They just murdered that wrestler in that sick game of theirs. I'm scarred. I don't won't to die over your foolishness. Please just do what they tell us to do."

"Hey Marc, could you have passed the talleywacker test," asked Hogan Lavin.

"Funny man, Hogan, but I'm serious as a heart attack. We can't just sit here and do nothing. It's a death sentence. Anyone can see that. We can overpower them if we all stick together and rush them in force."

"They'd drop us dead in our tracks before we could get out of these pews," added Tyler Myers, an employee of the local steel mill in Georgetown. "They're professionals, natural born killers, and we're what…a bunch of desperate vigilantes…unarmed and a tad bit insane if we try this bull crap. Count me out. I'll take my chances that they'll keep their promise once they have their money."

"And if they don't get their money…"

"Talk to me then, not now, Marc. I'm going to hold out a bit longer. I'm not ready to die either."

"You're all damn fools."

"Son, please give it a rest," said Penny. "This isn't anything to mess around with. These horrible people are stone cold killers and they'll kill us all and not even blink about it."

Trudy wasn't faring any better. She had long ago passed the antsy stage. She was somewhere between ready to talk more crap at Valdemar or kick his ass. She had similar suspicions, her instincts screaming that this was headed for a very unhappy ending for all of them. There might have been a glimmer of hope until the line had been crossed. The band of Poe were now murderers. Murderers tidy up the crime scene. They rid it of all evidence and never leave a witness behind. A silver lining if ever there was one; Valdemar hadn't recognized Brady. Brady was an actual witness. He could identify the man behind the mask. All bets were off if he made that connection. Still, would they murder as many as fifty people? Was the blood money worth something as heinous as that? Murder two or fifty, was there really a difference from Valdemar's point of view?

"Ligeia, time please…"

"Fifty-three minutes remain."

"Update please."

"Nine hundred seventy-five million…but we have more developing glitches…"

"Look," spoke up Trudy. "You're close to your original billion. Why not call it a day and make good your escape?"

"Escape, you make this sound so offensive, my dear. Your aggressiveness continues to intrigue me, Trudy Wagner. Does she always wear the pants in the family, Mister Wagner?"

"Hey, Frito Bandito," yelled Allison. "Leave my sister and brother-in-law alone, how about it? They have enough on their plate without you sticking your nose into their business. You want to mess with somebody, bring it on."

"I regret I never met your parents. You are both quite the pistol balls, aren't you? "

Buster stood up and prompted a warning from Valdemar. "Think long and hard before you dare speak, Sheriff Ferguson. I have little tolerance for the long hand of the law as you should be aware of by now."

Allison grabbed Buster by the arm and shook her head no motioning for him to please take his seat. Buster heeded his warning and complied with her request. He didn't like it, but he did it, figuring he was less useful dead.

"Wise man, Sheriff…but you must excuse me for a second while I investigate these glitches."

"What the hell are you doing, Allison?" whispered Trudy.

"I'm trying to save our butts. Brady said he knows him. You know as do I that if he figures that out, we're as good as dead."

"Thanks Allison, put the burden on me," said Brady.

"Sorry Brady. She's right, Pierce," added Buster.

"I know she's right, sir. I just want her to butt out. She's playing with fire. This man is a certified psycho. He'll murder and not give it an afterthought."

Trudy eyed Allison, "And you're not playing with fire pushing him like you're doing?"

"Allison, it's my job, not yours."

"You saw what happened to Buster when he discovered he was a cop, didn't you? Your smart-ass mouth is going to compound that problem when he finds out you're one too."

"Allison does make a compelling argument, Pierce," added Buster.

"Butt out…sir. This is between me and my sister."

"He's your superior, sis…you should show him some respect."

"I'm off duty and the sheriff is a guest just like the rest of us."

"You mean hostage, don't you?"

"Whatever, Allison…just stay out of it, please."

"Too late, you heard him, he has unfinished business with us."

"And whose fault is that, Sister Dearest?"

"Both of you, pipe down. Bickering is pointless. We need to unite and figure a way to save our necks. Everyone in this church is counting on that."

"You tell them, Brady. I'm behind you one hundred percent."

"Thank you, Sheriff, I wish I had a plan."

"Do me a favor though, take me off your invite list," said Buster.

"I think I'll be hard pressed to get anyone to accompany me to another event after this fiasco."

"VIP my butt," added Trudy, winking at her hubby.

"What now, Ligeia?" asked Valdemar.

"Fabio Fuentes would like a word with you."

"Mister Fuentes, Entrepreneur and Drug Lord, strange bed fellows we make. Speak, please."

"We should be on the same side here. You do realize that, don't you? "

"Enlighten me, teammate."

"Come on, I shouldn't have to spell it out for you."

"But I insist, Mister Fuentes, please by all means clarify."

"Call me Fabio. You can drop all that mister crap."

"Ah yes, we are best buddies, are we not, peas in a pod."

"See, you do get it."

"Indeed, I do, Fabio. I deplore and utterly despise drug dealers. You are the scum of the earth, taking advantage of those less fortunate, feeding their addictions, all for the sake of profiteering."

"I don't see you bitching and moaning too much right now, willing to take that money for yourself. That makes you an accomplice to my profiteering scum bag ways, doesn't it?"

"Actually, Fabio, I was looking forward to meeting you once I realized you would be among the guests."

"I'm honored."

"Don't be. My intentions are anything but honorable. My sister, Eva Lovelace, of course not her real name, died from a tainted drug purchase just six months ago. Sadly, she was addicted to the magical snake oil. My sources were able to track and identify the original supplier of the contaminated heroin. The trail leads directly to you, Fabio. I'm sorry. You were saying something about us being on the same side. Doctor Tarr, please administer the injection."

"Injection, what the hell are you talking about?"

"Fabio, please humor me. I just wish to test a theory of mine. Eva had more of the heroin in her possession. Could it have been a fluke occurrence? Possibly there was nothing wrong with the product she had purchased. Ensuring utmost quality control must be first and foremost in your process, correct? Maybe she miscalculated the dosage, or the years of abuse just caught up with her. Never promote a product you're not willing to try. Standing behind the brand is critical PR, wouldn't you agree?"

"You can't be serious?"

"Do I detect a bit of hesitancy in sampling what you so willingly sold to others?"

"Listen to me. I'll up the ante to an additional two billion if we just call this even."

"My sister's life for an extra two billion dollars insults my integrity and her memory."

"Doctor Tarr…"

"No, please, I beg you."

"That's the spirit, Fabio. I would have expected nothing less from worthless pile of dog feces. Please secure him Professor Fether. The convulsions lend to spastic and most deplorable results. That is, if what you have pushed off on my dearly departed sister isn't FDA approved so to speak."

Fabio was restrained while Doctor Tarr administered the injection as instructed.

"My, that was quick and quite distasteful, wasn't it? In the words of Edgar Allen Poe, a potpourri of quotes appropriate to the circumstances…*we loved with a love that was more than love…I have no faith in human perfectibility. I think that human exertion will have no appreciable effect upon humanity. Man is now only more active - not more happy - nor more wise, than he was 6000 years ago…That man is not truly brave who is afraid either to seem or to be, when it suits him, a coward.*"

"Blah…blah…nevermore…nevermore…"

"Shush…Allison…"

"Sorry, this is my dime, Trudy."

"But why push this to the limit?'

"I have my reasons."

"Does this have anything to do with your attempted confession?"

"I guess we reap what we sow, don't' we?"

"Allison, what's really going on here? Do you have a death wish or something?"

"Ding…ding…ding…cigar to the lady in front."

One Down, Seven to Go

Never shall I fail my comrades. I will always keep myself mentally alert, physically strong, and morally straight and I will shoulder more than my share of the task whatever it may be, one hundred percent and then some.

Those gathered, except for Leo now pulling substitute sniper duty, waited for Ranger Felix Malone to lay out the next course of action. Noah stared at the bloodied body of the former sniper, and even after removing his mask, they were no closer to identifying him. A search of his clothing had revealed no identification credentials either. These were not your everyday ordinary fly by night criminals. Woody was banking that finger prints would not reveal the dead man's identification either. He looked over at Malone. The man stood there expressionless, hard to read. He had just taken out the sniper and displayed no emotions whatsoever. Woody broke the silence.

"Mister Malone, sir, how do you recommend that we rescue those inside now that you have taken care of their rooftop lookout?"

Noah, squinting and then blinking rapidly, the Mighty Malone focused on the source of the chatter. "This will require additional recon. We cannot storm the chapel without first determining where the others are posted and the extent of the weaponry."

"You've already seen their weapons."

"I saw them from a distance, enough to realize they were not amateurs. I didn't see everything they unloaded from those golf bags. Count on them being strategically posted inside."

"How do you propose that we catch a sneak preview?" asked Woody

"We go inside and look for ourselves."

"Right, we just waltz right in there," commented Sly.

"Exactly and I'll require another volunteer."

"You're joking, right? He is joking, right?" asked Drew. "Please tell me he's joking."

"This will require another distraction. Someone will have to enter the church, become a hostage."

"How does this volunteer escape to report what they have seen inside?" asked Tim.

"They don't. As mentioned, they will be the decoy."

"Humor me," said a frustrated Woody Anderson. "Would that not tip off those inside that their sniper had most likely been compromised?"

"It would if the decoy entered from the front entrance. The volunteer will instead wander in from the back. Those inside will not be expecting anyone gaining access from the main entrance, as you pointed out."

"Then why don't we all crash the party from the front entrance?" asked Parnell.

"Risky without viewing the lay of the land inside…but the diversion would allow front door access and assessment."

"Maybe, but only if no one is posted directly inside," added Tim.

"Positioning an extra man there would be redundant given the sniper's assignment," replied Malone. "No, the others are in the chapel corralling those inside. No one is at the front entrance."

"Might be one or more guarding the back entrance," suggested Woody.

"No, they're not concerned about the back. There's no reason for them to suspect a sneak attack. You and your men are posted at the highway. You're supposed to be oblivious to the unfolding events if they stick to their timeline."

"Then it sounds to me we can rush them from both directions," said Parnell, just itching for a fight.

"I don't deal in unknowns. Those inside wouldn't appreciate the blind gunslinger approach either. Going in guns blazing might result in the same outcome, death and carnage to those being held. Recon will validate my suspicions. Once we know the positioning of the seven inside, then you're dead on. An assault from both directions might be an option. But when we do, specific targets will be identified and assigned to those deeming themselves cracker-jack shots. One misfire and all hell will break loose. Do I have that volunteer?"

"I've been there, done that. I may as well do it again," said Dallas.

"No. I'll be the decoy," said Summer.

"I don't think so," spoke up Tim. "This plan is too risky for anyone."

"Do you have a better one, detective,' asked Malone.

"Yeah me," said Woody.

"Sorry, but you'll be better utilized as a shooter. Besides, I think your security uniform would be a dead giveaway."

"It will be okay, Tim. I've done undercover investigative reporting before."

"This is insane. Do you think they are going to welcome you with open arms?" questioned Tim.

"Leave your ID here, Miss Knight. Your credentials would tip them off. What's going to be your cover story for stumbling in there? Your arrival will be highly scrutinized, and you will be grilled extensively. That is a given."

"I got it." Summer then explained, and Malone prompted her to go with it.

"I really wish you would reconsider."

"Tim, I'll be okay." Summer then kissed Tim, a deep passionate kiss, one that meant without a doubt that they were indeed in a relationship.

"Please be careful."

"You better do the same. They'll be shooting at you, not me when this goes down."

"Positions everyone…"

Readily will I display the intestinal fortitude required to fight on to the Ranger objective and complete the mission, though I be the lone survivor.

Truth or Dare

Trudy watched as Hop-Frog dragged the body of Fabio Fuentes out of sight. Bodies were being stacked somewhere like cord wood. The drug dealer had been executed for past transgressions. She now wondered had that been Valdemar's prime motivation for this little caper. Possibly this was his best opportunity to ambush the unsuspecting drug lord. Maybe the money was just a bonus. There seemed to be a loosely enforced code of ethics, honor among thieves. The more disturbing fact, this man continued to murder and didn't give it a second thought. Who was this man behind the mask? Brady had seen his face but who was he, really? It was time to find out.

"You don't blink an eye, do you? Seems to me you keep killing off your money makers."

"You're determined to position yourself in the center ring, aren't you Mrs. Wagner. Your constant distractions are becoming somewhat annoying. Yet…you have this charisma about you. I'm so easily drawn into your little sidebars. Why is that, Mrs. Wagner? Of all the people gathered here, why do you yearn to be a standout? You've so graciously pointed out how my actions disturb you, but you press onward. What do you hope to gain by this? Are you searching for my inner self, a man who possesses morals, show a little compassion, might not be a monster after all? Do you just want to know what makes me tick? What exactly is your game? Please enlighten me and dispense wiyh all this silly rhetoric."

"It's tough talking to a mask. Maybe you're Poe's version of the Phantom of the Opera. Your face might stop a clock. I just like to know who I'm dealing with, face to face so to speak."

"Be careful what you wish for Mrs. Wagner. Removing this mask would be a game changer. Are you willing to jeopardize the lives of everyone gathered here just to satisfy your selfish curiosity? I'll show you mine, if you'll show me yours?"

"Hey pervert, you've seen everything I have. You're way ahead of the game already."

"Bravo…bold and beautiful…in another life who knows…"

"In your dreams and my nightmares…I know."

"Seriously…who are you, Mrs. Wagner? My instincts have me leaning towards a couple of possibilities. You are head strong, a doer, and a problem solver with investigative skills. You stand up and somewhat take responsibility when others refuse. You don't hesitate in taking the leadership role, even under surmountable adversarial circumstances. Why is that? Why is it so important to you to gain control of the situation?"

"What…I'm a girl. I'm supposed to be afraid of the *Big Bad Wolf?*"

"Not you my dear…no matter how much huffing and puffing I do seems to put the fear in you. Time, Ligeia?"

"Forty-three minutes…and we're still shy by nearly 450 million."

"I shall allow you ten minutes Mrs. Wagner but we'll play a new game, you and I."

"Hold on masked man, what about me?" interrupted Allison.

"Stay out of this Allison," warned Trudy.'

"No please join us. You and I have unfinished business too. Besides, what I have in mind requires at least three participants."

Trudy gave Allison 'The Look', as only a female can muster. Her sister really needed to butt out and allow her to handle this. Time was dwindling, and this could be the last opportunity any of them might have. She had to crack this nut at all cost. Pun intended. The fact that he was willing to engage in dialogue with her gave them hope, slim at best, but anything was better than nothing. It rested on her shoulders. Having exposed Buster as a sheriff had taken him out of the game. He could and would only intervene if the worst-case scenario raised its ugly head. In less than an hour would signal the end game for their money harvesting.

The six remaining naked celebrities were frantically manning the phones, their every move policed by Doctor Tarr and Professor Fether, with Ligeia monitoring the totals and more importantly, the time clock. Now, of all things, Valdemar wanted to play a game. His games were usually deadly. Allison needed to bow out, but instinct told her that the host would not allow a gracious exit.

"Ladies, what I have in mind has existed for centuries. As early as 1712 it was referred to as Questions and Commands. The commander prompted his subjects to answer a question. If the subject refused or failed to satisfy the commander, the subject forfeited or had their face smutted, dirtied in a shameful manner. Madonna made this famous and more current, Truth or Dare."

"You have got to be kidding? Look around. Haven't you toyed enough with these people's lives?"

"They are our captive audience, Mrs. Wagner. Surely they could us this welcome distraction."

"Your distractions have been death sentences. You're not exactly building any faith for those snared in your mad house."

"Life is not always filled with choices. Sometimes you must simply go with the flow, correct? Shall we begin?"

"What's in this for us," asked Trudy.

"Ah…you require rules, boundaries by which to play then?"

"I want your guarantee that if we do this, no one else will be harmed."

"Quite demanding from one in your precarious position, don't you concur? I like that about you, so very persistent and predictable…alas…this is not a democracy. You are not enabled as a co-chair. However, I shall pacify you. We shall have rules if you wish."

"Just get on with this," demanded Trudy.

"Very well…one player shall start…choices are Truth, Dare, Double Dare, Kiss or Torture. The first player will pose the question to player number two. If the player chooses "truth", then the first player poses a question, which the second player must answer truthfully. If the player instead chooses "dare", then the first player sets a task, which player two must perform. After answering the question or performing the dare, that player asks Truth, Dare, Double Dare, Kiss or Torture to the next player, and the game continues. A player cannot choose truth more than twice in a row, and dares cannot be repeated. Failure to complete the task will result in most unfortunate consequences."

"Define unfortunate consequences."

"A member of the congregation will be punished."

"Define punished."

"Any assortment of possibilities administered by my host of actors…at my command…"

"What if one of us is asking the question? It seems unfair that something would happen to a member of our viewing audience. You could throw the contest intentionally."

"Oh, the pain, you are actually questing my ethics. Very well, what would you counter?"

"As contestants we play by the same rules. If you fail to complete your task or answer honestly then we can choose the punishment for one of your henchmen."

"Absurd…I like it. One stipulation however…to even the odds I shall have two turns each round. My game…take it or leave it…and yes, I start, followed by your sister, then me again and then you. Game ends once our fundraiser deadline has expired. I shall start. Allison, Truth…what is your sister's occupation?"

Allison looked over at Trudy, seeking guidance. If she refused to reply, someone in the congregation would be harmed, could even been killed. If she told the truth, where would that leave her sister? Valdemar gestured and mouthed answer please. She did the only she knew to do.

"She's a private investigator, mostly contracted for insurance fraud claims."

"Ah…so that explains her assertiveness and intuitive tendencies."

"My turn now," claimed Allison.

"Not quite so fast… Prospero, please locate Mrs. Wagner's credentials. We must validate her sister's claims."

"More rules," bitched Trudy.

"Validation my dear…we must keep the playing field even."

"Are you calling my sister a liar? Tell me. How will we be able to validate your responses?"

"Compromise…we shall continue the game while Prospero searches for your ID. If her answer matches, then all is well."

"I'll save you the trouble. I'm not carrying Private Investigator credentials."

"Is that not a legal requirement?"

"Not on my day off it isn't."

"Very well then…Prospero based on Mrs. Wagner's sincerity, please continue your search. Your turn, Allison, let's hope there are no discrepancies in either of your responses."

"Valdemar, I dare you to remove your mask."

Valdemar chuckled. "Were your not listening to our early conversation. If I do, you are jeopardizing the lives of all those around you. You do fully understand these consequences, don't you? I shall give you one opportunity to withdraw your dare."

"Dare stands."

"Very well…"

"Sir, I have located Mrs. Wagner's purse. There are discrepancies."

"What are these discrepancies, Prospero?"

"First, her name isn't Wagner. She is Trudy Pierce."

"Pierce…interesting…"

"I didn't lie. Wagner is my maiden name."

"Anything else…?"

"Oh yes, possibly you would like to see this for yourself."

"Very well, bring it to me. Sisters, do we have any additional secrets you feel obligated to share with the congregation?"

The entrance door behind the pulpit burst open. In stumbled a somewhat disoriented female carrying a wine bottle in one hand and a cigar stogie in the other. Her jeans were filthy and torn. Her top was stained and in the same condition. She wore no shoes. Her face was smudged, twigs entangled in her head. Weapons clicked into action, all pointing towards the intruder. Hop-Frog reached her first, grabbing a hand full of hair, jerking her to the floor, twirling her to a face down position with his boot rested in the center of her back. She mumbled some incoherent nonsense.

Malone entered the front entrance simultaneously. There was no guard in the entrance way just inside. As suspected, the sniper would have deterred anyone from gaining access. None were posted. Malone eased to a pair of double swinging doors with glass portals. He could see the ensuing commotion but not Summer Knight. Best he could tell she must be on the floor, her condition unknown. He began visually perusing the inside perimeter. Seven gunman and their positions were quickly noted. Two were on each side of the chapel, just behind the back pews. Three more were posted at what appeared to be half dozen totally nude guests. Three more were near the front. Eight…that can't be right he thought. The eighth had been on the roof. He was sure he had seen eight, two each in each in the four golf carts. There were nine. Where had the ninth one come from? Could there be more?

After searching the woman, Hop-Frog yanked her to her feet. She wobbled about, seemed to struggle to hold her standing position. The woman reeked of urine and alcohol. "She's clean. Well…she's at least free of any weapons. She has no identification."

"Who are you madam and why are you here?" demanded Valdemar.

"You're not the preacher," replied the lady in slurred tongue. She giggled. "Why are you wearing the funny mask? Is this a masquerade party? I love parties. Where's the bar?"

"I ask questions. I expect answers. I repeat, who are you and why are you here?"

"The preacher always gives me food and lets me crash in the church. He's a nice old man. He's so kind to me. Oh, there he is…hey preacher. I didn't know you had a masquerade party going on in here today. Should I leave and come back later?"

"Dispose of her Hop-Frog. We have no time for this."

A disruption from the front of the church caught everyone's attention. Another person had stumbled through the doors. He was immediately met with the butt of a gun, dropping him to the floor. It appeared to be a second wondering derelict. Malone couldn't stand idly by and allow them to kill Summer Knight. He did the only thing he could do, improvise and hope for the best.

Dispose of her, she poses no value," ordered Valdemar.

Noah overheard the order and was witnessing the unthinkable. Mighty Malone had options, leave immediately and report to the others, and then plan the assault or prevent the murder of Summer Knight. Ranger training had taught him that the mission must be completed. He was no longer a ranger though. This wasn't really his problem. No, he had made this problem his business. The commitment had been made. Others depended on him. How could he help the others if he intervened in this situation? Much more was at stake than one single life.

The enemy didn't play by his rules or anyone else's. Collateral damages should always be expected. Use unsound judgment and lose the war. There was no room on the battlefield for personal emotions.

This wasn't a battlefield or a military encounter. This was a police matter. No police had been notified. The responsibility fell on his shoulders. She had volunteered and had understood the risks…hadn't she. Sure, she had. Walk into the bowels of hell and expect the worse case scenarios. Summer Knight would die a hero. The mission must be completed.

Energetically will I meet the enemies of my country? I shall defeat them on the field of battle for I am better trained and will fight with all my might. Surrender is not a Ranger word. I will never leave a fallen comrade to fall into the hands of the enemy and under no circumstances will I ever embarrass my country.

Can Swimmers Tread Shark Infested Waters?

"What's taking them so long?" asked Detective Tim Burroughs

"Calm down, Tim, it's been less than five minutes," said Woody.

"I should have never allowed her to do this."

Dallas placed her hand on his shoulder. "You couldn't have talked her out of it any more than anyone could have talked me out of doing what I did. We analyze and rationalize and, in the end, we do what must be done."

"If anything happens to her…"

"It could have been any of us in there, Tim, including you," added Sly.

"I'd rather it had been me than her."

"And would you have preferred Summer being here anguishing over your safety?"

"I get it Woody, but it doesn't make it any easier to swallow."

"Focus son," added Parnell. "We have a hell of lot of folks depending on us right now. We are the Calvary, remember. We do this right or it all turns ugly real fast. Let the Mighty Malone do what he does best, and this will wash out clean as a whistle in the laundry. The bad guys won't know what hit them."

Woody wasn't feeling nearly as confident about this. Too many variables existed. Any one of them could blow this thing up in their faces. He had seen too much death over recent years at the hands of ruthless serial killers. People like these got their jollies from murder and mayhem. They had already murdered Al. They most likely wouldn't hesitate to do it again. He tried to envision what Trudy might be doing inside. He knew her too well. She wouldn't take this lying down. Would those inside put up with her crap though, that's what worried him. You can only push these types so far before they gobble you up.

Woody took a deep breath and then enlightened the others. "Maybe we should call this in. We might be biting off way more than we can chew. We've been down this road before and we're damn lucky it turned out as well as it did."

"I sort of agree," added Sly. "But I think we're committed now. There might not be time to bring in reinforcements before they attempt to pull out of here."

"We're not even sure what they really want. This could be a planned murder-suicide mission, just a bunch of crazies wanting to make their point and immortalize their names or cause."

"Malone is a pro, a friggin ranger. He's not going to let that happen," defended Parnell.

"This is not the movies, Stallone's Rambo against an army. He's one man and we're not exactly a swat or navy seal team." Woody extracted his cell phone from his pocket.

"We can't risk Summer being harmed by doing something stupid, Woody. Think about Trudy, her sister, Brady and the sheriff."

"I've been doing just that Tim."

"Man, you're the one who got us into this. Give it a rest. You're no longer a cop. We are though," fumed Parnell.

"You have no more jurisdiction than I do. This is Georgetown County, not Horry."

"Why did you call us first then," pushed Parnell.

"Felix laid it out, you know that. Any sign of law or news media and they would slaughter those inside."

"That hasn't changed to my knowledge," replied Parnell.

"He's right," said Dallas.

"What are we going to do, boss," asked Drew.

What are we going to do pondered Woody Anderson, all eyes glued on him?

Beat the Clock

"Who the hell is this Bozo?" asked Dupin, pressing the end of his assault weapon against the temple of Malone.

"I'm Noah," he announced as he grabbed the barrel of the gun and in one quick move and slammed the owner and the gun into the wall. Before anyone could react, he escaped back through the door he had just entered.

"Don't kill him," screamed Summer.

Dupin had righted himself and was about to pursue the intruder when Valdemar called him off. "Let Tamerlane deal with him."

"Tamerlane…he let him in here in the first place," yelled Dupin.

"He's obviously homeless, just like this one. Tamerlane probably figured why shoot and alert the country side."

"You don't want me to go after him then?"

The blast rattled the windows. "Tamerlane had second thoughts. Problem solved."

"What about this one?" asked Hop-Frog.

"Find her a seat with the others."

"One billion, three hundred million…fifteen minutes remaining," announced Ligeia.

> *And the Raven, never flitting, still is sitting, still is sitting*
> *On the pallid bust of Pallas just above my chamber door;*
> *And his eyes have all the seeming of a demon's that is dreaming,*
> *And the lamp-light o'er him streaming throws his shadow on the floor;*
> *And my soul from out that shadow that lies floating on the floor*
> *Shall be lifted—nevermore!*

And the Raven, never flitting, still is sitting, still is sitting

On the pallid bust of Pallas just above my chamber door;

And his eyes have all the seeming of a demon's that is dreaming,

And the lamp-light o'er him streaming throws his shadow on the floor;

And my soul from out that shadow that lies floating on the floor

Shall be lifted—nevermore!

And the Raven, never flitting, still is sitting, still is sitting

On the pallid bust of Pallas just above my chamber door;

And his eyes have all the seeming of a demon's that is dreaming,

And the lamp-light o'er him streaming throws his shadow on the floor;

And my soul from out that shadow that lies floating on the floor

Shall be lifted—nevermore!

And the Raven, never flitting, still is sitting, still is sitting
On the pallid bust of Pallas just above my chamber door;
And his eyes have all the seeming of a demon's that is dreaming,
And the lamplight o'er him streaming throws his shadow on the floor; And my soul from out that shadow that lies floating on the floor
Shall be lifted- nevermore!

"I have in my hand the key to unlock a plaguing mystery." Valdemar smiled. "Welcome Detective Pierce. Truth be damned, my dear Allison. Now we enter the penalty phase of the game. Liar…liar…pants on fire…"

"You better not harm my sister," warned Trudy.

"I have no intentions of harming a hair on your sister's head. Brady Pierce, we have met, have we not? You are the proprietor of that quant golf shop. Do I not do you justice sporting this rather unique outfit? I shall forever cherish the knickers and argyle socks. Unfortunately, forever is not in your future. A Jersey boy must dispose of all loose ends and I'm a Wise Guy at heart, a regular Tony Soprano. Yes, Virginia, there is a face behind this mask, and you know it all so well, don't you, Mister Brady Pierce, spouse of Detective Trudy Wager-Pierce."

Brady stood from his wheel chair. "Do what you must but think about this; more saw your sorry mug besides me that day. It will be just a matter of time before you are identified."

"The difference, you purposely deceived me, as did your wife and the sheriff. Allison even lied to me, refusing to follow the rules of our game. I cannot merely turn my cheek and allow these atrocities to go unpunished. I have a reputation to uphold."

Trudy took her position beside Brady. "Cops and robbers…it was never intended for us to get along. You have your job. I have mine. Mine is to stop you at any cost. Call that deceit if it eases your conscious. I was hell bent on stopping you. Take it out on me, not the others."

"Commendable argument, Detective, but rules are rules, and we all must abide by them or chaos prevails."

"It's your turn, Valdemar. Truth or Dare, challenge me."

"Very well…we do have a few moments." Valdemar retrieved a pistol from his belt and proceeded in unloading it. He then handed it to Trudy.

"One bullet remains. I dare you to point it and shoot your husband."

"Well played," replied Trudy. "Or not…" She pointed the gun at Valdemar's head instead.

"So predictable…breaking the rules runs in the family."

"Have your people stand down or I put this between your eyes."

"Fire away my dear. You win, I'm dead. You're out of bullets and everyone here dies along with us."

"You're bluffing."

"You have the weapon. I am currently unarmed. Are you bluffing or are you calling mine a bluff?" Valdemar held out his hand. "Honor, dishonor, good, evil, who can say what lurks in the hearts…correct…the gun please, Detective Pierce."

Trudy clinched the fist of her free hand, not so willing to just forfeit the gun back over just like that. It gave her strength and offered her hope. Pulling the trigger seemed the natural thing to do. Sadly, if the others were sincerely loyal, then this would end as a blood bath. Training had taught her to never turn over her weapon when other lives were at stake. What good would the one bullet really serve? Besides, this wasn't her police issue. There was a difference. Valdemar had made this point. Question. Once she was unarmed, where would that leave her and leave the others? She had but one choice. She handed it back to Valdemar.

In one fluid motion he accepted it and then plunged the six-inch blade concealed behind his back into the chest of Brady Pierce. Trudy screamed as her husband collapsed backwards into the wheel chair. Others in the congregation screamed, yelled and gasped, some standing, teetering on the brink of a full-blown mutiny.

"Lesson my dear, those wearing the badges should never trust those that are determined to disrupt the process. The good guys only win in the movies. Bad guys will improvise to save their asses and, in this case, prove a point. Follow the rules or pay the consequences, penalty phase, Truth or Dare, game over."

Trudy dropped to Brady's side, searching for any signs of vitals. She found none. Brady Pierce no longer suffered from Parkinson. His pain had ended while Trudy's had just begun. Circus boy was gone. She choked back her tears and then charged Valdemar, tackling him at the waist and knocking him to the floor. She quickly recovered the pistol and buried the barrel into Valdemar's cheek. Others in the congregation stirred, ready to rally to her support but rapid bursts of gunfire stopped them in their tracks. Luckily, they were indeed warning shots, none aimed at individuals.

"Lesson never let me get the upper hand a second time. New rules…new consequences…an eye for an eye…"

Trudy effortlessly pulled the trigger…click…she squeezed it over and over, nothing happened. Hop-Frog yanked her backwards, burying his weapon into her chest.

"A valuable lesson indeed Mrs. Pierce. Never voluntarily place a loaded weapon in the hands of your adversary for any reason," stated the masked leader.

"Time has expired. We are a half million shy of the goal, Valdemar" announced Ligeia.

"How disappointing for those in the congregation and those manning the phones."

Reverend Jonah Blackwood stood, hands raised to the air, "My brother, please be on your way. Has there not been enough bloodshed and suffering inflicted. Please do God's will and leave."

"Tsk…tsk…pastor…the Lord does not get a vote I'm afraid or have a say in what I do or don't do. Keep that 'deliver us from evil' nonsense to yourself."

Buster stood. "You exceeded your original demand. Why not be content? These people did the best they could to call in every favor that they had. The congregation is innocent. They are not to be faulted nor punished. Think about it. You don't really want a bloody legacy."

"There you go, typical thinking like a police officer and attempting to apply your logic to the criminal mind. It's much too easy being a criminal mastermind because of the ideological thoughts that go into capturing the criminals and solving the crimes. You can't pigeon hole us. Most criminal minds are much too complex and unpredictable. Show of hands, who really saw that coming with Brady Pierce? My guess is none of you did."

Valdemar smiled. "The author rarely kills off one of their main characters in the novel. You were so easily lulled. I eliminated a few random picks and then delivered the shocker. I take out the one person who can identify me. For the record, I recognized Brady Pierce immediately. A well-staged theatrical performance always saves a few unexpected twists. I intentionally allowed Brady and Trudy Pierce to squirm a bit, wiggle on that hook. Soon I had them convinced they were in the clear. I know you're all curious about what happens next. I laid it out, didn't I? Obtain the goal or everyone dies. We were short. Am I a man of my word you're asking?"

Members began weeping. Others vocalized their objections or begging for mercy. That small handful still wanted to rush them. Theorizing and implementing were miles apart and had too few committed to the cause to guarantee even marginal success. No one wished to sit idly by and be executed. No one was eager to be shot either. Time stood still for those seeking answers. Many just began praying, closing their eyes, intent on not witnessing judgment day, if indeed this ended up being the chosen path.

'The boundaries which divide Life and Death are at best shadowy and vague. Who shall say where the one ends, and the other begins.'

Edgar Allan Poe (1809-1849)

Regroup or Reboot

'I became insane, with long intervals of horrible sanity'

The bursts of automatic fire inside took those outside off guard. The jig had to be up. The bastards inside must be slaughtering those inside. Noah closed his eyes and then covered his ears, willing it to stop. It did. All was quiet once again. He opened his eyes to an audience of strangers. Each of the people assembled about were staring at him. What had he done or not done to prompt it? He perused his surroundings, but no instant answers popped in his head. He slowly edged back a step. One of them spoke.

"What now, Malone? We must do something. What did you see inside?"

Noah didn't recognize Woody Anderson. He didn't recognize any of these people. What did they want from him?

"Come on man, we need to go in there and kick ass or something," rallied Parnell Roberts.

Noah backed another step and then spun, ran like lightening away from this bunch of crazies' intent on blaming him for something. Parnell engaged in pursuit, confused by his actions. Woody froze. This had gone to hell in a hand basket. He was three people shy, counting Summer Knight now inside. Worse, he had no clue what had just happened inside. Had they just murdered Summer? He didn't dare share those suspicions with Tim Burroughs. He didn't have to; Tim was already on the move.

"Where in the hell are you going, Tim?"

"We can't stand here and do nothing."

"Getting yourself killed isn't going to help either."

"Woody, she's in there. You heard those shots. Hell is already upon us and the Mighty Malone just deserted us."

Parnell Roberts, younger and faster, not necessarily in better shape, was able to catch and overtake the Mighty Malone. He half grabbed, and half tackled the man. With his knee planted onto Malone's chest, Parnell stared directly into his eyes. The ranger's facial expression alerted Parnell that something wasn't right. He looked about wildly, resembling a trapped animal fearful of its life. Malone struggled to escape, but Parnell kept him penned easily, something he should have never been able to do to a seasoned ranger. He had never looked more homeless and abandoned as he did this very moment.

"What's wrong with you, man? What happened inside that church that upset you so?"

Noah said nothing, just continued to squirm. Parnell had seen this look before on one of his buddy's faces, an old timer, Vietnam Vet…flashbacks…trauma inflicted by real life experiences during war times surfacing once again. He hadn't expected the Mighty Malone to have been a broken solder. Rangers were supposed to be real bad asses and immune to this crap. This reinforced that everyone has their breaking point. Rangers are not superhuman. Parnell removed his knee from Malone's chest and stood down.

Noah scrambled to his feet, again looked about frantically before sprinting off. Parnell didn't follow him this time. His hero was no longer of any use to them. The rescue mission had taken a drastic shift, a serious blow, and it might be too late in the game to mount an offense. Typically, not one to give up, Parnell no longer felt confident in the mission and envisioned a punt, taking more of a defensive stance. Only fools would rush inside the church now and attempt overpowering those inside. There was nothing to do but head back to the others and formulate a Plan B.

Noah squatted behind a live oak, his back to the tree, listening for any sounds of pursuit. No footfalls followed. His mind replayed the sounds of automatic gunfire. He cringed, ducked and dodged as if under enemy fire. He found himself surrounded, under intense fire, with comrades falling one by one from the relentless onslaught. Wounded and losing substantial blood, Felix Malone had somehow been able to crawl to safety and hide in a camouflaged root cellar until the barrage had ceased and all members of his squad had been killed.

Readily will I display the intestinal fortitude required to fight on to the Ranger objective and complete the mission, though I be the lone survivor.

The thought played in his head. What did it really man though?

Readily will I display the intestinal fortitude required to fight on to the Ranger objective and complete the mission, though I be the lone survivor.

Complete what mission? Am I a lone survivor? Noah vaguely remembered but memories were just too fuzzy to justify actions.

Recognizing that I volunteered as a Ranger, fully knowing the hazards of my chosen profession, I will always endeavor to uphold the prestige, honor, and high esprit de corps of my Ranger Regiment.

Uphold the prestige, honor and high esprit de corps…Forest Ranger, Texas Ranger…Lone Ranger…it made no sense…these words playing in his head. What hazards were he supposed to know? He didn't remember choosing anything. One should remember choices if choices had been made. It was time for him to go, but go where…what direction…and for what apparent reason? He listened and waited a bit longer; why, he had not a clue. Run, hide, volunteer, all words making absolutely no sense. Finally, he gained enough composure to stand. He remained with his back to the giant tree trunk, head cocked, listening but listening to what...for what…

More gunfire penetrated his mind…shots fired from the deepest recesses this time; but to Noah, just as real as those heard earlier. He drew on every ounce of courage he could muster to leave the safety of his tree and run to the next one. This time he spotted vehicles ahead, parked and blocking the roadway. He could make out emblems on the side door panels. Unable to decipher their meaning, he surmised they must belong to the enemy. Who was the enemy? His mind would not formulate a logical response. He veered into the woods, giving them wide berth.

Complete the mission, though I be the lone survivor.

Parnell converged on Woody and the others. He informed them that Malone was long gone. He didn't share with them his encounter with the deranged ranger. He didn't like admitting what he had just witnessed so why repeat the experience. Woody confirmed that the church had succumbed to quietness once again. Leo was still securing his inherited sniper position. What was really going on inside though?

Woody had managed to calm Tim but still, they had to do something. He was short on answers and contingency plans. He had placed all his eggs in one basket, dependency on the ex-ranger leading the charge. Hindsight, allowing Summer and Felix to go inside the church had been a grave mistake. He was down two rescue members now and the uncertainly of what was going on inside remained. He cautioned the others that they should wait it out, not confident by a long shot that this was the best option.

A fleeting thought, life had been much simpler before Trudy Wagner had entered his life. Jinx or just murder and mayhem magnet, take your pick, but the Grand Strand had not been the same since she had come home to roost. He hadn't been able to escape her influence, even after leaving the force so it appeared. Counting him, Horry County was on a fourth sheriff since she had arrived, bad signs at every turn.

The only way things could be worse is if Lance Rocker was here. He shoveled that thought to back of his brain. He wasn't going to waste his time dwelling on that worthless piece of crap. Besides, it sounded as if Rocker had fallen on hard times. It couldn't happen to a more deserving soul thought Woody. He visualized Rocker with his Janice and then closed his eyes, pushing those images back where they had risen. Voices, these not from inside his head, seemed more persistent.

"What do you suggest we do now, Woody?" asked Sly. "Is just waiting for them to make their move the wisest counter?"

Woody looked at those looking at him and seeking answers. He wasn't a lawman now and he didn't have to take charge of a police matter; obviously having no jurisdiction, other than it occurring on his security watch. "Call it in, Sly. We've fooled ourselves long enough. This is bigger than all of us, as badly as I hate to admit it. I'm no gunslinger. I really never was."

Theatrical Chaos

"Detective Pierce, you flunked royally in your turn at our little game or maybe not. The end results were achieved, even if I had to assist you with your dare. I will bend the rules in this case. It is now your turn but choose wisely. This is the end of the game, round one."

"You son of a bitch, you just murdered my husband and you want me to play your silly ass game?"

"It is your turn, Detective Pierce. I'd not squander this opportunity. You do so enjoy stall tactics, don't you? Yes, I've been onto you from the beginning. Call it criminal intuition."

"You know where you can shove your damn sick game."

"Very well, you pass then. I will exercise my right to take the next turn. Allison, dear sister of our widowed detective, you are obviously a troubled soul. I request truth for you to complete your confession. After all, this could be your last opportunity to come clean. Nothing cleanses the human soul better than confessing to those who love you the most. Would you not agree, pastor?"

The pastor replied, "Son, you've buried yourself deep enough in the pits of hell already. Why not just give it a rest?"

"Allison...my challenge has been delivered."

"Don't humor this bastard, Allison. He murdered Brady. We owe him nothing."

The congregation remained silent...deathly silent. Their lives hung by a thread and many had come to terms with what most likely would play out eventually. The nude celebrities no longer manned the phones. They had been allowed to take a seat but hadn't been offered their clothing. Their host apparently found pleasure in the continued humiliation. The rich and famous took their medicine, already having witnessed there were no limits to the fiend's cruelty. Human life meant absolutely nothing. The rich held no advantage in the pecking order. Ace and Fabio were the proof in the pudding, both murdered. Valdemar having them all disrobe and remain naked had been the symbol that they were no different than those in the congregation.

Franco Morrissey saw it differently. The director/producer envisioned the story on the silver screen; that is, if they were granted clemency. He had already placed his fiancée, Julia Whitaker, in the Detective Trudy Wagner-Pierce role. Ex-Governor and TV Host, Marcus McDonald was even having Lance Rocker like aspirations. He could run with this over several episodes, bringing in survivors, witnesses, to his show, the ratings would sky rocket. Sponsors would pay out of the ying-yang for commercial time. The rich, regardless of the situation, always looked to take advantage and advance their agenda, capitalizing on adversity and tragedy to increase the portfolio. The viewing audience ate this sort of stuff up; reality and true life paid huge dividends.

Realestate mogul, Phil Locklear's wheels were turning too. He was thinking how this would become a tourist destination and how he might be able to purchase the adjoining golf course. He had visions of redeveloping the land as condos and townhouses, possibly even a themed resort.

Those in Valdemar's troupe were becoming a bit antsy. While they were accustomed to his eccentric ways and would never challenge him, the time table for completion had expired. A creature of the utmost discipline, he appeared to be wavering this time. Obsessive compulsion dictated he must complete the Truth or Dare game before he could resume the original plans. Ligeia might be the only one bold enough to speak up but even she remained silent but concerned and forever vigilant. It would have to run its course. Patience must be exercised.

The remaining captives were becoming anything but. She perused the various faces and feared someone was going to stupidly cross the line and when it happened, the unspeakable would play out, a tragic ending almost guaranteed. While murder was not new to any of them; slaughter on this scale was unimaginable and totally unnecessary. Their intent had never been to kill anyone, yet, nearly half dozen causalities had altered those plans. One line had already been crossed. All bets were off moving forward. No one wanted the blood of this many people on their hands.

"Remember sweet Allison, fail to complete your turn and complete it honestly and I will choose the punishment. I am quite unpredictable as you have previously witnessed. I shall promise you this; death will be delivered if you pass or if I have the slightest inkling you are lying."

"Screw it," she replied. "This is a piece of cake. I need to get this off my chest. It has burdened me long enough."

"Splendid," laughed Valdemar, clapping his hands.

"I was recently divorced. I kept the divorce from Trudy. I never gave her any reason to suspect that there were issues in our marriage. I know I hurt her dearly by saying nothing, but I had my reasons. Sis was concerned as to why I gave full custody of our two children to my ex-husband, without fighting tooth and claw for at least joint custody. That is an understandable reaction. She pried at first but then gave me breathing room. I thank her for that."

Buster reached over and clasped her hand with his. He wasn't sure why, but he just felt compelled to do so. He had only known her for mere hours, but the current circumstances had tossed them in the same boat. Buster wasn't sure who needed the comfort more, him or her. At this point it really didn't matter. The survival odds were not skewed in their favor based on what had transpired thus far. He couldn't even begin to fathom the hurt and hatred Pierce must be feeling. He hoped she didn't try the one-woman gang tactics again. The host's patience was wearing thin. She was safe for now as he hung on every word being delivered by Allison. He wished he could signal Allison to draw it out, make it a miniseries instead of a mere story. They were in short supply of time.

Summer Knight sat in her delegated pew, struggling to comprehend the viciousness of these maniacs. At least Felix Malone had escaped. Hopefully he and those outside would put an end to this madness before someone else fell victim. She wondered what was taking them so long. He should have easily already mapped out the chapel and identified the select targets. It all hinged on the element of surprise; each assigned a specific target. They must take out their foes before the bad guys could turn this thing into shooting fish in a barrel. Those outside had a distinct disadvantage to those inside. They weren't murderers. In this case it would be shoot or be shot. The rescuers better make every shot count. They'd not have a do-over to get it right. She hoped Tim wasn't harmed when all hell finally broke loose.

"Contrary to what some might believe this was the best decision for everyone. Don't get me wrong. I love my children and I loved my husband. Sometimes love isn't enough. We're supposed to protect those we love…right?"

Trudy stood there, starring at her sister and then glancing to her lifeless husband. She understood love and commitment. Brady had taught her both. Trudy had finally gotten her priorities straight and for what…just to have the rug jerked out from underneath her feet and left to tread water in shark infested waters again. Without him to keep her grounded would she fall back into a pitiful pattern of life driven by work? Why wouldn't she? That's all she had left. She shouldn't be thinking that. She had Allison and her sister sounded as if she needed her support to get beyond her personal tragedies. Just what the hell had happened to cause them to split up? They had indeed seemed so happy.

"I've been battling severe depression most of my life. Remember in school how I always had those bad headaches and locked myself away in my room. I never actually suffered any headaches. I didn't think anyone liked me. I'd just curl up in a ball on my bed convinced that the only thing I had left to offer the world was the removal of my ugly presence from it. At that moment I would be too exhausted to do anything about it. I would just sink into an ugly stupor while mumbling repeatedly, I need help... I need help... I need help…but I was too quiet, no one heard me. I finally crumbled into a frizzy-haired heap, my brain and body zapped of all its strength. I've ridden the roller coaster and have managed to conceal my worst episodes, blaming them on the headaches or other mysterious ailments. Mom never knew just how badly I needed help."

Mouth open, Trudy struggled to understand and to recall any signs but there had been none.

"After my first failed attempted suicide, one that only I knew about, because I took the cowardly way out and just slept through the ill-fated attempt at overdose. I sought out help, again discreetly, telling no one, not even my husband."

"Or me…" added Trudy.

"For years I blamed you for my woes. You were successful, a professional, living the life of a crime scene investigator. I dropped off the planet. I became a mom and shackled housewife. I hated it and was miserable at both. My shrink listened to my pathetic existence, offering me wonder drugs to block out the mental anguish, tricyclic antidepressants that seized up my bowels and caused my tongue to click from lack of moisture. My brain was too occupied, thrumming with guilt, stupidity and embarrassment. Nothing was physically wrong. It's all in your head. This ache, this low, this sickness, this sadness, they are of your making and there is no cure."

"I never knew."

"No and why I often made my family's lives a living hell, they didn't know the extent of it either. Sure, my beloved husband questioned the doctor bills and prescriptions, but I concocted lies to cover my tracks. I don't think he believed me but if it helped me, it helped all of them, so he never pushed it. I've lost too much time and too many people to feel any shame about the way my psyche is built. Now from time to time, for no good reason, it drops a thick, dark veil over me to block out air and love and light. It keeps me at arm's length from the people I love most. The pain and ferocity of the bouts have never eased, but I've lived in my body long enough to know that while I'll never snap out of it, at some point the glass will crack and I'll be free to walk about in the world again. It happens every time, and I have developed a few tricks to remind myself of that as best I can when I'm buried deepest."

Valdemar propped on a banister, captivated by the tale. He allowed her to go on. After all he requested the truth. He must allow her to finish. Ligeia strolled over to him and whispers her concerns in his ear. He waved her off. The congregation remained church mouse silent, either hypnotized by the story or enjoying the welcome relief from chaos. Trudy had taken a seat, her legs no longer able to support her, the double whammy, Brady's murder and Allison's confession taking its toll. Brady dead, it just couldn't be.

"Mom's death was the final blow. I became guilt ridden because I had remained at arm's length, unwilling or maybe just unable to cope with her illness. I neglected my responsibilities as one of her children. I sent her packing back to you at the first sign of just how severe her illness had progressed. I couldn't take care of her and me both."

How sad and ironic thought Trudy. She too had reacted in a similar manner, avoiding her responsibilities, putting work and her developing relationship with Brady ahead of Amy, her mother. The professional self-serving detective had let both her mother and now her sister down.

"Please continue my dear but condense it if you could or I shall impose a time limit. We do have other matters to tend, not that yours is not important, understand."

"After mom's death I fell into the deepest darkness but then you and I began connecting. I weaned off the pills and stopped seeing my shrink. For the first time in my life I thought positive thoughts and looked ahead to a brighter future. I had some wonderful times with you and my family. Then one day, out of the blue, Perry, a man I had shared group therapy with, lost his battle and killed himself. Suicidal thoughts crept back into the picture. I thought about it constantly, all the different ways I could do it. It consumed me, those morbid thoughts. Finally, I settled on a way."

"Apparently you failed miserably at it again," scoffed Valdemar.

"I am so thankful I did. I had retrieved my husband's hunting rifle. I loaded it one afternoon and just sat there in the bedroom with it propped underneath my chin, my finger on the trigger. I had wanted so badly to pull that trigger. Hours must have gone by and I just held it there, maybe wishing reflexes would kick in and I'd eventually end it. I heard my husband and kids arriving home from a day at the beach. I had made excuses for not being up to going with them."

Trudy sighed, glad she had not done the unthinkable.

"Footfalls told me they were heading for the bedroom. I removed the rifle from my chin and pointed it towards the closed door. No doubt in my mind, I would have killed all three and then me had the door not be locked, preventing their entry. I was willing to murder my family and then take my life for what…? It was then that I decided I could no longer be married or be around my children. I packed my bags that night and left them. I never admitted to any of them what I had almost done. I told him I no longer loved him or the children and after much dispute, he eventually gave in and granted me my wish…a divorce."

"Bravo, my dear Allison that was worth the delay. Tormented souls have been a main ingredient of Poe's tales. I thoroughly enjoyed your classical ditty. You can't fabricate tales like that. You have suffered enough at the hands of depression. No penalty is required." Valdemar took center stage and quoted from an article concerning the dreadful disease, delivering an artful articulation.

'Depression is the grand imposter, posing as all powerful. It can be defeated, every time, if you or the person you care about confronts it like the grand imposter that it is. It is always, to an extent, a psychotic illness. It steals reality, which is, in large measure, defined by the completely justifiable hope in tomorrow's possibilities and replaces it with a world in which one doubts his or her abilities, discounts to zero his or her past successes, doubts love, doubts friendship and doubts God. In its worst forms, it is much more than profound sadness; it is the conviction that nothing good will ever occur, sometimes coupled with horrific and constant anxiety that something unspeakably terrible is about to happen in a minute, or this very night, or tomorrow. If life is, for all of us, a labyrinth, with sometimes frustrating twists and turns on the way to the center, depression makes life seem, instead, like a never-ending and inescapable maze, with dead ends, frustrations and traps in every direction.'

"If you're that depressed, reach out to someone. And remember: Suicide is a permanent solution to temporary problems'…Robin Williams as Lance Clayton in World's Greatest Dad. Now back to reality, well for those not depressed…"

Trudy walked over and the two sisters embraced. No way was she about to allow a mass slaughter. She had offered herself as a hostage before, why not try it again? She had nothing to lose, plus she wanted to stay as close to him as possible. She had a score yet to settle. Justice would be delivered by her and her alone. A loud commotion at the front of the church drew everyone's attention. A badly beaten but still breathing Associate Pastor Garrett Moore stumbled through the door. His voice, barely above a whisper, requested a private moment with Valdemar. Hop-Frog threw up his hands, having thwarted this request once already.

"Very well, Pastor Moore, make it quick."

Moore motioned for him to come closer. Valdemar, weapon pointed, granted the request.

"I hired you. I'm your client, the silent partner," whispered Moore.

Houston, We Have a Problem

"Something is going on," announced Drew. "There's activity at the backdoor."

"Hold that call, Sly," requested Woody.

One of the gunmen had exited the back. From their hiding place Woody and the others watched as he nonchalantly strolled to where the golf carts were concealed. He retrieved something from the cart, a bag, contents unknown. Woody was tempted to ambush him but that would only tip off those inside if he failed to return. It was wait and watch mode, Woody teetering toward not calling backup, fearful they wouldn't arrive in time or worse, would arrive in the middle of their exit plan.

"Uh-oh," added Drew. "Someone just stepped outside the front entrance and it appears they're hailing the rooftop sniper."

Leo froze at the sound of the voice below. "Tamerlane, Elvis is about the exit the building. Hold your position until and then join Dupin, take the van and meet us at the rendezvous point. I'm guessing you bagged that homeless dude earlier."

Leo didn't know what to do. He had no idea how the original sniper sounded or talked. He tapped the roof with the butt of his gun to hopefully let the one below know he had heard him. Seconds later he heard the door close. Prospero had stepped back inside. Leo had pulled it off flawlessly. He wiped sweat from his brow, beaming with pride as he signaled thumbs up to the others. Parnell responded with thumbs up. The others looked to Woody now, waiting for the plan.

"No need to rush this," advised Woody. "If they are about to exit, then we wait, and we'll have the advantage on them. We might be able to pick them off and minimize loses."

"Lock and load, baby," chimed in Parnell.

"Tone it down, Rambo," cautioned Woody.

"Woody, what do you think they have in mind? They can't possibly transport nearly fifty hostages," said Tim.

"Unfortunately, that's where we are at a disadvantage. We have no clue as to their motive for doing this. If any demands had been made, we'd probably have seen signs of local law enforcement by now. That tells me they're still in the dark and we're the only show in town. Malone said they warned against any law or news media being contacted."

"Given that a-hole's desertion tactics, can we really believe anything he has said. He may have concocted the entire scenario," said Parnell.

"One of my men is dead. We've taken out a sniper and we've heard shots inside. Based on those facts I'm compelled to believe Malone."

Leo, as the sniper before him, heard the ambush just a second too late. Dupin had the knife to his throat, whispering don't make a sound, or you die. The others were too preoccupied to notice. Dupin backed Leo from his position, while Prospero took his place, sniper advantage to the bad guys once again. Worst still, Prospero had scoped out the rescue team. He moved the cross hairs from one head shot to the next, counting six; seven with the one they had just captured for interrogation purposes. He motioned to Prospero, indicating six with hand signals. Dupin pushed Leo ahead of him, entering from a side entrance.

Let's Make a Deal

"Associate Pastor Garrett Moore, you are my client, indeed. It's rare that I ever actually meet those who have enlisted my services. It works much better that way for all parties concerned," whispered Valdemar.

"You weren't supposed to kill anyone, just get the money. That was the deal."

"You apparently didn't read the fine print. We have no written contract, do we? Nevertheless, it is my prerogative to deviate as necessary to ensure the mission is successive. I regret abusing you, but you played your part extremely well. Have you had previous acting experience by chance?"

"You have the ransom, more than we had agreed to, so please, don't harm anyone else."

"And this should remain our little secret, correct, Silent Partner?"

Dupin crashed through the doorway, pushing his captive ahead of him. He had Leo drop to his knees in front of Valdemar.

"You'll have to excuse me, Partner. I have more pressing matters to attend to; more spontaneity I'm afraid. Mere coincidence, doubtful," said Valdemar. "Bring the woman here too." He pointed to Summer Knight.

"Tamerlane has either been captured or is dead. There are six more just inside the wood line, all armed" stated Dupin.

"I'm in no mood for games," Valdemar said, yanking Leo to his feet. "What is your intent?"

Leo remained silent. Valdemar repeated the question, this time holding his blade to Summer Knight's throat. "Answer or be responsible for the bloodletting of this young lassie."

Leo crumpled and spilled his guts. Summer shook her head, unbelievable how quickly the spineless guard had given in and told them everything, including the skinny on Felix Malone. Valdemar released Summer and stepped face to face with Leo, smiling his approval of the snitch.

"We do seem to have quite the ensemble just itching to become unsung heroes, don't we? Detectives, an ex-detective, security guards, news personnel and a washed-up ranger. We do attract a variety pack indeed. You have been most cooperative, Leo, but playing part in Tamerlane's death is unforgivable." Using the same blood-stained knife that had ended Brady Pierce's life, he made quick work of Leo. He then glanced over at the associate pastor, giving him a courtesy shrug.

"Summer Knight, is that your stage name for the viewing audience? Do you moonlight as a Myrtle Beach pole dancer?"

Summer didn't reply.

"I'm surprised by your silence. You should be excited. You have an exclusive. Surely you must have some questions. Where's that reporter spirit?"

"Why are you doing this?"

"Ah yes. You weren't present for the opening monologue. We acquired a substantial contribution to my favorite charity, me. Our nude celebrities over there did a phenomenal job but fell a bit shy of our goal of two billion dollars."

Summer looked over at the nudist colony seated on the first pew. She recognized a few of the…faces. "So, what happens now?"

"This has been an ever-changing scenario thus far and not to my liking I assure you. Your presence and those outside have further complicated the intended outcome."

"Give it a rest, Bozo," interrupted Trudy.

"Ah, Detective Pierce, still trying to rally the troops I see. Those outside wouldn't happen to be some of your cohorts, would they? Perhaps we should open our doors and invite them inside the Lord's house, collect their tithes and offerings. Or better still, I could have Prospero dispose of them. Which is the more appropriate choice?"

"Kiss my ass, how is that for an appropriate choice?"

"While an inviting proposition, given the fact that I have previously viewed your bare bottom, Truth or Dare has expired. I choose option II. Dupin, give Prospero the signal to proceed, please."

"As for the rest of you, I have a deal to offer you that you should not refuse. Those photos, that you so graciously posed for earlier, are set to be downloaded to all the social media sites as well as news feeds. Your most prize possessions and family jewels will be seen worldwide unless you follow my explicit instructions to the letter. You must remain here for an additional hour after we leave. If any of you leave or attempt to contact the authorities, those photos will be distributed. I'm sure some of you couldn't care less. Peer pressure is suggested. As an insurance policy, because the honor system doesn't always work, Dupin and Prospero will remain behind and keep you company for a short duration. The cast of risqué flaunters shall accompany us in the limos until we have assured save passage. I have the staged nude exposé of them to launch as well to warrant against any private investigations or personal vendettas. All's well that ends well, do you not concur. Splendid."

Dupin exited the side door and was met by a crashing tree limb to his head, instantly killing the man in the mask. With cat like prowess, Malone was back on the roof, making quick work of the second sniper. He fired six quick blasts from the sniper's rifle, Woody and the others ducking for cover.

"Cracker-jack shot that Prospero, no wasted ammo," smiled Valdemar, unknowingly now down three men.

Just when Trudy thought she could sink no lower, her heart ached for her friends outside. Summer collapsed in the pew, envisioning what had just transpired, Tim and the others now dead.

The Associate Pastor, now an accomplice to these murderous ways, pounded his fist against the wall, sickening of the senseless killings. He had never intended this to be blood money. He also smelled double cross. He had seen it in Valdemar's eyes during the confessional conversation. The man had no intensions of taking his mere cut when he could have it all. Revealing his identity and connection had been a grave mistake.

Sheriff Buster Ferguson, still holding Allison's hand, perused the chapel for any opportune advantage, He saw little that rendered an opening. He'd never felt so hopelessly helpless.

Woody prepared to return fire when he spotted Malone now standing on the roof top, rifle held above his head and pointing down to the second dead sniper. He scampered off the roof and quickly joined them. Offering no excuses or explanations for his earlier departure, he quickly laid out his plan. The others listened, nodded, allowing him to once again take charge. Here were no objections from any of them. The deal had been struck. They had few precious minutes to act. Any prolonged delay of the other two men returning would tip those off inside that something had gone wrong.

Parnell whispered, "Welcome back, sir."

Till Death Do Us Part

Shots rang out prompting many in the congregation to duck in their pews, others to run. Doctor Tarr, Professor Fether and Ethelred were taken out in the first burst of gunfire. Malone, Parnell and Tim had entered from the front of the church while Woody, Drew, Dallas and Sly entered from the back. Legeia had taken refuge behind the naked celebrities. Hop-Frog had yanked the associate pastor in front of him for cover, but not before taking out Drew. Trudy quickly and intentionally positioned herself to ensure Valdemar would utilize her as a shield and he had. She had unfinished business. Six faced off against the remaining three. Legeia had regained her footing, now using world renowned cardiologist, Doctor Paula Cameron as her hostage and shield.

Valdemar, not accustomed to failures, fumed at the mere thought of anyone gaining the upper hand. "I regret using this dreadful overused line but unfortunately it is the only one appropriate. Drop your weapons or we shoot the hostages."

"Everyone, stand firm," ordered Malone.

"Ah, you must be the esteemed ex-ranger then. My compliments, you have played your hand quite well." Valdemar then shot Sheriff Buster Ferguson. Allison quickly ducked behind the pew. "Didn't see that one coming either did you, Mister Rescue Ranger? Drop your weapons or I execute my next draft pick."

"Stand firm," barked Malone.

"You are really taking this ex-ranger bravado a bit too seriously, aren't you? How many will it take to gain your attention? Hope you brought plenty of body bags to our little performance."

"Wait," interrupted Trudy. "You have me as a hostage, why not just leave."

"Thank you for being so gracious, Detective Pierce. I must clarify your role, however. You are a shield; the congregation are the hostages. I'm no negotiator." Valdemar dropped Faith. "Now, that one just tried my patience earlier, cheese crackers indeed."

"Drop your weapons, Woody, please, before more are murdered."

"As suspected, these are your friends, commendable of them to come to your aide."

"Drop your weapons," ordered Woody.

"Don't do it," countered Malone, Parnell standing his ground beside the ranger.

Detective Tim Burroughs delivered a blow to the back of Malone's head with the butt of his gun sending him face first onto the hardwood floor. Then he buried the barrel into Parnell's ribcage. "Drop it, now!" After Parnell compiled with his request, Tim dropped his to the floor.

"Well done. Newcomers, please step into the aisles and disrobe to your birthday suits please. We must have no concealed weapons. Don't be shy. The congregation has undergone this drill already."

Tim looked over at Summer, thinking he had hoped the first time would have played out differently, disrobing in her presence. Reluctantly he, as did the others, complied. Only Parnell acted indifferent, not ashamed or impacted by being naked. He stood, arms crossed and defiant, beckoning to gawkers to take a long hard look if they liked. Others attempted to cover the best they could with their hands and arms.

"Join the nudist colony to your left please," Valdemar motioned. Ligeia, the cardiologist in tow, joined Valdemar and Hop-Frog up front, each maintaining their shields, the associate pastor and Trudy. Hop-frog was then delegated to confiscate the weapons.

"We shall be leaving momentarily. Please observe the device that I am placing here on the alter. It contains explosives, enough to flatten this wonderfully old nostalgic church. I will activate it as we make our retreat. Be forewarned that it is both sound and motion sensitive. I can disarm it remotely once I feel we have substantially distanced ourselves from this location. Those who foolishly think they can exit or disarm the mechanism to avoid the big boom theory, please heed my warning. You have mere seconds to react before it delivers the final curtain call. That is, if I am being truthful. Somehow, I don't envision a complete evacuation occurring within that timeframe, do you? Sure, a few might make it unscathed, but most will perish. Consider and exercise brotherly love for thy neighbor before making poor choices. Ta-ta for now and I do appreciate your due diligence and hospitality this afternoon. Regretfully I apologize for crashing the wedding, Mister Morrissey and Miss Whittaker. Keep in mind, I do have some explicit pre-wedding photographs that the paparazzi would die for."

Valdemar opted to backtrack and utilize the secured golf course next door. The limos would be too easily identified. Their van would not. The fools should stay put to allow them plenty of time to make the interstate and travel at a normal speed down 95 towards Jacksonville, Florida. There they would board a cruise ship as mere tourist, destination, Ochoa Rios. No one would suspect a getaway on board the Sensation. Trudy pretended to be a model hostage, shield or whatever. She'd pick her time to take him out. Luckily, they had not restrained any of them yet, guns pressed to their backs as a constant reminder though.

"I'm one of you," whispered Associate Pastor Garrett Moore to Hop-Frog. "Check with Valdemar if you don't believe me. I arranged it and subcontracted the venture." Moore didn't want this Hop-Frog guy to do something foolish. He just hoped he believed him.

Doctor Paula Cameron had difficulty maneuvering the terrain, thorny plants ripping at her skin and sharp objects lacerating the bottoms of her feet. She had not been allowed to retrieve any clothing. Ligeia pushed her along, not tolerant of her handicap or its painful results. Those inside the church remained quiet and motionless, mere seconds from certain oblivion.

The Five Second Rule

Allison hovered over Buster Ferguson. The sheriff was still breathing but was in bad need of medical assistance. She comforted him the best she could, concealed behind the second-row pew. Others of the congregation whispered to one another while trying to remain as motionless as possible. Front and center, shoulder to shoulder, less than six feet from the explosive device, stood Malone, Woody, Parnell, Sly, Tim and Dallas. Tim envisioned somewhere behind them, Summer Knight getting an eyeful of his backside. At least she hadn't been pegged for this most embarrassing moment. A man thing, Tim shifted his eyes, comparing and assessing the other men, hoping Summer viewed him objectively. Odd to be thinking such thoughts but Tim had always suffered from self-esteem issues. IQ didn't always counter for anatomically proportioned inadequacies.

Felix Malone, wheels turning, contemplated how he could disarm the bomb or at least remove the explosives from the church to minimize the causalities. Precious seconds allowed little time to snatch it up and reach an exit. Parnell was just plain itching for a fight. He was so excited thinking about it, almost too excited, his excitement becoming all too noticeable in his exposed state. He couldn't control it and presently wouldn't be able to conceal it either. Woody did what Woody always did, rethink the situation and second guess his decisions. He should have called this in and let it be someone else's headache. Sly tried to rationalize the circumstances. The current circumstances hampered his thought process. Dallas blocked out the world and focused on profiling the leader.

Malone assessed that at least ten minutes had expired. Ten precious minutes could be just enough of a head start to ensure a successful escape. Waiting was not cutting it but too many lives hung in the balance to act irrationally. He mentally calculated the distance he could cover in five or so seconds. No matter how many times he tried, he could see no way of clearing the church before the device detonated. The leader had said there were enough explosives to level the church. If he could shift the center point, possibly the damage could be minimized. Not knowing what type of explosives, he was dealing with posed an insurmountable problem. Before he could finalize his plan, a voice broke the silence.

Wounded and woozy headed, Faith pulled herself to a standing position, "What happened? What did I miss?" Motion and sound…

That did it, decision made. Malone raced for the device, scooped it up, the display already counting down from ten, not five. Realizing this was a death sentence he ran as fast as he could towards the back exit. He shouldered the door. It didn't budge. He fumbled with the locks. The locks weren't the issue. The door was barricaded from the outside. Three seconds…Mighty Malone plunged headfirst through a mural side window. Before his body crashed to the ground the explosion obliterated the ranger, along with the back portion of the old church. It had been as powerful as Valdemar had described.

Smoldering debris strewn about covered the screaming and moaning souls. The pulpit, piano and organ were gone, as was Reverend Jonah Blackwood, nowhere in sight. That section of church no more. When Malone had bolted, so had Woody and the others realizing what was about to happen. Too many in the congregation hadn't. The rafters and walls were miraculously in tack in the back two thirds, all widows blown out, and the first half dozen pews toppled. Bloodied and battered bodies began to emerge from the rubble.

Still naked as the day he arrived in this world, Woody assisted those nearest to him. He located Dallas, bleeding profusely from the side of her head but alert. Tim had found his singed clothing and had slipped on his pants before seeking out Summer. She was pinned under a pew with several others but was alive. Those on top of her had not fared so well. One would later be identified as Franco Morrissey, the other, Ex-governor Marcus McDonald. Fortunately, they would be the only two causalities besides the Reverend still missing and the Mighty Malone.

Sly had located a cell phone and had called it in, too little, too late. He requested ambulances and additional back-up and explained the perils still yet to be faced. He then located Allison, her body shielding Sheriff Buster Ferguson, both breathing but unconscious. He tended to them, hopeful the ambulances would be here soon. Faith looked about, nursing her non-life-threatening gunshot wound, still asking anyone around her that would listen what had happened?

After assessing the situation, Woody and Parnell, too unlikely partners, had clothed themselves as best they could and although unarmed, had taken up pursuit. A stone's throw away from the church they had located an assortment of abandoned weapons. They retrieved a small arsenal and readied themselves for combat. Two against three seemed much better odds. Hostages did pose a problem though. He counted on the predictable, the unpredictable Trudy Wagner. She'd not welcome her hostage situation with open arms. First chance she would make this scoundrel pay, hell or high water; he knew his ex-partner, she'd find a way.

Blue Light Special

Valdemar had not been surprised by the explosion behind them. The odds had never been in the favor of those inside. As anticipated, motion or sound would do them in easily. It had been all too predictable. What did trouble him however was the sound of approaching rescue and law enforcement vehicles, the sirens announcing their presence. Gambling making it to the van might be a bad move now. They had reserved the golf course for a private function to ensure it would be closed to the public. Upon arrival they had neutralized the staff. While there would be no one at the clubhouse to thwart their escape route, Valdemar could not help but be concerned that the authorities would block off the roadways leading in and out. The carnage from the explosion should preoccupy the rescuers, providing there were no survivors to set them straight.

"Not as you envisioned it, I assume," said a sarcastic Trudy Wagner Pierce.

"Minor technicality I assure you, Detective. We shall proceed as planned."

"You're screwed, and you know it."

"I feel your pain. Sadly, our renowned cardiologist cannot mend your broken heart. Your beloved Brady is gone my dear but be brave. Take away something positive. I carry his legacy sporting these knickers and he no longer suffers from his illness."

"You carry nothing but a death sentence around your neck."

"Cynical, it aptly becomes you."

"I hope you have an heir, one who can aptly enjoy the money you have stolen."

"You are a feisty one, aren't you, Detective Pierce."

"Facts, I deal in facts and fact is your ass belongs to me and only me, sooner or later, one way or another and that is a promise not a threat masked man."

Valdemar placed his blade underneath Trudy's chin. "One thrust and face facts. Your quest for vengeance will be no more."

Trudy placed her hand on top of his. "Save the theatrics for someone who gives a shit, Shakespeare. This isn't my first rodeo on the hostage circuit."

Valdemar applied pressure, the point pricked her chin, just enough to draw blood. Trudy could feel the warmth trickling down her neck. With the fingers of her other hand, she touched the blood, coating her index finger and thumb, and then she applied it to Valdemar's masked lips.

He responded by licking his plastic lips through a slot in the mask and smiling underneath it. "Death has never tasted sweeter. The tongue, like a sharp knife, kills without drawing blood."

"Red marks the spot. Val, take that to the bank, you, sick bastard."

Ligeia stepped forth and placed her hand on top of Trudy's. "Please end it. Time is slipping, Valdemar."

Valdemar chuckled loudly and then snatched the knife away from both women. "In due time. Let's proceed to the clubhouse. Our chariot awaits us there."

With Ligeia momentarily distracted, Doctor Paula Cameron did the unthinkable, she bolted. Assistant Pastor Garrett Moore promptly tripped her, sending her face first to the ground. Trudy from her position hadn't seen the interference maneuver. Hop-Frog delivered a boot to the cardiologist's ribcage and then yanked her to her feet by her hair.

"Naughty now, aren't we," said Valdemar, motioning for Ligeia to watch Trudy as he approached the nude unruly doctor.

"Don't do it," warned Trudy.

"Naughtiness must not go unpunished. Work ethics and reputation restoration are pertinent in these situations."

"Hostages are no good dead," warned Trudy.

"Did I imply death, Detective? Don't judge me for past discretions. Diversity can be most effective."

"Then punish me, not her. I provided the distraction."

"A valiant offer," replied Valdemar as he backhanded Trudy and then buried his blade into Paula Cameron's chest. "Being predictably unpredictable is an art form overlooked. The doctor's fate has succumbed to a heartfelt ending. Humor brings insight and tolerance. Irony brings a deeper and less friendly understanding. I think that you can fall into bad habits with comedy. It's a tightrope to stay true to the character, true to the irony, and allow the irony to happen. Ben Kingsley never spoke truer words. Two hostages shall suffice."

Sirens blared from the property next door. Blue lights could be seen flashing ahead in the parking lot of the golf course. The getaway van was no longer an option. Ligeia was tempted to scorn Valdemar for wasting so much valuable time but it would be a moot point at this juncture. Even she knew better than to rile him further. He had sunk into one of his darkest moods, the depths of which could not be reasoned with or rationalized. She had witnessed this behavior far too many times, as had Hop-Frog. His thirst for bloodletting could not be deterred. There was nothing to do but go with the flow and allow it to run its course; and hopefully it wouldn't lead them down a path they'd all regret later.

"Boxed in, run rabbit run," smiled Trudy, blood trickling from an open gash on her lip delivered by Valdemar's backhand.

"You will find peace not by trying to escape your problems, but by confronting them courageously. You will find peace not in denial, but in victory...J. Donald Walters, internationally known author, lecturer and composer; widely recognized as one of the world's foremost authorities on meditation and yoga. Do you engage in yoga, Detective Pierce?"

"You will find death becomes you, asshole...Trudy Wagner-Pierce...detective, vengeful wife, widow, grim reaper for all those pretending to be Edgar Allen Poe characters."

"Your wit and sarcasm are indeed your best assets. I shall miss them both once the journey has ended."

"Not to worry, I shall recite something quite witty and sarcastic at your funeral. I get dibs on the first shovel full for your hole in the ground. Isn't it about time you removed those stupid idiotic Halloween masks? It's easier when I can place a face to the stiff."

"Valdemar, please cease all this senseless dialogue. Perils await us at every turn. Can't you see she is only baiting you, delaying our departure?"

"Of course, I do, my dear Ligeia. Don't take me for a fool. Flashing lights and sirens, the mere implication of pursuit and capture enhance the suspense and build to a climatic final act. It is what I live for..."

"And die for...dishonorable mention among the rolling credits, a-hole..."

"Very well...that way," he pointed. "Lead us to salvation Hop-Frog."

Act III

"Four carts, all accounted for," stated Woody. "They're still on foot."

"But which way," asked Parnell.

"There's nothing but swamp and water tributaries in that direction, so I'd guess the golf course clubhouse. That's the way they got in, so they must have transportation for a way out."

"I don't get it then. Why didn't they take the carts?"

"Maybe it offered too much exposure, open ground."

"It would still have been faster than hoofing it with hostages. I say screw it, let's take a couple, we can split up, cover more territory and a hell of a lot quicker."

"Providing we don't make ourselves sitting ducks; maybe they're baiting us for that very thing."

"Hell, my bet, they won't be looking for anyone to follow. They had to have heard the damn explosion, game over as far as they must be concerned."

"You take one then, follow the cart path and backtrack the golf course. "I'll take the direct approach to the clubhouse, but I'm doing it on foot. Hopefully one of us will be lucky if the Georgetown troopers sealed off the road in time to box them in. Don't do anything foolish, Roberts. Don't you dare put those hostages in any kind of jeopardy. I mean it."

"I'm not a damn rookie. I can handle what is shoveled out. Besides, these guys can't be too damn swift, look how they have botched this thing up so far."

"No one wants them any worse than me. I've lost two men and a dear friend, but underestimating might get you killed, Roberts. These are not fly by night criminals. The situation might have been an entirely different outcome if not for Malone stumbling into it."

"Never shall I fail my comrades, the ranger creed. He saved us while sacrificing his ass."

"He was a ranger. You're not. Keep that in mind before you go all hero to zero, cowboy."

Parnell just rolled his eyes. This was his fight to win. He'd do whatever it took to bring them down, hostages or no hostages. He was feeling it. He was born for this very moment. He would show the world he was every bit as qualified as any special opts personnel. Rowdy Roberts kicked ass. He saved the taking names for those less qualified. Woody Anderson was just a washed-up cop. He didn't take his marching orders from a man that couldn't take the heat, one that had resigned from the police force to be a damn watchman. He checked his inventory of weapons. He had more than enough fire power to do the job.

Woody skirted the cart path, just inside the tree line, cautiously making his way towards the clubhouse. This Parnell Roberts was potentially a loose cannon. Hindsight, he probably should never have allowed the detective to venture out alone. He could be a serious liability if he caught up with them first. Either way, he didn't have tight reins on him. His read, this guy was going to do what he wanted, when and how he wanted, hell or high water. Woody had been there too many times in recent years, being caught up in renegade mode. That's why he had opted out of the police force, a job he had so thoroughly loved. He could no longer count on himself abiding strictly by policy and law. He had crossed that line one too many times. He had even allowed it to cloud his judgment in this fiasco. He should have called it in, but old habits die hard.

Woody kept the cart path in sight as he slowly but meticulously approached the club house. It was in view now, but his cover was running out. He was so focused on his target he almost stumbled over the bloody body of the nude female lying face down. He took a deep breath and then rolled her over. It was the cardiologist and not Wagner thankfully. He instantly regretted thinking that. Still, why had they decided to murder a hostage? It just didn't add up. Nothing about this case added up. Were there no more text book crimes and criminals? From the road rage serial killings to now, the bad guys had tossed their playbook, making and breaking new rules of engagement. It made it tough for the good guys to decipher the patterns, the usual signs and motives. A new breed of lawbreakers had crashed onto the scene.

Eyeing the clubhouse for any signs, Woody prepared to make his jaunt across open territory. The next hundred or so yards would offer no cover if they were holed up in the clubhouse and watching their backside. Taking a deep breath, he sprinted as fast as he could, zigzagging hopefully making him a less easy target to hit. He cleared the distance with no shots fired, his back against the clubhouse, catching his breath. Either they hadn't seen him, weren't in the clubhouse, or didn't want to alert anyone with any unnecessary gunfire. Woody was thankful of any of the possible scenarios. While determining his best route of entry something caught his attention, movement from the corner of his eye. Focusing he didn't see anything at first but then there it was again, reflecting in the sunlight. It was them; one of their weapons had given away their route. He just caught a glimpse of them disappearing into the woods near the end of the first fairway.

Woody briefly hesitated, tempted to go inside and call the troopers. No, he couldn't gamble away those precious moments; not when he had them in his sight. Besides, the direction they were heading might bring them in contact with Roberts. He had to get to them before Mister Gung-ho did. Woody decided to opt for one of the electric powered golf carts this time to close the distance. He'd hug the far side of the fairway to at least offer some concealment. He hoped for the best but expected the worst. These were vicious and unpredictable foes. Killing meant absolutely nothing to them. Pierce was his ace in the hole. She'd not go down without a fight.

Detective Parnell Roberts motored up the cart path of the third hole, a par 3. A scorecard clipped to the steering wheel provided the perfect layout. It indicated he had a par 5 and a par 4 between him and the clubhouse. He had seen nothing but an abundance of Canadian Geese and huge grey fox squirrels along his route. He had slowed down and had taken evasive action, had altered his route so as not to stir the flock of geese. Honking geese would have been the kiss of death, alerting anyone close by of his approach. Parnell sped up the number two fairway, attempting to make up for the detour. The crosshairs rested on his temple making him an easy target. Parnell wasn't a golfer. He drove directly onto and over the number one green. The crosshair followed his progress, but no gunshot broke the silence. To do so would divulge their location. Parnell never knew just how close he had come to being just another token cadaver.

Hop-Frog lowered his scope and then picked up his pace to join the others. Ligeia and Valdemar herded Trudy and Garrett Moore along just in front of them. They no longer followed the golf course, the terrain becoming much thicker and more treacherous. Twice already Trudy had caught the telltale sign of something slithering through the brush and out of their way. Rattlers, cottonmouths and copperheads were common venomous snakes in the area. Brady had killed a large copperhead near their backdoor this spring. She had almost stepped on it. It struck but luckily, she had been wearing high top sneakers and not flip-flops or it would have most certainly struck pay dirt.

Garret Moore willingly played up his role as a defenseless hostage. He couldn't drop the ruse in the presence of the detective. He wanted his lion share of the ransom free and clear, and no part of being identified as an accomplice, especially not with all the murders that had been committed. Unfortunately, he was presently at the mercy of the masked Valdemar. All the money had been transferred to an unknown account. Keeping Valdemar alive was of the utmost importance. Stumbling aimlessly about in the swamplands did concern him. Obviously, all contingencies had been exhausted. They were winging their escape. Sadly, he didn't know any more about the lay of the land here than did those with the weapons. His footing had become increasingly more unstable, the ground almost squishing underneath his feet. They were traveling deeper into swampy conditions, never more evident than by the swarming gnats and mosquitoes.

Garret stepped into a spot and mired up to his knee. He came to a screeching halt, the muck holding him in place like quicksand. Ligeia pushed at him with the barrel of her gun. He pointed to his leg but that didn't prevent her from nudging him even harder. He pointed again, telling her he was stuck in the murky gunk. She held up her hand signaling those behind her to stop. Hop-Frog had caught back up with them and took the point. He pulled Moore free and then pushed him to the left, altering their direction. Within twenty more yards they were all splashing forward in brackish water quickly reaching to their thighs. Open swamp lay ahead as far as the eye could see. A huge cottonmouth slithered into the water to their right no more than two paces away. It swam away instead of toward them.

Valdemar nudged Trudy, the gun barrel digging into the nap of her back. She gave him 'The Look'. He responded with an evil eye and concealed smile, her stare having no impact. He was tiring of the relentless and ever deepening wetlands, but he would never reveal this to the others. One can never be perceived as weak. Weakness equated vulnerability and lack of leadership. No such traits existed in his perfect world. The humidity was taking its toll on them underneath their masks but at the same time it offered welcome relief from the onslaught of insects buzzing relentlessly.

Trudy was forever thinking, scheming, determined she would make the man behind the mask pay dearly for murdering Brady. There was no place for this bastard in the judicial system. An entire congregation had witnessed his crimes, guilty your honor, death sentence issued and guaranteed. He'd not have the luxury of a tedious trial or humane death sentence, not if she had anything to do with it. There would be no electric chair, lethal injections, firing squad or a hangman's noose. Trudy would not allow this bastard to idle on death row for twenty years. She wanted to administer a slow and torturous death to him, make him suffer, look into his eyes, see his face as he gasped for his last breath. She should be disturbed by these thoughts. She wasn't, not even close. Hungering to be his executioner kept her going, alive and more determined than ever to make good on her promise to Brady and to herself.

Detective Trudy Wagner Pierce had always been pegged as the one damned and determined to color outside the lines. This time she would be crossing a line no police person was supposed to cross, sworn to an oath to enforce and uphold the letter of the law. Woody had it right. Screw this profession. It was thankless and besides the crooks didn't play by the rules. Why should she be handcuffed by them too? She would be doing mankind a favor, ridding the world of a creature that should never have existed in it in the first place.

Judge and jury, maybe she would just go rogue and become a crusader taking out the garbage, saving the taxpayer, a vigilante force to be reckoned with like *Charles Bronson* in those *Death Wish* movies. No, she had no aspirations of becoming a super hero, an avenging angel, living a double life, fighting crime by her rules. She had only one mission and when she had completed it, she would face whatever consequences resulted. This time her priorities were spot on. The fate of family justified her actions. Reality seeped into her thoughts; the explosion…her sister…was Allison okay? What about Woody and the others? This just fueled her rage and justified her pending actions. At this moment she fully understood just what had pushed people like Tim Ford and Joe Preston over the edge, avenging their loses, road rage unleashed. Obsession and revenge were powerful motivators for cruel intentions.

"Haven't you tired of all this sloshing about, masked man?" She stopped in her tracks, time to toss a monkey wrench in this traveling freak show.

"Detective Pierce, I must give you credit, you are the constant wise ass, aren't you, even under the most deplorable conditions."

"Hey, I say if you can't make life fun…but seriously, this is over, and you know it. There is no escape in your future, hostages or not. You don't even have a clue where you're heading. Trust me when I say this; these swamps are no place for a rambling man. YOU continue playing with fire, YOU will get burned eventually."

"You must learn to exercise patience. My success rate speaks volumes, 100% guaranteed presently."

"I get it. You murder and steal for a living. So what? The best always stumbles sooner or later, and the law gets their man. Your time has arrived, Poe. Convince yourself all you want otherwise, but the scales are tipping in my favor every second you remain on the run and lost in this dangerous swamp. One misdirection here or there and we wander about in this glorious landscape for days, or until death do us part."

 "Death do us part has already become your mantra, hasn't it, Detective? To be determined if you are the better half, I suppose."

The fire inside of Trudy hit the boiling point with that last little zinger but like the commercial goes, never let them see you sweat. "Tick tock, eye on the clock, we're approaching the two-minute warning and you're down by two touchdowns. A Hail Mary will not ensure you of a 'W', too little, too late, little man."

"Football analogies, I applaud you. Remember, Sudden Death awaits you."

"Keep your eye on the highlight reel; it ain't over until it's over."

"Now baseball, Yogi Berra. How quaint. Yogi's Mets trailed the Chicago Cubs by 9 ½ games in July 1973 when he spoke that gem. His Mets rallied to win the division on the final day of the season. Do you know any other Yogi-isms, Detective? One of my favorites...*I really didn't say everything I said.*"

Trudy shrugged, uninterested in most of what came from her captor's mouth. Then again, keeping him distracted and engaged might offer her an opportunity to catch him off guard. "*You can observe a lot by watching.*"

"Nice Yogi-ism, Detective. Are you originally from the New York region?"

"Southern Belle but I lived in Ohio for a while before returning to my roots."

"*Lawdie*, an exclamation frequently used by the southern persuasion; did you know that *Lawdie* was Yogi's nickname, derived from his mother's difficultly pronouncing his God-given name correctly, Lawrence or Larry?"

"Lawdie no Mister Poe, say it ain't so."

"Two more of my favorites and quite appropriate given the current affairs, '*You can observe a lot by watching*' and '*Always go to other people's funerals, otherwise they won't go to yours.*'

"Valdemar, I fear the detective has bewitched you. We must focus our attention on escaping this gosh awful environment"

"Indeed, he's been smitten by me, southern charm conquers all, Ligeia or whoever the hell you really are...jealous, are we?"

"Move along, Detective Pierce. While I do enjoy the volleying, I'm not blind to these obvious attempts to delay our progress. We can converse as we walk, or slosh as you have so eloquently noted," interrupted Val.

"Truth...tell me something about the man behind the mask."

"Ordinary...chameleon...perfect for blending in a crowd...a police line-up's nightmare...has served me well in my chosen profession."

"So, you chose to be a murderer and a thief; couldn't cut it in an honest man's shoes?"

"Dishonesty, no my dear, I deal in deception. As for the murdering, it's just a mere by-product of my services. I am and have never been a hired assassin. Those positions are a dime a dozen. For the right price anyone can be employed to commit murder. Those who specialize avoid apprehension. I am good at what I do. I set the benchmark. I raise the bar for all who strive to fill my shoes. My reputation speaks volumes."

"You were hired to do this?"

"Indeed, contractual obligations apply."

"Who would hire you do something so despicable?"

Valdemar chuckled loudly. "Despicable indeed, *all religion, my friend, is simply evolved out of fraud, fear, greed, imagination, and poetry*, Edgar Allen Poe; greed is the inventor justice as well as the current enforcer; lust and greed are more gullible than innocence, Detective Pierce."

"Must you always speak in riddles and quotes?"

"Very well, the child's game…you are getting warm and are closer to the truth than you could ever conceive."

Trudy scanned the remaining three. Two were murderers. The third…unbelievable… '*All* **religion** *is simply evolved out of fraud, fear, greed, imagination, and poetry.*' "

"You bastard…why?"

Garrett Moore ignored her comments, never turned to face her, and just trudged along in the wetlands. He wasn't about to confess his part in this ever-growing catastrophe. Sure, he wanted his money but until they were safe and secure from the long arm of the law, he would continue to play the part of the hostage, even for the audience of one. He figured sooner or later Valdemar would tidy up loose ends. The detective would be of little value once they had successfully escaped. He had played his role to perfection, chameleon like too. No one would ever suspect an associate pastor as being involved, one who had been beaten and taken hostage. Regrets, sure; no one should have been killed. Clear conscious, there were no blood stains on his hands. He had not committed murder, nor had he granted permission to murder anyone. He certainly hadn't known anything about the drug lord's connection to Valdemar's sister. *I'm innocent on all counts, Your Honor.*

The Defiant Ones

Woody Anderson and Parnell Roberts stood at the edge of the swampland. The trail they had been following abruptly ended at the brackish water's edge. Nature had all but consumed the route. Parnell had a bit of bloodhound in him but trailing a bleeding and mortally wounded deer offered hope to the hunter. Here he had nothing. Neither conversing, they each widened their search pattern, looking for any signs to indicate which direction the others had taken. Occasionally they eyed one another. Woody wanted to proceed with caution. Parnell wanted to simply proceed and engage, a challenger itching for a gun fight to prove he was the fastest gun in the east.

Unlikely partners at best, similarities to the 1958 movie classic, *The Defiant Ones*, existed. Sure, they weren't shackled together, nor were one white and the other black, as depicted by *Tony Curtis* and *Sidney Poitier*, two escaped prisoners, but similarities existed. To be successful they must learn to cooperate with one another. The warden in the movie would be saying right about now, '*don't look too hard as they will probably kill each other in the first five miles.*' Both were pigheaded, but their different approaches and assessments hadn't evolved to physical blows, at least not yet. It still resembled a schoolyard competition. Toss teamwork out the window for now.

"You're stirring up too much crap, Roberts. We'll never find their trail if you don't stop trampling down the surrounding vegetation."

"It beats having both thumbs up my butt. You couldn't cut it as lawman, so you opted out. Leave the crime scene investigation to the experts. Remember you called us when you got in over your head."

"Don't hang that on me. I didn't call you, wise guy. I enlisted the help of friends. You might want to hold your voice down, Deputy Dog. Did they not teach you that in obedience training? By the way, I have bent reeds over here. Lucky for me you haven't destroyed it already. They went that way."

"I'm not familiar with these parts, but instinct tells me that will take us deeper into the swamp."

"Who said they know where they are going anymore than you do?"

"Why don't you go back to the church and point the Calvary in this direction? I'll dog them without you, Mister Has Been."

"That's all I need on my hands, losing them and YOU in this swamp."

"What's the matter, you can't backtrack your ass out of here, boy?"

"I've seen your type. You'll screw up a wet dream. I'm going this way. You do whatever the hell you want to do, Cowboy. I warn you one last time you'll answer to me if you botch this up and get them killed."

"Old farts like you are dinosaurs. Good thing you up and quit before they put your ass out to pasture. You're lucky they didn't lock your ass up with all that crap you pulled with those two high profile cases."

"When this is over, this old fart is going to teach you some manners. Respect thy elders, you son of a bitch."

Woody turned away and headed in the direction he felt most confident. Parnell refused to follow in his footsteps but moved in the general direction, fanning out and looking for his own signs. Neither was equipped with the shoes or clothing suitable for negotiating the swamp. The relentless buzz of gnats and mosquitoes deafened their sense of hearing. Both were too macho to slap at the blood thirsty predators, at least not in view of each other. The further they ventured into the swampland, the more convinced Woody became that he had again made a terrible decision. It wasn't his job. He wasn't the law and certainly wasn't accountable for crimes in Georgetown County. Still, this had blown up on his watch and he felt accountable to a certain extent. Plus, Pierce was out there somewhere, heaven help those murderers. With no radio or cell phone the burden had never weighed heavier.

To make matters worse he had to deal with this foul-mouthed redneck yahoo. He would most certainly screw this up for everyone. Malone had been able to keep him in check. This boy had no respect for him, so it appeared, ignoring his years of police experience. Woody wasn't sure why Roberts had such a hard-on, but he recognized the type, headstrong, bulletproof and ready to make a name for themselves. He had busted their balls many times and he'd find a way to take him down a notch or two eventually.

Woody had this eerie feeling of being watched. It wasn't like him to have a case of the jitters. Maybe he was just rusty. No, he trusted his instincts. Trusting and reacting to them kept you alive on the job. Alive on the job, alive on the police force maybe; but he was no longer on the force, as the smartass bubba had pointed out. Nope. Like riding a bicycle, you don't forget this crap.

You went with your gut. His gut quickly warned him this was a hell of a predicament. These bastards were more ruthless and deadlier than any he had ever encountered. They didn't blink an eye when it came to murder. Look what they had done to Brady Pierce. His stomach soured just thinking about how Allison had described what had happened. The fuse had been lit. It would just be a matter of time before Wagner exploded. He sure hoped his ex-partner picked her spot wisely.

"I got something over here," said Parnell.

Woody sloshed over to where Parnell was crouched. He pointed to a strip of cloth hanging from the cattails. The sliver of fabric wasn't weather worn. It was fresh, and it had been planted. It dawned on him. It was the color Pierce had been wearing. Gretel was leaving them bread crumbs. Woody confirmed this with Parnell but refused to give him an official 'attaboy'. The little smirk on Parnell's face told him the detective took liberty to accept one just the same.

They were indeed heading deeper into the swamp. Woody didn't confirm Parnell's suspicions on this either. Partners didn't have to vocalize every little finding. Partners…Woody choked on that thought. Soon they discovered a second sign, another piece of her clothing. Reality, she couldn't flaunt this much longer, or her captors would take note. Woody knew it, as did Parnell. They'd have to close the gap quickly, before the trail went cold again.

Parnell broke the silence. "Why did you do it?"

"Do what?"

"Up and quit the force instead of retiring and drawing your pension. You could have retired on a sheriff's if you would have just stuck it out."

"I had to do what was right for me…my family."

"I read what happened to your wife, what that road rage serial killer Joe Preston did. That must have been tough."

"I don't really want to talk about that."

"Got it. Sorry for being so nosey, the detective in me I reckon."

"I know you're not a rookie but let me give you some advice. There is a fine line between doing what you've sworn you will uphold and doing what your gut sometimes tells you is the right thing to do. Take it from one who knows, they're miles apart in a lot of situations. You cross over that line too far and it's tough to find your way back. You know where the line is all right, but too often it's easier to do what feels right than to do the right thing according to the book. The letter of the law is just that, not much wiggle room and certainly no place for convenient interpretation."

"Is that why you quit, you took it too far?"

"I know the difference between right and wrong, no matter how blurred it might seem. I don't care how you want to spin it, taking matters into your own hands, circumventing protocol and justifying your actions for something as simple as revenge is wrong. Some can live with that fact providing that in the end the job gets done. Live by the sword, die by the sword. Good intentions often turn sour. It's a dice roll at best. Gambling just wasn't my thing. I had ventured too far off the beaten path and I just didn't have what it took to right the injustices. I didn't take any bribes or do anything along those lines. I just did what it took to solve the case and catch the bad guys. Bending rules didn't seem so bad as long as we got our man."

"So where does that put us now?"

"It puts you at the crossroads. You're a cop. I'm not. You're held to higher standards than me right now. I can choose to color outside the lines, but you better choose wisely. I had no business asking any of you to come here, to circumvent the system and play rescue rangers. I put your asses on the line, not mine. Detective Wagner…Pierce is my ex-partner and my dear friend. These bastards held her and her husband, her sister and these innocent folks' hostage. They murdered Brady Pierce and others for what…money? They did that under my watch. I have no choice in this. You do. Walk away. Let me handle this. That's pretty much it, Detective Roberts."

"I reckon I crossed that damn line when I decided to come here. Nobody twisted my arm. Sure, I got caught up in the adrenalin rush, especially when I recognized Malone. I'm a sucker for a good fight. I always fight to win, can't remember the last time I lost one. Fairness is for losers. That's my superior officer they held hostage and shot up back there. Let's go catch or kill the bad guys. Hell, it doesn't make much difference to me one way or the other. I'm too friggin far in this to give much of a damn anyway. I can promise you one thing; however, this shakes out, I won't be dropping my weapons next time. They'll have to pry 'um from my cold dead hands after I've busted loose on'um."

"Well partner, it sounds like it's time for us to go kick some butt then."

"I'm right behind you, Sheriff."

"Sheriff my ass, I don't need no stinking badge for this one."

The thunderous crack brought down a world of hurt. Woody plunged face first into the swampy waters. Detective Parnell Roberts splashed some ten feet behind him, launched backwards by the impact of the sheer force and velocity of the rifle's bullet. He was dead before he landed in the watery grave. Woody's gut had been 'spot on' as always. They were being watched. Hunkering down was his only defense from the sniper. Hop-Frog eyed his view finder, ready to align his next shot.

Woody remained as low as possible, taking in enough water to guarantee a bout of dysentery, that is, if the next bullet didn't take him out first. How had they been so careless, allowing those ahead to wait in ambush? Both men had been convinced escape had been their priority, tossing caution to the wind. Parnell lay dead and Woody didn't exactly like his odds of faring better. He and Parnell were just bonding and just like that, it was over. Mourning the dead man served no purpose right now. There would be a time for that later, that is if he survived.

To better his position and hopefully conceal his location, Woody began crawling towards a stand of cypress and reeds, pulling himself along the bottom with his hands. He resembled an alligator. That thought put him on high alert, especially with Parnell's bloody corpse ringing the dinner bell. These waters were infested with gators, huge gators. While he couldn't ever remember any attacking people, people didn't usually venture on foot this deeply into swamps. They certainly didn't crawl around on their belly offering up opportune easy prey to the giant aquatic lizards. Gators or a bullet, pick your poison. He probably had a better chance wrestling a gator.

Woody made it to his destination with no more shots being fired. What did that mean? Had the sniper moved on or was he just waiting for another clear shot? Possibly the shooter was moving in for the kill. While simply laying here momentarily offered him hope, staying here forever was not a viable option. Sprinting in sucking muck offers an easy target for a blind man. Crawling about, while safer, isn't exactly the best plan either. Woody was screwed either way.

He still had weapons and ammunition, if he hadn't ruined both while exposing them to the water during his wetland's belly crawl. Military style guns were supposed to be designed to survive the elements, better so than him. Woody decided to chance a peek, but peek at what? The sniper could be anywhere, perusing the perimeter with his scope. He turtle-necked a slow look but could see very little of the surrounding landscape hugging the ground like a log. Luckily, he drew no gunfire. Again, what did that really mean?

Woody eyed another spot, maybe forty yards away. It appeared to be a patch of denseness, spindly trees and brush, possibly even a small island, solid ground if that was possible out here. Should he chance it and by chance, he meant run for it. Crawling would take too long. Not crawling might end it quickly. He opted to crawl, not ready to concede just yet. He had those rug rats that still counted on him being around to take care of them. Just as he started to pull himself along, he paused and cocked his head. What was he hearing? Something or somebody was moving towards his location. The sloshing was quite noisy.

The shooter or shooters must be confident that they had the upper hand. They weren't even attempting to mask their approach. It was judgment time. Should he stay put and fire when they were close enough or should he act on impulse, catch them off guard and spring to his feet, automatic weapons blazing? Obviously, they would be in ready fire mode regardless of what actions he decided to take. To hell with it, he decided to time it and spring into action.

Death approached him from behind. He turned to position himself for its arrival. Too late, there they were, less than ten feet away, silhouetted in the blinding sun. Indecision had cost him dearly. He was in no position to fire at will. Taking a deep breath, Woody Anderson prepared to meet his maker. A gambit of memories flashed through his head; those of happy times with Janice and the kids, life on the force before and after Trudy Wager's arrival, that big old bear of a man, Sheriff Hank Singleton, and of all people, Lance Rocker, that sorry bastard. He closed his eyes and readied for the death sentence. Second thought leap up Woody and try to get off a few shots.

"Is he dead?"

"Eyes are closed, can't tell from here."

"I'm living and breathing but y'all better get your asses down. Sniper has already taken out Roberts."

"The view is crappy down here."

"Glad to see you boys. How are things shaping up back at the church?"

"Total chaos," replied Sly.

"State troopers are blocking off all access roads to this area. They're bringing in a chopper," added Tim Burroughs. "This is Deputy Kyle Roswell and that's Officer Parker Huffman."

"Do you have a bead on the gunman," asked Roswell.

"Not hardly, but he took out Roberts with one clean shot. I've been snaking along ever since."

"The shooter must have vamoosed, or we would be dead meat too," added Huffman.

"You're probably right," replied Woody.

"I say we go catch the bad guys then," Huffman stood, tempting fate. Fate didn't kill him, so the others followed suit.

Swamp Fox Players

"There were two, now there's just one," reported Hop-Frog. "I don't think he'll be too eager to follow us."

"Let's find a way out of this dreadful marshland then," said Valdemar.

"You're screwed, and you know it. They're onto you. Face it, your little drama is over."

"Detective Pierce, you forget, you are my bargaining chip."

"You've murdered too many for me to be worth much on the bargaining table. I'd wave the white flag if I were you. You'll make twenty or so years sitting on death row, pretty good deal considering."

"I might possibly have a little Francis Marion in me, my dear."

"College, I liked it better when you quoted Poe."

"Even in the face adversity you still possess a savvy attitude. I admire that about you, Detective."

"Savvy is going to kill your ass. It's my day off and I feel like bending the rules just a tad. I don't think anyone back at that church will condemn me as a sinner when I do."

"Heebie-jeebies…your threats intrigue me even more. You are from the south, are you not? Francis Marion was a military officer who served in the American Revolutionary War. Acting with Continental Army and South Carolina militia commissions, he was a persistent adversary of the British in their occupation of South Carolina in 1780 and 1781, even after the Continental Army was driven out of the state in the Battle of Camden. Due to his irregular methods of warfare, he is considered one of the fathers of modern guerrilla warfare and is credited in the lineage of the United States Army Rangers. He was known as the Swamp Fox. American history is an obsession of mine. Yes, I have my vices."

"I know who the hell the Swamp Fox was and you're not even close. Play your silly pretend games. I'm still going to kill you."

"Bravo, you stay true to your character, admirable but that will be the death of you, Detective."

"Valdemar, you must stop allowing her to lure you into these senseless debates. She is vying for time, delaying our progress."

"Ligeia, I tire of your persistent mothering."
" Shouldn't we be going?"

"Pastor, you are a hostage, remember. You have no say. You're supposed to be the silent partner."

"After I kill you, I'm going kill the mastermind."

"Mastermind, preposterous…liability possibly…"

"I contacted you. We have a contract. You knew nothing about this until…"

"Show me the money. I have always wanted to incorporate that quote into my dialogue. You should have never exposed yourself, Pastor or whoever you are supposed to be. Breach of…I never meet my clients face to face. It works better on all accounts."

"Please…Valdemar, we must go," pleaded Ligeia.

"Hop-Frog, gag him and secure his hands. He might still be useful under the right circumstances."

"Not to worry, I'll play hostage. There's no need to bind and gag me."

"I fear that will be a stretch for you now. Contract has been nullified. Very well, Ligeia, lead us to our salvation. Haste makes waste."

Trudy made her move, desperate as it was, she shouldered Valdemar, and then took him down with a leg sweep. She snatched the knife from his belt, the same one he had used on Brady. She now held it to his throat, her knee resting on his chest as he lay on his back.

"Tell them to back off."

"Or what…you make good on your threats and kill me. We've journeyed down this road already, Detective. Hop-Frog, shoot her."

"Froggy, I would stand down if I were you," Trudy warned, now drawing blood from the tip of the knife, a returned favor.

"Hop-Frog, end this…now!"

Guns blazing, Hop-Frog staggered about, his bullet riddled body danced with the likeness of a marionette before plunging face first with an impressive splash. Valdemar ceased the moment and countered, gaining the upper hand on Trudy. He now lay underneath her, blade pressed against her ribcage. Ligeia stood defiant, Associate Pastor Garrett Moore serving as the perfect shield. The gun fire went quiet.

"The ole Swamp Fox lives," bragged Valdemar.

Valdemar rolled Trudy off him and cautiously stood, keeping the detective between him and the perceived direction of the shots. He hailed those hiding, threatening to kill both hostages, maiming them first, slow and painfully he promised. No one responded. No one offered to disclose their location. Valdemar smiled underneath his mask. He appreciated their tenacity and determination. Evil required good counter roles. Life was but one huge play to him. While the ending to this one could be anyone's guess, ole Swamp Fox had a few cards up his sleeve yet.

"I'm guessing these are friends of yours," he whispered to Trudy. "Mere constables would not be so eager to flit about in this environment. They would wait us out, cut off all escape reroutes, and perhaps even employ aerial surveillance and recon. This poses new challenges now doesn't it? Ligeia, demonstrate to our secluded gawkers that there are consequences for their disobedience and untimely persistence. Deliver a painful reminder to our associate pastor."

Ligeia retrieved a knife from her belt and promptly severed Garrett Moore's right ear and held it above his head for all to see. Garret's scream was muffled by the gag. He weakened at the knees, about to fall but Ligeia promptly grabbed him by his belt and buried the point of the knife into the base of his spin, altering his decision to crumble in a pile at her feet. She tossed the ear aside and then placed the knife just above his other one.

Valdemar shouted out, "Your continued pursuit will result in us dismantling our two hostages, one painful segment at a time. All the king's men will not be successful in putting them back together again. Here's fodder for your thoughts, however. Point us toward the nearest escape route and hail a vehicle for our departure. Better still; arrange a helicopter as our taxi. I'm sure you already have one on the way so why waste it. I'd not ponder frivolously if I were you. Next up on the dissecting table will be Detective Pierce. Thirty seconds…"

"Not such a good feeling is it, being all hemmed up like this," whispered Trudy. "Let's save the tax payer. Why don't you remove that silly trick or treat mask and then you and I can have us a little mud bog, one on one duel, until the last man or woman is still standing. You're not afraid of taking on a woman in a fair fight, are you?"

"Not at all and that proposal does intrigue me, but, I win, I still lose. They'll most certainly unleash hellfire on the standing champion. You serve my purposes better as a carving turkey. Once we escape, I might grant you your dream match." He then shouted fifteen seconds.

As time expired a voice yelled back, "Ground or air?"

"Let's go with what's behind door number two…air for $200 please." He then turned to Trudy and whispered, "I have a weakness for those classical game shows. *Monty Hall*, *Bob Barker* and *Gene Rayburn* and *Allen Ludden* were icons. I bet you didn't know that *Betty White* was widowed by *Alan Ludden*. Little known fact, *Ludden* proposed to twice-divorced, *Betty White*, whom he had met on *Password*, at least twice before she finally accepted."

"You're a certified psychopath. One minute you're committing the most heinous, vicious acts and then next you are rambling on like a damn walking encyclopedia."

"Thank you for noticing. I have all the answers."

"A pilot is twenty minutes out," yelled the mystery voice. "Rendezvous is half mile to the west, which would be to your right; a soybean field. I'd suggest you head there immediately."

"You lead, and we shall follow. Show yourselves and disarm immediately."

Woody and Tim stepped from the overgrowth, hands up, guns held over their heads. Trudy had already identified Woody's voice during the exchange. She sighed. This bastard would never allow any of them to live. Was there no end to this insanity? This was unfolding like one of those thousand-page *Steven King Dark Tower* novels. She had to finish this before he had the chance to notch his gun with more murders. Her wheels were spinning. Four on two did improve their odds.

Woody whispered to the others, spoken like a true ex-sheriff, "Hang back, bide your time, but under no circumstances allow them to board the copter. Take the shots when you have them. He'll kill us eventually if you don't stop him now."

"Just do what you can to give us an opening," replied Sly.

"Change of plans," shouted Valdemar. "It doesn't digest well, pre-selected locations. It's a bit too convenient for lawfully justified ambushes. Have the chopper come here. The pilot can certainly hover close enough to allow us access. Make the call, please."

Woody motioned to Tim to use the cell phone had had brought with him. Tim nodded and complied.

"Nicely accomplished, now snap to and move briskly in our direction, officers."

"Hold your position. This is where we make our last stand," whispered Woody.

"It might work to our advantage," replied Sly. "They won't be expecting it here."

"Don't underestimate him," cautioned Woody as he and Tim began walking towards the duo and their captives.

Keeping the hostages directly in front of them, Valdemar addressed the approaching men, "Ah yes, I recognize you; two of the assassins who murdered my supporting cast at the church. Tell me, just how did you survive the explosion?"

"Just lucky I guess," shouted Woody.

"I do apologize for the collateral damages and most certain loss of lives, but sacrifices are often necessary for the greater cause. You must admit. I am full of surprises. I have to rank up there as one of your toughest foes, if not the ultimate and undisputed king of the hill."

"You don't even rank as dog shit on the underside of my size 10 1/2s," replied Woody.

"You southerners have a unique way of spinning an anecdote. Tell me, how do you know Detective Pierce? I am assuming you are friends or at least acquaintances. Spare no details, we have plenty of time."

"Get your jollies elsewhere. I'm not here to converse or entertain you."

"What about you, young man?"

Tim took a deep breath and then answered, "Discarded day-old gum on the underside of a desk…that would be you all right."

"Original I must say. This is where the Red Queen orders, *off with his head*," smiled Valdemar with a little wink.

"Stop it," snapped Trudy, the knife point still buried in her back, Valdemar's other arm draped over her shoulder, his hand brandishing the automatic weapon. "Leave them alone. They've done what you asked."

"Truth or consequences, they really had no choice, now did they? Well, they could have watched helplessly as you died, I suppose, dissected bloody body parts piece by piece."

Garrett wobbled on unsteady legs. Ligeia held him in place, whispering if he wavered, he died. The hole where his ear had been had almost stopped bleeding. Tears flowed freely down his cheeks. Selfishness had cost him dearly. He so regretted ever speaking up. If he somehow survived this nightmare, he would spend the rest of his life behind bars, but only if proof linked him to the crime. So far, the detective had only heard the ramblings of a mad man, nothing that would hold up in court. The offshore accounts offered no trail in his direction. The money no longer seemed so important. He just didn't wish to lose any more appendages or his life. Give them their damn helicopter and let them escape. Let the madness end now.

"Time to kill, no pun intended, and you can't fault me this time, Ligeia, for conversing with our captive audience while we await our winged chariot's arrival."

"Chatting with you one last time makes me want to cut cartwheels. I could focus better though if you remove the sharp object from my spine."

"How's this?" Valdemar put his knife away but then buried the barrel of the assault weapon against the side of her neck.

"Perfect," Trudy replied, flexing her body and relaxing her muscles.

"Names of your two companions, please?"

"*Merle Haggard* and *Kenny Roger*," replied Trudy.

"I'm Merle, he's Kenny," added Woody.

"Catch us on tour at the Alabama Theater next month. Ask about the local's special," said Tim, not to be outdone.

"Improvise, your little troupe are naturals, a regular *Robin Williams* and *Jonathon Winters*. I will be so saddened when the final curtain eventually drops." The volley even prompted a slight smile from Ligeia, not that anyone could see it.

"Take off the mask and I'll spill my guts."

"Detective Pierce, my identity or should I say, lack thereof, prevents you from an untimely departure. Regretfully I offer no witness protection program and the life insurance benefits are deplorable. Listen, my dear. Is that the whirly bird I hear approaching? Tick…tock…"

The helicopter appeared in the distance, just coming into view above the moss laden tree tops. The chopper wasn't what Valdemar had hoped for, on the small side, but it would have to do. On a positive note, it was a naval chopper, with pontoons equipped for landing on the water. There would be no ladder climbing required. It landed thirty yards away. Valdemar positioned himself strategically shielded by Trudy and *Merle Haggard*, while Ligeia did the same with the pastor and *Kenny Rogers*. Slowly but meticulously they approached their escape pod, the Swamp Fox smelling something rotten in the gentleman's agreement. Constables didn't just roll over without a fight.

Now standing a few feet from the chopper and their freedom, Valdemar ordered the pilot to exit. He searched him. Satisfied he had no weapon, he instructed him back inside. Valdemar turned to Ligeia and gave the command, "End it. Take them."

She released her grip on Garrett and immediately the defrocked associate pastor collapsed to the marsh. Next, she turned her focus on the two officers and without so much as a smile she raised her assault rifle. She took a shot to her forehead, the mask shattering to reveal a bloody but beautiful face; death delivered by Officer Parker Huffman, a marksman of extraordinaire caliber. Valdemar lunged for the chopper's door, dragging Trudy in behind him. Sly, Parker and Deputy Kyle Roswell rushed as fast as they could slosh towards the lifting chopper. All they could do was watch along with Woody and Tim as the chopper headed eastward, destination unknown and their friend still held hostage.

'*The death of a beautiful woman is unquestionably the most poetical topic in the world.*' *Edgar Allan Poe*

The Final Act

The bastard was on top of her, Trudy pinned face down inside the helicopter. The pilot glanced back but there was nothing he could do. The masked man had his weapon pointed directly at him, barking no instructions, but those eyes spoke volumes. He quickly refocused on the horizon. Valdemar smiled underneath the mask. He had gotten his revenge; the money was safely tucked away offshore and he'd not have to split it with anyone. He could never have envisioned this outcome. Lady luck sometimes works things out for the better bad. The idiot clergyman who had contracted him would take the fall alone and even he could not connect any dots that would lead back to him, a perfect and just ending. Sadly, this had come at the cost of his entire assemble of actors.

Trudy had survived worse, not much worse, but she was a survivor just the same. Valdemar appeared to be in no hurry to dismount her. She feared that the sicko was enjoying his current position, pressing a tad too close for her liking. His weight suddenly shifted. He was positioning to stand-up. Just as he did, Trudy pushed off with her hands and managed to spin and flip over. In one fluid motion, more instinct than calculated, she grabbed at his mask while at the same time, with her legs recoiled, she gave him the double barrel push kick. Valdemar completely caught off guard, lost his balance and fell backwards. With her fingers clutched through the mask's eye holes, Trudy managed to pluck the knife from his belt.

She buried it in his thigh, gave him another double kick and this time he fell through the open door of the chopper. She had plucked the mask off his face just before he disappeared through the door, the knife he had used on Brady still buried in his flesh. Trudy saw the man behind the mask. There was nothing distinguishable or outstanding about his face. His was one that could easily be lost in any crowd and never picked out in a lineup, certainly not the face of a heartless, ruthless killer. His neighbors if he had any would probably be the first to profess what a nice guy he had always been.

Trudy eased to the chopper's door. Swampland and somewhat of a lake spread out seventy feet below, but she didn't see him anywhere. The chopper had been moving at a reasonable click so most likely he was further back. She instructed the pilot to go back. She wasn't going to be satisfied until she spotted a body, dead or alive.

The chopper made several passes but nothing; he had seemingly vanished. Oh crap, the thought hit her, and she immediately hung out the door and looked underneath the chopper. Unlike in the movies, the villain was not hanging on the pontoon's underneath. After one or two more passes, she motioned for the pilot to head back to where the others probably needed to hear some good news. Well, good that she was alive, bad that his sorry carcass had not been located. One thing for sure, this wasn't over until she had a body. She at least owed Brady that.

Valdemar hunkered underneath an old petrified tree, bruised, battered and bleeding but very much alive. He smiled and even tossed the departing chopper little air kisses. This was far from over. He would still have to escape this swamp and they would most certainly continue their search, but never underestimate the master.

"Never to suffer would never to have been blessed. Believe only half of what you see and nothing of what you hear. I became insane with long intervals of horrible insanity…ah yes Poe, it is you and I…even in the grave, all is not lost."

Valdemar stood, gathered his bearings and then began to trudge towards where he believed would offer him the best advantage, the wider tributary, a river, a current swift. Ride it to the end. The water had gotten nearly waist deep. He had applied a tourniquet to his bloody leg, a reminder that he and the detective would indeed cross paths one more time, his choosing of course. The knife also served as his only weapon. It would be of no use against automatic weapons if his pursuers were lucky enough to gain ground. Organizing a search in this terrain would be no easy task; advantage Valdemar. These backwoods constables had not proved to be much of a threat.

Valdemar vanished underneath the murk before bobbing back up like a fishing cork. He laughed, having stepped into a deep hole. Now treading water, he swam along, constantly feeling for a footing. A loud splash caught his attention to the left. The water showed signs of a ripple, no more. His right toe touched bottom. He maneuvered in that direction and soon had emerged to his breast, finding higher ground as he crept along cautiously. He spotted bubbles just to his left. The pain, the yank, the thrashing all happened spontaneously. The roll really caught him by surprise.

The thirteen and half foot alligator, an ancient one calling this swamp his, full throttle now in a death roll, had closed its massive jaws around the torso of its prey. Bones crushed, and massive amounts of flesh shredded from the helpless form. Nature had delivered southern justice but not before Valdemar had buried the knife into the reptilian skull.

The boundaries which divide Life from Death are at best shadowy and vague. Who shall say where the one ends, and where the other begins? Edgar Allen Poe

Encore, Encore

Trudy sat on the back deck of the Pierce Beach House sipping Jack on the rocks. She had just buried her love and life, Brady her one and only husband. Others were gathering inside, Tim and Summer, Woody, Sly, Dallas, Marion, Faith and Reverend Jonah Blackwood. Yes, somehow the man of the cloth had survived the explosion, a miracle indeed. The ancient live oak pulpit had shielded him from certain death. She had asked for a few minutes alone, one last toast to Circus Boy. No, she hadn't seen this one coming. It seemed someone was always dying on her watch. She was back where she had started, before she had moved back from Ohio to South Carolina. She had nothing left but her career. How easy it was to slide back into old habits. She had no time for a pity party. Her mission in life, find the bastard who murdered Brady. She'd not rest until she did, or his sorry rotting carcass had been found.

Myrtle Beach, fun in the sun, a must go tourist destination, why hadn't she experienced any of that? Well, selfishly she had when she had allowed herself to; but too often she had gotten her butt caught up in the next greatest crime spree. Maybe she needed time off as a meter reader. Too much crime fighting can take it out of you. Bitch and moan, how about it; you're among the living, gal. Take what the Good Man above has given you. She downed the drink and then tossed the glass as far as she could throw it.

"Can I join you?"

"Sure Allison, my mourning is over. How are you holding up?"

"On the mend, sort of…I checked in on Buster after the funeral. Hospitals aren't his cup of tea, but he will recover with time. I like your sheriff."

"I can tell. You've been there checking on him constantly."

"We never finished Truth or Dare."

"I did."

"But I didn't. I want to finish it now if you will hear me out."

"I'm not sure this is…"

"It is, trust me, it is."

"Have a seat then."

"I asked for the divorce and asked him to take the children. It was for their protection."

Trudy didn't follow but remained silent, something not so easily done. This was Allison's time, not hers.

"I'm broken, really screwed up inside. I have been like this for a very long time and it was just getting worse. I couldn't stand to be around my family, my kids, my husband, even you and mom. At least you and mom lived far away from me. That might have saved you now that I think of it."

Trudy almost spoke up but bit her tongue and remained quiet.

"The head doctor did what he could, counseling and medicating me. Nothing helped long term. Everyone was so demanding of my time. Someone always wanted something of me. I hated all of them; feeding them, bathing them, taking them here and there, homework, office parties, grocery shopping, clothes shopping, sex, him wanting sex all the time. I wanted them all to just go away and never come back, and just stop bothering me. I was suffocating, dying inside and I wanted them dead too."

Trudy couldn't fathom what her sister was confessing. This was too bizarre.

"I stopped going to the doctor and tossed all those stupid medicines. I began scheming day and night, visualizing how I could end it. Death was the only solution."

"Allison, you didn't attempt suicide again so don't beat yourself up."

"No silly, I planned to kill my husband and children. I lied during Truth or Dare to Valdemar about putting that gun to my chin. I had a much different plan. I had it all figured out, even practiced it. The night that I walked away was the night I had envisioned doing it. I watched him pull into the drive with them. They were laughing and having a good time as they exited the SUV. They were so happy and full of life. I chickened out thankfully. They didn't deserve to die. I ran out the back door and ran and ran and ran. I never went back. If I had, they would be dead. I never told any of them what I had planned to do, what I thought I was capable of doing. I miss my kids and I miss him too, but I can never return to that life for their life's sake."

Trudy, tears running down both cheeks, did something she didn't ever do. She pulled her sister tight and hugged her, promising her she was not alone in this. Trudy had a new family crisis to balance out her life. Everything was back to normal.

Epilogue

Sheriff Buster Ferguson sat behind his desk, never happier to be back on the job. He had summoned Trudy to his office. He sipped an ice-cold sweet tea, compliments of Conway's Maryland Fried Chicken, his newest favorite place to dine. He'd save the fried chicken livers for later. He'd almost weaned himself off the frequent stops at the shooting range, combo of being debilitated and distracted. The sudden change was growing on him. A rap on his door summed him back to earth.

"Pierce, come on in and have a seat; you too Anderson."

"I hope you two didn't conspire to get me here. I'm not interested in rejoining the department," Woody warned them.

"Don't flatter yourself, Anderson; I wouldn't have you under my watch. I can only contend with one loose cannon at a time. I have some news I think both of you will be interested in hearing."

"Don't mind him, sir, please continue."

"Duck hunters stumbled into something down in Georgetown, two rotting carcasses intertwined so to speak. Big mother of a gator, knife stuck in its head, had attempted to make a meal of a yet to be identified man. I've seen photographs of the scene, including the knife. That bastard tangled with one of our locals after you sent him flying without a parachute. He's this Valdemar chap all right. We'll know his identity soon enough."

"Fitting end," said Woody.

"For Brady, I can't be happier, but I hate an innocent alligator got caught up in it," added Trudy.

"Associate Pastor Garrett Moore is squirming but still not talking. We'll nail his butt in due time; still no lead on the money though."

"Easy come, easy go," added Woody.

"One more thing, law over in Walterboro still hasn't found hide or hair of that newspaper friend of yours. They do suspect foul play. Two good ole boys are thought to have been involved but nobody down there is willing to speak up against them. Some hate Lance Rocker more than helping the law."

"I still find it hard to believe just how far the mighty Rocker has fallen from his glory days on television," said Trudy.

"Got no use for the SOB, but not having him around does sort of leave an empty spot.
Guess that's different from the bad taste I normally have," said Woody.

"Is that all, sir?"

"Well, you can tell that sister of yours I'll come calling around six."

"Will do Sheriff. Take care," Trudy replied, taking in a deep breath, "and enjoy your chicken livers."

Exiting they saw Tim. He was on his cell phone grinning like a lovesick possum. Trudy decided not to disrupt the love birds. Obviously, Summer Knight must be on the receiving end of the conversation.

"What's next for you Woody; hear you're out of the security business."

"I never really liked those stupid uniforms I picked out. I sold the business and gave shares to the families of the men I lost."

"You still haven't said what's on the radar next."

"I might just try my hand out as private investigator."

"You're not thinking about heading to Walterboro, are you?"

"See you partner. You take care and try to stay out of trouble, how about it. I'm getting tired of bailing you out."

"Bailing me out?"

"Try keeping your clothes on for a change, no one ever said you had to do police work in the buff. Maybe that's the way they do things up in Ohio, but this is a family vacation destination for heavens sake."

"Tell Marion and her hubby I hope they find that beach condo they're seeking. It will be real handy having her here at the beach."

"Hey, lay off my babysitter."

"Don't be a stranger, partner."

"And you call me when you need a shoulder, any time, day or night."

"I have work and a neurotic sister to keep me busy. I have no time for a private dick. Take care, Woodrow Anderson."

"Down the road, partner…"

Trudy collapsed at her desk. The loss of Brady was taking its toll, a constant gnawing from the inside out, relentless and gaining ground. Her work…she must focus on her work…what else did she have left? At least his murderer had found a fitting end, identity known or not. Trudy Wagner, southern belle, what would the future toss her way next?

> THE BEST AND MOST BEAUTIFUL THINGS IN THE
> WORLD CANNOT BE SEEN OR EVEN TOUCHED.
> THEY MUST BE FELT WITH THE HEART.
>
> *Helen Keller*

Here's a sneak preview.

Trudy Wagner, Southern Belle

The 4th edition in the Detective Trudy Wagner series is somewhat of a prequel, introducing Trudy before she became the Grand Stand crime fighter. Do not fret though. This will be covered in a series of flashbacks while Horry County's finest continue their quest to rid the riff raff from the tourist community and solve crimes that plague the Palmetto Coast. Mourning the death of Brady, Trudy escapes, remembering her past.

Love begins with a smile, grows with a kiss, and ends with a teardrop.

Detective Trudy Wager had taken a leave of absence, a contradiction and far cry from how she normally reacted to adverse conditions. These were not normal conditions though. Widowed and tittering on the brink of depression, she hadn't coped well in the early going of losing her husband, her soul mate, Brady Pierce, ruthlessly murdered, knifed as she stood there helplessly and unable to prevent it. Immersing herself in her work had typically been her mantra, family always taking the backseat and second fiddle. Boy how things had changed. Her move back to Horry County had been her worst and best decision, a decision she couldn't really take the credit for, not that she would really want to claim it as her idea. Her ailing mom, a situation she could not just turn her back on, had quilted her into returning to where she had been born and raised. She had surely screwed up that, poorly prioritizing the role of a caregiver, placing too much credence on her career instead. Lessons learned she had paid dearly for that ill-fated decision. What goes around comes around.

Police work had always been enough to sustain her. That Trudy hadn't needed anything else to complicate her world. Becoming the best at what she did had been enough. Such had been her life in the buckeye state before returning to the South Carolina Grand Strand. Work, with just the right smidgen of social life, and being far removed from responsibilities associated with family, had been her perfect recipe for survival. The rigors of a committed relationship compounded with the neediness of family posed unwanted boat anchors, Trudy not willing to be hampered or strapped with either inconvenience. If that labeled her one cold bitch and an insensitive and awful daughter, so be it. Learn to deal with it. It was no skin off her back if you didn't like it or couldn't understand her philosophy. That was then, and this was now. Those days seemed a distant memory. Then why was she wallowing in them? Could it just be part of the healing process or was she on the brink of a complete emotional collapse? People do see shrinks for these situations, but not one as pig headed as Trudy Wagner…detective and crime scene investigator leader of Horry County's finest.

Trudy sat on the back deck of the beach home, one of hers and Brady's favorite spots, sipping on her third adult cocktail. No amount of alcohol seemed to dull her senses or improve her serious bout of melancholy. Too many cancerous what ifs and whys devoured her, sucking her dry of her life force. She had never ever been faced with a lack of will to go on but giving up seemed so much easier than doing what needed to be done to put the past where it belonged.

Nothing much mattered anymore; dealing with it included. Nearly a week away from work had not improved her disposition by a long shot. If anything, she had sunk further into the pity abyss, a hole deeper and darker than any she had ever experienced. Nothing was more evident as when she rubbed her hands up and down her folded bare legs; briars from days of neglected shaving, feeling prickly to the touch. Personal hygiene had fallen completely off the priority scale. Alone, she had no one to 'pretty up' for. Well, she wasn't exactly alone. Allison her sister was still living with her. Even with sis around, she was becoming a psychotic basket case, one who should probably not have guns easily accessible, not that she had experienced any suicidal tendencies…at least not yet.

Perhaps the saddest irony of depression is that suicide happens when the patient gets a little better and can again function sufficiently. Dick Cavett

The Pierce Beach House

That constant sound was quite disturbing. Make it stop. Quiet, peace and quiet, that's all that is important right now. The answering machine picked up. Inside through the open window Trudy could hear her voice greeting the caller. She had regretfully erased Brady's and had added her personal greeting. Her recorded, perky, gleeful tone grated on her badly placed disposition. If she would have been inside, she might have yanked it from the wall to restore order. She wasn't. At the sound of the beep the second voice intruded on her privacy. This new world without her husband was not a happy place.

It was her sister, Allison, inviting her to dinner at Bovine's. She and her new love interest, the current sheriff was hitting it off quite well, so it seemed. Unlike her, her sister Allison and Sheriff Buster Ferguson had recovered from the physical and emotional scares caused by the same ordeal that had taken Brady from her. After all, they had each other to lean on. She had no one; at least no one she was willing to allow into her life right now. Granted, Allison had good intentions, she just wasn't ready for a coming out party right now.

Funny, in the few precious weeks following Brady's death, Trudy had sucked it up, had even shown interest in Lance Rocker's disappearance. Slowly but surely the ominous dark clouds had formed. As unpredictable as a funnel cloud dropping from the sky, she had been whisked away to the Land of Oz where the daily ho-hum life no longer made sense or required processing. So, what did the road hold ahead? Standing, Trudy sloshed about the melted ice cubes in her glass before emptying the glass over the railing, now feeling the need for another refill. Catching a glimpse of her reflection in the glass storm door just before entering the house, she toasted it with her empty glass. The phone rang again, apparently Allison wasn't going to take no for an answer or at least not be satisfied until she talked to her. As before, Trudy allowed it to cycle through, fending off the urge to snatch it from the wall as previously envisioned.

"Hey partner, Woody, just what the hell is this I hear about you taking a leave? I know you're there so pick up the damn phone how about it? Your choice, but if you don't, I'm coming over there pronto, if you catch my drift."

Trudy took a deep breath, rolling her eyes, looked towards the ceiling for answers before flinging her glass at the *pain in the ass* machine. The insulated mug missed its mark and ricocheted harmlessly off a lampshade. Trudy ran her hands through her hair, tempted to pull it free by the roots, before gasping and then pressing the Speaker button, barking her response.

"What do you want, Woody?"

"As testy as I remember you, who crapped in your mess kit this afternoon?"

"And the smart ass I remember too, why are you calling?"

"Okay, I'll cut to the chase. I've been missing your smiling face lately and the calming affect you have on me. I thought maybe we could grab some supper tonight. I'm buying. You just name the place; that is providing it doesn't require reservations and cost me an arm and a leg."

"Sorry, not hungry, not in the mood to venture out into the land of the lost right now, but thanks for the invite."

"No is not optional. I can be a pain in the ass too, partner."

"That you can, but really, I'm fine."

"Fine, I don't think so. If you were fine, you'd be on duty busting someone's balls."

"I just need a little break. Beach life has worn me down; too much fun in the sun, sand and the sea. Besides, the bad guys could use a little alone time without me. Tell you what, why don't you let me tag you in, knock off the rust and you can give the bad guys hell for a while."

"Sorry, I've worn out my welcome on that side of law and justice. It became way too predictable and boring after you cramped my style. Any hoot, Myrtle Beach has hopefully run out of serial killers. My services are no longer value added. Where do you want to grab some chow, The Hot Fish Club? I know that's one of your favorites."

"No, anywhere but there…"

"My bad partner, I forgot that was yours and…"

Trudy interrupted him, not really wanting to hear the Brady explanation. "Look, I don't feel much like seafood, all right."

Woody caught the hint. "What about a big juicy cheese burger? River City or Hamburger Joe's, both are excellent choices."

"I'm not hungry and I would be shitty company."

"You're always shitty company. I'm used to it. I'll pick you up in forty-five minutes."

"Make it an hour. I need to shave my legs."

"Man, fifteen minutes for a shave, you're grossing me out, partner. Please do your arms pits too while you're at it. I don't want any surprises."

Trudy held up her free arm and took a peak. She almost gagged at the sight. She ended the call and then mixed that drink; that is after she retrieved the mug from behind the loveseat. Dread overwhelmed her. Just thinking about doing anything wore her slap out. Her mind briefly drifted to the Hot Fish Club, her first sighting of Circus Boy. She almost mustered a smile visualizing Brady Pierce in that gaudy knickers outfit.

Trudy recalled how she had summoned the waitress, asking about him and then had sent over one of those drinks with an umbrella just to make her point about his Ringling Brothers appearance. Little did she know then how the crossing of their paths would be the best thing that ever happened to her? Crossing paths with that bastard Valdemar would undo what they had once had. Trudy poured another drink, a double shot of Jack. Somehow, she had to numb the pain or go insane. Poetic justice she whispered, realizing her rhyming thoughts.

She sat on the edge of the tub mowing through the briars on her legs, unfazed by her recent neglect. The Wagner sisters, what a pair? They had put the 'D' in dysfunctional, so it seemed. Trudy had not noticed Allison's downward spiral any more than she had seen her own coming. How had their lives become so screwed up? A shrink could have probably helped her solve the mystery. Funny, a crime scene investigator can't even solve her very own crimes. Crimes…it seems like such a harsh thought. What she had done and was presently doing was not criminal by definition; not when compared to the decisions she had made during the Road Rage case. Obviously, she had colored outside the lines of the law then and had drawn *Mister Play It by The Book*, Officer Woodrow Anderson down a path of unlawfulness. Once lines have been crossed…

Now she contemplated if she should remain in law enforcement. Untrue, she wasn't even thinking in those terms at all. For once her career was the least of her concerns; so far on the back burner it was not even a blip on her radar screen. Brady, she so missed him and couldn't get beyond the fact he was gone. People always struggle with loses she attempted to convince herself. Get through the mourning process as quickly as possible, pick up the pieces and move on; easier preached than practiced. Walking in those shoes had been much tougher than imagined. She didn't want to be over it apparently. Wallow, wallow and wallow some more. See where that gets you, detective…damn ugly situation. Suck it up she tried to tell herself. Her self just wasn't in a listening mood quite yet. Where did her life go so terribly off the beaten path?

The next in the Detective Trudy Wagner series, Novel 4, Trudy Wagner, Southern Belle.

About T. Allen Winn T. Allen

Winn began writing in 2003 while being cooped up in hotels during business travel. Completing a 650 page so called novel he became hooked. The homegrown Abbeville, S.C. boy embraced the experience completing one novel and then leaping into the next one, fun and therapy at the time. That changed in 2011 when a chance encounter brought stranger and new neighbor Bob O'Brien to his Pawley's Island doorsteps. Bob didn't realize the neighborhood home had been sold and apologized when Tom greeted him instead of the man he had expected to see. Book in hand, Bob had just published his first novel, The Toppled Pawn and explained the previous neighbor had shown interest in writing. Tom remarked he dabbled in writing to which Bob asked, do you have a manuscript? Tom replied ten. Bob had just started Prose Press, a publishing company and suggested publishing one. You can't make this stuff up.

T. Allen Winn's first novel, Road Rage joined the ranks of the published a few months later, and he owes a special thanks to Bob O'Brien for making this possible. His first seven books were published by Prose Press. In 2016, T. Allen Winn established Buttermilk Books, his publishing company. Ten books have now been published under Buttermilk Books. He and his wife reside in Myrtle Beach, South Carolina.
Ole T doesn't write under any specific genre. He writes what strikes his fancy. If you don't see something that fits your reading wheel house, just tell him what you like, and he might just write it for you.

Books are available on Amazon or on line where books are sold. Select books are available in Tabor City, N.C. at Grapefull Sisters Vineyard. Or *Message* T. Allen Winn on Facebook to arrange delivery of signed copies.

Fiction from T. Allen Winn

The Detective Trudy Wagner series

Road Rage
North of the Border
Tithes and Offerings

Foot Series

Foot, Tree Knockers and Rock Throwers (1st in the trilogy)

More Fiction from T. Allen Winn

The Perfect Spook House
Dark Thirty
Lou Who
Raw Ride, a Wild West Zombie Apocalyptic Shoot'um Up
The Man Who Met the Mouse
Mister Twix Mystery, a Cat Scene Investigation

Non-Fiction from T. Allen Winn

Being Bentley, A Dog Like No Other
It's All About the 'A', Faith, Family, Football and Forever to Thee
with coauthor, Benji Greeson
December's Darkest Day, While I Breathe, I Hope
The Hardwood Walker of Port Harrelson Road (based on true events
in Bucksport, S.C.)
Cuz, My Brother, Life is Good, God is Good

Memoirs

The Caregiver's Son, Outside the Window Looking In
Cornbread and Buttermilk, Good Ole Fashion Home Cooked
Nostalgic Nonsense

Short Stories

For Your Amusement featured in Beach Author Network's book titled 'Shorts'

Ciled Me a Bar featured in friend and author, Danny Kuhn's Headline Book's
Mountain Mysts, Honorable Mention in Fiction at the 2015 London Book Festival and the book is endorsed by *Joyce Dewitt* of the sitcom *Three's Company*

Short story about Granny Bowie in friend and author Robert Sharpe's book, *The Heart and Soul of Caring*, about caregivers and their challenges

www.ingramcontent.com/pod-product-compliance
Lightning Source LLC
Chambersburg PA
CBHW072127250626
47159CB00007B/2596